D1826315

THE WATERMARK

SAM MILLS

GRANTA

Granta Publications, 12 Addison Avenue, London, W11 4QR

First published in Great Britain by Granta Books in 2024
This paperback edition published by Granta Books, 2025

Copyright © Sam Mills, 2024

Illustrations copyright © Christiana Spens, 2024

The right of Sam Mills to be identified as the author of this work has been asserted by her in accordance with the Copyright, Designs and Patents Act, 1988.

All rights reserved. This book is copyright material and must not be copied, reproduced, transferred, distributed, leased, licenced or publicly performed or used in any way except as specifically permitted in writing by the publisher, as allowed under the terms and conditions under which it was purchased or as strictly permitted by applicable copyright law. Any unauthorised distribution or use of this text may be a direct infringement of the author's and publisher's rights, and those responsible may be liable in law accordingly. Please note that no part of this book may be used or reproduced in any manner for the purpose of training artificial intelligence technologies or systems.

A CIP catalogue record for this book is available from the British Library.

1 3 5 7 9 10 8 6 4 2

ISBN 978 1 78378 967 2
eISBN 978 1 78378 966 5

Typeset in Adobe Garamond Pro, Albertan Pro, Marcia, Bookman JF Pro and Utopia Std by Iram Allam

Printed and bound by CPI Group (UK) Ltd, Croydon CR0 4YY

The manufacturer's authorised representative in the EU for product safety is Authorised Rep Compliance Ltd, 71 Lower Baggot Street, Dublin D02 P593, Ireland. www.arccompliance.com

www.granta.com

SAM MILLS is the author of *The Quiddity of Will Self*, a novel, and *The Fragments of My Father*, a memoir about being a carer. Sam has written for a number of publications, including the *Guardian, Independent, 3:AM* and *London Magazine.* She is the co-founder of the independent press Dodo Ink.

'A story about stories, an ingenious genre-tumble through literature, artistic expression, free-will, and how far – how deep – we will go for love. A compulsively readable, dizzyingly inventive novel that is both gloriously immense, and immensely, heart-wrenchingly intimate' Glen James Brown

'There are books within books within books in this inventive fantasy with echoes of *The Matrix* and the works of Susanna Clarke' *Mail on Sunday*

'If you've ever heard the phrase "lost in a good book" and thought, "Great, where do I sign up?', this one's for you . . . An impressively confident performance with a very clever ending' *SFX*

'I was absolutely blown away . . . There are elements of *Inception*'s several-layers-down trickery here but it's also a set of charming and well-done pastiches of everything from J. G. Ballard to doorstopper Russian novels. Let yourself get lost in this, as we all imagine we might get lost in a good book from time to time – Mills will transport you' *Lit Hub*

'A deeply ambitious work . . . a proper page-turner . . . The individual stories are entertaining and inventive, and masterpieces in authorial ventriloquism . . . the ending . . . is a five-star triumph' *Bookmunch*

'Mills' ambitious work of metafiction, packed with characters gone awry and a romance tested by a whiplash trajectory, offers a colourful, dizzying adventure plot, but also philosophical questioning of our connection to reality and truth' *NB*

'Kaleidoscopic . . . an imaginative tour-de-force, one that never collapses under the weight of its hugely ambitious structure. In a breathtaking, captivating page-turner full of surprises and gloriously inventive narrative devices, Mills deftly demonstrates how enormously entertaining metafictional novels can be' *Booklist*

'*Inception* meets *Stranger than Fiction* in this ambitious meta adventure . . . [Mills'] fluid command of each vastly different genre serves to highlight what stays the same in each – the strengths, faults, and deep bond of Rachel and Jaime'
Publishers Weekly

For L. K.

My mother, 1946–2011

And the love of my life, Andrew Gallix

'Dying is pointless. You have to know how to disappear.'

BAUDRILLARD

The Prologue

1

I left my flat at six that morning to catch a train to Wales to interview Augustus Fate. It was the first interview he'd given in nine years. When I boarded at London Paddington, I threw my rucksack into the overhead rack, slumped into my window seat and shuffled through my Spotify, from Sufjan Stevens to Bowie to Beethoven's fifth. None of them helped me forget my troubles: the patronising, enigmatic comments – supposedly worth nine thousand pounds a year – that my tutor made while 'supervising' my thesis; the drudgery of my weekend job in the local pizzeria, where every one of my tips, mostly earnt by flirting, were nicked by my plump French boss; the sapiosexual physicist I shared a flat with, whose trysts stole much of my sleep; Rachel.

I attempted to quieten this white noise by reminding myself that I was about to interview one of the most famous and celebrated authors alive today. That millions of readers and writers and journalists would sacrifice body parts to be in my place. That I had to produce four thousand words, which would be published in *The Times* and syndicated across the world. I flipped open my iPad, where I had typed the heading 'Interview Questions'. The rest of the page was blank.

I gazed out at the suburbs greying past. The stranger opposite me was giving my foot an irritated glance, for it had been tapping out a nervous piece of jazz. Blushing, I crossed my legs and locked my hands in my pockets. How I missed the body of my teenage years, which had been such a graceful, languid thing, slumped in T-shirts, stretched out over a bed or a lawn, catlike in the sunshine. The divide between those two eras, between my sixteen-year-old self and the present day, had created two Jaimes who existed in entirely different worlds. The first Jaime lived in a society aswirl with money, happily borrowing to study for a BA, since the reward of a good job in exchange for my 2.1 felt like a certainty. The second Jaime was a man who went to the cafe in Waterstones Piccadilly each week to sip espressos and fill in form after form, only to find out – over 540 job applications later – that he wasn't good for cleaning (overqualified), flipping burgers in McDonald's (doubly so) or publishing (I attempted five internships but it was clear that I just didn't have the right connections).

We were all in the same flimsy, leaking, waterlogged boat. My friends who ought to have been physicists were working in call centres; friends who were qualified engineers were banging on doors, selling tea towels and oven gloves. We bought food from supermarkets laid out on pallets, lacking any slogans or fancy packaging; we shunned the expense of TV licences by borrowing a Netflix login; we rented small rooms with rashes of mould growing across the ceiling for extortionate sums and when we couldn't afford those anymore, we moved back in with our parents, extending our childhoods like our overdrafts. We surfed the internet for hours with zombie eyes and latched on to causes that were miniature – an offensive advert, the actions of a particular landlord – because to attempt to address the bigger issues was to feel helpless and hopeless, to sense that the world had been reshaped for those who lived in grand houses and played golf at weekends.

My interview with Fate had the potential to change my limp destiny and achieve that near-impossibility: a journalism job that paid. The pressure was worse than anything I had endured; no wonder my nails were non-existent.

The scenery softened: London brickshit was replaced by countryside, hawthorn and birdsong. I changed trains at Newport, then picked up a local service from Craven Arms. As the train rattled across Llandrindod Wells, the sun became a red glow on the horizon and snow began to fall. The austere landscape took on an eerie beauty; churches became poetic, trees silhouetted with white. Occasionally I was pierced with an ache in my stomach, a wish that Rachel was with me, that we could wander into those dark snowy woods together; but there was a kind of pleasure in my wistfulness. By the time the train pulled into Pen-y-Bont, twilight was smoking the sky. I liked the small, quaint feel of the station: the stone walls and the murmurs of people chatting in Welsh; the sheep beyond the car park.

The taxi the paper had booked was waiting for me. The driver was a stout man with a pointed beard. When I passed over my rucksack, he looked me up and down. Should I have worn a suit and tie? I had opted for my usual jeans and red checked shirt with the thick black trench coat I had picked up in the local Oxfam, but now I was back to fretting that Fate might be a proponent of the industry's formalities. In the back of the taxi, I fingered the dark prickle of my stubble, pushing back my uneven fringe from my forehead. We were mute for five minutes before I asked him what it was like to have Fate as a neighbour.

So much had been written about Fate that he had become more myth than man. He'd once been a fixture on the London literary circuit, after winning the 1993 Whitbread and receiving his first of many Booker nominations, but for the past decade he had eschewed all company and shut himself away in a remote Welsh village. In the latest photo of him – from five years ago – he looked as though he belonged in the title role of *King Lear*, hurling obscenities into the wind.

I was hoping the driver might tell me all sorts of exotic stories about how Fate sacrificed local sheep, or sewed pansies into his beard. Instead, he shrugged and said that the only book he enjoyed reading was his Bible. The press sometimes sent helicopters flying overhead to spy on Fate's cottage, he added, which spoilt the silence for everyone.

He parked his taxi on the curve of a country road.

'I can't take you any further.' He pointed to the fence, a jagged gap cut into it. 'Just go through there and carry on up for two hundred metres.'

I followed a trampled depression through the snow-strewn grass and bracken. I was already translating my experiences into Times New Roman; I noted the detail of some rabbit fur and blood caught on the fence. The sound of a Welsh 'Silent Night' echoing out from the village church down the lane. The icy purity in the air that made my eyes water and my skin feel raw.

The trees here were different from the ones I saw every day in London parks, where they were pruned to meek prettiness. These trees seemed to jostle me, like locals who find a stranger invading their town. My body began to defy the cold; sweat burnt under my armpits. I couldn't help picturing a simple lane and neat gate on the opposite side of the thicket, which I had somehow missed. If it did exist, I'd have to pretend I never saw it.

As I pushed my way out of the woods I spotted a trill of smoke rising up into the snow-flurried sky from a chimney. I paused, swallowing. Did I really deserve to be here? I wasn't a journalist or a book blogger. The Fate fanatics had, unsurprisingly, reacted badly to the announcement that I had won the competition to interview him. Twitter, Facebook and various forums had been buzzing with conspiracy theories detailing how I had cheated by bribing or seducing the organisers. One account had even unearthed my birth certificate to prove some form of cover-up: apparently, a smudge on my place of birth revealed that I was actually born on Bardsey Island, which meant I was Fate's illegitimate son, a revelation that would be officially announced when my interview with him was published in *The Times*. It was all so bizarre. The embarrassing truth was this: I didn't even like his novels that much. The main reason I was here was that I'd fallen in love with Rachel. It was Rachel who had invigorated my interest in Fate's fiction: we'd exchanged dozens of messages about our favourite authors, and she had posted me a dog-eared copy of *Glossop Inn*. The pleasure of reading it had been intensified by the thought that I was turning pages her fingertips had once brushed, savouring lines she had once marvelled over.

The snow spread out before me was a clean blanket, and when I looked back I saw the messy trail my boots had left. As I drew closer, I saw that Fate's cottage was large, with squinty windows and an ugly door for a mouth.

The competition entry form had been minimal. They had asked applicants to attach a sample of their writing – something that demonstrated *a vigorous intellect and a passionate love of literature, the sort which would involve staying up all night to read Fate's latest volume in a frenzy, rather than making twee observations over tea and biscuits at your local book group. Eccentricity would be considered a desirability rather than a disability.*

'Disability?' I had messaged Rachel. 'Jesus. What kind of insensitive boomers are running this competition?' But she coaxed me into entering, and so I cut and pasted four thousand words of my thesis-in-progress into a Word document and emailed it off.

Death in fiction: that's my speciality. My favourite fictional death has to be that of Mr Krook, the shopkeeper in Charles Dickens's *Bleak House*. The death itself is a crazy, wonderful thing – Mr Krook's lodger enters his room to find *a smouldering, suffocating vapour in the room and a dark, greasy coating on the walls and ceiling*. Even better is the pompous preface that Dickens wrote a few years on, in which he asserted that there were over thirty well-documented cases of spontaneous human combustion, including the famous death of Countess Cornelia de Baudi Cesenate.

Fate also had a penchant for the dramatic, quirky death. He even included his own death by spontaneous combustion in *The Beetle Fossil*, one of his early novels. In another, characters were infamously killed off at random intervals with casual, throwaway sentences: 'Kay was playing tennis when a ball smashed into her skull'; 'Gerard was walking down the street when he fell under a bus'.

My sapiosexual physicist flatmate was there when I got the call to say that I'd won, sitting at the kitchen table in her negligee, smoking a Sobranie and eating a bowl of cornflakes. She declared that someone had to be playing a joke on me. When I informed my supervisor, Professor Millhauser, he congratulated me in a tone of astonishment. He added that they'd probably received very few entries for the competition, and though I had broken a certain ancient college rule by using part of my thesis, he would kindly abstain from reporting me. My fingers were shaking when I emailed Rachel the news, but she never replied; I emailed her seven times more, but still didn't hear back. The last email I ever received from her sits on my computer, dated six weeks ago:

'I have forgotten my umbrella.'

My interest in her ought to have faded by now. Instead, it had intensified into a pathetic obsession: she was the backdrop to my days; she laced my dreams at night.

I had reached the door of Augustus Fate's cottage. I could no longer hear 'Silent Night', just the sound of my teeth chattering and the harsh uncertainty of my breath. I raised my fist, slowly. Above me, the light was already dying, stars lonely in the pale blue twilight.

2

Augustus Fate's author photos depicted him as a giant in a black cape. In real life, he was a few inches shorter than me. He was wearing a navy jumper with holes in it, a pair of brown corduroys and sandals, displaying a row of large, gnarled toes.

'Mr Lancia!' His voice possessed the maturity of the snow-soaked oaks that curled over his cottage. 'Do come in.'

The cottage was delightfully strange: perfect article fodder. There were little tables carved from wood stumps. Tree branches framed a window, forming a curtain rail, from which hung two orange sheets patterned with sequins. There were so many candles, it was surely a hazard, what with so much wood and paper teasing flame, but I liked the atmosphere of eerie romance they created.

Clapping his hands, Fate declared that he would fetch some tea for us. I listened to him clattering in the kitchen and smiled, warming myself by the open fire. I felt at ease, as though I was in the home of a kindly uncle I had known for years. I can do this, I thought, I can actually do this.

I wanted to post some sort of faux-casual update on Twitter, the sort that always fucked me off when I stumbled across them in my newsfeed: 'Some news! I am thrilled to announce . . .' Now it was my turn for revenge. My tweet this morning, 'Off to meet the big man,' had already prompted an orgy of retweets.

I'd read somewhere that Fate had never been online, that he typed all of his correspondence on an Olivetti. I pulled my mobile from my pocket: no reception. I snapped a few surreptitious photos. The walls were lined with bookcases, crammed so tight that the spines visibly strained. There were books on every subject, from every century: Dickens and Eliot, Hitler and Nietzsche, Darwin and Marx, Plato and Virgil. There were books in piles on the floor which propped up tables. Books laid in circles which served as stools, with cushions balanced on the top. Suddenly one of the cushions came to life. As she stretched, the flick of her verbose tail sent a book-tier tumbling to the floor. I was quickly reassembling them when Augustus came back in.

'Causing chaos already?' he remarked, setting the tray down.

'Well – no – your cat—'

'As though Dorothea would do such a thing.' Suddenly his weathered face was taut, his eyes steel. 'Apologise. At once.'

'Dorothea – I'm truly sorry.' I was already editing this moment out of the article. 'I—' Then I saw that his head was tipped back, his mouth rich and wet with laughter. I forced a laugh too, relieved, but on guard now.

He patted the sofa and I sat down on the opposite end. I opened my rucksack and pulled out my iPad.

'No, no,' he said.

'I'm sorry?'

'It's a rule. My rule. No journalists are allowed to write things down while I speak. If you do, you'll only half listen.'

My grin faded when he failed to mirror it.

'I have a terrible memory.'

'You think my answers will be so very dull that you'll forget them?' More laughter. This time it grated. 'I promise to provide you with unforgettable answers.'

'I might not be fully accurate . . .'

'Your subjectivity is inevitable anyway. Misquotations are fine. I don't want people to know me too well. Come away from my cottage with me in your mind like a mist, rather than as a sharply defined creature.'

'OK. Well . . . I'm really chuffed to be here, Mr Fate.'

'Chuffed?' We both winced.

'I've wanted to meet you for just over a decade now, since I was fifteen. You were booked to speak at the Southbank Centre. A coachful of us turned up with our teachers. *Glossop Inn* was on the GCSE syllabus at the time. We waited for hours. One of the boys even sobbed and threatened to slit his wrists with his compass.' It was a slight exaggeration.

'Ah.' Augustus lifted his chin. 'I'm afraid I'm a recluse. That means I have no interest in talking to people.'

'Why did you agree to give a reading in the first place, then?'

'They should never have asked me,' Augustus said. 'If you invite a recluse to give a talk, you can't possibly expect him to turn up.'

I laughed.

'Well, you'll be glad to hear that Timothy's compass was too blunt for the task.'

'*Timothy*? He sounds like a pseudonym for a certain Mr Lancia.' Augustus raised a hirsute eyebrow as I nodded uneasily, playing along. Then he confessed: 'I find meeting people rather difficult. Every time I encounter someone, I feel a nagging urge to put them in one of my books – and there simply isn't room for everyone. My head buzzes with all the possibilities. What might happen to them, I wonder, if I was to turn them into a murderer, or a detective, or put them into the middle of the Arctic.' He drew out a handkerchief, and wiped his forehead. I felt a little sorry for him: perhaps this was as much a strain for him as it was for me.

He reached for one of his hardbacks and pulled out a dog-eared typescript which had been tucked into the inside cover.

'Your thesis is very eloquent, Jaime.'

I could hear the echo of Professor Millhauser in his voice.

'To be honest, I didn't expect you to read it – I thought one of your organisers would be sifting through the entries . . .'

'Oh no. It was I who dictated that an essay had to be submitted. I thought it was better than asking my readers to write an arse-licking piece on why they're my number one fan, with a tongue most suited to the task.'

He looked pleased when I laughed.

'So, Jaime, how did you come to hear of this competition?'

'I saw it online.'

His expression seemed expectant, and so I continued:

'I often doomscroll, to help send me off to sleep – in theory, at least. To be honest, I hate that I do it, but it did lead me to the person who then alerted me to the competition . . . So it's not all bad.'

'And why do you hate that you spend so much time on the internet?' he demanded.

'Well, there was that brief Edenic period where it looked as though we were all going to connect and help each other, but now it just feels like the Silicon Valley geeks are the authors of our lives. And I hate the mob mentality, the pitchfork mania, all that . . .' I trailed off, swallowing.

'I see. You still haven't answered my question properly, though. How did you come to hear of the competition?'

'Right, right – I'm sorry. So, one night I decided to visit a suicide forum – it was a way of researching my thesis. Authors seem to avoid suicide as a plot device, don't you think? They prefer the *deus ex machina*, the glorious death, dictated by Fate or God or whatever. The Russian authors had no qualms about throwing their heroines under trains or young men hanging themselves, but I found it harder to find examples of suicides in Western literature . . .'

'Well, that's absurd.' Augustus crossed his arms. 'Virginia Woolf's *Mrs Dalloway*. Lily Bart in *The House of Mirth* and Jeffrey Eugenides's *The Virgin Suicides* – to name a few . . .'

'Of course, there are *some*. But I'm talking about the ratio of suicides to natural deaths . . .'

'But this is true in life, no?'

'Of course, but there's such drama to suicide – it's a wonder that it's still underrepresented . . . In any case, that's how I met Rachel.'

'So, when you joined this forum – you stated that you were a student seeking help?'

'Not exactly.'

'Oh.' Augustus looked pleased. 'You masqueraded as a depressive?'

'I told them that it was my wish to end my life by throwing myself on to a funeral pyre, in the manner of Dido in *The Aeneid*. It impressed some of them.' I felt sheepish at the memory. 'Rachel saw right through me. She sent me an email telling me to get the hell off the site. And then I emailed her back and asked her why she felt that her depression was more profound than mine and why her choice of death – hanging – was so superior. We started chatting, and she turned out to be one of the most fascinating people I've ever connected with.' I broke off, feeling the sting at the back of my eyes.

'You care very deeply for her?' Augustus's tone was that of a caress.

'I've never met her,' I admitted, my eyes fixed on the carpet. 'But I guess that's why we could open up to each other. It was as though we'd known each other all our lives. And then, one day, the emails stopped. I've been checking the headlines in her home town every day, thinking she's gone missing or something, but I can't find anything.' I sat up, formalising my tone. 'But enough about me. I'm here to interview *you*.'

My mouth was thick with thirst. The tea tray sat on a pile of books, carrying a quaint teapot and two delicate cups, decorated with a Japanese sashiko pattern.

'Shall I serve?' I asked.

'Not yet, not yet.' Augustus shook his head. 'I can assure you that this will be the finest cup of tea you've ever tasted. It's called Grand Kuding and it's an extremely rare tisane, strained from holly leaves. I have augmented it with a few medicinal herbs of my own from Bardsey Island.'

'Your birthplace.' I decided to show off my research.

'Indeed. It takes a little longer to brew than your average cup of Earl Grey.'

The grandfather clock warned me that it was now half past six. I had only been allotted an hour to interview Augustus and I had already wasted a third of my quota.

'Bored?' Augustus remarked, making me jump.

'Not at all! I just – I'm dying to hear about your new book, *Thomas Turridge*.'

'I'm afraid it's not going to be published.' Augustus sighed.

'But – isn't the new novel the whole point of this interview?'

'I handed the book in and my publishers complimented it so excessively that I knew something was wrong. My editor confessed that my adolescent narrator did not convince – he was "too knowing for his years". She asked if I could "tweak" it, and so I have withdrawn the book for the time being.'

'But everything you write is genius,' I cried, and in that moment I actually sounded sincere.

'What genius do you see in my books, exactly?' Augustus narrowed his eyes.

'They transport me into other worlds. I don't like novels that are strictly contemporary, observational – I have enough of real life in real life.'

'Oh, so you think I write escapism, do you?'

'I don't think that it has to be a pejorative term,' I replied hastily. 'We spend twenty-four hours a day stewing in our thoughts, hopes and insecurities. Our minds are forever scurrying on the wheel of thought and dream. Who wouldn't want to escape that?'

'Do you, Jaime? Do you want to escape?'

'Yes,' I answered. 'Sometimes I don't like my life very much.' I felt both vulnerable and irritated at feeling vulnerable. It felt like the confession had been extracted from me. 'But this is a good moment,' I added quietly.

'I think that the tea is nearly ready,' Augustus announced.

It was unlike anything I had seen before: jet-black and as dense as ink. I sniffed it surreptitiously. It smelt like midnight.

'It contains *Scapania undulata*, river startip,' he said. 'Very beneficial for relaxation.'

Little balls floated in my cup before fading into black.

'So when can your readers expect *Thomas Turridge* to be ready?' I asked, taking a sip and hiding a wince at its bitterness.

Augustus, who had raised his cup to his lips, set it back down on his saucer with a sigh.

'I intend to spend several more years on it. As I said, my adolescent narrator refuses to obey me. In that respect,' he gave a wry smile, 'he truly is adolescent.'

'Perhaps you should stop being a recluse for a week and visit some schools. Let their adolescence seep into you.'

'I abhor modern teenagers. They have no idea of where to place an apostrophe and believe that a smiley face can symbolise the exquisite complexity of a heart. They will only pollute me.'

'You could go online, do some research.'

'I lack a modem. I have no wish to connect.'

'I'd love to be a teenager again. Just for the simplicity of it all. I think your teen years are still a time of innocence. You don't understand people. You see girls as sex objects, adults as enemies. Things are black and white. I feel fragmented now. As though I am so many different selves with different people . . .' I trailed off, noticing that Fate's attention had wandered. It was clear that when it came to my life, Augustus was happy to dissect me, collecting data for his novels. But when it came to the cerebral and the literary, he wanted to talk and me to listen; he wanted to be the guru, and for me to be his disciple. I felt a sense of disappointment grey over me. Perhaps this would be the slant of my piece: how we seek out our idols in the hope that they will espy something special in us, and elevate us to their rarefied level. They, meanwhile, need confirmation that they are worthy of worship. Meeting an idol involves an inevitable crash, as the concrete splats into grey shit around their pedestal.

'Well,' I said, 'if the character won't obey you, maybe it's best to let them take on a life of their own?'

'But what a *ridiculous* concept,' Augustus shook his head

sternly, and set his cup down. Judging by the copious splash in his saucer, he had hardly touched his tea. 'Do you know what Nabokov said about Forster? He said – and I quote him word for word – *It was not he who fathered that trite little whimsy about characters getting out of hand; it is as old as the quills, although of course one sympathises with his people if they try to wriggle out of that trip to India or wherever he takes them*. Characters cannot *get out of hand*. Nabokov saw his own characters as galley slaves. That is as it should be.'

I was definitely back with Millhauser now. Fate seemed determined to show me how sharp the whip of his IQ was. I stared down into my teacup, swirling the last dregs of black liquid.

'Rachel,' Augustus said, his voice softening.

'Sorry?'

'It's an interesting name. Of course, if you look back through history, Rachels have never come off well. Jacob's wife – the biblical Rachel, the original Rachel – was cursed unknowingly by her own husband when she stole her father's idols, and then died in childbirth. The Rachel of Martin Amis's *The Rachel Papers* – her name is virtually an anagram of his narcissistic narrator, Charles, who can only bear to love her as an idealised caricature. He learns that she shits; his love dies. Who else? *My Cousin Rachel*, Du Maurier. A possible murderer, as I recall. No, Rachels do not fare well . . . But *your* Rachel? She may surprise you yet.'

I downed my cup and asked tersely if I could use the toilet.

'Aristotle says that every character has a superobjective. I wonder what yours is, Jaime?' Most of the candles had burnt down to a stub; the room was becoming more shadow than light.

'It could be love, perhaps? And yet you chose to fall in love with a woman whom you have never met. A fear of intimacy, then? Perhaps Rachel was, in effect, your erotic muse. Perhaps you are no different from Charles.'

In a flat voice, I asked once again if I could excuse myself. Fate relented with a faint sneer on his face.

The stairs were rickety, rearing up ahead of me like a set of leering teeth. Upstairs, I discovered that the cottage was larger than I had realised. The hallway, covered in a bumpy plum carpet, veered off in three directions. I paused, then followed his instructions: *Turn left, second door on your right*. Inside the bathroom, I examined my unhappy expression in the mirror. *Aristotle says that every character has a superobjective*. From now on, whenever he asked me about Rachel, I would make up a story. The thought of him stealing my lies and weaving them into his prose, confident all the while that he was turning life into art, made me smile: now I had a secret weapon. But I felt sad that I had to fight at all. I had wanted him to like me; I had wanted to like him.

The thought of going back downstairs exhausted me. I flushed the toilet, slipped into the hall, and wandered further down the corridor. There were a number of doors leading off; the house had the feel of a warren. The handle of the furthest door was an ornate, beakish curl. The door opened into an old-fashioned bedroom, a four-poster in the centre, its pillars leaning drunkenly, so that the lace drapes were muddled and doubled. As I entered the room, I became aware of a blackness fogging the periphery of my vision. My body whispered that it would be quite happy to slip between the covers and take a nap.

It was only then that I noticed that there was someone lying on the bed. I immediately cried out in apology, but the room stayed silent. When I lifted the veils, I saw a young woman. Her hair was in a bun, stray wisps coiled around her face. Her ears had multiple piercings, but she was dressed in a black satin dress that was more suited to a Victorian wake. Something scuttled across her cheek and I jumped; a spider had found a home on her lashes and skin. I leant down over her purplish lips. Against my cheek, I felt the slightest flutter of breath, like the last trill of smoke from a dying fire.

'What the hell . . .' I whispered. Why would Fate leave this door unlocked? Was it all a macabre set piece? The woman a hired actress, displayed so that my experience might become legend, so that a thousand blogs might speculate about the Mysterious Woman in Black in Fate's Spare Room? I stared down at the still of her lashes, hoping that her face might convulse with laughter. Then, as my eyes travelled down to her hands, my smile died. They were crossed over her chest, more bone than flesh, and there was a terrible twitch in her joints, as though she was locked in a nightmare, or tapping a helpless Morse code. A catheter had been inserted into one hand, and a thin ribbon of tubing looped down the bed, disappearing under a door into an adjoining room.

I became conscious that my name was being called. I left the room in a daze, closing the door gently behind me, and then hurried down to meet Fate.

'Lost, were you? It's a jungle up there, with all those doors and that ocean of carpeting.' I no longer took his sneer personally, now I knew what he was trying to hide. He held my gaze for too long and then looked away abruptly. Perhaps it was guilt. It wouldn't stop me ringing the police.

'Feeling OK?' His tone was unnaturally jovial.

'I'm fine,' I said, though the blackness was returning, lapping at the edges of my consciousness. For a moment his face was a blur of storm clouds.

'You look as though you ought to drink more tea – it will make you feel better, Jaime.' He clapped his hand on my shoulder, his expression suddenly tender. I thought then that I had misunderstood him, seen him through the fractured prism of my fears. My heart reminded me of Forster's dictum: *Only connect.* I opened my mouth to speak of superobjectives – the word now an olive branch between us – when the world tilted, the blackness fluttering around me like paper birds. My body slid to the floor. I heard a distant mew; fur caressed my ear-tip. I felt the ooze of my bladder involuntarily spilling its contents. His face a moon above me. My saucer in shards on the floor. I called out for Rachel, told her I was losing the fight. And then he had me.

The First Story

OXFORD, 1861

I

'Jack, Jack, show me your light!'

Darkness. I found myself in a corridor behind a moth-nibbled red velvet curtain, holding a candle in my right hand. Wax seared my skin, cooling and solidifying in blotches on my knuckles. The flame was a barometer of my heart, trembling nervously on its wick, threatening to blow out but clinging on as best it could. Yet I realised that I was deriving pleasure from it too; the race of my heartbeat, the damp of my brow all giving rise to a state of heightened awareness.

'Where am I?' I whispered.

Everything seemed both familiar and unfamiliar. Then, once again, came the voices. They were childish and they rang out with threat and thrill:

'Jack, Jack, show me your light!'

My body acted with a will of its own, as though it knew entirely how to behave. My hands wrenched aside the curtain; my feet hurried across the wooden boards; the golden halo of the candle shimmered. At the far end of the corridor, in the grey gloom, I saw the face of a young girl, not yet fourteen, her rosy cheeks framed with fair plaits. My hand curled around a doorknob; I twisted it.

'One . . . Two . . . Three . . .' A voice was counting in the distance. 'Four . . . Five . . . Six . . .'

The room was a chaos of silhouettes which my candle was too weak to give substance to. Stepping forwards, I tripped and thereupon grabbed at the closest mystery to save myself from falling. My saviour began to rock, emitting a repetitive squeak. The rocking horse was dappled grey in colour, and when I held the candle close to its eyes, I perceived a sadness in the glass. It made me yearn to press my cheek against its neck, but when I stroked its mane the desiccated feel of the wool made me feel foolish.

A rattling sound at the door! Out, out, I blew the candle. The dark shape that appeared in the doorway was unmistakably the girl with the fair plaits: Eleanor. Her breath was dramatic, rapidly rising and falling with the thrill of the game; she seemed unable to deduce whether my silhouette was human or toy.

'Jack, Jack, show me your light . . .' Her voice was soft and lyrical now, as though she was singing a hymn in church; yet firm too, possessing the threat of a governess. Closer and closer she tiptoed. The uncertainty of whether she had seen me caused my heart to become so loud, I feared it would give me away.

Only once before had I been in such close proximity to a girl, to the possibility of a kiss.

Last summer, when Nanny had been quite sick with a fever and Father had been attending a lecture by Mr. Darwin, I had been taken on an adventure by Ruffles, the boy who worked in our kitchen. I had just turned thirteen years old, and if someone had asked me to sketch a map of England I would have drawn my genteel Oxford as large as a continent, and the rest of the country would have appeared as but a crumb, separated by my ocean of ignorance. The wider world that Ruffles introduced me to was one of dark alleys and back streets possessing lurid smells. There were children who shocked me with the dirt and dust in their hair, and I fear Nanny would have had a fit at the very sight of them. They had been playing football with a pig's bladder (Ruffles said they had been gifted it by the butcher) until they broke off and squealed, 'The Hurdy-Gurdy Man is coming!'

Ruffles led me down an alleyway in the shape of a crooked finger. Up until then, I had only seen women who were drab as a dreary winter's day, like Nanny, or parcelled up in feathered hats and swishing dresses. These women showed flesh I had not seen before, dirty skin revealed by soiled white hems; these women lacked teeth and had hair that fell about their faces; these women possessed a sort of recklessness, prowled with mischievous menace.

One woman, poised in a grimy doorway, beckoned us. As we drew closer, we saw that her beauty was a mirage, painted on to a face that ill fortune was already marring with premature scars and lines. The children's distant voices became a chant – 'The Hurdy-Gurdy Man is coming! The Hurdy-Gurdy Man is coming!' A sweep of her skirt; a flash of her thigh, around which was tied a red ribbon. She informed us that if we paid 6*d*., she would allow us to touch her skin. I begged Ruffles to pay for us both, and he did, his eyes starry, and I wondered if this must be how it felt to imbibe laudanum, I was so drugged with desire. She examined me as though *she* were purchasing *me*, and I stood very tall, cheeks so red I feared birds might mistake them for cherries and peck at them. Having counted out the money, she stowed it in the rim of her dress, before warning us that we had better be gone, or she would inform the police what services we had paid for. A shady figure appeared at the end of the alley and, fearing our throats might be slit, we turned and ran. I tumbled back home with bursting ribs, my eyes bittered with tears, for I was convinced that the Hurdy-Gurdy Man was chasing me, ready to toss me straight into the pits of Hell for the sin of lust.

As I stood there in the nursery, this remembrance came rushing back vividly. Eleanor was but a few paces away from me now. She seemed so solid – the white flashes of her eyes and teeth confirming her presence despite the persistence of darkness – that an uneasy sensation crept over me; though I knew her failure to acknowledge me was part of her game, I felt as insubstantial as a spirit, as easily blown out as a candle.

Our breaths caressed. I remained still, so as to make her believe that she was safe. Then I quickly grasped her by the shoulders and pressed my lips to hers. The moment was over before it had begun. The door opened. It was the Hurdy-Gurdy Man, ready to punish me, to whip me to death. I let out a cry that Eleanor took up as a scream.

'Children! What is all this noise and fuss!'

Curtains were yanked open; light flooded the room: reality asserted itself. Nanny, peevish, declared that we were disturbing my father, who was working below in his study. What did we think we were doing, playing with such savagery of spirit?

'If you play, then you must play quietly, with your toy soldiers. Soon you will be home, Eleanor, and I hope then that you will pick up your Bible and pray.'

The other children crept into the nursery, meek and shrunken. We settled down in a muted manner, whispering, self-conscious. I picked up the lead soldiers and pretended that I was fighting the Russians. Eleanor set herself down on the rocking horse and forced it on at an exuberant pace. From her furtive glances, I deduced that she was trying to ascertain whether Nanny had seen our illicit act; she appeared tortured by the uncertainty.

Through the window I gazed across at the dreaming spires, picking out the tall, spiked one where the Vicar preached. My soldiers clashed and bashed and battled, until I could bear my agitation no longer – I stood up, grabbed Eleanor and pulled her down from the rocking horse, declaring that it was my turn to ride him.

'Goodness me, Thomas, you rude boy, how dare you behave like a savage!' Nanny sprayed fury over me.

I enjoyed the trembling relief of admonition, like the absolution at the end of confession – even if it did mean the end of playtime for us all. The other children were sent home, Eleanor sobbing loudly, and I was told to clean up the nursery. I felt calmer then, as I gathered the soldiers in their tin and the rocking horse's violent pace became slower and slower, until it finally came to a rest.

My father's study was a place that I was forbidden to enter without permission. It possessed towering bookcases filled with scientific volumes whose titles were either difficult or silly, like *Zoonomia*, which made my mouth trumpet into a funny shape when I spoke it. By the window there was a desk covered in a messy heap of Father's papers. The room had a heavy, ponderous feel; the grandfather clock ticked as though it was forever marching on the spot. I wondered how a clock died and if its death would sound like the slowing of footsteps. I was in the hallway, pretending to be a flying machine, my lips reverberating with the thrum of an engine, when my vehicle crashed into the door of Father's study. It opened a few inches.

I stood very still, gazing at a fragment of Father's face, crumpled and made wet with tears. Nanny – with her artful predilection for silently appearing – was suddenly behind me, whispering, 'Come quick, Thomas,' and drawing me away up the stairs.

'But – Father – he needs my help,' I cried, wriggling against her grip.

'You know it is the most difficult time, with it being the anniversary . . .'

For once, Nanny did not berate me for being so slow to change into my bedclothes. I lay in bed and recalled some advice that Father had given me about thoughts being like trains; if one was upset, the best cure was to simply switch to a superior carriage and find a nicer journey. Thus, I pictured a train with *Eleanor* painted on the side, puffing smoke and charging forth at a glorious speed. The thought of when I might see her again was a vexation, until

I realised that tomorrow was a Sunday. For the first time in years, I ardently looked forward to attending church.

'Father,' I asked, 'do you think Mother in Heaven hears us singing hymns when we go to church?'

I regretted the words the moment I uttered them. My father had been pulling gloves on to his hands and he paused, so that the leather half hung from his fingers like a bat, and addressed me quietly: 'We'll visit her grave after the service.'

I loved my father beyond anyone or anything else in the world. If God had made man in his image, then I longed to be made in the image of my father; indeed, I felt as though he had created a mould for me to fill as I grew up. He was a tall, formidable personage. His face was habitually set in an expression of stern grandeur, from the firmness of his jawline to the two large eyebrows that fierced above his eyes. Yet if one looked a little closer, one might detect a softness, perhaps even a nervousness, in his smile, as though his commanding countenance was a cultivated front. His frock coats and waistcoats were always spotless, and his hair never had a curl out of place. He was precise about the value of manners and there were numerous etiquette guides hidden in the drawers of his desk, which advised on whether or not to remove gloves when shaking a lady's hand or how to respond if one's nemesis greeted one with a bow. His cane had only ever been used to tap me gently as a child, and if a fly entered his study, he would refuse to swat it, but wait patiently for it to zizz its way back through the window.

In recent years, his interest in science had grown ardent. Many a thrilling experiment had been performed in his study. For example, there was the evening he left a female butterfly in a cage on his desk and awoke to find the room veritably wallpapered with the male of the species, a key breakthrough in proving his theory that insects attract through scent. My father regularly exchanged correspondence with Mr. Darwin, Thomas Henry Huxley and Émile Blanchard. He lived life with zeal, though he was so absorbed in his ideas that I sometimes felt jealous of them. So often did the door of his study present its stern face to me that when I did spend time with my father, I felt anxious to elongate it, to be wise enough to earn his attention. Ever since the death of my mother, there had always been a palpable tension between us before Sunday service.

Outside, the church bells were echoing among the rooftops and spires, weaving into the rattle of carriages and the patter of hooves. The men strolling past looked so tall in their top hats, while the women yanked their shawls tight around their shoulders to see off an unexpected chill. As they reached the entrance of the church, they formed one body that flowed through the stone gate.

I pictured my mother's grave beneath the hawthorn tree. The loss had made me vividly aware that anyone I love might be seized from this world at any time. Fears beset me: that my father would not manage to reach the entrance of the church, for a carriage would suddenly veer from the road and crush him, the horses' hooves painted red with his blood; or else a chimney might crumble from a house and tumble on to his head, splitting his skull. His body might easily share the earth with my mother, their bony fingers inches apart. By the time we reached the church, I had devised thirty or so unfortunate ends for my father and was clutching his arm with my trembling hand.

Various neighbours greeted us and I noted that while the men were respectful and cheerful, the women were unable to resist smiling. I felt relieved, as though all the love that was being directed towards my father would sustain his place in the world, ensure that he lived for many years to come; yet the dilution of his attention also filled me with unease, and I tugged gently at his sleeve, prompting him to smile down at me in reassurance.

We sat three pews from the back. I spotted the blonde head of Eleanor shimmering in the congregation; she gave me a cool look, one that did not thaw even when I smiled at her. Nanny pinched my hand, and filled it with a hymn book. She often spoke of how the Vicar's youthful charisma had drawn a new throng to the Sunday service, though at the age of twenty-four he seemed ancient to me. She was so attentive to his address that I was able to let my eyes venture once more across the pews, without her noticing. Next to Eleanor sat a young woman in possession of chestnut hair, held in a bun that was escaping its pins. There were rows of candelabras at the front, and the flickering light danced off the choirboys' faces, haloed the statues of angels, sparked in the colours of the stained-glass windows. When the light reached her hair it seemed to slow down and linger lovingly on the curls straying down her back.

II

The Vicar broke off from his speech to frown and tug at his ebullient mutton-chops, before resuming his impassioned tirade:

'Imagine yourself in the Garden of Eden! Imagine the moist fruit hanging from the branch, the seduction of the forked hiss in your ear, advising you to taste its succulence – can it be said that it is possible to resist such temptation, day after day? Nay, I say it is! As Ecclesiastes reminds us, "whatsoever thy hand findeth to do, do it with thy might". Eve's decision cannot be deemed purely one of inevitability – nay, it was her choice to pluck the licentious bloom, to sink her teeth into its flesh, to gain awareness of her nudity, and may I surmise that she no doubt found its taste was bitter with consequence. Thus, like all sinners, she made the assumption that she knew best, forgetting that it is God who knows best, that we should choose to surrender our will to his commandments, and choose to become the blank page for his dictation . . .'

The parishioners clasped their hymn books as though they anchored them to the earth, or tugged their shawls more tightly around their shoulders, and mouthed a silent prayer; no doubt even the bats in the cloisters were wrapping their wings about their ears. I was confused by their foolishness. If God was dictating our lives, as the Vicar had so often expounded in his sermons, then we could be happy, safe in the knowledge that He was looking after us. The thought was so reassuring that I began to feel bored, and an urge came over me to shuffle my feet. I peered down at my hand. *Move*, I instructed my forefinger. It disobeyed and then, as though with a will of its own, it shuddered. What power made it still or lively? Was I the God of my own body? Or had He written down all of humanity's actions in a very large book and on some page, maybe page 32,989,122,000, it was written that *Thomas shall move his finger*? I glanced once more at the lady sitting by Eleanor and wondered if God had been in an especially good mood when he made her; Nanny, meanwhile, had obviously been composed from bile after the consumption of some particularly indigestible food.

'For those brave men who have fought in the Crimea, their fate is in God's hands. Only He and He alone decides the hour of our death . . .'

I was startled to observe a blur in Nanny's eyes that she quickly dabbed away. Father had said that she had a sweetheart whom she wrote to, who was fighting at the front; when I remarked that he was probably glad to escape her, he chided me for being unkind and I felt quite meek.

The service over, the congregation trailed outside, lingering to converse and gossip. How gratefully did I breathe in the air, chirpy with birdsong and sugared with summer delights. I observed that my father was quite engrossed in chatting with his friend, Mr. Gwent. Eleanor waved at me and I sidled over to her. The beautiful woman stood beside her, and I was quite shocked, as I noticed her plain clothing, to realise that she was Eleanor's governess. When she flashed a smile down at me, I was unable to speak, and as for perusing her – well, a glance that lasted more than a few seconds became unbearable. Perceiving this, Eleanor laughed and her governess gave her a firm look; not the caustic type that I had become accustomed to from Nanny, but one that contained affection, like a pinch on the waist or a tickle under one's armpit.

'Come,' said Eleanor. 'Let me show you something.'

I wanted to linger near her governess, but she smiled and encouraged us: 'Do explore. Enjoy yourselves!'

I replied with a knowing glance, asserting that we were the adults and that I was engaging in this theatre only to humour Eleanor, before following the latter to a large grave:

IN LOVING MEMORY OF
WILLIAM FEVER BERRIL
BORN ON 17 NOVEMBER 1796
WHO ENTERED INTO REST
1 SEPTEMBER 1856

'Look!' Eleanor touched the stone. 'This man lived until he was sixty! So very old!'

I knew that the correct return was, 'Well, he is now at peace in Heaven'; words which had been spoken a hundred times to Father and me, often with so little feeling that I wanted to spit and roar. Instead, I turned to Eleanor and solemnly replied with, 'I suspect he is now in Hell, his feet being devoured by rats.'

She looked aghast and giggled. Everything that I did and said felt as though I were parading on a stage beneath a spotlight, gazed at by an audience of a thousand chestnut-haired governesses. But when I glanced over at her, she was with my father, addressing him with that deferential air that he inspired in all.

'We may be visiting *her* grave soon,' Eleanor said in a cold voice.

'Your governess has scarlet fever?' I asked fearfully.

'Oh no.' Eleanor picked up a piece of briar, touching its thorns with the tips of her nails. 'She is quite mad. Mother says that Rachel hears voices.'

'Rachel? Is that her name?'

'Did you not hear me? She hears voices.'

'She seems kind enough to me,' I remarked. 'She looks like an angel. God will surely cure her.'

Eleanor pressed the briar against my skin so that I cried out.

'She will soon be in an asylum,' Eleanor whispered. 'And you can send her love letters there, if you like her so much!'

That night, as I lay in bed and gazed through the gap in my curtains, up to a slit of starry sky, I mused on a telegram I wished to send to God. It would enquire as to why Mother, aged twenty-eight, had died of tuberculosis when she was such a kind woman, while other, cruel and unpleasant folk lived until they were sixty. In church we had been assured that everything was fair and just, yet it seemed to me as though God, having laid down a set of rules for writing our lives, had decided to disregard his own plan.

If I was always agitated after our trips to the graveyard, my father often had a softer look in his eyes. On our journey home, he gazed up at the billows of wandering clouds, pointing out stratocumulus and other formations, as well as species of birds such as honey buzzards and magpies, for he was as well acquainted with the landscape of the sky as with the creatures that flew in it, and was beginning to inspire in me a love for our feathered friends.

During my first year at Eton, I had missed my father very much, and written him frequent letters. When we had travelled back to school for Hilary term, he had bade me farewell with a stern countenance, pressing a letter into my hand. The instructions therein had advised that I should refrain from ever touching my member with the intention of extracting idle pleasure from it, for such an act was degenerative and poor marks in my studies would ensue. It had concluded with the words: 'We will never speak of this letter or acknowledge its existence.' When I arrived home for the summer holidays, I blushed in his presence, but his face remained set; he behaved as though he had never dipped his pen into the inkwell and committed such words to paper.

Lying there, my hand twitched in temptation for one brief moment, but a triptych of correction loomed above me, formed of the Hurdy-Gurdy Man, Father and Nanny. I wished that I could take leeches for lust, that they might be applied to my mind and suck out the sins therein.

Nay, it was more than lust. I was in love with Rachel. When I thought of Eleanor presently, she was like a wildflower from a meadow set next to the rarest species of orchid. I felt sad at the thought that my love might be

God's creation, an emotion that did not really belong to me – that I might just as easily have fallen for a chambermaid. Yet when I recalled Rachel's beauty, I felt determined that this love was mine. Like my father with his experiments, my heart had combined a medley of chemicals to form a frothing, beautiful feeling; one that contained colours beyond the rainbow's spectrum.

I fixed my eyes on one of the more prominent stars visible through my bedroom window. Its beauty intensified the amorous joy in my heart, such that an energy seemed to fire through me. When it happened, I was quite stunned – the sudden drop of gold, a star falling to earth as though unable to disobey my command; I pictured it lying in some field, leaving its echo burning in the night sky. Quickly, I pulled my covers over my head, suddenly afeared by my power, and ardent to tell myself that it was just a coincidence.

III

On the following Friday evening, Nanny ordered that I dress in my best suit, for Father and I were to partake of dinner at Mr. James Gwent's house. Travelling by carriage, we passed a procession of stone colleges, their dark doorways resembling elderly, cross fellows sitting in hunched judgement. Every time I saw a woman with chestnut hair peeking out from beneath the brim of her hat my hopes were first raised, and then rudely dashed.

Five days had passed since I had last seen Rachel, and yearning had hollowed out my stomach. Every night when I knelt down beside my bed I made desperate pleas to God that, in his book of the world's destiny, he might scribble a few lines whereby Rachel and I became ardent lovers. I attempted to please our Creator with good deeds, each conducted with slightly less ardour than the one before, and with a sinking feeling that our Heavenly Father was unimpressed by such trivial acts. My gesture needed to be grand, and so when Nanny happened to tell me the story of how St Francis of Assisi had built a church with his bare hands, I had run into the garden, found three small rocks and placed them beneath the willow tree, declaring that they were the foundations of a church that would pierce the clouds with its spire by the end of 1861.

We disembarked from our carriage and approached Mr. Gwent's abode. As always, I was tickled by the note that hung upon his gate:

> I MUST ASK ANYONE ENTERING THE HOUSE NEVER TO CONTRADICT ME OR DIFFER FROM ME IN ANY WAY, AS IT INTERFERES WITH THE FUNCTIONING OF MY GASTRIC JUICES.

My father rang the bell and the front door was opened by the maid. Mr. Gwent, on his hands and knees, gazed up at us with a quizzical expression and proceeded to bark loudly, then turned – so that I fancied a tail frisking behind him – and crawled down the hallway, his trousers squeaking on the polished boards. My father bowed and offered the maid his coat and top hat. I ventured to pat our friendly canine on the head – only to cry out when he gently nipped the pudge of my palm.

'Good Lord, James!' My father admonished him for his display of eccentricity. 'That is quite enough – the game has gone too far, I fear.'

Mr. Gwent jumped to his feet, looking far meeker as a human than he had as a pet. He apologised, and after vigorously shaking our hands invited us to join him for tea.

Mr. Gwent's parlour was my favourite place in the entire world. It was not so much a cabinet of curiosities as a museum dedicated to preserving the mind and heart of a true eccentric. Candelabras lined the grand mantelpiece, their twisted branches reaching towards the silvery light of a large mirror. In the room's shadowy corners lurked all sorts of treasures – a skeleton hanging in a glass cage, a stuffed dodo perched on a card table, and the original Pandora's box, if Gwent's boasting was to be believed. His bookcases were filled with every volume of Dickens and H. G. Wells, along with Gwent's own novels and dusty tomes describing magic rituals from ages past. Even the fire had a mysterious crackle, as though inviting one to cry, 'Open Sesame!' and see the flames leap apart.

His large méridienne, covered with skins and furs, reminded me of the pictures of shaggy wildebeest in our schoolbooks, and there we reclined while the maid entered to serve us tea. Mr. Gwent insisted on making us pause to savour its aromas before we sipped it. We sat with our fingers curled around our teacups, as though we were trapped in a still life, inviting the scents from our cups to parlay with our nostrils. My father, who had learnt to recognise herbs, began citing traces of rosemary and bergamot. I, meanwhile, could only translate the smells into colours and impulses.

'Nostalgic,' I murmured. 'Silver . . . A long way from home.' My father rolled his eyes, but Mr. Gwent beamed at my fancy.

'Come, where is it from?' my father finally asked, impatiently.

'It is Tie Guan Yin, a Chinese oolong tea,' Mr. Gwent informed us. He went on to explain that the tea was less dramatic than black tea, but more provocative than green. My mind began to drift and I quietly set down my cup, drawn to the large mirror above the fireplace, which possessed a gilt frame and was scritched with age. I fancied that it stored countless memories of my face, from a chubby, angelic cherub to a thirteen-year-old boy on the verge of adulthood, and beyond that too: a prediction of my elderly self, with whitened hair and craggy lines storing secrets of a life well lived.

'Dinner time, Thomas,' said Mr. Gwent, smiling down at me. Under his arm was tucked the dodo, which eyed me with a curious gaze.

We entered the dining room, a dark, stuffy room, sickly with candlelight. Heavy oils adorned the walls, of men who seemed as old and creaky as furniture, looked upon by various animal heads perched on cabinets. I had once heard my father declare that they were the worst examples of taxidermy he had ever seen. There was a stoat which seemed to have welcomed death as a relief from some sort of terrible constipation, a cross-eyed deer, and an antelope whose neck was so long that he clearly aspired to be a giraffe. The table was set for four, and on one velvet-cushioned chair, Mr. Gwent set down the dodo; this was a habit that my father had tried to dissuade him from for some time, but to no avail. We were served mulligatawny soup, the dodo included, though he obviously found its scent unsavoury, for he did not lift his claw to his spoon. Mr. Gwent proceeded to speak, with increasing vehemence, of overcrowding on trains and the profit the train companies were making from our discomfort. He spat out little pellets of soup as he spoke: mulligatawny exclamation marks. This was very typical of Mr. Gwent, who regularly alternated between railing against the mundane injustices of the world and consoling himself with the magical and the extraordinary. He was also malignly scathing about Dickens, his literary rival, whom Father had to pretend to dislike when in truth he devoured every instalment of his novels.

'Tell me, then,' my father said, attempting to redirect the train of conversation, 'how is your latest novel progressing?'

'Oh!' Mr. Gwent sipped his soup as though becoming aware of its flavour for the first time that evening. 'Very well indeed. I am close to finishing.'

I had seen the covers of Mr. Gwent's novels, sporting monsters and machines; I had been told that I would be allowed to read them only when I became a man, a fact that Nanny had asserted and my father had confirmed.

'In what year is your latest novel set?' Father asked, as the servants brought in the beef steak.

'2014,' Gwent declared. 'There will be all sorts of glorious inventions present in my tale. Men will have machines which will enable them to fly, for instance.'

'We can already fly,' said my father, with a twinkle in his eye. 'Why, we have the hot air balloon.'

'In 2014, they will invent hot air balloons that will outpace even the birds in the sky,' said Mr. Gwent.

I had never had the opportunity to travel in such a balloon, though Father had promised to take me to see the one at Cremorne Gardens. I envisaged the hot air balloon of 2014 with great feathery wings, flapping so that it might soar higher and higher.

'Will it be another sensation novel?' My father enquired.

'It will be a love story,' said Mr. Gwent, his eyes acquiring a dreamy hue. 'The man shall be chasing the woman, hoping for her hand in marriage, but she will rebuff him, for she prefers her independence.'

'What a perverse creature such a woman would be,' said Father. 'A woman doomed to spinsterhood and wilful loneliness.'

I saw a familiar look pass between them, as though both were removing their top hats and rolling their sleeves up.

'Take Darwin's *Biston betularia*, the speckled moth,' said Mr. Gwent, his voice rising. 'Its dark colouring is quite different from the moth of pre-industrial times, when it was able to survive as a speckled white. So too will the species of woman be quite different in 2014, in reflection of the changing culture. Why, her very mind, her physique, her chemical being will be an entirely different concoction.'

'*Homo sapiens* is not a butterfly,' said my father. 'We contain certain fixed traits that God created when He made us. Why, I was recently reading a novel written in 1746 that spoke to my heart in its themes of love, of marriage, of parenthood. The stories of people do not change so very much.'

'What will churches be like in 2014?' I asked, thinking of my own paltry tower of stones in the garden.

'Oh, the churches will have all become haberdasheries and coaching inns,' Mr. Gwent sighed. 'For God will be dead in 2014.'

I froze, my knife half embedded in my steak. My father did not look quite as shocked as I might have feared at such blasphemy, which only served to exacerbate my alarm.

'It is entirely the fault of your friend,' Mr. Gwent went on, giving Father a sly glance. 'He is the man who is killing God.'

'Charles Darwin is a most misunderstood man,' said my father. 'He is a devout fellow whose scientific discoveries are truly an act of propitiation.'

Mr. Gwent's expression looked most dubious.

Mr. Gwent concluded the evening with his regular treat; we gathered in the living room, the lamps subdued, the curtains drawn tight, and his magic lantern projected its eerie phantasmagoria on to the wall. I habitually adored such shows, finding that they poured bizarre colours into my mind and cleansed me of my cares, but, on this occasion, it only seemed to inspire anxiety. I pictured God scrawling on his sheet of paper, and dipping his pen into the inkwell to find there was no ink, his sentences dwindling to the strange marks ancient tribes might have made, when we lived in caves and wrote on walls. The images flew as though Mr. Gwent had wandered the streets at night, collecting dreams to pour into his lantern: lions that leapt on to the backs of galloping horses; monkeys exchanging stovepipe hats; the goblins who stole the sexton Gabriel Grubb. I pictured God lying down in a bed, tired and old, a tear trickling down His cheek as the people of 2014 laughed and chatted and cared not what happened to Him, unaware that He was drawing His last breaths. On the wall, an image of a gentleman in his bed ended my daydreaming: a giant beetle with spindly legs was climbing up the sheets. I cried out in fright. My father chided Mr. Gwent and declared that it was time for me to return home.

In the carriage, I asked Father if Mr. Gwent's theories were true. He laughed.

'Why, of course not! Do you think man has the power to destroy or create God? God was here before us, and will continue to be after we have gone.'

I stared out of our carriage window in order to hide my blurred eyes from him. My mother would not suffer a Heaven of cobwebs and fading light; God would look after her still. My father went on to tell me that I should not mind Mr. Gwent, because he had become an eccentric ever since he had lost his wife, Mary, before he moved to Oxford. That sad fate had occurred twelve years ago, my father explained, and that was why Mr. Gwent put a dodo on the table, in her place, as a sort of mourning gesture.

IV

On the 3rd of July, my father and I, together with the Carmichaels, set off on an excursion to Margate Sands. We travelled first class on the train. I sat by the window, and while Rachel was the furthest away from me, I was attuned to her voice, detailing her patient and sweet manner, as she supervised Eleanor's needlework. It was almost painful, the intensity of this sinful thrill in my blood.

The guilt was accentuated by the concert my father had taken me to the previous evening, where I had heard Beethoven for the first time. I had expected his ninth symphony to be as polite as the hymns we heard in church, and so the rousing torrent of music – being dashed from calm to storm and storm to calm – had astonished me. Several times, I had glanced up at my father to make sure he had brought me to the right concert hall, amazed that I should be permitted to experience such emotion; but his eyes remained fixed on the orchestra, his jaw fierce; and in the finale, as the choir stood and sang from the depths of their souls, I clenched my fists to fight the tears in my throat. Was it a blasphemy that no hymn in church had given me faith in God the way this music had? Surely it was not: for music of such truth, such beauty could not exist unless there is divinity in the world. As though to assuage these concerns, God had opened his book and concocted this visit to the seaside, for which my gratitude was a sweet ache.

There were sighs and shivers when we stepped out on to the platform. Back in Oxford the sky had stretched out like a big billowing blue sail, from which a benignant sun had shone down; here the sky looked as though it was in a most foul temper. The foaming waves seemed to toss forth gusts of icy chill. On the beach, we huddled together beneath several parasols, sharing round pies, lemonade and sandwiches thick with roast beef and Worcestershire sauce. I thought the food was delicious but I noticed that Rachel treated it as though she was a despondent bird: every mouthful was picked apart into crumbs, before finally being surrendered to her mouth. An ache spread through me; I longed to fill her with such a happiness that she would treat every meal like a joyful feast.

A shrill wind slipped under our skin and whistled through our blood as Father guided us children on a brisk walk to the rock pools to search for fossils. They glimmered with scuttling curiosities; upon being the first to discover one, Eleanor let out a cry. Observing that Rachel had wandered away from our party, I stole over to the larger rocks – and there I found her, weeping vehemently.

I felt frightened then, though Father had told me that women cry very often, prompted by little reason. Kneeling down beside her, I dared to reach out and touch her hair, the way that Father consoled me when I fell and cut my knees. She emitted a sigh. When I curled my hand away, she smiled through her tears and whispered a request for me to continue; we sat in this pose for a while and I kept on stroking the same place, until it felt quite warm.

A most curious sensation of déjà vu came over me. I imagined that we had spoken together like this before, while strolling across a wide green park, beneath a row of thick-leafed oak trees. Rachel's expression then was morbid, but when I nudged her and pointed out a fairground on the horizon, a flicker of delight passed over her face, as though reminding her that happiness was possible.

Finally, she spoke:

'Do you ever feel as though you are living in the wrong century? As though you were born at the wrong time?'

I immediately felt lost; then I considered a book that Father had recently shown me, which included some cave paintings. 'Well, I suppose it must have been jolly fun to have a spear and hunt animals . . .'

She frowned.

'Look at you,' she said. 'You are so natural in this world. Perhaps it is because you are a man in a man's world.'

'We are in *God's* world,' I corrected her gently. 'But I don't think he's being very fair or kind to certain people—' I broke off, muttering a silent apology for any possible blasphemy.

'Perhaps God is punishing me,' she said, sluicing sand through her fingers.

'If you went to confession, then perhaps you might feel better,' I said. 'In the Bible, you know, many of God's Chosen Ones heard voices. Moses did, and Cain. And Elijah too.'

She gave me a sharp look, clearly furious that her secret was so well known, and then wept a fresh bout of tears.

'Oh God – I do hate to cry . . . As it happens, I heard the Voice this morning. He said to me, *Rachel awoke on*

Thursday morning to discover that the Carmichaels had planned a trip to Margate Sands. The day was interrupted, however, when they were disturbed by a sudden flurry of snow.'

'But there is no snow,' I said softly. 'Snow would be absurd. It is just a little chilly.'

'Yet I had no knowledge of this trip to the beach, for Mrs. Carmichael is apt to forget to tell me anything, and Mr. Carmichael – well, I do my best to avoid him. The Voice spoke true.'

'Then you are God's special messenger, his Chosen One!' I cried. 'Why, if the Vicar knew—'

'No!' Her eyes widened. 'You must *never* speak of it to him. Eleanor's mother already mentioned my . . . concerns, and do you know what he said? He said I could not possibly be hearing the words of God, for God only speaks to male prophets. Jesus had ten disciples who were all men.' At this, she let out a small laugh. 'What is a gift for men is a curse for women. The Vicar would gladly drown me as a witch, or have me locked away in an asylum until I rot. This must remain our secret, yes?'

'Yes,' I cried. 'I do promise you, Rachel. But my father is friends with Mr. Darwin, and he says that the world is changing and we must grapple with our faiths and allow them to adapt too, no matter how painful. If I were to speak to him, he might—'

'Perhaps sometime soon, but only when I am ready. For now, be careful what you say. Do you understand? Or you will never see me again.'

'I promise.' I offered my hand and she shook it, sniffing back the threat of further tears and nodding vigorously.

'My father says that there is no better cure for an ill than a holiday. Perhaps Mrs. Carmichael would allow you to leave Oxford and visit home for a few days?'

'Oh, I cannot go back,' Rachel murmured, and I wondered if she was referring to Manchester, where Father had said she was born. 'I cannot go back and I cannot stay. I feel at home neither there nor here. Mrs. Carmichael says that one makes a home in the heart and there peace is to be found, but I cannot feel any.' And to my shock and consternation, she suddenly picked up a rock and dashed its edge against her left hand. A series of red welts welled up on her knuckles and blood trickled over her fingers.

A shadow fell over us.

'An accident, I presume?' Father asked, but there was something knowing in his tone, and I noted that Rachel kept her eyes downcast. I felt a surge of anger towards him, wondering how he could be so callous, when he commanded: 'Well, then, Thomas! Pass her your handkerchief – be a gentleman!'

I hastily pulled it from my pocket and watched as Father knelt down and slowly bound her hand with surprising gentleness. There was no pin to secure it, so he removed a brooch from her shawl. A faint pinkish snake appeared on the handkerchief, just as I felt something wet touch my forehead. In my enervated, jangled state, I thought that it had been placed there by the lips of the Virgin Mary in order to reassure me, but when I glanced up I saw that it was snowing.

V

My father once made the following observation with regard to his dear friend: 'Mr. Gwent is not the sort of charismatic hero that he chooses to pen in his adventures. Nay, Mr. Gwent is the type of man who might go out having forgotten to tie his shoelaces and then, having taken a wrong turn down an avenue of unfortunate kismet, trip over them and fall into a disquieting calamity.' Thus, I was only a little saddened when my father informed me that he would not be attending our planned trip to London to see *The Colleen Bawn* with Mr. Gwent, for Mr. Darwin had asked for his assistance regarding some insectivorous plants. It was my hope that under Gwent's sole care, I too might be thrust into a thrilling, calamitous adventure.

Our journey to London took much of the day, and I must confess that I slept for the greater part of its duration. A week had passed since the Margate excursion, during which I had been frequently disturbed by the memory of our hasty departure, prompted by unexpected snowfall. The journey home had bustled with perfidious whispers and pantomime looks. Subsequently, I had asked my father if Rachel and Mr. Gwent were of a similar mind and malady, but he had replied, '*He* is eccentric – that is quite a different thing!' While Gwent's madness possessed a lightness, like a giddy, brightly coloured kite that one cannot control, there was something more earnest about Rachel's 'peculiarity', which I could not help picturing as a sort of sickly grey miasma with a palpitating black heart in its centre. I recalled how I had often felt eccentric in my love for her – those sickly, spoony days, the wretchedness in my stomach, the exhaustion of rapturous yearning – and decided that a quarantine from her might be a sound idea.

My father had taken me to London on previous occasions but I had forgotten just how violent the noise of carriages and horses and chatter was, and how thickly the dusty air tickled my throat and nose, and how many boys there were waving advertisements on the street corners, each touting a different product: Macassar oil for the eradication of freckles, Keating's cough lozenges, Hugon's beef suet, and numerous others.

We were staying at the One Tun tavern. Upon arrival there, our trunk was taken to our room, and we dined on a supper of bread, cheese and fish. I was always a little nervous of making conversation with Mr. Gwent, for I often found it hard to deduce if he spoke in earnest or in jest. I longed to ask him more about his prediction of God's death in the next century, but I was so afraid of the answer that I changed my question at the final moment.

'Father says that your new novel will be set in London – is that true?' I hoped that my conversation sounded very grown-up.

'It shall be set in Canary Worf.'

It was such a curious name for a place that I could not help but fall about laughing, endeared by his invention.

'And will this Canary Worf be a dangerous place?' I asked.

'There will be men who make so much money that they could afford a dozen castles and a dozen carriages each and still have much to spare. They will drink too much ale and be in the possession of magical machines. Such as one that I have in my possession.' Mr. Gwent lowered his voice and became conspiratorial. 'I can show you, if you wish, for I have been able to obtain one from the future. But it must remain our secret.'

This time my laugh was one of incredulity; I was struck by how aptly I imitated my father. In truth, however, my heart was beating frantically with curiosity.

Mr. Gwent removed a small object from the pocket of his coat and, with an air of great secrecy, slid it across the table for my perusal.

It was the size of a small, slim book and possessed a sort of blank lens, beneath which were little buttons, upon which the alphabet and various symbols of punctuation had been painted. Above the lens was the word *BlackBerry*, which seemed the oddest name for a machine and quite undermined my belief in it. One of the larger buttons had a curious green symbol on it, which I fancied was a tiny dragon, and so I pressed it. To my alarm, the machine appeared to wake up, glowing like a lantern and emitting an ethereal light; I was so startled that I dropped it into my lap, eliciting glances from nearby diners. Hastily, I passed it back to him under the concealment of the table. In a trembling voice, I asked if it was a miniature phonograph. Mr. Gwent laughed and said, 'When I said that it was from the future – you understand that I was only jesting. It is simply a zoetrope, portable and easy to use.'

Before we departed for the theatre, Mr. Gwent and I returned to our room. I had noticed at the start of our journey how unfeasibly large his trunk was, presuming that he liked to travel with plenty of spare frock coats and breeches. Now, as he opened it, I saw that it was filled with leaflets. Mr. Gwent passed me one with a proud smile:

THE MARVEL OF THE SKIES
A beautifully bound book,
Its fun is immortal – worth reading twice.
Of all the books by the great humourist,
this is the one that will make his name a household word
in the English-speaking language.
Everybody can afford it.

He proceeded to secrete large quantities of his advertisement into every available pocket of his coat, and when I copied him he gave me a grateful look. Soon we were quite heavy, as though we were walking, breathing novels and our coats book covers.

Outside it was still light, even though it was eight o'clock. We queued for a hackney cab and to my surprise and delight, he ordered the driver to take us to Cremorne Gardens.

'In the play, there is the most marvellous scene where Colleen Bawn is thrown into the water and all but drowned

– you will relate this to your nanny and father?' Mr. Gwent asked me.

I nodded eagerly. Mr. Gwent squeezed my shoulder so hard that it hurt, but I adored the beam of his expression. I believed that he was one of those characters who only felt truly alive when he was in the midst of some adventure.

Cremorne Gardens was a place that I had heard Nanny speak ill of, but I could not see any evidence of sin there. There were puppet shows, an American Bowling Saloon, a Chinese bandstand; and, to my joy, there was the famous hot air balloon that I had always longed to see, pinned to the grass like a leashed wild beast, caressed by the last of the day's sun. The tight feeling in my heart that had been predominant over the last week eased, and I found myself wishing that Rachel had accompanied us. My reproving intellect swooped down and advised caution, but even at my tender age I was becoming aware that in quarrels between the head and heart, the head rarely triumphs. All of the feelings I had been attempting to repress now flew free, and I found myself preserving every spectacle in my mind, knowing that I must convey each and every detail to Rachel; and with every new discovery added to this list, I fell a little more in love with her again.

Twilight was seeping into the gardens; the balloon lost its colours and became a silhouette against the embered sky. I felt a chill and a change in atmosphere as the dappled trees became purveyors of shadows and the faces of passing strangers were made luminous by the eerie glow of lamps. There was a change in the women too, for the ladies of pretty bonnets and rustling crinoline were replaced by women with wild eyes and explicit bosoms, who reminded me very much of the woman in the alleyway where the Hurdy-Gurdy Man had danced. I thought of that moment when Adam and Eve, playing so happily in the sunshine, were flung out of the Garden of Eden and into the wider world, to wander in twilit uncertainty, not knowing if they were still falling or if they had landed.

What occurred next was wholly unexpected, and I am glad that Mr. Gwent did not give me any warning. As it was, I had no time to consider whether I wished to be his accomplice. I had been wondering why he was lingering so close to the hot air balloon, and why he had checked for the sharp scissors in his inside pocket, and why he had bade me stand in front of him so that he might cut the balloon free from its ties. Yet when he cried, 'Jump in!' I stood frozen in confusion. He clambered into the balloon and entreated me once more – just as a group of men, noticing his misdemeanour, began to laugh and shout. He attempted to lift me into the basket; this he failed at, for he was a slight man and I was a tall boy, but he did succeed in alerting me to my choice, and into the balloon I vaulted.

The balloon danced upwards; the nearby leaves of a tree brushed my hands. Mr. Gwent was already busy relieving himself of the advertisements in his pockets. As I leant over its edge, I saw several policemen running towards us, and a voice inside advised me to adhere to the laws of society; yet the very awareness of this voice also gave rise to a joy in disobeying it. With a spirited yelp, I released my advertisements into the air, creating a snowstorm in the midst of summer. As the policemen drew closer, however, I found my courage was all too brief. How I cowered and prayed to our Father, *Oh, please let us not be in trouble, please let us escape!* Mr. Gwent was entirely unabashed. He merely called out to them, 'Bless you, merry gentlemen, do purchase *The Perilous Mr. Petticoat*, the finest book you shall read this year, or I shall refund you!' and tossed over a further flurry.

Up, up, up went the balloon – and what a spectacle it was, to see London spread out before us, the horses small as toys, the streets a muddle of people, the rooftops a patchwork of puffing chimneys! I saw an order in the chaos of landscape and architecture – a Creation sustained by harmonious laws – and it prompted within me a fresh understanding of God; not as a fearsome father who would mock my church, but someone rather more mysterious, who hid behind the beauties he created and even chuckled at our misapprehension of him. But this was a fleeting thought, for Mr. Gwent was soon crying, 'Hark!' and tossing out the last of his advertisements. It was unfortunate that a gust of wind chose to send them down a nearby chimney pot, but Mr. Gwent was stoical: 'Well, they shall make for good kindling!' As a frightened bird swerved to avoid our balloon, Mr. Gwent hailed him: 'Would you, perchance, like to purchase my latest masterpiece?'

Mr. Gwent turned to me, his eyes sparkling as brightly as the stars on a clear night, and I laughed with wild joy. As the balloon proceeded to sail higher and higher, we found ourselves surrounded by a curious white mist. I had sometimes imagined what it might be like to be a bird passing through clouds, and envisaged that they would feel like wet flannel, but now I discovered that they evoked very little sensation at all. Mr. Gwent expelled a rapid series of exclamations – 'What a splendid view!' – 'Why, good day to you, Mr. Albatross!' – 'Why, we seem to be ascending rather rapidly!' – 'Goodness, at this steady rate, we shall reach the moon!' Sensing his inner consternation, I suggested that he study the central mechanism, and he cried, 'Fine plan, Thomas, fine plan!' and then expelled the most curious curse – 'Bollocks!' – before finally recalling that one needed to open a flap to allow the hot air to dribble out. My stomach felt as though air was whooshing up through it, as the balloon rapidly dropped a number of yards; we both turned and emitted a screech as we narrowly missed a church spire by a matter of inches.

Down,

down,

down

the balloon sank.

It became clear that although Mr. Gwent had chosen a fine place to disembark, a green field where some resting sheep were rapidly scattering, he had little idea as to how to land it. The basket swayed and bumped and sent us rolling around its bottom and then we were drowned in striped fabric, from which we had to untangle ourselves.

No sooner had we brushed the grass and sheep droppings from our clothing, than Mr. Gwent set forth across the field in the manner of a country gentleman taking a stroll. However, this time I could not be wholly convinced by his optimism, for the sounds of the nearby sheep seemed insidious, the moonlight pale, and the boggy ground was sucking at my feet. I was also afeared we were lost, due to the manner in which Mr. Gwent repeatedly looked up and down the nearest lane. I found myself crying, 'Father would not be very happy with me at this moment!', rather meaning that Father would not be at all happy with *him*, at which Mr. Gwent patted my shoulder and drew out the portable magic lantern that he had showed me earlier.

'This shall offer us some light, at least,' he said, and pressed a button, its ethereal light beaming brighter than any gas lamp I had seen. Mr. Gwent seemed to touch the screen and punch in some instructions, frowning and glancing up and crying, 'We are in Surrey! Not too far from Carshalton.'

'Your magic lantern can tell you where we are?' I asked, though, to be honest, the whole day had become so fabulous and peculiar that I was starting to believe that anything was possible.

'Oh, well, no – that would be absurd – and yet – and yet!' Mr. Gwent cried. 'It has some remarkable insights into certain matters, does the magic lantern. And it has suggested that we walk down this lane, turn left and continue down it.'

As we strolled, I became suspicious that Mr. Gwent was treating me like some sort of child, spinning a fairy story so that I might be consoled.

'And how is the fair Miss Levy – fair Rachel?' Mr. Gwent suddenly asked me.

I jumped then, wondering how on earth he had seen the contents of my heart.

'Does my father know?' I asked. I was perturbed that it might be the work of his magic lantern, but he returned with the assurance, 'Why, as a writer, it is my duty to notice such matters. I do not judge you, Thomas, for we have all been in love at some point in our lives, and you are at that tender age when a first love might well afflict you.'

'I did love her,' I confessed, 'but I fear that she is quite mad. She is not eccentric, as Father says you are' – the observation brought on a smile from Mr. Gwent – 'but truly insane.'

'Perhaps those who are mad are the ones whose doors of perception have been the most cleansed,' said Mr. Gwent, 'and they are still becoming accustomed to such clarity.' Although I did not fully understand his words, I absorbed their sentiment, and felt reassured, as though he had given me permission to love her, a permission I had been wanting someone to grant me.

VI

If the reader is wondering what on earth became of Mr. Gwent, having conducted such a stunt, then behold this account: we were able to find ourselves accommodation in Carshalton that evening, after waking up an innkeeper and his truculent wife. The following morning, we journeyed back to Oxford, Mr. Gwent chuckling to himself as he turned the pages of the newspaper, for on the front page was the headline STOLEN!, accompanied by a picture of the hot air balloon suspended above the city. Drama and retribution soon followed our arrival back in Oxford, however. I heard the servants gossiping about the news first and then Father confirmed it over our lunch of mutton: the constabulary had presented themselves at Mr. Gwent's house and arrested him. Father said he was still uncertain as to why this injustice had occurred, and I quickly busied myself with my mutton, declaring that Mr. Gwent had been a well-behaved guardian in London, for after we had wept heavily over the drowning scene in *The Colleen Bawn*, he had sent me to bed early.

Every newspaper soon carried the story of his balloon adventure, and all painted him as a dashing, heroic eccentric. *The Times* declared him the 'chevalier of the skies', while the *Telegraph* argued that all authors would be hastening to mimic his innovative methods of advertising.

Every bookshop sold out of *The Perilous Mr. Petticoat* and his publishers, John Murray, hastily and frantically arranged its reprinting, and then another, and another. Indeed, its sales were now surpassing that of *Great Expectations*. Mr. Gwent, locked away in his cell, heard the clamour of crowds outside Gatehouse Prison, calling for his release so that he might sign their copies of his 'masterpiece'. When Queen Victoria announced that she was reading certain passages from it to Albert at night in bed, Mr. Gwent was released with an official royal pardon, and found his mantelpiece filled with invitations to every dinner party in the country.

While I was vivified by all this amusement, I ached to see Rachel again, to apologise for my distant manner to her following our beach excursion. However, when I asked to pay a visit to the Carmichaels, I was informed that Eleanor was sick and no visitors were permitted.

How long would it take her to recover, I wondered, and would I even have a chance to see her governess before I left? I would be returning to Eton in less than three weeks. I do believe that my mind was so coloured and blinkered by the revival of my love that I failed to attribute much meaning to the curious events that were occurring in the city. There were no more sudden flurries of snow; but the governess of Miss Fairchurch, a grim and discontented woman, was found in a bedchamber, reduced to no more than a severed leg surrounded by a layer of ash, and the room smelling foully of burning flesh. When I heard from my father that she had suffered from spontaneous human combustion, I am ashamed to admit that I fell into a fit of laughter, for it seemed like an ailment that Mr. Gwent might invent for one of his novels. The Vicar's Sunday sermon warned us that it was a sign of devilry in our midst and thereafter I became anxious every time I felt any sort of heat in my body.

The day after the sermon, I took a stroll down to the churchyard, distressed to see how quickly the grass and brambles had writhed their way across my mother's stone, obscuring the carving. There, stumbling across the sunny hillocks of the graveyard – the mounds formed as though those restless souls had punched up the earth and grass – I chanced upon Rachel. Thrusting my hands in my pockets, I edged towards her. Her expression was drawn, her eyes hollows of sadness, but when she saw me they lit up.

'My dear Thomas!' she cried. 'I am glad to see you fit and well, for poor Eleanor is still in quarantine.'

Her tone was yellowy with a forced brightness, and I desired that she might forget social customs and confide in me. I stated in a solemn tone that Divine Will had led us both to be present in the same place at the same time and that to ignore it, to fail to seize it, was to induce it to become lazy in creating such marvels and find more willing subjects. In short, I requested that we sit on the grass so that I might make a confession.

Under the cool green of the hawthorn we sat, Rachel bisecting a dandelion stem with her thumb so that its juices glinted on her nails.

'I – I love you,' I confessed. The words were huge inside me, but as I spoke them they seemed as light as a thrush hopping between branches. 'I love you!' I attempted to add gravitas by increasing the volume of my voice.

'Shush, Thomas,' Rachel whispered, looking around furtively.

'I love you,' I whispered. This tone seemed more fitting, as though the words became concentrated in their quietness. 'Oh Rachel, I do love you.'

She reached out to touch my cheek with her fingertips. I flung her hand away.

'I know you think I am just a silly boy, but I am more than that!' I cried.

'Oh Thomas, I can see that,' she replied. 'There have been times when you have seemed like a man beyond your years. But we have to accept reality. I am ten years older than you, and I am only a governess. By the time you are fit for marriage, I shall be a grey-haired spinster with prissy habits and an over-fondness for escaping into novels, while you will be a man in your prime. Your father will want you to marry a beautiful young woman.'

'I can persuade Father!' I reached into my pocket and extracted a dog-eared roll of paper with trembling fingers. 'Look, I have written down why we must be together. Father says that Mr. Darwin did this when he was debating whether to marry his wife, Emma. If I can prove to my father that sound scientific logic supports my desire, then in a few years' time, when I am of marrying age, we can be together.'

My gaze was fierce on her as she perused the list. In the 'Pros' column, I had written 'fiery beauty, bizarre mind, energy like a thunderstorm'. Father had said that Darwin's list had included virtues such as 'constant companion

(& friend in old age)' and 'better than a dog anyhow'. The 'Cons' column of my list was a blank.

I saw the liquid in her eyes as she let out a small laugh. She folded up the list into a square the size of an insect. I was afeared that she would give it back to me, but when she tucked it into the pocket of her skirts, I was filled with hope; I seized her hand and gently traced the pattern of lines, as delicate as the veins of a leaf. Slowly, she raised her eyes to meet mine; they seemed to be offering permission. Yet now that I was on the brink of such exquisite fulfilment, I became paralysed. The heat that burnt inside me was not a pure flame, for it felt familiar, coloured dirty by the song of the Hurdy-Gurdy Man. The clouds passed over the sun, rendering the graveyard overcast, so that the church behind us acquired a portentous air. A crow swooped and stared at us, as though an agent of the Vicar's.

Rachel leant forwards, furrowed my hair roughly with her fingers and kissed me. I was shocked by the fluttering that sullied her breathing, for I had expected desire to be something I would gradually unpeel, petal by petal, coaxing it into a bloom. I was about to push her away and demand to know if she had ever kissed anyone else, when physical sensation overwhelmed this scatter of thought. We lay down among the graves in sweet pleasure, nervously glancing about for strangers, and then laughed and kissed and then kissed again; an insect flew on to my nose and she blew it away with a gusty breath, and we laughed and I asked if I might speak, but she silenced me with another kiss, and I was aware of the pleasant tickle of grass beneath my skull, and the hot blue of the sky above us, and still we kissed. It was intoxicating, to go on and on like this, to sink into a state where speech was no longer possible, where emotions had become shades of colour, impulses an intuitive blur.

A voice, deep and hoarse, announced: *And so Thomas kissed Rachel and they burnt with a fiery, illicit passion*. I broke off in a fit of horror. The voice had sounded akin to the Vicar's, only more sly in tone. Yet there was nobody to be seen; I thought the culprit must be hiding behind a gravestone, or perhaps the trunk of an oak tree a few feet away.

'What's the matter?' Rachel asked, caressing my cheek.

'Did you not hear it? It seemed—' I broke off, for once more the voice sounded, this time speaking with a grandeur and authority: *Thomas began to search in vain for the source of the mysterious voice*.

'Can you not hear it?' I rose to my feet. 'There is a man, speaking. He seems to be watching us, narrating our every move!'

'I heard nothing,' Rachel insisted.

Rising to my feet, I paced around the graveyard, searching for the source, but it only confirmed my suspicion: we were alone. I turned back to Rachel in dismay.

'What have you done to me?' I said. 'I have caught your madness. Now tell me how I shall be cured!'

Rachel fixed me with a look of the bitterest disappointment. She reached into her pocket and unfolded the sheet of paper I had penned for her, passing it back to me. I nodded stiffly, then turned and hurried away without bidding her goodbye.

I ran through the streets as though pursued by crows, terrified of being pecked by the voice again. Back home in our garden, I sat on the wall and listened to the soft murmur of the clucking chickens and the distant sound of rolling carriages, but my heart still felt like a wound-up spring; I expected the voice to return. The anticipation was so great that to have heard the voice would have been something of a relief. I turned to my neglected church, and brushed away a few leaves. It was still only as high as my knee. In a fit of anger I kicked at it savagely. As the stones collapsed in a cacophony my father appeared.

When he asked what the matter was, I wept. My father's lips trembled and I wished I could have laughed with him, for it felt so painful to conceal my terrible truth. He lectured me to stop my tears and be a man.

'But I am worried, Father,' I cried. 'What if I have caught Eleanor's illness? She has caught the illness of hearing voices from her governess, has she not?'

'Not at all,' my father returned, surprised. 'Eleanor has a simple case of measles. As for her governess, she has inherited her mother's affliction.'

'Her mother?' I asked, conscious that Rachel had never mentioned her to me.

'She resides in Hanwell asylum, in London. She has neurasthenia, which means she can suffer from terrible fits of hysteria.' Father touched my cheek softly. 'Rachel will follow in her footsteps and be committed to the Oxford asylum a week today. Mrs. Carmichael is due to sign a lunacy certificate any day now. Do not be sad, Thomas, for they will seek to make her well again.'

VII

Mr. Gwent's waistcoat, ever a barometer of his mood, was most resplendent that evening: a tartan silk the colour of a kingfisher's feathers. The moment that we entered his house, my spirits improved, for a curious sense of dread had overshadowed me since my amorous confession in the graveyard two days prior. Gwent led us into his drawing room, gabbling that he had discovered a tea which he thought was the finest yet, not just in its flavour, but in its ability to bring enlightenment to the mind. While we reclined on the méridienne, waiting for the maid to bring his latest elixir into the parlour, my father drew a picture from his coat and passed it to Mr. Gwent. 'Perhaps you can enlighten me as to the meaning of this, then.'

I felt my visage redden, feeling wilfully betrayed, for I realised that my father had passed over my picture of the helicopter. I cannot say quite how the inspiration had struck me, it had simply been present when I had awoken. A tingling in my fingertips led me to seize a pencil and sketch the curious image. It was shaped like a large metal apple, with four propellers on its top. Within the apple was a glass cage, like the interior of a carriage, where the pilot might sit and adjust his metal reins, for the helicopter was rather like a flying horse crossed with a bee. When I had interrupted my father in his study, he had declared that it looked quite absurd. I had been spending far too much time with Mr. Gwent, he added darkly.

Mr. Gwent's initial reaction to the picture was quite a curious one. He jumped as though there were pins in the cushion beneath him. But as the maid entered with the tray of tea, Mr. Gwent composed himself and set aside the picture, declaring that it was 'fanciful'. The cups were passed around, and this time the liquid poured from the pot was so black that my father jested whether Gwent had obtained it from an inkwell. It seemed to me to taste of cloudy imaginings, eerie dreams and tattered scrolls. I found my gaze wandering to the mirror above the fireplace, where the smoke from the fire, misdirected by a chimney draught, was hazing into the room, imbuing the mirror with a tremulous quality.

'How do you like the Soma tea?' Mr. Gwent asked my father.

'It is very rich, a little smoky – and even a little erudite,' he said, playfully. I thought perhaps he was relieved that my picture lay forgotten.

'And you, young Thomas?' Mr. Gwent addressed me. 'Do you find my tea to your satisfaction?'

'It tastes a little like . . . Coca-Cola,' I heard myself say. I frowned, while my father muttered that I was warping our fine English language into nonsensical words.

'Coca-Cola, you say?' Mr. Gwent's eyes were very bright and intent on me. 'And what is that, Thomas? What is Coca-Cola?'

A memory came wriggling out of its chrysalis, flying about my mind.

'It's . . . my favourite drink. It's black and it's fizzy and if I drink it too fast it makes my nose feel like there's a feather in it.'

'I have heard of no such beverage,' said my father.

'Actually, I believe this fine tea tastes something like a cross between Coca-Cola and a latte, maybe a latte from Caffè Nero, perhaps,' I declared.

'What is Caffè Nero? I have not visited such a tea shop,' my father asserted. 'I presume it is named after the emperor, though?' His eyes were performing a rigorous exercise, hurrying to Mr. Gwent and then hastening back to me, suspicious that we were sharing some private jest. I felt unease shiver over me, for these words made no sense, yet were as familiar as they were unfamiliar. It felt as though Mr. Gwent himself were Pandora's box, about to impart a horrifying knowledge; and that the very room quivered and shimmered like the smoke before the mirror.

'I was studying literature,' I said in a rush. 'I was studying death in literature – and I looked at death in Dickens's *Bleak House* – and *Our Mutual Friend* and *The Mystery of Edwin Drood*.'

'*Our Mutual Friend? Edwin Drood?* There are no such titles by Mr. Dickens,' my father contended. He snatched away my teacup and, striding to the window, lifted the sash and dashed its contents out into the air. Turning, he announced in an icy tone: 'I cannot allow you to misuse your new-found fame and good fortune to befuddle the mind of my child, Mr. Gwent.'

'It is just a tea from the East India Company that I bought in Piccadilly,' said Mr. Gwent calmly, gesturing that we should join him on the méridienne. He was already pouring out another three cups. 'In fact, I wouldn't have been able to afford it, had I not sold fifty thousand copies of my novel!'

My father looked a little sheepish; though when Gwent tried to pass me more tea, he prevented him and asked, in a trembling voice, what subject matter his latest novel concerned itself with. From there, my attempts to concentrate on their conversation were stricken, for I was beset by a curious self-consciousness. It is hard to convey the exact sentiments, but pray, consider this: when you are shopping for groceries or other routine activities, you are often entangled in an ongoing spool of thought. You get on a train and you fail to see the scenery sailing past, for you are thinking of your destination and what you shall say to the person you are meeting at the other end; you sit at your desk and stare at your inkwell with glazed eyes, engaged in an imaginary, robust dialogue with your boss; you retreat to the lavatory and wash your hands and stare into the mirror and wonder if everyone likes you or is only pretending to. In these moments, your mind is like a goldfish in a bowl, circling around and around the same worries. But every so often, the spool stops. You are gripped by a self-awareness, a consciousness of the present moment, uninhibited by the past, and not foreshadowed by the future. The experience is often accompanied by a sense of distance; the world seeming theatrical, surface, spectacle. Perhaps it is an elevated state – various religions and spiritual movements have, over the centuries, named it so. It creates a kind of questioning wonder: *Who am I, but one person engrossed in my universe of petty, pointless thoughts on a planet of billions of others who are doing the same?*

The mirror above the fireplace shimmered as though it had been crafted from air rather than glass, and I found myself rising, ignoring my father's troubled attention, and seeking to stand before it.

I heard the sound of dashed crockery, and felt the splatter of liquid against my breeches as I dropped the teacup. The reflection did not paint a picture of a young boy in his best suit, but a man of the future, in a sleep so deep it seemed as though he were suspended between the worlds of the living and the dead. The room he lay in was a dark room in a cottage, piled high with books. In the corner sat a large bearded man with his back to the sleeper. He was writing. A cry of recognition escaped my lips.

'Thomas!' My father's presence behind me shattered the vision. 'I will not tolerate this kind of behaviour!'

I turned to him and thought of how silly he looked, with his collar stiffly starched to prove to the world that he was a gentleman; he looked like the leading actor in a Sunday night costume drama.

'You are not my father!' I cried. 'My dad is Italian and I have not spoken to him in years. I know what this is about, Augustus Fate! Pray, be a man – tear down this illusion, and show yourself!'

My father's hand came down in a slap across my cheek. I stumbled backwards and stepped on a shard of shattered china, my cheeks damp with tears.

'Come, may I suggest that you have a lie-down,' Mr. Gwent said, taking a firm hold of my arm and whispering in my ear, 'Enough of this melodrama! Calm yourself and I will tell you everything soon enough.'

As Mr. Gwent led me into the hallway, my legs buckled.

I glanced down and considered, with a cool surprise, that I did not fully believe in them: they were about as persuasive as the flitting goblins in Mr. Gwent's magic lantern show; why, they felt as incidentally useful as an umbrella that I might pick up from a carriage stand. I willed my feet to lift up on to each step of the staircase, but, as though insulted by my lack of faith in them, they refused to obey. My father resolved the issue by half dragging me up the stairs. The pain I suffered in my shins as they scraped against the wood made my body seem slightly more convincing.

I was taken into a cold, dark bedroom, where a nervous maid lit the gas lamp and the covers of a freezing bed were drawn back and then tightly pulled over me. Mr. Gwent and my father spoke harshly to each other, and resolved to leave me be while they sent for a doctor. The moment they had departed from the room, I pushed back the covers and ran to the dresser, on which was perched a small ornate mirror. I reached for my ears, pulling at them to see if I could peel off my face like a mask. But my skin remained obstinate. What a stupid, boyish face, devoid of gravitas, lacking in stubble – why, what a prison sentence, to be locked in the body of a child when I possessed the soul of a man!

I moved over to the window. An affliction of temporal synaesthesia overcame me – the drum of the horses' hooves were the sound of a bass note in a rave; the rattle of a carriage on cobbles was a supermarket trolley being dragged over concrete. *This world is all an illusion!* Such was the revelation that washed over me again and again. I gazed out to the horizon, seeking gaps in that thinnest of veils which separated this world from the one where men hailed motorised taxis, where an electronic missive, sent to a friend, was opened within seconds rather than days.

I sat on the edge of the bed with my head in my hands. The tea was still syrupy on my tongue, sticky on my teeth; how I craved to clean them! I nearly wept at the thought of a line of clean artificial mint paste, squeezed from a tube on to my voltaic toothbrush, which would buzz pleasantly around my fillings, while the radio informed me of football results, or the chatter of *The IT Crowd* played in the background. The last time I'd had Coca-Cola was when eating pizza with my mother, after she had attempted to cook a roast chicken, and had instead produced a black, smoking carcass; thus we had notified the local Pizza Hut of our request for several slices of their finest deep-pan. 'Oh, Mother,' I wept, 'oh my poor Mother.' As always, she had been kind to me during my visit. She always had a gift for me. On that occasion, she had given me a box of red berry tea and had asked after my studies; she spoke of the narrative of my life as though she was as anxious as I about what might happen next. Given my current absence, she would have telephoned the police, desperate to ascertain my whereabouts; she would be suffering amid nights of sleepless worry, and pills, and fears that I have deserted her.

With this thought, such a fury overwhelmed me that I rose and picked up the mirror, this harbinger of dishonesty, and tossed it at the wall. It shattered, and spun icicles of glass across the floor. I closed my eyes and focused the sound of my breathing. I struck my forehead with my fists, crying, 'You will not have my memories! You might have everything else, but my mind belongs to me!'

My tirade was interrupted by the sound of my father

and Mr. Gwent quarrelling. Eventually, however, my father was persuaded that Mr. Gwent needed to address me once more. I looked up, wiping my eyes, as he closed the door behind him. I could not be certain whether Mr. Gwent's charm and knowledge were a fabrication or not, whether he was akin to me or spun from the imaginative thread of Mr. A. Fate.

'Is Father preparing to fill out a lunacy certificate on my behalf?' I asked in a trembling voice.

'Your father is merely concerned for you,' said Mr. Gwent. After casting a furtive glance at the door, he continued in a whisper: 'I can assist you with your escape, but you must be careful.' He lifted his eyes to the sky. 'We are under the command of a cruel deity. *As flies to wanton boys are we to th' gods: they kill us for their sport* – only, he does not *kill* us for his sport: he much prefers to pull off our wings in slow torture and watch us struggle. Remember, you cannot control what he does to you, but you can control how you react to him. Adaptation is necessary for survival.'

'I can go home?' My voice cracked into splinters of relief.

'Yes, I can assist you with a safe passage,' he assured me. Then he sat down beside me on the bed and seized my hand. 'I hope that I am not forgotten in the real world, either. What is your real name?'

'Jaime.' My voice rose in boldness: 'Jaime Lancia.'

'I am Gareth Saint.'

'The writer? But I remember you . . . You won the Hugo and retired, supposedly . . .'

'That is poppycock. I lie in the cottage of Augustus Fate, in the basement beneath his living room, while my poor wife, Mary, no doubt frets and wonders what has become of me. I have been trapped here for more years than I can count.' Tears filled his eyes and he shook his head.

'And my father? Is he real too? Are we all prisoners in this plot?' I cried.

'No. Your father is, I am afraid to reveal, a creation of Fate's. There are very few of us who are truly *real* – our bodies in the modern world, our souls bound into the pages of Fate's books like a corset.'

I recoiled at the concept of 'the soul', for I had departed from 2019 as an avowed atheist, and now regarded my recent devotion as a childish embarrassment.

'Call it consciousness, if you prefer,' said Mr. Gwent, looking sympathetic.

'And – Rachel hears Fate . . . Well, that explains everything! She is not mad. Why, she is more sane than I have ever been, walking around in a state of denial . . .' I hissed.

'Hush, lower your voice,' Mr. Gwent warned me. 'At first, I was also convinced that she was real, but when I attempted to speak to her she seemed so . . . mysterious. I cannot be sure whether she is a daughter of Fate's pen or a woman of our world. She might betray you yet.'

My father entered the room at this point, else I might have defended Rachel. I was convinced that she was too rich a character to be invention; though perhaps I was simply longing for her to be the Rachel I had conversed with in the suicide forum, before being forced into this untimely narrative.

A look from Mr. Gwent persuaded me that I should maintain an act with my father, and so I slid back beneath the covers. Initially, the sensation of my father's hand on my brow caused me to shudder, but the gentleness in his touch and the look in his eyes made me sorry to have perturbed him. Against my will, I felt myself being woven back into the world. The maid entered, carrying a tray, and my father seized a glass from it, pushing it to my lips.

'This will help you – just a little of Godfrey's Cordial. Then you shall sleep restfully while we wait for Dr. Adams.'

My head swam with a new-found urgency to escape, yet the cordial was working its will, filling my head with woozy smoke, placing weights upon my eyelids. Father began to mutter a prayer in fear that an unholy spirit had taken possession of me; I wanted to laugh at him and cry that there was no God. Then my father's hand was on my cheek again and he was asking me questions, ignoring Gwent's insistence that it made little sense to address me after I had been fed laudanum. I managed to croak the correct answer as to what day of the week it was, but when he asked me who was queen, I found myself replying, 'Elizabeth the Second.' My father rose, his brow contracted, and said that I should rest.

As they left, Mr. Gwent placed his stuffed dodo on the table beside me and said he hoped it would bring me solace. I watched the room slowly spin and fracture, furious with the drug for kidnapping my senses just when I most required them. Sensing the attention of the dodo, I gave it a bleary smile, and it advised me, 'It is probably best that you sleep and forget me. After all, you were happier – were you not – when you were innocent?' I advised the dodo that his voice reminded me greatly of Fate's and he replied that his voice must, in that case, be sensuous and baritone, and he proceeded to sing me a lullaby, and so I fell into the comfort of darkness . . .

VIII

At lunch the next day, we all dined together at Mr. Gwent's again, making bright conversation as though the past traumas were but a dream. It was not easy, persuading my father that the entire incident was not a case of devilrous possession. Mr. Gwent concocted a story in which he had received a telegram from the manufacturers of Soma tea advising – rather belatedly – that it should not be drunk, for their customers were complaining of all manner of side effects. Upon examination, Dr. Adams concluded that it must have been a passing fever, which assuaged any lingering doubts my father had.

But everything was different: I was no longer blind; I could see. I became aware, for example, of how theatrical Mr. Gwent's manner was, a consequence not just of eccentricity but of being out of joint with the present age. I wondered, however, why he had remained in Fate's novel for all this time. Was he really trapped, or was he choosing to stay? His writing career was far more successful here than the real world, I noted. Was his body dead and buried in Fate's basement, or being kept alive in some way, perhaps through some sort of preservation in an icy tomb?

And how did a character in Fate's book age? Did time run in natural rhythms, or did Fate manipulate it according to his whims? If I was imprisoned in this novel for another three years, for example, then would I only become 'seventeen' by the conclusion of my sentence? The thought made me feel so pale inside that I could barely eat; but, upon descrying Mr. Gwent's urgent expression, I forced the veal down into my churning stomach. Just before I departed with my father, Mr. Gwent whispered to me, 'Do not fret. I will be able to get you out of here. Soon, I promise.'

Oh, how I clung to those words. I spent that night hardly able to sleep, for I drifted in the eddies of shallow dreams and every time I rose to the surface, the remembrance pierced me again: *This is all illusion, you are lost, in the real world your body remains a hollow*. The next morning was heavy with knowledge. For these past six weeks, I had risen and put on my shirt and waistcoat with the same ease that I had once yanked on my Levi's jeans and Primark T-shirt back in Brixton. It was disturbing, how easily I had followed Fate's dictates, with the mindlessness of a sheep. Was I really so dull, so susceptible to suggestion? Was that why Fate had picked on me? When I considered the past weeks, I realised that I had some memories of the real world – there was the familiarity with Gwent's mobile telephone, the automatic sketch of the helicopter. Or was I just rewriting these events in hindsight, imbuing my past self with greater awareness?

I should be angry, though, not self-flagellating. Fate was the abuser; I was the victim. *You are not to blame*, I kept repeating.

As I cleaned my teeth with dentifrice, I pictured the sink in my old flat, which had always been stained and strewn with gunk. A thought wrenched my gut: my flatmate would never be able to afford the entire place by herself, and my standing orders from my Co-op bank account would have started to bounce long ago. By now, she would have solicited another young man as a lodger. My belongings had probably been bagged up in black sacks and taken to my mother's. She would have unfolded all my clothes and put them into the chest of drawers in my old bedroom. Tears streamed from my eyes, tears that mingled with my dentifrice and ran down my neck. The world knew that you were going to interview Fate, I reassured myself as I wept. The police will have been called, an investigation will be underway. They will surely find you.

The snow that fell in flurries over the next two days, icing rooftops and choking up chimney pots, blanketing streets and bringing carriages to a standstill, would have been most picturesque, had it not been for the fact that it was the middle of August. Roses were being killed early; a baby bird, frozen, was found on the edge of our lawn, its mother singing a melancholic lament from her nest above. As the church became veritably swollen with anxious townsfolk, I wondered if Fate was concocting adversities in order to bring his creation under control. Exorcisms were performed daily as though the church had been converted into a theatre, its audience hungry for melodrama. Half a dozen monks had also arrived in Oxford, their purpose unclear. They remained silent at all times, drifting across the cobbled streets like grey ghosts, their faces entirely shadowed by their heavy hoods. They occupied the vestry space behind the Vicar during the services, like a celestial army.

I was ardent to speak to Rachel. I had become convinced she was the very woman I had spoken to online and speculated that she needed a spur to inspire her awakening, just as Mr. Gwent had assisted me. When I pleaded to my father that we should pay a visit to the Carmichaels, I felt as though I was auditioning for the part of his son; my voice was an embarrassing juvenile whine. By and by, he yielded to my entreatments. On arrival, however, we discovered a terrible sense of unrest.

We were shown into the parlour, where we sat sipping a tea that tasted so plain Mr. Gwent would have died of disgust. Mrs. Carmichael pointed surreptitiously to the window, which overlooked the street in front of the house.

'Do not look directly, just out of the corner of your eye. Do you see the monk? He has been here these past five hours. I hear their purpose is to locate those who are possessed.'

I risked a full glance and saw indeed a hooded figure across the road, still as the oak tree he was standing beside. More of this world's religious absurdity, no doubt, I thought; I sensed that a sneer was taking hold of my face. I had become very conscious of my features during this past week, of attempting to manipulate them in the way a master might his puppet. How hard it was to resist the modern malaise of irony; it afflicted my every action.

Fortunately, my father spoke sense: 'I doubt very much that is their purpose.' I saw a meaningful look pass between him and Mrs. Carmichael. 'Thomas,' he ordered, 'why don't you go up to the nursery?'

I obeyed him, though outside in the hallway I lingered on the pretext of tying up my shoelace, whereupon I overheard Mrs. Carmichael telling my father that Rachel's exorcism had failed, and that the lunacy certificate had now been signed: the doctor would be here for her tomorrow. She spoke as though his arrival would immediately bestow the whole of Oxford with the blessings of blue skies, sunshine and birdsong.

I found Rachel upstairs in the nursery, where she was pouring out tea for Eleanor, who was still frail and scarred from the aftermath of her sickness. I did not bother with pleasantries. It was a relief to speak as a man:

'Eleanor,' I snapped. 'I have an important matter to discuss with Rachel. I would be grateful if you left the room.'

Rachel widened her eyes at me in warning, no doubt assuming that I was contriving to solicit her solitude for amorous pleasures. Eleanor glanced at each of us in cool curiosity.

'Does it concern her mother?' she asked. 'Mama says that they will soon be united.'

I was briefly confused, before recalling that Father had said her mother was also resident in an asylum.

'I visit her in Hanwell with gifts,' Rachel said quietly. 'That is all.'

'I wish to address another matter, Eleanor,' I said firmly. 'One that you are far too young to understand.'

'If I leave,' Eleanor pondered, forcing her doll into a coat by the fierce manipulation of her arms, 'then I will be forced to use my imagination and so I will have to tell my parents what I can only assume to be true.'

'You are a true daughter of Fate,' I informed her, testing her reaction, but she merely looked bemused and returned to the nonchalant torture of her doll.

Rachel stared down at her lap, spreading out the tassels from her shawl. If I did not act with due haste, she would be jammed into a carriage and parcelled into a strait-waistcoat. There was only today; only this hour. The frantic pressure drove me to find an answer; I would play at being a storyteller.

'Rachel – I'm going to tell you a story. I recently visited Mr. Gwent's house and he allowed me to sit in his parlour and read his latest novel. By chance, the girl in the book is also called Rachel.' I forced a grin, and she returned it quizzically. 'Rachel lives in the year 2019 – you know that Mr. Gwent does like to write science fiction. She loves to read, but she is also very sad. One day she decides to visit the house of one of her favourite authors, Augustus Fate. He lives in Wales, in a remote village, and so it entails a long, cold journey.'

'Where is Wales?' Eleanor interjected. I was furious, having briefly convinced myself of her absence. Rachel quickly smoothed the tension away, advising Eleanor that Wales was a far-off land where sheep thrived and the rain fell in abundance. Eleanor nodded and carried on pretending to play with her dolls, listening intently all the while.

'Upon arriving at his cottage she knocks on the door, hardly daring to hope that he might let her in, and so when he does she nearly weeps for joy. He gives her some tea and says to her, 'I am stuck on my new novel. My characters are simply not convincing and I fear that I need to make them more realistic.' The tea makes her drowsy and she tumbles into a slumber. A stupor, a coma, a state that is not quite living but not quite death – a sort of twilit consciousness. Fate carries her up to his bedroom, and he dresses her in Victorian clothes—'

'Does he *undress* her first?' Eleanor asked, with great interest.

'That is not important,' I snarled. 'He lays her down on the bed and pulls up the covers and there she sleeps, so still that spiders dance over her face. And while her body remains sedated, her mind enters one of Fate's novels. It is set in the Victorian era – that is, the present, in 1861. She is a . . .' – I sought for a word that would resonate with Rachel – 'a soul trapped in his book, and she might not even have realised this, were it not for the fact that every so often she can hear her narrator: *Rachel awoke on Thursday morning to discover that the Carmichaels had planned a trip to Margate Sands*. She fears that she is mad, but actually she is simply a very sensitive soul – she is sensing a reality that others are blind to.'

There was a brief pause, before Rachel snorted, laughing dismissively.

'What an absurd story,' Rachel said, but I saw panic born in her eyes like the flare of a candle's flame.

'It doesn't make sense,' said Eleanor, her forehead crinkled. 'How can a soul be trapped in a book? Do you mean like a flower in a press?'

'No, the soul roams the world of the book, while the body remains behind. It is done by a certain magic,' I said. 'And having her soul imprisoned in a fictional character causes her to suffer great discomfort, for she is shaded with 2019: she rubs against her age, and it causes a constant friction that sparks unrest in her mind. At the same time, she cannot admit that this is her reality, for to face such horror is more than she can bear. Perhaps she even feels happier telling herself that she is mad. Perhaps believing she is mad is a comfort of sorts, a way of hiding.'

'But if such a character did exist,' Rachel's voice was trembling, 'then surely she has forsaken all freedom. Surely her escape is impossible?'

'The question is one of free will versus fate,' I said. 'Mr. Gwent instructed me that the characters in the book are free to react to events as they please – after all, the author himself wanted real people because he lacked inspiration, because his own creations were so two-dimensional. They can do as they please, but they are knitted into the society and age of the book's setting. The author too can do whatever he likes, whether brewing up a storm or causing snow to flurry from the sky in the midst of summer. It is his amusement. He is a cat with mice between his paws.'

'He is a sadist too,' Rachel said, with unexpected venom. 'He is cruel and mocking—' She broke off and glanced upwards briefly; at that moment, happiness rang in my heart, for I knew that she not only believed me, but had sensed these truths for some time.

Eleanor broke the silence.

'This is all very strange. I think you might end up in an asylum as well, Thomas.'

'Oh, I don't give a fuck,' I snapped.

Eleanor screwed up her face. '"Fuck" . . . what does that mean?'

'Nothing,' I said roughly. I heard the clatter of a carriage pulling up below, the impatient neighing of our belligerent horse. Nanny climbed out and glared up at the window. 'Rachel, the situation is urgent. I am certain that Gwent's heroine is able to escape.'

'But what about the other people in the book who aren't real?' Eleanor asked.

'They are sketches. Paper-thin. Lacking any depth or soul.'

Eleanor went pale and turned away from me, feigning fascination with a tangle in her doll's mane. I turned back to Rachel.

'Time is pressing. We need to get back to 2019 as soon as possible. But I'm not yet sure how we do it. Maybe it is simply a case of breaking the spell through knowledge of it.'

Rachel was silent for a few moments, and I sensed her inner consternation. But then she shook her head.

'But there is no spell,' she asserted. 'This is all just a story.' She forced her pale lips into a tight smile. 'And as sweet as it is, it is disturbing young Eleanor and you must cease the telling of it. Gwent intended his story for adults, not children.'

I blinked, exasperated by the fierceness of her wilful denial.

'2019 is a very fine era for women to live in,' I said hastily. 'They are free to live as they wish – to choose whether they want to marry or to have children, they can be doctors or even prime minister.'

Rachel turned to the window, glancing down at the monk by the oak, who had latterly been joined by several others.

'You might consider that asking such questions is

angering our Lord above. Have you not detected a sudden change in the atmosphere around us?'

'I care not for any change! I care not for his anger! I believe that it would be better to exist in the present!'

'I like 1861.' Her tone was defiant. 'I am very happy here.'

I heard footsteps on the stairs: Nanny was coming. I played the only card I had left.

'And will you remain happy when they put you in an asylum on Friday?'

Rachel's terrified expression haunted me throughout my journey home. I felt certain she was the Rachel I knew in the world outside. A silence permeated the carriage and I found myself engrossed in memories of when we had first exchanged pleasantries in the suicide forum. It seemed such an odd coincidence that we now both found ourselves ensnared in Fate's trap; there was surely a reasoning behind this that I had yet to ascertain.

Gazing out at the world around me – at the snow falling in the smoky twilight, at the Oxford colleges with their impervious stone – I wondered at how solid it all seemed despite being nothing more than an idea in a man's mind. We had discussed similar ideas in our debates. Rachel had pointed out that much of contemporary civilisation was based on ideas: a legal contract is little more than gobbledegook without our species's belief in the *idea* of it; money too had no material reality, it was based on a trust system, a shared belief. Rachel had spoken of life with such detachment: she said she could not be sure if she was ascending to enlightenment or sinking into the depths of depression.

My father interjected, announcing that the asylum would surely be a 'tonic' for Rachel, as though she was about to take the sea air or a batch of smelling salts. My acidic sneer no doubt silenced him, but the remorse that then filled his eyes provoked a guilty meekness in me. I waited for him to admonish me, but a curious air arose between us. For in that moment, my look had irrevocably turned the tables of the relationship, as though he was the child and I the parent. I was no longer in awe of his words, but judging and dissecting them.

I felt a nostalgia then for my prelapsarian state, for the six weeks of childhood I had enjoyed in 1861, however illusory, had possessed a sort of sweet innocence that I had not been privy to in real life for some time. In the true world, my mother had been a constant, but my father had frequently been absent. And just when I had grown used to that absence, he had habitually reappeared, upsetting our balance by creating a familial triangle with sharp edges. By comparison, my childhood here had been a fairy tale, and the man who sat beside me was the father I had always dreamt of having. That I had loved a fiction with such unconditional delight disturbed me, and even as I glanced at him then, the complexity of character behind those features was so persuasive that I found myself smiling back at him. Once more, we were father and son.

IX

The next day began with the invasion of his voice: *And Thomas attended church later that afternoon, in innocence of the terrible calamity that was about to befall the city of Oxford . . .*

Despite my determination to ignore his narration, I longed for more elaboration on the phantasmal figures that followed Father and me to the evening service. The monks shadowed our shadows, some six feet behind us, their hoods drawn so tightly that their features were scribbles of darkness. My father glanced back too and immediately reached for my hand; in spite of all my internal reminders that the true age of my soul was a manly twenty-six, I found myself gripping his tightly in turn. He muttered a reminder that the monks were here to protect us, thanks to the compassion of the Vicar and our Father above, but even so, neither of us dared to look back again as we sped towards the church.

It was so congested that every pew was soon filled, and a crowd were forced to stand at the back. A place had been saved at the front for my father and me. There I sat and attempted to calm my nerves by reminding myself that the monks were a fiction. Then I caught sight of a cut on my forefinger that I had acquired last week, and which was slowly healing. It had hurt and I had bled. I was not exempt from suffering in this place, and neither was Rachel. I considered her view that the 'atmosphere' in this story had darkened since I had gained awareness of my situation, and frowned: was Fate trying to beat me down? My gaze was drawn back to the minacious throng of monks standing behind the Vicar and the fear of what these mysterious beings were, of what they might be capable of, trembled in my heart.

I found myself close to praying so that He might help her, and then recoiled. Only I could help Rachel, and only through my own choices and actions. My father had let slip that she would be collected in a carriage at five o'clock: an hour from now. I had intended to slip out midway through the service, run to the Carmichaels' house and save her with my own hands, so I felt troubled when I saw the monks closing the heavy oak doors. My departure would now be conspicuous; yet if I remained trapped here for the entirety of the service, I might be too late . . .

'Beloved Brethren! The figure of Satan, whose presence has come to be felt so keenly among us, has in recent years become a matter of buffoonery – a dancing fiend at the Punch and Judy show, a lurking menace in a ghost story – and it is this dangerous levity when we ought to be solemn, this laxity when we ought to be guarded, that has led to our present calamity . . .'

So began the sermon. The Vicar, standing on tiptoes in his pulpit, focused his gaze approximately a foot above the congregation, as though he perceived a flickering army of spirits above our heads, poised to seize on weaker souls.

'The snow continues to afflict our skies and defy the season of summer.' The Vicar's voice quietened to a portentous whisper. 'And while it strikes terror into the heart of each believer, it also behoves us to respond with the sweetest compassion, to award cathartic release to those who writhe under the galling yoke of the beast, and purify our parish . . .'

The congregation, pierced by orgiastic fear, let out sighs and cries that infuriated me with their ovine ignorance. Turning to my father, I whispered that I was not feeling sound, and he gave me a look of such tenderness that I found myself smiling up at him; then that look began to dim with disappointment. Rising to his feet, he addressed the Vicar thus:

'I am afraid that, as much as I love my son, he has not been well. Dr. Adams pronounces him fit in body and mind, but I am conscious of a sickness in his soul that has been afflicting him over the past week. I beg that you help my dear Thomas. He speaks of imaginary beverages; he is possessed by troubled thoughts I am not privy to.'

'Father – no!' I cried, but my protest only delighted the congregation further. 'Be logical, be wise – you are a man of science! Would Mr. Darwin agree with such a verdict?'

A flicker of doubt passed over his features, but it was gone quickly, and replaced with the pink skin of embarrassment. My father was not the same man outside the church as he was under this roof.

'Father, I am your *son* . . . If you love me, protect me!'

Two of the hooded monks departed from their shadowy line beside the choir and swept towards me, silently gliding down the aisle of the church. My footsteps echoed like gunshots as I fled down the centre aisle; the crowd at the back scattered; the doors refused to yield, even when I flailed at them furiously with my fists.

Above me the voice of Fate boomed: *And so Thomas was forced to undergo an exorcism, helpless to save his loved one, as she was hurried away to the asylum. There they would shave her scalp and apply leeches to her temples to cure her melancholia*.

'Fuck you, Fate,' I whimpered into the heavy oak of the door. 'Fuck you.'

The monks' grip was fiercer than I had anticipated. I could not detect the sketched outline of a nose or chin as they led me back towards the Vicar. Once more, I glanced at my father, cut by his betrayal, only for him to respond with an encouraging nod.

The Vicar stared into my eyes as though I was no more than a vessel playing host to a demonical parasite. A hot anger rose up inside me and I whispered, 'Look at me, you fool! I am not the devil: I am real.' At my protest, he became wildly triumphant, interpreting my words as an act of satanic ventriloquism.

In that moment, Gwent's dictum returned to my mind: *Remember, you cannot control what he does to you, but you can control how you react to him. Adaptation is necessary for survival*. My weapon would be rationality. The congregation desired a Spectacle; and I would give them one. I must perform it swiftly – to delay, to argue, would be to let Rachel down. I let my hands fall slack, my shoulders rounded, and I began to walk in a figure of eight, occasionally exposing an armpit so that I might scratch it, while pursing my lips and emitting the hoots of a chimpanzee. Our audience made suitably horrified noises. The Vicar seemed pleased, until I feigned to remove some fleas from his head.

'You are infected with Darwin!' he cried. 'You see the consequences of Darwin's words. What devilry he has created. Darwin is a man who requires an exorcism!'

He brandished a large glittering cross at me while ordering the spirit to be gone from my body, and I feigned torture, as though a narrow beam of energy were tunnelling into my heart. My monkey chortles evolved into howls, such that my voice filled the building. It felt satisfying to vocalise the rage I had been forced to repress these last few days, to let Fate hear my rebellion. Then, as the Vicar swirled his hands about me and recited some Latin, I allowed my cries to soften. As I fell silent, the Vicar concluded his exorcism, and turned back to the congregation, his chest puffed, whereupon he was met with weeping and applause.

The service concluded thus, and each member of the congregation rose with the dazed look of one who has read a particularly gruesome penny dreadful, before they all trailed out into the graveyard. Despite my cleansing, they treated me as though Darwinism was a contagious ailment. I cared not; all that mattered was Rachel.

I was about to hurry away, when my father caught my arm. Snowflakes gently mocked his cheeks. He wiped his face, his eyes clouded, and I saw him visibly slump with confused disappointment: they had followed the ritual, so why was the world still one of disorder and chaos; why was God failing to maintain his side of the bargain? His hand curled on my shoulder. He did not look at me – for his eyes were fixed on the distant curve of his lost love's grave – but I sensed his impulse towards regret. I shook away his hand, still raw from his betrayal. I wondered if he was not so very dissimilar from my own father after all.

A carriage was hurrying past the church; I recognised the black silk of the horse's coat. A face appeared at the window of the carriage and I cried out, 'Father! They are taking her! Rachel!'

My protests were drowned out by the noise above us. At first, it sounded like a torrent of bees. The Vicar, who had just exited the church, gazed upwards, and his congregation followed suit, for the cacophony amplified until it seemed that a steam train was hurtling through the sky. A wild laugh tumbled from my mouth, for the recognition was a joyful one – 'A helicopter!' I watched it swirl, slicing air, blowing the hats from the heads of the congregation and sending them tumbling across the graveyard. I might borrow it yet; I might fly and swoop down and save Rachel. Could it be – could it be that Fate had decided I needed relief from torment, and given flesh to the machine I had recently drawn?

'You!' My father's hand flew from my shoulder. 'What have you summoned? What new devilry is this?'

As the helicopter swung and circled back to us, its beam fell upon the crowd, lighting up an array of visages pinched by horror. But the congregation's fear could no longer settle on a target, for they were too bewildered, too preoccupied with dodging its peculiar illumination. Someone cried, 'Surely this is a sign of God! It is not a demon, but an angel!' A few crossed themselves and many looked relieved.

I saw that Rachel's carriage was now stationary in the middle of the road, the coachman gazing upwards, while Dr. Adams peered out from his window, stunned by the sight above him. I wanted to run to the carriage and tear open the door, but I too was mesmerised, rooted to the snowy ground in a gasp of fear and wonder. The helicopter swooped down toward the crowd, its propeller spinning at a wild velocity, and I glimpsed the pilot – laughing, crazed, as though Fate's doppelganger – before he did slam the vehicle into the church.

The thunder of this collision was so noisome that every grave appeared to shudder. I heard the crash of masonry; a flock of birds took flight, cawing. Then fire erupted. A fountain of smoke poured forth into the sky. Flares roared across the church roof and the Vicar descended into hysterics, sobbing lines from the Book of Job. My eyes were fixed on Rachel's carriage, for Dr. Adams had flung open his door and was running into the graveyard as fast as his portly figure would permit. I saw her pale figure emerge and hover, ghostly, on the road. I made to run to her, but my attention was seized by the man Dr. Adams was tending to: my father lay sprawled in the snow.

I ran to his side and he clutched my hand, whimpering boyishly. Tears trickled down my cheeks and on to my sooty neck. He must have been gashed by the falling masonry, for his forehead was dizzy with the flow of blood; I tore my handkerchief from my pocket and attempted to stem it. I told him that I loved him and he whispered, 'My son.' All around me was a chaos of screaming and fleeing parishioners, but I pushed them into the shadows, fighting to hold my father's gaze.

'Make haste, Thomas, we must go!' Mr. Gwent appeared, chiding me. His face was smeared with smoke, and there was a hole burnt into his waistcoat, as though a cigar had been plunged into the silk.

'But my father!'

'Let me tend to him, Thomas,' Dr. Adams advised, glancing up in horror at the church, before jumping violently as another chunk of burning stone toppled and missed him by a few yards.

'He is not real,' Mr. Gwent whispered in my ear, kneeling down beside me. His expression had never looked so sombre, his usual gaiety had entirely dissipated. 'But you and Rachel can be freed – we must seize this moment.'

'But—' I turned back to my father and attempted to untangle my hand from his, but his eyes flew open and he clutched me all the more tightly. I wept.

'It is surely my doing, not just Fate's – I drew the helicopter, I drew it into the story—'

'This is Fate's cruellest trick,' Gwent hissed. 'Your father is only an illusion and you must tell yourself this, over and over. We cannot control the tragedies that Fate bestows upon us, but we have the free will to react to them.'

In their repetition, these words seemed less like wisdom and more like a dictum, created to make life survivable in this world.

'I know that Fate has found a way to harness your weakness, but you must fight it! Remember your real name: Jaime, Jaime, Jaime.'

Drowning in grief, I could not believe in his words; Jaime was but a dim, shadowy memory. Dr. Adams intervened, forcing my hand away, and begging Gwent to assist him in dragging my father away from danger. As I watched them do so, smoke frothed about me, and a trembling beset me: my heart begged me to chase after them while reason ordered that I must let my father go. I became conscious of someone calling my name. I turned and I saw her, holding out her hand to me: my dear Rachel.

Mr. Gwent returned to our side and we made haste to his house, stumbling along the streets, choked with smoke and chilled by the snow.

X

The door banged behind us and we tumbled into the parlour. Mr. Gwent drew the curtains shut, lit a gas lamp, and called out to his maid in a panting voice: 'Prepare the Grand Kuding tea at once, and make haste! Only one teaspoon of leaves – it must be mild!'

He rang the bell several times, its silvery shimmers echoing in my quivering body; then he hurried to his desk, leafing through sheaves of paper covered in his slanting scrawl. To quell my erratic breathing I employed a technique a counsellor had once taught me, to interrupt a potential panic attack: a short, sharp inhalation followed by a long, deep exhalation. Rachel looked so frail and fragile that she might have been composed from paper. I clasped her hand and spoke words I was not even assured of myself:

'Everything will be all right now, everything. We will return to 2019 safe and sound. This time tomorrow we'll be . . .' I thought of Fate's cottage and how we would awaken there; he might attempt to overpower us, but our rage would fire us with superhuman strength. I pictured us victorious over him and stumbling out into the true snow – but no, winter would surely be over now. The thought that the landscape might be one of green hills, of emerging bluebells and snowdrops, caused a dizzy disorientation to assail me.

The maid had brought in some tea, and was attempting to pour it when Mr. Gwent shooed her away. He lifted the pot's lid and buried his face in its steam, frowning and muttering that it must be the correct intensity, otherwise parts of us would be 'lacking punctuation, with full stops all over the place'. Once more, a quivering beset me and I turned to Rachel, feeling her grip my hand tightly, and then she began to speak – quite the longest and most heartfelt speech I had ever heard her make:

'I remember that it was Christmas 2019 when I left and came here, to Fate's world. I couldn't stand it anymore – the gap between who I was and who I wanted to be – the life I *wanted* to live. I could see it everywhere; I went out shopping for presents for my friends, and behind all the frantic bustling and rushing, there was this despair behind everyone's eyes. I realised that the biggest lie of civilisation is that we are happy. We say "Hello" and "How are you?", and "I'm fine" is the standard, automatic reply, even when we're not fine at all, even when we're insecure and panicked and worried about money and thinking, "What the fuck am I doing here?" And I just wanted to escape it all . . . But I didn't think – it was still a shock – I drank his tea and then – *this*.'

A silence filled the room, for both Mr. Gwent and I felt touched and a little embarrassed at this confession. She did not appear to expect anything from us, however, for she merely lowered her eyes, her shoulders rounded with exhaustion. I felt there was nothing I could do but lean over and kiss her in consolation; her lips did not move in response. At first she seemed abashed, but a glow began to pulse in her face.

'*This* indeed,' said Mr. Gwent. 'We used to dine with Fate from time to time – Mary and I, before all this happened. We were among his few friends. We thought him charming and eccentric, if a little sinister. I enthused to him about William Blake and he became enchanted by my ideas on consciousness. At one meal, he would not speak of anything but the newspaper report he had read that day, which detailed how in ninety per cent of miscarriages of justice, the wrongly accused has been convicted on the basis of witness testimony – not spite, you see, but delusion. Fate thought this hilarious: unreliable narrators, he called them, and he became obsessed with the science of reality as a hallucination, so highly subjective and warped that it can be manipulated. And so he found a means with which to do so.'

I sensed that Mr. Gwent had been waiting a long time to share his story, perceived how loneliness had increased its weight with every day.

'But how did he manage to find such a means, concoct such a drug?' I pressed him.

'This he never fully disclosed to me. But look, we are running out of time,' Mr. Gwent said, with a fierceness to his voice. 'Now, my novel will not be anything like this world. It will be a place of complete freedom. I shall set it in 2014, and you will be entrusted with the plot: shape it as you wish; unlike Fate, I will not treat you like a father punishing his errant children.'

I turned to Rachel, expecting her to share my horror, but her expression was one of animation.

'But you promised that we would be returning to the present day!' I cried.

'Why, and so I shall. I might have lived in Fate's world for the last decade, but I recollect everything beautifully – I made extensive notes, I can assure you that all the details will be accurate. I left reality in 2007 but 2014 is not so very hard to imagine.' A look of wistfulness came over his face.

'But I am referring to 2019, the real world that exists outside any novel,' I protested. 'I thought that we would drink this tea and it would reverse our current ailment.'

'Dear God,' said Mr. Gwent, his forehead glowering into a frown, 'I am afraid that my powers do not extend that far. My novel is but a refuge from this world.'

I recollected my earliest memory of this world, poised behind a thick velvet curtain: my identity held down like a jack-in-the-box with the lid fastened tightly.

'And what will you make me?' My voice rose in anger. 'A foetus or a forty-five-year-old? An aristocrat or a bus driver? I want to be myself again. Why, we may as well stay here – I would rather be me and live out this agony than lose myself again.'

'Listen: that is precisely what I want for you, my dear boy,' Mr. Gwent soothed me. 'I too know that craving well. There is little time to explain the rules of literary metamorphosis, so I must be quick: an author who wishes to impose a strong storyline, when using a real soul in their book, will force amnesia on a character, negating their past, just as Fate did to you – your true self works merely as a subconscious, pressed down. It requires a strong dose of Grand Kuding.'

'Grand Kuding?' I exclaimed in dismay, haunted by

memories of sitting in Fate's cottage, sipping at that noxious liquid. 'What was the tea that you used to awaken me?'

'Ah, that was *Soma* tea. Soma awakens, Grand Kuding drugs. But you require the latter for the transition, and while Fate gave you a very high dose, I shall give you a weaker strain – enough for the journey only, I promise you. I will not plot you; you will be you. Our memories make us who we are, and you will have all of them!'

'I see,' I said, doubtfully, looking to Rachel for her opinion.

At that moment, Mr. Gwent's maid entered the room, her face flushed.

'I am sorry to interrupt you, sir,' she cried, 'but there is a trio of hooded monks at the door. I advised them that you were not receiving visitors, but they have been persistent in lingering. They gave me quite a chill – and when I next glanced out of the front room windows, I saw that they had doubled in number. Now they are entirely filling up the path!' Her hand fluttered against her heart as she furtively drew open one of the curtains. We all turned, and all gasped. There, in Mr. Gwent's back garden, were half a dozen more of them. They strolled to the glass, appearing to stare in and peruse us.

Mr. Gwent raced to the window and violently redrew the curtain.

'You must both drink the tea and be hasty about it.'

'But even with our memories, we're still entering a book within a book.' I held Rachel's hand tightly. 'This is no solution at all! What if we were to let Fate destroy us? Would we wake then, free, in his cottage—'

'If you die in Fate's book, you will not return to your former world,' Mr. Gwent said bluntly.

'But these are not our real bodies!'

'No matter – the psychological shock of a death here will result in the true death of your body in the real world. And I have not seen Fate in such a vindictive mood in all the years that I have been trapped here. Drink the tea; take refuge; then seek the Storyteller. He will be able to facilitate your return home, should you still desire it after you've spent some time in my world.'

Rachel reached for her cup and began to gulp it down. I hesitated and took a sip. The taste immediately brought back the most unpleasant sensation of déjà vu; I recalled the look in Fate's eyes as he first saw me drink the tea in his cottage, as though I was some rat he was anesthetising for his experiment. I wanted to approach every single one of his wretched monks and tear off their heads. I took another, much larger gulp, and complained that my tongue was burnt.

'A burnt tongue is better than death by a hooded monk!' Rachel said quietly.

'I will give you both your real names,' Mr. Gwent insisted. Beads of sweat were glistening across his brow and he unfurled a handkerchief to dab at them. 'You will be Jaime, Rachel will be Rachel. You will have free will.'

'And this Storyteller?' I cried.

'Find him – they say he is the only answer.'

'So he is no more than a legend? Why have you not found him?'

Rachel showed me her cup – all that remained was one final mouthful.

'All legends are rooted in truth!' Mr. Gwent's hands furrowed his hair. 'Pray, drink!'

His words were interrupted by the shattering of glass. A chill blew into the room and swirled around our frozen forms; there was movement beneath the velvet curtain, the sound of a hand undoing the latch of the window. Rachel downed the last of her drink and set down her cup with a querulous bang.

I took a gulp of tea, and another, and another. Every mouthful filled me with the rage of surrender, the despair of defeat. Mr. Gwent lifted the sheaves of his novel and began to read, *Jaime woke up to find himself in his flat in Manchester, a small room above the record shop that he owned . . .*

One last gulp. The curtains whirled; the shadows laid out by the gas lamps slanted into italics as a monk climbed into the room. But Rachel and I were already fading, like candle flames being extinguished, fire turned to smoke. Mr. Gwent's narration was filling me like a liturgical chant. I lifted my eyes to the housekeeper and saw in her face an expression of Fate's, a parting message from him: a look of scorn and fury and, perhaps, sorrow, for the loss of his playthings. The room was losing colour; sound was losing meaning, becoming noise, and the air was all wind and I could no longer tell if the screams I heard were mine or Rachel's and I found myself crying out for my mother, and then all was gone and there was peace, and dark and a sense of new beginning, and in that beginning was the word . . .

An Interim

The telephone is ringing again. I listen to the click of the answerphone, followed by my message, recorded in Latin, and then a breathy, girlish voice speaking:

'Hello, Mr Fate . . . It's Eleanor Bates from Jonathan Cape here, and we were just wondering how you were progressing with *Thomas Turridge*. We're all so – well, we're dying to read some more, even if you just have another chapter. There's no rush, of course. I just wanted to – well, touch base – and – we look forward. Very much. OK. Thanks. Bye for now.'

Eleanor Bates: an unfamiliar name. Perhaps she is the new girl. Last month I received a message from a Miss Rose Harriet-Jones. I found it to be more than a little demanding in tone and after I complained about her, I was assured that she would be fired. My editor, a Mr John Sturgeon, sent me a letter after reading the recently redrafted opening of *Thomas Turridge*. It was penned in blue ink and the stiff, awkward flourishes, the gloopy twists of his Gs and Js, suggested that he was uncomfortable without a keyboard. I suspect he thought that it was an old-fashioned touch which would impress me. He congratulated me at length on the first twenty-three thousand words. He informed me that the character of Thomas was beautifully conceived – *a vulnerable, sweet and deeply sympathetic protagonist*. He was moved by the loss of Thomas's mother and is eager to know if he might save Rachel from being sent to the asylum. He added that Mr Gwent is a hilarious creation and he never grows tired of his cameos in my novels. The crisis involving the helicopter came as a surprise, he concluded, and he wonders if it might be best to maintain the tone and atmosphere of the Victorian era, which I have sustained so well. Then the note of melodrama: *We are keen to publish and capitalise on the recent surge of interest in your work.*

He is referring, of course, to the newspaper pieces on the missing Jaime Lancia. I have been announced as a suspect, which has served to give me cachet: the idea of the author as murderer supposedly upset my fans; the fact that all my books went back into the *Sunday Times* top ten suggests otherwise. (After a recent plateau in my sales, this has been a welcome revival, the sort of resurgence in popularity usually only experienced after one has died. Alas, I have begun to worry of late that I might be a breed in danger of extinction: the mature male novelist. Literary fashion has unexpectedly taken a perverse swerve in favour of gossipy, slim novels by young women exploring romances with unkind boys, bodily angst and the delights of Marxism.)

I sit down at my desk for my morning session. I weigh my paperweight, Gwent's carpal bone glinting in its fissured centre. I open my Moleskine notebook, I dip my Montblanc fountain pen in my well of deep-blue ink; I fire my mind with two espressos and soothe it with tobacco pressed into my favourite pipe; I imbibe several chapters of *David Copperfield*, adding words such as *querulous* and *phlegmatic temperament* to my list of Dickensian flourishes; I play Beethoven. Several hours pass. Desperation wearies me. Now that Jaime and Rachel have fled, the characters of Thomas Turridge and the governess revert to little more than mannequins. The pages I produce are fit only for the fire. Once more, I curse Mr Gwent for assisting in their escape, ushering them into his inferior text. He will suffer punishment for that, but for now I shall follow Dickens's advice and *make them wait*: let him writhe in vexed anticipation of possible tortures.

Eleven times, my grandfather clock chimes, reminding me that it is time to feed my characters. I shuffle into the kitchen and remove two packets of Nutrifeed from the cupboard. Gently kicking Dorothea's dirt-tray to one side with my slippered foot, I peel back the newspaper, and unlock the wooden trap door. *Dimitte me*: it is such clichéd villainy, to lock them in the basement! And I am too old to risk daily descents down such a steep staircase without a rail: one slip and I would require a new hip. However, it remains the safest place for the present. When the police calm down, I shall return them to the bedroom.

I check on them five times a day, my visits as regular as a devotee attending to his prayers, whether in person or on the live feed from the CCTV playing out on a twelve-inch black-and-white TV screen in my shed. There is something so peaceful about seeing them there on the mattress, laid out like the dead, wandering in my created world. My little ducklings. Then I recall this morning's creative frustrations and the urge to slap them tingles in my fingertips. I busy myself with unscrewing tubes, adding nourishment to the drips that flow into their catheters. They are fortunate that I am a benign caretaker of their souls, for when they fled into Gwent's book the temptation to stop their feed briefly assailed me.

Gently, I stroke away a curl that whispers over Rachel's forehead. It is the boy that I blame for their flight. Jaime and Rachel are the pulsing heart of my novel, the bloodflow of its plot. They were not as foolish as I had anticipated and the Grand

Kuding tea wore off more quickly than I had expected too; when Jaime became enlightened that he was trapped in my creation, I thought he might join Rachel in the asylum. He had told me of how he loathed the mob mentality of social media; I gave him its Victorian equivalent in the form of a congregation. He rebelled against me no matter how outrageous my plotting became, even as the centuries collided. I concede that my editor might be correct on this front: the incident with the helicopter will, perhaps, need to be rewritten, for I got rather carried away. Their resistance to me was such a thrill. I understood then how much fun the God of the Old Testament must have had, tormenting nations with surreal weather, thunderbolting tragedies at Job. It was the friction between Jaime and I that created the flow of words. I never allowed them to suffer boredom; I tested them to the very depths of their souls. But no, they prefer other plots: they've opted to laze in Gwent's tepid sub-Ballardian nonsense.

Upstairs, I return to my desk to discover another message burbling through on my answerphone. Two calls in one morning: *O bonitas misereatur mei!* My telephone's shrill is such a rarity that it usually makes me jump vehemently with the sudden awareness of its existence; I am ill-used to such popularity. But it is only the Welsh constabulary, with some tedious request that I attend another interview to discuss 'the ongoing investigation into the disappearance . . .' and other such rot.

I dip my pen's tip into my well. An ink blot drops on to the paper, spreads, dries. My pen trembles. I know that they will return soon, and I will finish *Thomas Turridge*, and it will be my masterpiece.

The Second Story

MANCHESTER, 2014

one

I'm walking down Oxford Road, Manchester, when I become aware that my eardrums have thinned to the finest of membranes. Everyday white noise – students chattering, buses trundling, cars picking up speed between traffic lights – is a headache of heavy metal. I dive into a shop called 'The Eighth Day'. It sells healthy food: crisps made from pulses, expensive snack bars containing around ninety or so super-immune-boosting ingredients and oxymoronic 'fun-filled' chocolate bars without a trace of chocolate or sugar in them. I wander down the vitamins aisle, wondering if I should be brave and make an appointment with my GP to test my hearing. I'm only thirty-two, for fuck's sake, and I've not been to enough gigs to explain this tinnitus. I pause by the snacks; I have a craving for bonbons. A memory, smudgy: a dim interior, the shelves filled with glass jars of humbugs and toffees and butterscotch drops, which are weighed out and put into paper bags. Where did I last see a shop like that? Maybe down in Rusholme?

A noticeboard by the shop door. It is thicketed with leaflets for protest marches and gigs and writing collectives. YOGA

EVERY SATURDAY, one cries. Another memory, clearer: my tatty copy of the Penguin Classics edition of The Upanishads. The Taittiriya Upanishad states that a human quiddity is surrounded by layers: ego, emotion, intellect, senses, the mind, the body. I used to find succour in meditation and yoga. The classes I attended weren't full of the clichés you see on sitcoms; there were no chakra-obsessed women with ponytails carrying scented candles. Most people who attended looked twitchy, earnest, in need of answers. Meditation nourished my soul, for a time. It felt like a 'fuck you' to capitalism and its tiring maxim that happiness is a sterling sign. Then I suffered periods of doubt: that I was naive and foolish, that faith was pointless in a world of chaos, that there was no narrative to be fashioned from its madness, and my practice faltered.

I've got a nagging feeling that I need to be somewhere.

'The Corner House, 6 p.m.,' my calendar app tells me.

I can't remember who I'm meeting, though. Add senility to my list of ailments; my inner hypochondriac is having a fine day.

Halfway across the road, they come at me: a zoo of honking vertebrae with metal skeletons and tails of exhaust. I reverse back on to the pavement, wondering at my stupidity as I watch some students facilitate the use of a traffic light. The green man fails to reassure me. As buses pant at the lip of the crossing like a herd ready to stampede, I hurry across. My heartbeat gradually slows as I head towards the Corner House, the quirky arthouse cinema that sits on the corner of Oxford Road.

I grew to love this place while doing my Masters in Fine Art at Manchester uni. There's an exhibition on upstairs. The last one I caught was by David Shrigley, I believe. I don't go to exhibitions anymore. I once believed in the art world as a divine, benign cultural force that was devoted to the dissemination of beauty. Freud advises that illusions save us from pain and allow us to enjoy pleasure; I miss the Maya that the Rachel of my early twenties believed in.

Whoever I'm meeting doesn't seem to be turning up. As I'm climbing the stairs for the toilet, a man wearing a dark suit over a black shirt and a black tie greets me. His face is scarred and his eyebrows are verbose. He kisses each of my cheeks, blasting me with aftershave that smells of money.

'You're a little late,' he chides me. His eyes are almost yellow, like those of a fox. 'But you look beautiful, as always.'

As he pulls me up the spiral staircase, I am conscious of the smile on my face. Such is the fate of being a woman: a strange man is dragging me into a room, and for all I know he could be a rapist, but here I am, anxious to please, keen to show the world that I'm happy.

A poster on the wall: I stop, tugging him back, and examine it. *The End* by Rachel Levy.

'It's *my* exhibition!' I cry.

'You on the coke again?' he whispers in my ear.

During my twenties, I staged various exhibitions. They ranged from *The Hollow Man*, hosted by my local library, tucked behind a stand advertising local walks for the elderly, to my most famous show, Metamorphoses, in the Serpentine

Gallery. There's even a photo (still preserved on Google) of Bowie visiting the exhibition and staring at *The Gaze of Orpheus* very intently. I have no recollection of ever putting together a show called *The End*, however.

I enter the gallery. Smiles float as though the Cheshire Cat has been replicated in pop art, mouths open and spout congratulations, hands curl around glasses of bubbly. I am thrust before a microphone and the room falls silent. I still the impulse to press my knuckles to my eyelids and crouch down in a ball. How can I not recall painting these huge canvases, the result of what must have been months of graft? Hemingway in oils, shotgun tip between his teeth, cut-up slithers of *For Whom the Bell Tolls* spurting from the side of his head as though anticipating the blood-splatter. Thick oils of a dark figure snagged in river-web, the silhouette of Virginia Woolf looming above the waves. A painting, post-impressionist in style, of a counter-narrative: bright-yellow dabs and dashes depicting two boys playing with a gun in a field of irises; the ones who shot Vincent van Gogh, only for the murder to be rewritten as suicide. I wish there was a straightforward explanation for my amnesia. I dread that this is the result of a night that became too dark: a white room, pills forced down my throat, a bed and electrodes placed on my temples, a thread that snapped inside me.

'Thank you all for coming,' I begin. I manage to make a polite speech, but I detect a faint disappointment. Did they want me to be an enfant terrible? I hear laughter from the back of the crowd. A young guy with dark hair has a pet duck by his feet, tied to a lead. He grins at me intimately and I raise an eyebrow, figuring he might make a good post-show fuck, then round off my speech.

Everyone surges forwards to congratulate me. It's odd, being beneath the spotlight of your fifteen minutes of fame, knowing life will always conform to cliché and fortune's wheel will turn. People say, 'Well done, well done,' but their eyes are all shades of sadness, jealousy, hunger. A man from the *Manchester Evening News* asks me what my influences are. I explain that, at the age of sixteen, I saw my first ever Francis Bacon. I don't want to talk wank about technique or concept or how the sight of *Head VI* – a man trapped behind the ghost of a glasslike structure, a face screaming into an airless void – was a visual translation of my adolescent angst. So I simply say that I had wanted to love Bacon's work even before I saw it, ever since I'd heard that Maggie Thatcher described him as 'that man who paints those dreadful paintings'.

The guy with the pet duck approaches me.

'Hey, Rachel,' he says. 'It's me, Jaime.'

'Hey, nice to meet you,' I say, smiling. 'Nice to meet your duck too. What's its name?'

'I don't know. No, I do. It's Tim. Look, should we find somewhere to talk about next steps – about fate?'

His tone is light but his eyes are a little frantic. I wonder if he's an art student seeking contacts.

'Sure, soft boy,' I laugh. 'I also believe that everything is meant to be.'

'Do you not—' Jaime begins, looking puzzled. 'Gwent said we'd both remember—'

Daniel, the gallery owner, cuts Jaime off, saying that we should go on to the after-party at the Warehouse. As we leave, Jaime calls after me, something about how we once romanced in a graveyard.

two

Lights strobe in neon flashes, so that the figures on the dance-floor appear to move in slow motion. The music takes my puff-clock cares and gently blows them away. We came to the club from the gallery in several taxis, ordered by Daniel, all of which he filled with attractive twentysomething females. We moved in a group at first, conscious of his power, like dancing girls undulating around a king. Then I drifted away. The pleasure of dancing is transcendent, as though I've been released from the machine of my body. All the best experiences – dancing, music, art – negate the body, even while they stem from it. Beyond my happiness, there still lingers an unease that is vague but more permanent than my immediate cares and concerns – a sense of something being wrong. But I'm used to that being the backdrop to my life. That *is* life.

The guy with the duck reappears, tunnelling through the dancers, his feathered friend in the crook of his arm. God knows how he managed to talk his way past the bouncers. He whispers once more that his name is Jaime and that he knows that my name is Rachel and that he really, really needs to speak to me.

Outside, we stand in an alleyway fogged with cigarette smoke. He keeps trying to tell me that we're in a book. As chat-up lines go, it's certainly zany, but also cheesy as fuck: I'm waiting for him to add that it's a romance novel. Then I see the intensity in his eyes and I fear that his eccentricity, so endearing in the gallery, speaks to something more dangerous. I recognise it and sympathise with it, but its familiarity also repulses me. Undeterred, he carries on, telling me about Victorian England and someone called Gwent, and I smile politely, nodding all the while, thinking, Why do I attract these types? It's followed by a more superficial thought: It's a shame too, when he's so good-looking. Then he tells me about Fate again. Fate: the word snags me with a feeling of unease.

I ask him to describe how on earth we got here.

'You don't remember that kind of moment,' he replies scornfully, his voice rising. 'The same way that nobody remembers the split second when warmth and darkness give way to the shock of air and screaming and a surgeon in your face. You only ever remember some time later, lying in a nursery, watching the swirl of a mobile.' He says the word 'fate' once more and suddenly there's a prickle in my throat. I swallow it down.

'I get what you're trying to say,' I reply, waving my cigarette around idiotically. 'Life is all about narratives, right? We edit our pasts.'

'It's not a metaphor. I saved you, remember? You were in a carriage, being taken away to an asylum, and I saved you.'

'What about your duck?' I ask. 'Does he think he's in a book too?'

'Oh God – I knew I shouldn't have brought the bloody duck! I'm just duck-sitting, that's all. Look, I know the duck really isn't helping here, but just hear me out—'

'Actually, if it wasn't for the duck, I think I might have scarpered a long time ago.' I bend down to ruffle the duck's head with the tip of my finger. Then Daniel comes out and asks if Jaime is bothering me. It's easier to say yes, and soon the bouncers are dragging away both the protesting man and his duck.

Daniel's Deansgate flat must have cost him at least several million. Peering through the green lattice of his houseplants, I eye up Manchester's sprawl with affection. I might have been born in Camden, but I'm a Northerner in my soul. His living room is busy with fancy sofas, black lamps and bubble-wrapped pieces of art. Daniel offers me a tab with a smiley face on it. I only pretend to take it: the night already feels as though someone has slipped something into my drink, and adding another drug into the mix might break me. Daniel invites two of us – me and a girl with honey hair (am I girl A or girl B, target or back-up plan?) – to look at his study, which he says contains all sorts of gems for a forthcoming exhibition on Victorian erotica at the Lowry. The other girls sprawl across the sofas; two of them start kissing, willingly becoming an exhibit. Daniel smirks at them, then turns his back.

He points to the Bouguereau hanging on the wall and says, 'Do you remember John Berger's essay, *Ways of Seeing*? Berger said that the female nude was never a woman truly naked, but a woman lined up for the male gaze. A passive woman with an active male protagonist looking at her.'

'Bouguereau was a Victorian painter . . . It wasn't a great time for women,' I say, wishing my voice wouldn't slur so. 'In *The Descent of Man*, Darwin said that the "intuitive powers" he found in women were characteristic of "the lower races and therefore a lower state of civilisation". The bastard.'

The girl with the honey-coloured hair stares up at a Bronzino print: Cupid cupping Venus's breast.

'Me, I love women,' says Daniel. 'I love to surround myself with them.' He seems to presume that his natty tie and Hugo Boss suits divide him from the men in frock coats and waistcoats of 1861. 'Come.' He puts his hands on my shoulders and guides me towards a humped shape. When he pushes me down, beneath a black cloth, I try to resist, but he shushes me and promises that I will love this. 'It's a mutoscope,' he explains.

I stare through the lens at the circle of film projected on to the screen. A caption: *The Mouse in the House*. It runs in sepia, its images jumpy, as if the film itself is winking lasciviously at its subject matter. Two women, frightened of a mouse, jump on to a table and raise their skirts. It was considered terribly risqué back in 1900, Daniel informs me. Then, a series of images: a topless woman draped over a chaise longue, her fingers entwined in pearls; two maids lifting their frilly white dresses to show off their bums. The women are plump, their skin as soft as ripe fruit, and there is a bashful innocence to their poses that today's porn stars have given up trying to imitate. I am embarrassed to feel a pulse between my legs, but the shame is also part of the pleasure. And then I see – me. Or rather, the Rachel of 1861, right there in the kaleidoscope of sexuality. I'm posing with a peacock feather, my governess's dress slung on to the chair behind me, and I can hear Mr Carmichael's voice cajoling me to lower the feather just a little more, just a little more, his excitement measured out in inches. The picture clicks. I am replaced by a topless woman in a tatty mermaid's costume.

I stand up, reeling. I would have hit the floor if Daniel hadn't steadied me. In moon-eyed shock, I look him up and down as though searching for the pencil sketches beneath his suit. *You're not real*, I mutter.

'What the hell is the matter with you tonight?' Daniel hisses. He instructs the other girl to take me to the bathroom, but I tell her that I need a taxi. She escorts me down herself. Now that I am no longer her rival, she is ready to be kind. In the lift, she keeps giggling and posing in the mirror, twisting sheaves of hair across her lip in false moustaches.

'Are you one of us?' I ask her. 'Are you one of Gwent's refugees?'

She lifts an eyebrow and applies some cerise lipstick.

His flat is next to the Hilton; I head to the taxi rank outside it. My lips recite an address on autopilot. I slip in, slam the door and panic again: How the hell am I going to afford a taxi all the way to Chorlton? Digging around in my handbag, I locate my purse. There's a rainbow of credit cards in the wallet section. I pull out a spray of notes, and a draught blows them over the seat and floor. The driver glances at me in his rear-view mirror as I scramble about, collecting them.

I close my eyes, rest my head against the seat. Beneath the disorientation is a relief, of sorts. I'm glad I'm in Gwent's story, rather than the 2019 I left behind. But I'm not sure who the Rachel Levy of this world is meant to be. I feel as though my body is a sketch, and I need to block in the colours. I'm too close to being myself again. That moment when I entered Fate's world was euphoric. The Rachel that Fate superimposed on me put her hands around my neck and suffocated me. I was able to lie in the back of her consciousness in a blissful coma, in a forgotten room with no visitors. She dictated my script; and the strictness of the society around us dictated our actions.

I pull my mobile out of my bag and check the contacts folder. It's empty. I look out into the night and wonder after Jaime: he must be cursing me.

'Here,' the cab driver says.

I have a feeling he's said that to me several times and is losing patience. I get out of the cab and notice, through the smear of his window, how tired he looks. He's probably keen to get home to his family and a warm bed. I give him a ten-pound tip and his face lights up. The act feels like an anchor; I want my new self to be kind.

I stand in the cold night, looking up at my new home. It's a big Victorian house, with a flaky face and black beams like shaggy eyebrows arched over its porch. Inside, tatty carpeting on the stairs leads me to the second floor and my flat, number 27.

three

I walk about on tiptoe, feeling like a burglar invading a stranger's home. It's hard not to feel insulted by the generic nature of my new place. A pink bedroom with tasselled curtains; a wardrobe filled with high-heeled shoes and filmy floral dresses, rather than the trainers and jeans I'd usually favour. I remind myself that Gwent hardly knew me, but I can't help but feel that his perception of women seems to be inspired by the clichés of women's magazines. I think of Mrs Carmichael, back in 1861, of the hooped skirts she wore that made it hard to sit down, of the corsets that crushed her ribs. Clothing designed to restrict women, keep them at home, keep them in their place. She wasn't a kind boss to me when I was governess to her daughter, but I saw why; with so little power in her life, she lorded it over her staff; it was the only domain she was allowed to express any sort of control over.

As for Mr Carmichael, when his wife and daughter were absent, he would sometimes coax me into being photographed in his study, in return for favours that I desperately needed: time off to visit my mother at Hanwell; the money for the travel there and back. Though I suspect that Fate introduced the subplot for titillation, I didn't feel like a victim; as a poorly paid governess, I became so invisible that I often felt like a ghost. At least Mr Carmichael made me feel like flesh and blood, even if it meant becoming a caricature of his lust.

I check my inbox. There are emails from an Emily, a Daniel, a Mary, but nothing from Jaime. I hesitate, then type in 'Mum' to see if I have a mother in this story. 'No results,' my email informs me. The little clock on my Mac tells me it's 1.32 a.m.

Water sluices over my body in wave upon wave of bliss. After months of using a pail of warm water to wash, the shower feels like regal decadence. I stand naked before the mirror, examining my reflection. My hair is the same colour as it was in real life, dark brown, but it seems to have been highlighted and possesses a glossy sheen that I never used to have. I used to cut my own hair with the kitchen scissors and, if it went wrong, pretend it was meant to be a jagged, layered look. I felt like hacking at the neat ends now, but perhaps I ought to play along with Gwent's world.

A scratching noise. I open the door; a black-and-white cat purrs around my damp ankles and I pick it up. Its fur becomes wet with my tears. The day I went to visit Fate, I left my dog behind with my neighbour. I know he loves Tommy and will have adopted him by now, but still, I miss his cuddly warmth, his gruff barks, the thump of his tail when he's happy. Sometimes I would stare into his eyes and feel ashamed at the thought that I loved Tommy more than any human I knew.

When the cat streaks back through the window, pads along the windowsill and into the flat next door, I watch her go with a wistful heart.

Yawns are curling up my throat but I'm afraid that sleep's oblivion will beget a fresh amnesia. I sit in the living room with a notebook on my lap.

'Gwent?' I say to the empty room. 'Gwent? How can I get in touch with Jaime?'

Silence. Just as he promised: no intervention, only free will.

I hate this humming noise in the background of Gwent's novel, modern machines perpetually reminding us of our dependency on them. I've grown used to the clatter of hooves on cobbles, the dominance of birdsong.

My fingers are tingling, but there are no canvases in this flat, and it's been a long time since I last picked up a brush. I pick up a notebook, click a ballpoint pen, smooth the blank page, and begin to write:

My name is Rachel Levy. I was born in Horsham, Surrey, in 1987.

I pause, afraid to spill the emotions welling up inside me, to assert my own narrative. I am used to shaping my ideas through images, colour, texture. But then, in jerky script, the words find their flow:

Here's a childhood memory: when I was six years old, I showed my mum a sketch of a robin.

It's lovely, she told me. She asked where I'd got it from. When I said that I had drawn it myself, she went very quiet. That evening, she gave me bread and margarine and jam to eat, but didn't make any for herself. As I devoured mine, she assured me that she wasn't hungry.

This went on every night for ten days. I began to feel scared that she wasn't eating because she was sick and going to die. I was sitting at the table sketching when I heard her come home from work. Her face was flushed and she said, 'I've got something for you.' It was a box of twenty-six colour pencils. I drank the shades in like milkshakes. Even then, I had some sense of the sacrifice she had made, and I tried to give her a clumsy hug. She wasn't a tactile woman, so she gently pushed me away and set me down before a sheet of paper with a stern look.

~~*I am an artist.*~~

In 2010, I took a trip to Assisi with my mother. She was much better around this time; still a pale version of herself, but able to survive in the world. I feel guilty about my resistance to going on that holiday, fearing we would regress into teenager and parent. But we had a beautiful time swimming, eating and lounging on the beach. She brought Augustus Fate's The Beetle Fossil *as her holiday read; I had brought* The Baronet. *We both declared Fate our favourite author. We enjoyed his historical novels the most. He wrote books that you could drown in; if you were immersed in one long enough, you would look up and be startled by the fact that the world around you possessed planes and mobiles, so deeply did he take you into his Victoriana. His characters felt as familiar as family, and as for his use of language – well, I am no critic, but I could see that if Fate were an artist, he would paint in oils, layer upon layer, the colours rich as wines – a slow and patient craftsman.*

In the weeks before I visited Fate, I stayed inside my flat and disconnected my phone. I got my neighbour, Joe, to take Tommy for a walk, explaining that I had developed agoraphobia; every time he returned and passed the lead back, he would emphatically ask if I was OK. My blinds kept the sunlight distant; I might have been living in some post-apocalyptic landscape. I would sit before my computer, staring at a stream of tweets where it was impossible to distinguish truth from fiction. Sometimes I even tried to compose one myself, but only managed a fragment, a few words that hung in the blue box in pure potentiality. Then there were the news pages, which were often skeletons of stories strung together with the bones of tweets. Once offering essays and analysis, journalism had now devolved into children's stories. I would wake and think about how I might progress the narrative of my life. I might work at an animal hospital, where every day would be sweet with compassion. I might travel for a year, find dissolution in disorientation, reshape myself.

The Vedas state that we are in the depths of Kali Yuga, that darkest hour when the positive laws of humanity lie dormant, where demons thrive and misery is the median. I visited suicide forums because they were honest places, filled with people who, even with their trauma, had the sanity to see that the world was not as it should be. Tommy had taken to lying by my feet and whimpering, unable to understand why the love I used to lavish on him was gone. But I could not stroke him, because to feel the warmth of his flesh, the beat of his heart, would be to connect with a world that I ~~refused to could not~~

What do you do when the narrative of your world is one that you can no longer believe in? When you no longer want to be part of it? You can slit your wrists. You can say 'fuck you' to the world, mimic its cruelty, and strap explosives to your waist. You can find religion and pull its tatty, thin coat around you in the hope of protection, conscious of its holes, of the winds of life that keep blowing through. Or you can seek a place in which to hibernate, to . . .

The last trip I made after leaving my flat was to Wales, to the home of Augustus Fate. I cannot recall the moment when Fate gave me the tea, but I know that I needed no persuasion to drink it.

four

I sit on the train to Liverpool, sifting through a crumpled copy of the *Metro*. The news, a weave of reality and unreality, feels more disorientating than depressing: Blair is still PM, Jordan's boobs are indecisive, the only manufacturing industry alive and thriving is *X Factor*. I glance up at the June sky. In winter, cities look man-made: the trees are anorexic, the skyline dominated by bleak buildings, the flowerbeds bare and tragic. In the summer, Nature wins: the train rattles past houses obscured by trees of foamy blossom, brick made elegant by ivy. The date on the paper says 5 May 2014.

I used to find summer a little bit cheesy, like an American smile that tells you to *have a nice day*. But this blue sky is persuasive. Gwent is a benign deity. This morning I found a filing cabinet in my flat that contained my bank statements. I brought in twenty-eight thousand pounds from my last exhibition. People who say money doesn't buy happiness have never been poor. Yet this new-found sweetness feels fragile. Can I really start afresh here? Or will I just fall into the same fucked-up patterns?

I get off the train at Liverpool Lime Street and stroll through pools of sunlight up to the high street. I check the address on my smartphone once again. The Post-it on my fridge was backed up by a diary entry: *3 p.m., Stanley House, Lord Street.* It had been underlined three times. When I get there, the building gives me no clues as to why: there is no plaque above the dirty white buzzer.

I arrive with twenty minutes to spare, and so I cross the road and enter a cafe. To my surprise, it has a smoking section at the back. As I order a lemonade, I notice a guy with dark hair sitting at a nearby table.

'Rachel!'

It's Jaime.

'I'm really sorry,' I say as I sit down, but he cuts me off.

'Look, I know I must have sounded crazy last night, but—'

'I know,' I say. 'We're in a book. I remember now. I behaved like a dick—'

'But were you trying to get rid of me? Or did you forget?'

'I forgot, of course!' I say, accepting a cigarette from him.

We exhale smoke in trembling lines; they meld into one anxious fog. I hold up my glass and remind myself that it belongs to the imagination of Mr Gwent. I picture us as though from a long tracking shot, like figures in a snow globe. I look at him through the tumbler, and Jaime fractures and blurs; becomes an impressionist portrait of dark hair and pale skin. After knowing him as Thomas, all puppy eyes and a dimpled smile, he seems to me so grown-up, with his firm jaw and smattering of stubble and the faint lines etched around his eyes.

'So, how come you forgot? Gwent said we'd have free will.'

'I don't know – I was just on my way home, and it suddenly clicked – I felt so stupid. I used to live in Manchester, so I guess it felt like being back in normal life again . . .'

'I'm just glad I found you again.'

We smile at each other.

'Well, I got a note saying I should be at that place across the road at three p.m.'

'I had the same note!' He rolls his eyes. 'So much for free will.'

'You think Gwent is trying to matchmake us?' I feel relieved. Last night, before I got into bed, I automatically fell down on my knees and recited the Lord's Prayer. Halfway through, I realised that it was unnecessary but I carried on by rote.

'Perhaps he did,' Jaime replies.

There's an awkward pause during which I wonder if I'm imagining the flirtatious tone in his voice, and then he eyes the clock, brisk again: 'I'm hoping we're about to meet the Storyteller.'

'Uh huh.' I finish my cigarette and immediately reach for another, but he takes my hand in his. There is something authoritative, possessive about the gesture.

'We're going to be OK,' he says emphatically. 'We just need to follow Gwent's advice, and find a way out. Simple.'

I pull my hand away, for his confidence seems misplaced, his decision-making too presumptuous. He folds his arms, frowning.

'Can you remember what happened with you and Fate?' he asks, after a pause. 'How did you end up here?'

The memory makes me feel like crying.

'I just wrote him a fan letter,' I lie, 'and he asked me to visit.'

'That fucking *cunt*,' Jaime says, making me jump. A few of the other diners glance over at us. 'Sorry. But – God – he nearly had you put away in an asylum.'

'At least an asylum has some drama about it,' I reflect. 'I mean, in the present day you just get sentenced to tranquilisers and a life of quiet desperation.'

Our laughter is forced. I realise that I am back to turning everything into a joke, using wit to make tragedies bearable.

'I just can't believe the police haven't got him,' Jaime says. 'He's a fucking psycho. He's like Fred West or something.'

'That's a bit strong.'

'Is it? We're being held captive. He's stolen time from us, and we'll never get it back.'

'Or perhaps it's like Narnia in here, and time stops for us?'

'Time didn't stop. You were missing, Rachel. You've been missing for some time—' He swallows, his eyes filming again. 'My poor mum . . . Sorry, you must be worried about your parents too.'

'Um, yeah,' I agree, vaguely, for I am quite certain that neither of them will be concerned about my absence. Jaime must read my discomfort as grief, for he quickly changes tack.

'In the real world, I'm meant to be doing an MA at UCL with Professor Millhauser. In this book, I run a record shop, in the Northern Quarter. I live in the flat above it.'

'That's so cool.'

'I've got to admit, it is a dream job. But it's not real.'

Jaime seems to have lived in the Victorian era without samskaras taking root in him.

'But then, how much of our lives was ever real?' I ask. 'How many of the thoughts we had were truly our own, and how many were white noise, suggestions planted by films and adverts and the articles we read and the society we lived in? OK, so Blair's still in power here, but so what? It's still the same old bullshit.'

Jaime looks at me with worried eyes and then nods at the clock. 'Well, I think that you'll feel differently when we get to go home. I think you'll feel much happier.'

He stubs out his cigarette and is about to rise, when I say:

'Do you remember that moment when the helicopter crashed into the church?'

He laughs and says, 'God, yeah. Mad.'

It's as though we've just been to the movies and are reliving the best moments.

'I was in the carriage, passing by, and Dr Adams kept trying to slip his hand up my dress and I was fighting him off. I was willing something to happen and then there it was.'

'God, what a bastard. Those fucking pious professionals with crosses around their necks. That was the worst thing about that time – all that religion, and the way even non-believers were still trapped in Christian imagery and ideas and all that. At least here I can be a proper atheist again.'

'So you're an atheist?'

'Sure? Aren't you?'

I shrug. I feel a little disheartened by his revelation; just another typical guy reflecting all the clichés of Western enlightenment. I'll bet he reads Steven Pinker in his spare time, maybe Hitchens, and all those big, clever white men who think they've got the world sussed out.

Then, as we depart, he opens the cafe door for me, and says, 'After you, Ms Levy,' in a mock-gentlemanly voice, shy and sweet, and I find myself smiling back at him.

Out on the street struts a magpie. I look for its twin.

Across the road, outside the building, we stand close to one another as I press the doorbell. A crackling noise. Then a pale voice:

'Yes?'

'It's Jaime Lancia and Rachel Levy,' Jaime says. 'Can we come up?'

'Why?' A male voice; young, Liverpudlian.

'We were told to come today. We have an appointment.'

The white noise of bureaucracy. Then: 'According to our diary, your appointment is in ten days' time. 3 p.m. on Thursday the *fifteenth* of May.'

'Ask him what it's for?' I whisper, and Jaime nods impatiently.

'So we're due to see the Storyteller then?' he asks.

'Well, we can discuss that when you come for your appointment,' comes the reply, but it's careless, automated, and I wonder if he knows what Jaime is referring to. 'See ya later,' he adds in faux-American and cuts us off.

'Fuck!' Jaime keeps crying, chain-smoking in shock. 'I thought we'd be home in, like, two hours. Ten days! It's ridiculous – why the hell is Gwent keeping us waiting?'

I tell him there's nothing we can do but be patient, but he frowns, shaking his head. I remember the devotion in Thomas's eyes when he looked at me. It's hard not to look into Jaime's and see a coldness in equal measure.

We exchange numbers, and agree to meet up the next day to plan our next move. We both lean in as though to hug each other but we lose our nerve at the last minute. We've kissed and exchanged secrets, he's even told me that he loves me, yet that intimacy has the shame of a drunken one-night stand. Now, in the sober daylight, I'm not sure how to behave, nor what Jaime is feeling. We say our goodbyes with a wave.

Back in the cafe, I order an espresso, smoke some more and worry about Jaime's eagerness to find the Storyteller. Perhaps he's keen to return to a girlfriend back in London. He never mentioned it when we first chatted in the suicide forum, but the internet is all about technological smoke and mirrors, the editing of personas. As the initial kick of the caffeine wears off, my mood starts to slide. I remind myself that Gwent must have brought us together; that we are being looked after, even if only a little. This is a relief; a world of complete free will, where our choices dictate our actions, is terrifying to me. I'll always pick path B when I should have chosen A. I console myself with the thought of my bank balance. I picture myself returning to my flat with a medley of glossy bags – but that would be vulgar. Instead, I decide to have another consequence-free cigarette.

five

A text from Jaime: 'I might be 10 mins late. I've hailed a carriage but my horse is belligerent.'

I grin and text back: 'I'm about to hail a hackney cab. See u soon.'

On the tram into Manchester, I recall a fragment of last night's dream: I was in a lift with my mother, ascending floor after floor, up into the clouds. I flick through another free paper. The stories remain puzzling. In Gwent's 2014, there are no tragic tales of disabled people suffering the bedroom tax, or the poor walking miles for food banks, there are no students rioting on the streets. The line between the rich and the poor, so defined in a depression, is still blurry here. The rich are not yet creating a world within our world where they fly private jets, buy up property in London and push everyone else into its Saturnian rings. Instead, I'm just met with photographs of celebrity weddings: the things we read when life is OK and we have to blow up gossip several sizes in order to make some news.

I hear the singing of church bells as I step down from the tram. Without thinking, I follow their thread, weaving through streets until I find the source: St Mary's. In the modern world, graveyards are oases of Old England, time slowed down. Inside the church, I'm shocked by the thin smattering of people. I have grown used to this being a place where everyone presents themselves to the world, their piety a spectacle for all to see. Here, the priest is jolly and jokey, mentioning Buddhism, meditation, even making self-consciously hip references to *The Simpsons*. I want to laugh at him for wanting to be one of us, rather than wanting to rule over us. Closing my eyes, I listen, for Fate's narration has always been loudest in church. But Gwent remains silent. God sleeps.

I arrive to find that Jaime is waiting for me. We hug each other and begin to stroll up Market Street, where buskers line the pavement, dancing or feigning superpowers. I notice Jaime's stubble, his dark quiff, the blue of his eyes. His body language is already more relaxed; after three days, he is starting to seem more at home in this world. He says that he's been searching online for books that mention the Storyteller, and I change the subject. As we drift through the high street, we notice shops that went extinct a long time ago: a Jessops, an HMV, a Books etc. Jaime snaps pictures of everything on his iPhone.

'Gwent got kidnapped by Fate at the end of 2007,' says Jaime. 'That's where the present day stopped for him.'

'So I guess we're in a 2007-style 2014, where forty per cent of the world's wealth hasn't been wiped out.' I feel brightened by the idea.

'I guess the whole boom *was* a fiction anyway, everyone just materialising money out of nothing,' Jaime muses, but his unease seems pervasive.

As we walk through Woolworths, we revel in sweet nostalgia. Jaime misses Nerds, those fizzy particles of rainbow, while I want Quality Street to bring back their Peanut Cracknell. We muse on retro sweets that amuse us: Road Kill gummies, which were in hilariously bad taste and deserved their ban; candy cigarettes, which died out with the glamour of smoking. Jaime suggests going on a tour of all the extinct shops, as though we're in the retail equivalent of the Natural History Museum.

'I feel like neither of us is taking this seriously,' I complain.

Jaime's laugh is anxious. Then his tone bitters: 'If we're going to be stuck in this book for another week, we may as well have a laugh. I mean, I think we need to. Last night I woke up in a night sweat, freaked out. I just kept staring at my bed and thinking, It's not real.'

'I had a panic attack last night as well,' I lie. 'We are going to get home, and while we're here, well . . . this is home.'

He frowns. 'I admire your stoicism.'

'It's just that . . . while we're here,' I say, the 'while' designed to placate him, 'we should just try to enjoy it. I mean – this is a really good 2014, where we don't need to suffer or worry about money. But if we mooch around being really ironic and postmodern about everything – well, it's no way to live. We should embrace it.'

Jaime looks doubtful but he shoves his hands in his pockets and nods.

We decide to go to the Cornerhouse cinema, where Jaime insists on buying both tickets even though I offer to pay half. He gives me a sheepish grin as he passes the ticket over. Neither of us comments on the choice, *The Aviator*, and the fact we have seen it many times before. Afterwards, we go to Home Sweet Home, a cafe in the Northern Quarter. One wall is covered in paintings by local artists. There's a little sticker by them saying they are going for £50 apiece. I'm upset that nobody is looking at them; everyone is too busy chatting and munching on paninis.

The waitress brings us our toasties and milkshakes, and Jaime gives her a warm 'thank you'. I'm noticing how polite and sweet he is with everyone. He always flips coins at buskers and never leaves a cafe without leaving a tip.

'That suicide forum, where we first started chatting. I wonder if it's still online.'

He looks up at me and it's too early in our friendship for me to be able to decipher his gaze.

'We were both fraudsters,' I say. 'You researching your MA, me researching my exhibition.'

'So you're an artist in the real world too?'

'Yeah, I had a few exhibitions. The big breakout one was called Metamorphoses.'

'But I remember that.' Jaime screws up his face. 'I read a rave review about it. You're famous.'

'Not everyone reacts to my work like that,' I say, because I feel so pleased that I'm embarrassed.

'But you're *the* Rachel Levy! I never clicked in the suicide forum . . . You were just "Rachel" to me back there.'

'Now you're being over the top. Nobody would ever put a *the* before my name . . .'

'Why did you keep it quiet all this time? Didn't David Bowie pay your work a visit?'

'Uh huh. That was the high point of my career,' I say sadly. 'It was all downhill from there.' I glance up again at the paintings on the wall and an ache fills me.

'I guess Fate fucked everything up for you,' he says angrily, and I nod, knowing that I fucked up everything long before Fate ever did. 'Even more reason to get back home. You should be painting! And to think that chauvinist had you corseted up as some governess . . .'

I smile, liking Jaime's feminist spirit.

As we continue to chatter, a waitress lights the candles on the tables. The room becomes soft with their flames, romanticised by the darkening, streaky sky outside. I watch Jaime's lips as he talks, the way he smooths his hair back from his forehead. I'm still trying to pin labels on him: he is left-wing and believes in Marx; he was once a God-botherer, before becoming an atheist; he used to sing in a band; he seems to love birds – or ducks, at least. He lived with a bubbly flatmate and was studying with a Professor Millhauser who was proud to be supervising his MA. He seems very together in his real life, as though he knows how to handle the world – as though he is heading somewhere. No wonder he wants to go back.

The town clock is chiming midnight as we head down the long stretch of Oxford Road that eventually becomes the Curry Mile. Neon signs firework their colours. Customers sit outside cafes, laughing and eating barfi and smoking hookahs. Our conversation skates along the surface. We are both preoccupied with what remains unspoken: when our eyes meet, there's a tenderness in our gaze, a retinal caress. Our elbows knock from time to time; our bodies lean in closer; our breaths interlace. In my jacket pocket, my fingers play with an old chocolate bar wrapper. I am trembling with the thrill of hoping that we're on the same page, that we want this story to go in the same direction.

My intellect is starting to kick in and spoil the party. It warns me: a one-night stand is all very well, but Jaime is your only ally here. The sex might be awful. Or: the sex might be great, but the next chapter might be a problem. He might want more than I can give.

A trio of beautiful girls passes by. I notice Jaime's gaze slip over them and then, with a faint trace of guilt, flick back to me. We reach the turning that leads to my road. I look up at the skyline: the spike of a church spire silvered in the moonlight.

'Do you remember that day in the graveyard, when you were Thomas?' I ask. 'You asked me to be your wife and you made a list, like Darwin.'

'I was only a boy,' Jaime says.

'It was kind of sweet,' I reply, and then wonder what the hell I'm saying. Am I mentioning marriage in order to project some kind of feminine stereotype, to lure him in before he finds out who I really am?

Jaime is looking at the stars.

'Did you know that up there is a cloud called Sagittarius B2?' I ask casually.

'What's that?'

'It's this cloud that floats in the Milky Way. It's full of dust and gas and it contains ten billion billion billion litres of alcohol.'

'We should party up there.'

'That'd be cool.' I laugh slightly too loudly.

'We could go tonight,' Jaime says, wincing at the cliché, and we finally look at each other, and I chew my lip.

six

My electric toothbrush shrills in my mouth. Jaime blots toothpaste on to his forefinger and lightly scrubs his teeth. I say goodnight to his reflection and his reflection gives me an awkward reply. I slip into bed in my pyjamas and he goes into the living room in his T-shirt and jeans, to huddle up under the sleeping bag I left out. We had a quick cuppa, messed about with my old guitar which I never learnt to play, and took turns to play each other favourite tracks on YouTube. As our yawns multiplied, he joked, 'Shall I take your bed while you sleep on the couch?' and I laughed back: 'What a gentleman.'

I feel peevish, stupid: have I misunderstood everything, misread his interest? Am I too scruffy, too weird, too ugly?

'Well – goodnight then,' he calls from the living room.

'Goodnight.'

'Sleep tight.'

'Goodnight.'

I wake in shock, aware of a figure in the flat. I nearly scream, and then I remember. I listen to the tinkle of his pee hitting the bowl. Jaime stumbles back to the living room; he sounds sleepy, hazy and disorientated.

An hour later, and I'm still awake. Tired of running on the wheel of insomnia, I switch on my light and pick up *Vasistha's Yoga*. I open it up at random. Tonight's story is about the three demons, Dama, Vyala and Kata. Created by the demon Sambara, they are invincible because they have had no previous incarnations. They are free from every other type of mental conditioning. They have no fear; they do not know the meaning of war, victory or defeat. When they fight with the gods, they are often victorious, and leave terrible destruction in their wake. Gradually, however, the demons begin to weaken. They develop the notion of *I am*. Once this ego-sense arises, they develop desires: for the acquisition of wealth, the prolongation of life in the body. This *I am* then gives rise to *this is my body* and *this is mine*. Objects bring them pleasure, but diminish their freedom, and they begin to lose their courage. They begin to fear that they might die. And so the demons are defeated and take refuge in the nethermost world.

Desires create actions. Actions create experience. Experiences leave latent impressions. Samskaras, the Vedas call them. Samskaras drift in our consciousness: the ache of a love affair cut short; the pang of an interview that never led to a job; the hollow left by a lost parent. With each rebirth, the kaleidoscope twists and casts a fresh pattern, shaping new desires, hungers that promise the illusion of happiness. And so we become trapped in incarnation after incarnation. In Satya Yuga, the Golden Age, our natural state was to fulfil desires with ease. In our current era, Kali Yuga, our desires are constantly thwarted. We puff and grind away at a promotion that is given to the candidate with the right connections; we fall for the lover who warps us. Fulfilling a desire involves either tremendous effort, or else we call it luck and we know that it is fleeting, out of character with our time. And so we get stuck in ruts, flailing, aching and praying and conniving and sighing, as the shattered hope of youth gives way to cynicism and resignation.

I hear Jaime in the living room, gently twanging my guitar. I put the book down, and I slip out of bed.

'Sorry if I woke you, I can't sleep,' Jaime says. 'I could teach you how to play this . . . If you're in the same boat, that is?'

He shuffles back, patting the spot in front of him. Armed with the guitar, I sit down stiffly on the lip of the sofa; he curls his arms around me, and his palms envelope my hands. He presses a trio of my fingers against the strings.

'That's an A major chord,' he says in a low voice. The outline of my body feels sharply defined against his. He complains that I'm not focusing properly and I tell him that he must be a very bad teacher. His lips touch the back of my neck. I turn and he gasps, catches a handful of my hair, and pulls me in tight as our lips clash.

Later, he smokes a spliff out of my bedroom window while I lie drowsy on the bed, and he says words into the night: something about how he'd hoped we'd get together but thought I wouldn't like him because of his – walk? ways? wisdom?

We lie in the double bed. I am acutely aware of his breathing slowing. It is as comforting as the sound of the sea. I look up through a gap in the curtains and the moon pours its silvery colours into me. I cannot stop smiling. I had forgotten what it is to feel happy. The distant beat of music from some party, the cry of a reveller, weaves beauty into my heart.

My problems are distant; I am buffered from the real world by hundreds of pages. With every day that passes, people will forget me, and, in forgetting, forgive the wrongs I've done. Jaime and I could hang out here for weeks, interrailing through prose. Then a sadness laps against me, for I know that he will return, back to a life rich in love and fulfilment, and how can I blame him? Our ending is inevitable: he will leave and I will shock him with a coward's goodbye and here I will stay, drifting through books as I grow old alone, seeping into these pages like a watermark.

seven

It's still dark when we rise and stumble into a taxi. A cat scampers down the pavement, chasing an unseen rodent. The air is chilly with fading night, and both of us have woken to the birth of our hangovers. We take it in turns to lay our heads on each other's shoulders; we take it in turns to glug from a bottle of Buxton. At Liverpool airport we irritably scan our passports into a machine to get our boarding passes. Once upon a time, buying a product meant buying a service; now, in the third act of capitalism, we seem to be serving the corps, so that buying their stuff also entails playing at being their staff. Our airline is called 'B'. Jaime whispers that this seems a bit unimaginative of Gwent. The woman at the check-in lacks detail; her fair curls are just an outline. It strikes me then how well drawn all of Gwent's minor characters have been until now, complete with the finer brushstrokes of tics and quirks. When all is well in Gwent's world, I forget he exists. In moments like this the illusions collapse, and I remember Fate's illusions and the illusions of my former world. I just hope and pray that he isn't getting bored of us.

We're travelling first class, something neither of us has ever done before. In the fancy lounge, we are served champagne that is more elegant in idea than taste, our sips tentative, as though expecting someone to tap us on the shoulder and send us back to our proper place. The dawn, breaking beyond the panorama of the window, interrupted by planes soaring into the sky, looks like a ruined painting: Turner's watercolours savaged by Marinetti. It seemed such a funny idea last night: after numerous cocktails, we'd made a bucket list of all the places we wanted to go. My top choice was Kauai, Jaime's Tangiers, but it turned out that Russia featured on both of our lists. We still had three days to go before our appointment with the Storyteller. Why not use them to see St Petersburg?

As we board the plane, a silence descends. We've been seeing each other every day for a week. We've gone to the movies, sat in cafes reading books side by side, hung out in his record shop chatting to customers. Maybe this trip is a step too far; too fast, too soon.

We float in a seascape of silvered clouds. In my notebook, I start to sketch Jaime without thinking. I tell him that my ex hated me drawing him.

'He told me to tear it up after I showed it to him.'

'The more you tell me about your ex, the more he sounds like a complete cunt. You've done well to get rid of him and find me instead.'

I grin, feathering strokes to shape his nostrils. Jaime's last relationship was a fling with a physicist, a girl he shared his house with. We're at the stage where our exes must be caricatures, clowns; a private joke; a way of defining our relationship in reply to them. If, indeed, we are having a relationship, or a fling, or whatever this is between us.

I tell him that my ex was a handsome 36-year-old German-Argentinian; I imply that I never really liked him. 'Half Lothario, half Nazi,' is Jaime's verdict on him. I don't tell Jaime that it was my first semi-serious relationship, that it concluded with a deep paranoia that I was being punished for the romantic misdemeanours of my twenties, when I chased lust and dismissed love. I pursued casual fucks long after I had begun to change, to crave meaning and intimacy, trying to ignore the shift in my psyche. I don't tell Jaime that my ex was the first person I said 'I love you' to, or that he revealed he had another girlfriend after we'd slept together; that he told me he intended to break up with her, but never got round to it. I don't tell him that, when tragedy broke me, my ex grew tired of my grief, which he described as 'suffocating' and 'tedious'. I don't tell him that I simply came home one day to find him gone, after eighteen months of living together, a notepad on the kitchen table with *Dear Rachel* scrawled on the first page and nothing more, as if summoning the inspiration for his goodbye note had entailed too much effort.

I had wondered, given Jaime's fling with the physicist, if he might be a womaniser like my ex. Before her, however, there were only serious relationships, each lasting several years; he speaks about them with an earnestness and maturity. I ask him what the real Eleanor – a girlfriend of two years – was like, and whether she differed from Fate's version. He tells me that she was very moody.

'You're much easier to be with,' he says, rubbing my arm. 'Much more relaxed. Eleanor didn't have your sparkly optimism and upbeat attitude to life.' I wonder if he is being ironic, but his eyes hold mine, and I smile awkwardly. Then he says, 'When we get back to the real world, we could do this for real. We could go travelling for a bit.'

I frown and Jaime slowly removes his hand from my arm. I unclip my belt, muttering that I need the toilet.

Our relationship has been a sketch taking shape on a raw canvas; now he wants to put a frame on it. I know that I'll have to tell Jaime the truth, sooner or later: I don't want to go back. But then what? When I was drawing him, he gazed at me as though there might be genius in my fingertips. I don't want to ever reach a point where he looks at me with irritation, or disappointment; I want this love affair to be an experience I can put in a locket and treasure with a wistful ache.

Pulling down my knickers, I note that I haven't had my period since the Victorian era and I've no idea if my cycle is muddled. A few days ago, a condom broke. If we were to have a baby inside this book, how would that work anyway? It would be half-real, half-fictional, a mixture of DNA, imagination and Times New Roman. Back in the real world, I was terrified of having children; that I would love the child with the depth that my mother loved me, and sacrifice my career for them.

I sit back down next to Jaime. His smile is strained. I feel sad and wonder if this is typical of me. As I grew up, I came to realise that happiness is not one of life's gifts, but something that you have to fight for, and carve out of the suffering of the world; I also began to realise that I was better at sculpting suffering.

As the flight attendant approaches us with a tray, Jaime lets out a gasp. She has a face which is more absence than presence: cartoonish, with exaggerated cerise lips and a Cyclops eye. I sing out an ebullient 'Thanks!' as she passes over an apple juice. This is one of my worst habits: laughing in the most inappropriate circumstances.

Now the flight attendant's mouth has disappeared. Her face is a blank oval which sits like a lollipop on top of her uniform, as though she is awaiting instruction.

I point at the window. The scenery outside has been leached of colour. Our seats are no more than pencil strokes; the view from the window is reduced to a draft.

'We're going to crash,' I say to Jamie. Funny how panic turns you into a narrator. We hold one another's hand tightly. We're going to die, I realise, and in dying together, our last breaths will fuse – a thought that creates a momentary, fleeting peace. Our eyes close, noses bump, the downward swoop of the plane looping in our stomachs.

A jolt; the skim and skid of the wheels; a violent halt. I open my eyes. We are in Liverpool airport, back in a world of texture and substance. The flight attendant is now a ghost who stands before us and announces that, due to a technical problem, we have returned to our starting point.

'B Airlines apologises for any inconvenience caused.'

Our taxi home keeps stalling, with endless traffic lights. Our early morning feels as though it took place days ago, rather than hours. It's all a punishment, I tell Jaime. We've grown to refer to Gwent as though he's the prime minister of a bad government, mockery our default position. But when I share this view, Jaime reminds me that Gwent is benign, that he's probably just ignorant of Russia and untravelled. He will have lacked adequate research facilities to create a backdrop for us – it's not as though he could pop down to his local library in 1861 and buy *The Rough Guide to St Petersburg*. We circle round it again and again, interpreting the story until we're tired of it.

Back home, our lovemaking is wild and passionate, edged with aftermath. Halfway through, Jaime breaks down crying. He smudges his palms against his face, laughing in embarrassment.

'I really did think we were going to die . . . I tell myself all day that this place isn't real, but suddenly nothing has felt more real.'

We lie together and discuss the moments in which we've been close to dying in real life as the room becomes more shadow than light.

eight

Jaime takes a length of my hair and folds it over his lip in a faux moustache, savouring my laughter. We get off the train at Liverpool Lime Street. As we wander past a wig shop with a window display full of mannequin heads sporting different styles and colours, I say: 'Look at all the people, beheaded in the name of commerce.'

Jaime roars with laughter and I look at him, his blue eyes crinkled up, his fillings on display, and think I might be in love with him. The sunshine dazzles over us; the sky promises happiness and a ban on clouds; in the sweetness of anticipation, the fulfilment of the past few days, I feel a potential for redemption, as though the self I am presenting to him might be made true. Once more, I ask him what my surprise is and he chides me for my impatience.

Jaime looks at me with mounting panic as we stop outside the Tate.

'I thought it would be a *good* surprise,' he says. 'Is it clichéd and boring, because you go to galleries all the time?'

'No.' My voice has shrunk to the size of an insect. 'It's fine. Thank you.'

'You've had to put up with days of me mansplaining music

to you, so I figured it was time for you to womansplain art to me,' he carries on ebulliently. I force a smile.

Inside, we enter a room with paintings from floor to ceiling, from wall to wall; like a church with too many stained-glass windows, such is the dazzle and colour.

I always hated going to galleries with other people. They are my private dreamworlds, places I ghost through alone, letting the masters seep into me through osmosis. When Jaime follows me and examines my profile, I feel as though he is fingering the pages of my diary.

The last time I visited an art gallery was just a few months before Fate took me. My creativity seemed self-indulgent after everything that had happened. I had walked through the Tate Modern in a state of intense bitterness, aware of colours inside me that could only be stillborn.

We stop to look at Klimt's *The Kiss*. It is luminous at first glance, with all that shimmering gold leaf. But then you notice how the lovers' pose looks uncomfortable, as though expressing an uneven relationship: the man clutching the woman, his arms a cage, his lips possessive. In the Rig Veda, unity is defined as the ultimate spiritual experience. Yet the thought of a serious relationship – of blurring at the edges, of picking up habits and turns of phrase – terrifies me. I think of that quote by Marina Abramović: 'I'm thinking an astronaut is my best choice as a husband, because he'd be in space doing anti-gravitational experiments, and I could work undisturbed.'

I leave Jaime and enter another room. Once, when I was seven years old, I fell off a swing and knocked myself out. As I came to, I became aware of life as a force, a gush and a rush of energy that was almost violent in its determination to keep oxygen flowing into my lungs and blood pumping around my body. For days afterwards, I wandered around the back garden, seeing its furious energy in the flutter of a butterfly's wings, or the arms of a tree reaching for the sky. I feel it now, gazing at a Waterhouse: in the weave and layer of oil and colour; in his attention to the tiniest detail, in those strokes which are so beautiful that they feel as though they were painted not by him, but through him. This is what I am, I think as I look at it. This is me.

I stand in front of Millais's *Ophelia*, my arms wrapped around my body, my face a wet mess of salt and snot, willing myself to get a grip before Jaime comes through and finds me. My mother loved the Pre-Raphaelites. I close my eyes tight and think of her funeral back in the real world. It was just a month before I went to see Fate. The Vedas state that there is a gap between death and rebirth, where the soul takes a rest, before it packs a new suitcase of karma for its next incarnation. The soul, the kernel of personality that is reincarnated in body after body, is called a *Jiva*: I picture my mother's as feminine, foetal, finally at peace. I believe, I hope, that she has forgiven me for the part I played in her death.

When Jaime appears a little while later, I chat away and hope that my eyes have lost their redness.

We spend another half an hour walking around the cafes, and then sit in the downstairs one, sipping Earl Greys. Jaime keeps giving me concerned glances. I stare into the distance, a smile on my face. Then I begin plaiting my hair, one strand far too thick, the others far too thin. He asks me what art college I went to.

'Goldsmiths,' I whisper, and clear my throat. 'And then I did my MA at Manchester. That's why I used to live here.'

'Tell me about your Metamorphoses exhibition,' he says.

I tentatively begin to tell him about my most famous piece: *Pygmalion's Girl*. In *Metamorphoses*, Pygmalion is inspired to become celibate when he sees the Propoetides: the first prostitutes, women who enjoy sex and are therefore seen as dangerously erotic. Ovid punishes them by turning them into stone. Pygmalion, meanwhile, creates a woman from ivory. But she is a daguerreotype, a copy of a copy, based on the Venus de' Medici marble statue which in turn was inspired by Praxiteles' *Aphrodite of Cnidus*. The statue I created was classical in its original design, but papered with photocopies of Page Three girls and images from *FHM*. She was a queen of plastic surgery, an ideal rendered in papier mâché. Jaime praises it for being 'feminist', but I shrug my shoulders.

'Before Metamorphoses, I had three exhibitions that were just as good, but nobody was interested. If you're a female artist and you call something "feminist", then responses become predictable. Men will be polite, even if they don't like it; women will be obliged to support you. It puts your work in a tidy box. It's far more dangerous and daring for a woman to simply create a great work of art in the manner of a man and be valued for it on those terms.'

Jaime smiles softly and tells me how much he loves debating with me. I smile back. I feel connected to the world again.

'What else shall we argue about?' I hold his gaze and raise an eyebrow.

'God.' His tone is one of jest, but there's an edge to it. 'Since you seem to like that fairy tale.'

I shrug and he looks disappointed. I feel no need to convert, nor to reprimand; as far as I'm concerned, faith is a personal matter. I tell him that I have tried reading some of the Western philosophers he admires, but that I found them neither 'ground-breaking' nor 'original'. Most of their ideas echo those explored in the East centuries earlier. I enjoyed being introduced to Baudrillard, but his point that the real cannot be separated from artifice reminds me of the concept of *maya*, and when you posit such ideas but strip them of their spirituality, the result is nihilistic: you end up with clever white men with dazzling names whose books look good on your shelf, and are fascinating to debate, but who don't actually nourish you in any way.

Jaime looks taken aback. 'I refute that.'

'Refute, then.'

'Marx, for example! I was eighteen when I discovered him. I'd gone from taking communion twice a week to chucking my copy of the Bible in the bin. There was this void there, like, what the fuck do I believe in now – and then I read *The Communist Manifesto* and it hit me with the power of a Beethoven symphony.' He presses his fist against his heart.

We debate back and forth for a while, and I am touched by his passion, even if it possesses an aura of youthful naivety and idealism. Then Jaime asks if we might return to the gallery. I hesitate and he backtracks. I quickly smile and say it's a fine idea.

This time, I am able to mute my heart and view the pictures from the bland perspective of a tourist.

Afterwards, we wander through the sun-streaked streets, enjoying the Friday vibe of the city winding down. Jaime stops. I recognise the cafe across the road and realise we're outside the big stone building that houses the Storyteller.

'Hey, let's try them again!' Jaime exclaims, pressing the buzzer. I open my mouth to say that we should wait until our official appointment next week, but he's already cajoling them, and something about the magic of the day is infused in his voice. We're in, both not quite able to believe it. A musty hallway; stairs patterned with faded black and white diamonds; a pool of warm colours from a stained-glass window. I feign excitement. Did Jaime plan this right from the start of today's trip, or was this just a whim? And how do I tell him that I'm not going home? I've composed eloquent speeches during sleepless nights, but now the lines are jumbled, cut-up fragments.

The third floor. We stand before flat 23.

He raps sharply on the door.

nine

The door swings open. The moment has all the dramatic tension of a movie, one that ought to conclude with the revelation of an iconic figure: a Darth Vader sporting a cloak made from book covers. Instead, the guy standing before us is bathos personified. He wears skinny jeans with a T-shirt stamped with a Mona Lisa smoking a joint. His hair is quiffy, his face stubbled. He looks us up and down, grins and says, 'Come on in.'

We follow him down the hallway to a reception desk. There's a rainbow of file boxes jammed up against a till, a noticeboard crowded with posters for cafes and classes. A girl with very short, dyed white-blonde hair looks up and smiles; as her neck twists, a tattooed lion leaps across her throat.

'You showing them the Surfer Rooms?' she asks. Her accent is Scottish.

'This your first visit, yeah?' Hipster Boy turns and asks us.

'Yes,' I say loudly, for Jaime is biting his lip. 'We'd love to take a look at the Surfer Rooms.'

Hipster Boy shows us the Reading Room first. The walls are lined from floor to ceiling with books that are more cult than mainstream: William Burroughs, Rachel Ingalls, Ann Quin. I open my mouth to ask questions, but Hipster Boy puts a finger to his lips. We must remain silent, he advises us, knocking gently on a closed white door, for now we're entering the Surfer Rooms themselves. As we go in, there is a twist in my gut and a desire to run out, back down the spiral staircase. I realise that I'm daring Jaime on, playing the brave cop to his nervy, cautious one, but I am in no doubt that we should not be here, that we should be back in the gallery, that whatever is in here will destroy our happiness.

It looks like a dimly lit hospital ward. Laptops sitting by each bed, their screens patterned with neuron light. Needles protruding from heads. Cracked blinds and a few plants wilting on dusty sills and bodies that don't lie still but suffer faint tremors in their fingers, a quivering jerk of limb. An acrid smell in the air, of sweat and unwashed clothing.

I start to back away, but Jaime pulls me forwards; I nearly fall on to a patient. Hipster Boy casts me a warning look. He removes a clipboard from the little white plastic pocket slung over a bedrail. It says *Dickens, 1853*. The guy lying on the bed writhes as though he is an addict suffering from withdrawal. It's then that I notice that the needles poking out of his head are not acupuncture gear: they are biros.

I overhear Jaime quietly asking about the Storyteller as I drift down the ward, gazing at the clipboards at the bottom of the beds: Margaret Atwood, *Oryx and Crake*; Will Self, *My Idea of Fun*; Angela Carter, *Nights at the Circus*. I think of Gwent's love of sci-fi and H. G. Wells. Then I jump as Hipster Boy taps me on the shoulder. As we leave I notice a spider, a silhouette on the dim blind; I shiver and clutch Jaime's hand very tightly.

Back in the reception, the guy says: 'So, I'll book you in for an appointment, then? Any idea which book you fancy?'

'Um . . .'

'We . . .'

The girl with the white-blonde hair looks up, fingers her earlobe and smiles.

'Digby, I think they're a bit shell-shocked. Maybe they weren't sure what it would all look like.'

'We – we thought we were going to find the Storyteller here,' Jaime says.

Digby and the blonde girl exchange glances and laugh.

'Who?' Digby asks.

'The Storyteller,' Jaime's voice falters.

'I'd need to know the title of the book he's in, if you want to meet him. Sounds like a kids' book,' Digby adds, sounding dismissive, even disappointed, as though he'd put us down as the sort to shoot up in a Hunter S. Thompson novel or slither into the slipstream prose of Anna Kavan.

'So, if we find out which novel he's from, we can meet him by bookhopping . . . Is that right?' Jaime asks. 'You'd put us in a trance and we'd hunt for him in a book?'

'Book*surfing*,' says Digby lightly, as though *hopping* is some terribly antiquated term that tickles him. 'For a four-hour session I can give you a first-timer discount of £30 an hour – but you can only get the discount if you book in now.'

'And there's no Storyteller *here*, in this world?'

Digby and the blonde girl shake their heads in unison.

'OK. But, really, all we want to know is how we get home,' Jaime says, his voice rising. 'We just need to get home.'

It's like that moment in a play where an actor breaks the fourth wall and the audience prickles.

'Home?' Digby chews his lip, exchanging glances with the blonde girl.

'I mean, are you guys even *real*?' Jaime sounds slightly hysterical and I put a hand on his arm. 'Are you like us? Are you stuck here?'

Another long silence. My face burns as Digby slowly lifts his hand and pretends to examine it.

'I don't think I'm made of plastic,' he replies.

'Sure you are, I first found you in a cereal box,' the girl fires back, fighting laughter.

I seize control. 'Just book us in next week. But we'll just try one hour to start with.'

'That's barely a chapter, I'd suggest—'

'We don't really want to commit to more just now,' Jaime cuts in. 'We need time to think about it.'

Digby looks pissed off but the girl with the white-blonde hair nods sympathetically and hands us a form to fill out.

'Sure – you can check out our library online. Just pick your book a minimum of four hours in advance, so we have time to upload it.'

We sit down on a big white corduroy sofa, over which is draped a scarlet cloth with an Indian print pattern. The questionnaire requests our date of birth, how many books we've surfed and whether we have any history of mental illness. Is Booksurfing Gwent's genesis, I wonder, or a tradition that has been around for a long time that only a select few know about? I glance over at Jaime's sheet, surprised to see he's scribbling, seems inspired. His choice is Leopold von Sacher-Masoch's *Venus in Furs*; I was expecting him to choose Martin Amis, B. S. Johnson, Orwell. I stare at my clipboard and I recall how, when I was a child, I wished that I could slip into the world of *Alice in Wonderland*. I used to dream that I was forever sliding down a rabbit hole, delights flying past, and I never wanted to land.

Once outside, I suggest we go for dinner and chat it through. Jaime replies tersely that he wants takeaway. The sulky girl who serves me bunches paper around the chips as though she is wrapping a carcass. Jaime and I find a bench and we squirt ketchup on to our chips.

'So, shall we do it?' I ask him, my tone light as a balloon. 'Will you waltz with me into a book?'

'We should just focus on finding the Storyteller. We're not looking hard enough. We've been here over a *week*. I keep having to remind myself, "It's a book, it's a book" – it's becoming a mantra. I can't keep it up . . .'

'Why not just . . . embrace it?'

'You've forgotten about the forgetting?' Jaime's voice sharpens. 'What if we die down here, with a kind of literary dementia, not even knowing our loved ones are above, looking for us?'

'That was because of the tea Gwent gave us – I must have had too much,' I improvise quickly. 'I hardly think we will forget *entirely* . . .'

'We have people waiting for us – families. I have my MA to finish and you have to paint . . .'

'You can do a degree any time,' I burst out in a trembling voice. 'How many people ever get to do this? It's pretty amazing, isn't it? You'll look back on this and regret it if you don't seize the adventure.'

'You have Stockholm syndrome.' His voice is shaking slightly too.

'This is amazing.' Oh God, I've used that word too many times. I change tack. 'I like being here, with you. Sharing it all with you.' Now I sound sentimental.

'It's a drug,' he asserts. 'You saw them back there – they're addicts. We have to get out of here before we become like them.'

We sit and smart and shovel chips into our mouths. The sun has set. Jaime puts his hand over mine. I feel the grit of salt crystals against my skin.

'If we can get back to the real world, we could get to know each other properly,' he says. 'There's no sense of anything moving in this world. Everything is static. And there's all this money sloshing around – it's a capitalist hell.'

Two days ago, Jaime organised a march, under the banner of his record shop, against tax cuts for the rich, but only three people turned up. He tried to laugh and shrug it off, declaring that it didn't matter because it wasn't real anyway, but I saw the hurt in his eyes. Politics is always personal.

'It's not so bad,' I say quietly.

'When did you last paint anything? When did I last sell a record? Yesterday we spent an hour googling "the Storyteller", then watched TV all day.'

I'm suddenly aware of the gaps between us. I have been too busy presenting an idealised version of myself to him. It's my fault that he doesn't understand my motives. And yet the thought of shattering my cool artist persona – of showing him how weak I am – is terrifying.

'I'd rather stay here,' I confess. 'I never see my mum or dad. It's difficult with them . . .'

Jaime looks shocked.

'You didn't tell me that.'

'I'm sorry. I'm happy here. I've got nothing to go back to.' I stare down at my chips.

'But you're an artist,' he says, 'and you're good. You can carry on.'

'My career is fucked. Everything went black-and-white,' I say.

'You haven't seen what you look like,' he says, rising and staring down at me. 'I've seen you in Fate's place and it's an awful sight – you're lying on a bed with cobwebs in your hair. We have to get you out of there.'

'It's only my body,' I say sullenly. '*I'm* here – my psyche, spirit, *Jiva*.'

'That's just hippie shit,' Jaime says. 'You're under the spell of an illusion, and you're calling it real. To carry on living here is to commit suicide up there.'

Silence. There's a moment between us, in which it feels like either one of us might just laugh it off. Instead, he kicks the bench and storms off. He glances back and in the dying light I can't place his expression.

ten

I slump against the window of the train carriage, watching it all pass me by: fields gushing, houses high-pitched, clouds on fast-forward. The list of stations is reversed; someone must have forgotten to reset it. We are heading to London, it declares, as we speed to Manchester. It makes me feel disorientated in the way I get when the clocks go forwards or back. I pull my sleeves over my wrists to wipe the tears collecting at the corners of my eyes.

I had visited the capital to meet Daniel, who spent half the lunch taking calls from other, bigger artists. Then he took me to the Saatchi gallery, and introduced me to a contact. I had wanted Jaime there beside me, looking proud of me in a way that my mother used to. But we haven't seen or spoken to one another in nearly a week. There's a sadness swimming inside me. Life seems to be falling into the patterns of my former existence: love souring into enmity and disappointment.

Behind me, two students are discussing the Russian revolution in very earnest voices. One is explaining that Rasputin led it. I smile and reach automatically for my iPhone to text Jaime, then I catch myself. This is what I've missed most: not being able to share little, everyday nonsense with him. This new samskara is not yet an algorithm; I am scrambled, malfunctioning, in old patterns. Now my inner dialogue can no longer dance between me and him; I must split myself in two and play both halves.

Once, it felt as though he and I were against the world. Now it feels as though Jaime is one of Them. Why is he so desperate to return? We could easily survive here a little longer. Maybe I'm not important enough for him to want to linger here with me. Maybe he wants to go back to Eleanor, or fuck his flatmate. After all, I'm just a madwoman who believes in hippie shit.

He has become a plot twist for me; a character whose super-objective is a mystery. It's hard not to look back over the last few chapters and want to screw them up and rewrite them. I misunderstood everything. That night, our first night: just a one-night stand. That moment when he looked at me with tenderness: my mistake. Where I saw depth and detail, he only intended a sketchy lightness.

I get off at Manchester Piccadilly. The platform board is winking, with journeys gone and journeys about to go. I spot salvation and suddenly my heels are clacking across the concourse and I'm leaping on to a crowded train. Heading for Liverpool.

Forty minutes later, I free myself from the commuter fug, and run all the way to Lord Street. I press the buzzer and say, 'I came to see you last week. I'm not booked in, but can I come up now?'

'We're pretty busy,' the voice says.

I remember how easy it was to get in when I was with Jaime. I'm troubled by superstition: that Jaime was the lucky amulet I'd been wearing around my neck, and that now the chain has broken.

'Please,' I say. 'It's urgent. I only need an hour.'

A tired reply: 'Well, OK. Come up and let's see what we can do.'

Upstairs, however, the girl with the white-blonde hair is smiley and welcoming. She takes me into the Reading Room, looking slightly surprised when I make a beeline for the 'F' section, picking out *Thomas Turridge* by Augustus Fate.

'So, will this be the proper book by Fate?' I pass it over to her. 'Or Gwent's imagining of it?'

She gives me a weird look.

'Fate's book, of course. We don't stock fan fiction, I'm afraid.'

I smile quickly, apologetically, and she gives me a form to sign. I squint at the small print disclaimer at the bottom.

'Um, this bit here . . .' I point to it. 'Does anyone ever die?'

'More often than you might think,' says the girl, and I can't tell if the look in her eye is a warning or a tease. 'Last week a man went into *Bleak House* and ended up dying of spontaneous human combustion.' She shudders.

Surfing without him, and returning to Fate's narrative of brimstone and fire: this feels like a glorious defiance of Jaime. For all I know, he might be returning to the real world, where I will be carried in his consciousness as no more than a memory, losing colour with every hour until I am pastel, until I am pale, until I am nothing.

When I sign the form, it feels like the flourish on a suicide note. But the girl just flashes the form a cursory glance and then files it away.

The Surfer Room is fuggy with other people's essences, their CO_2 forming a stale membrane. I lie down on the bed with reluctance, as though it is a dentist's chair; as I close my eyes, my meditation mantra slips into my mind. For a moment I am released from the buzz of thought, floating, observing. A presence close by; a male voice warns me that I might feel a slight sensation as he inserts the biros into my pressure points. 'Slight' is a misleading description; I have to keep my fists clenched by my sides to prevent them flying up to my face. They place a mask over my mouth. The gas whispers through me and panic thrashes inside as I fight the approaching numbness – *Oh, Jaime.* I long to be with him now, laughing and kissing, and my mind is a white fog as I leave Gwent and stumble back into the world of Augustus Fate . . .

HANWELL PAUPER AND LUNATIC ASYLUM, says the sign by the gates. I glance down at my long skirt, woven from cheap cloth and shaped by crinoline; beneath my bonnet, my hair is drawn back into a tight bun. I am a governess again. I did not want to enter the novel at this point in the story, following the chaotic pantomime in the church: I wanted the delicious shame of posing for Mr. Carmichael's photos; a Saturday outing in the countryside with the children,

followed by sweet chatter with Mr. Turridge. Fear beats in my breast as I enter the grounds and pass through the gardens, where there are two men turning over clods with their pitchforks, one singing merrily, another laughing in a wild manner. I pause in dread, but Augustus's voice-over dictates my fate: *And so Rachel, feeling lost and lonely, decided that she must see her mother*.

'Do be quiet,' I hiss in a whisper, and a passing nurse gives me a forbidding glance.

The last time I visited, I was not permitted to see her. The superintendent himself addressed me, an alienist called Dr. Charles Wentworth. His tone was clearly intended to be kindly, soaked in compassion, but it only instilled within me a desire to slap him:

'Your mother was painting in a group of patients when she rose to her feet and began painting on the faces of the others.'

I pictured blue streaked across a nose, hair striped green.

'Her hysteria comes and goes, with her cycles,' Dr. Wentworth continued, before speaking, delicately, of how a hysterectomy might be the kindest solution.

As I left on that drear September day, bereft at not seeing her, I heard distant screams echoing through the corridors and a queer trembling came over me, not knowing if they belonged to her. Today, I am led to a parlour, which serves as a recreation room. Therein I hear the tinkle of a pianoforte, notes flurried too fast and accompanied by an uneven soprano; I notice two women dancing close by; others gossiping; a few painting. Observing that my mother is sitting hunched and alone in a corner, I call to her. Suddenly I am wracked with guilt for my reluctance to visit her. The sensation of welling tears assails me; accompanied by the fervent urge to hold her tight and never let go. I gather my wits and sit down; she greets me with an indeterminate smile.

'Rachel,' she whispers, then trails off, glancing up at the ceiling.

There are weeks when she will chat merrily, and others when it seems as though she has climbed into a well and I am peering over the rim, calling down entreatments and hearing their melancholic echo.

'You are practising embroidery,' I observe. Her smile fades as her gaze traverses her lap; she jumps in the most peculiar manner, as though it cannot be her handiwork. Though she possesses an array of threads, she has chosen to stitch white thread on a white backdrop: an ill omen. When her mood is cheerful, she favours rainbow colours.

'Would you like to do more painting? Dr. Wentworth has given permission for you to return to it this week . . .'

She looks only more cheerless. I gaze at her hands, which are reddened and coarse from her daily work of doing the laundry, and I am at a loss for words of comfort. Six years ago, when she was first brought here by my father, the alienists were confident that she would only be incarcerated for a few months before being released fully cured of her mania and her melancholy, her tendency to hear voices. Every time I pass a gallery in London and in Oxford, I am beset with anger, knowing that my mother's efforts should be in there, that she ought to be stationed on a beach, or in a pasture, before an easel, not in this living tomb.

Surreptitiously, I remove a little twist of butter from my bag, which I stole from the Carmichaels' kitchen. I rub it into her hands, and she smiles winsomely and suddenly picks up her cotton bobbin, unrolling the thread and snapping it with her teeth. This she circles around her neck, tying it at the back.

'A pretty necklace!' I must try to resist adopting the tone of the condescending men, as though I am addressing her as a child. Behind me, the piano flurries grow more discordant.

'Oh! It is too tight!'

She appears to be having trouble breathing and I seek the scissors in haste, but there are none to hand – likely too dangerous a weapon to be permitted on this ward – and there is nothing I can do but lean in and bite through the cotton at her neck. When I turn, I see that the superintendent is watching me, a frown on his stern visage.

And so Dr. Wentworth's suspicions were confirmed, Fate's voice announces. *The Carmichaels were right to fear that mother and daughter were quite as mad as each other . . .*

I take my leave, making haste down the corridor. My mind is already anticipating the long journey back to Oxford, whereupon I must return to the Carmichaels: to Eleanor, who struts about like a queen, expecting me to play her faithful servant; to her father, who lusts after me; to her mother, who loathes me. And so I do not notice them creeping up behind me until it is too late; I am nearly at the entrance when, from both sides, hands seize me. Accompanied by two nurses, I am borne back into the office of the superintendent.

'I am afraid, Rachel, that your employee has requested your incarceration, out of concern for your recent behaviour,' he informs me, 'and your lunacy certificate has been signed by two doctors.'

As he approaches me, his face horrifically benign, I hear Fate declaring: *And so Rachel would soon find herself in a strait-waistcoat . . .*

I hear screaming. My hands fly up over my breasts: I am convinced that I am naked. As I turn my head, the biros twist in my pressure points. The guy on the next bed is suffering some kind of fit, his mouth frothing, and I hear myself cry out again, as though ventriloquising his pain. Then I realise that the screaming is an alarm. The girl runs in, followed by Digby. Biros are frantically yanked from the man's head – much too fast, it seems, for blood spurts out. When I reach for my biros, I force myself to withdraw them slowly. I sit up, free, but my machine begins to scream too. Digby is panicking, crying, 'He's going into paper arrest!' and then he turns and cries, 'Not you too!' I tell them I'm fine but my voice is tiny, my throat parched.

The rest of the surfers are all lying in their little worlds of prose, oblivious. And then I see something terrible. The man is feathering: losing parts of himself, which unfurl and float away from him. I nearly vomit, assuming it is skin, but as one lands near my feet, I realise it is paper, and that his body has followed his mind too far.

On the train home, I find a seat at the back of the carriage, and quietly weep. When I first met my Victorian mother in Fate's book, I was angry that he had drawn on my pain for inspiration, and fearful of what was to come. But there were softer moments of consolation too: the first time I visited her at Hanwell after arriving in *Thomas Turridge*, I held her hand and asked for forgiveness. It is too late to do so in the real world.

A sense of calm comes over me; the tears have been cathartic. But a sadness lingers still. I'd like to be able to dip back into *Thomas Turridge* from time to time, to visit her, but I know that it is now too dangerous to do so. Fate is enraged by our flight from his novel; I could taste his fury in the prose. Before leaving, I caught a glimpse of the chapter's ending: me, locked in a white room, my arms locked across my chest in a strait-waistcoat, as though laid to rest in a coffin. I could sense that he wanted to crush my soul, to grind me down to an absolute surrender. Now, I feel a greater resilience; I realise that, since leaving his world, I have become a little stronger. Hearing Fate's voice hour after hour, day after day, made me dizzy, wore me down. It gave me an insight into my mother's illness that I'd never had before, of how tormented she must have been, how she must have yearned to escape the chorus of those voices.

Back in my flat, I fill the kettle and wander over to my canvas. I pull the cellophane wrappers from the paints and brushes I bought in the gallery. My fingers are tingling, desperate to acquire calluses. I feel the threat of tears again, but I force them back and pick up a brush.

It has been a year since I last painted. I stand before the canvas for nearly an hour before I dare to dab a mark, terrified that my talent has rotted inside me. My first strokes are stilted, but then, slowly, my brush becomes firmer, more focused. I paint and paint as twilight becomes night becomes morning, and Jaime does not matter, and the past does not matter, and the Storyteller does not matter.

As the dawn rises, I can no longer fight the delicious delirium of sleep; I take a break, washing lapis lazuli from my fingers. I feel sheepish now about my temper, my angst on the train. I want to treasure my time with Jaime. I go to text him to apologise, only to find a message from him: 'I'm sorry.'

eleven

I am being irrational; I know this. Jaime and I arrived at Daniel's party twenty minutes ago. We crunched over gravel towards the house, the sort of grand, ivied mansion that you see in BBC Sunday night dramas – Jaime in a pinstriped suit, me in a red silk dress, both of us wearing eyeliner and feather boas. The scents of summer flowers in the air; the moonlight splashing over us like a warm sea. There was a moment, at the start of the party, when we were united in our shyness. We took little sips from fluted glasses, whispering together, giggling at Daniel's guests. I eyed up the tattoo on the inside of Jaime's wrist: the small R an echo of the J on mine; a private joke, done while we were drunk. (It seemed hilarious at the time.) Then Daniel invaded our bubble and asked me how my new paintings were coming on, while a woman pounced on Jaime.

Now I am having a conversation with Daniel where I am only half present, watching Jaime chat to the woman who is watching his lips as he speaks. I overhear her name – Eleanor – and my heart skips a beat. She is nothing like the girl of Fate's tale, nor Jaime's ex, from his descriptions of her. This Eleanor is very slender, with pale blonde hair, and a sharp mouth.

The last few weeks have formed a concentrate inside me. Since making up after our row, we have barely spent a day apart. During the day-time, when Jaime is managing his shop and I am painting, we text every few hours. Silly pictures, quotes, politics, jokes, or sometimes just trivial details: a weird customer, a brushstroke gone awry. One day, after Jamie left me to dream in his bed, I drifted through the flat and became a composer. I told him that it was a love song about him that I would never sing in his presence, but he would always be able to hear its echo in the walls. He hugged me very tightly when I told him this. After lovemaking we lie in the dark and words smoke between us, surreal and childlike. I ask him what colour his soul is and he says dark red. I tell him mine is the blue of the sea. Before sleep our noses bump as we say goodnight. I always borrow a T-shirt from his chest of drawers, normally one decorated with an obscure band's offensive logo – and his tracksuit bottoms, which are too large and bag around my ankles. They are infused with his scent, which is catnip to me. I take him to galleries and he takes me to concerts. We find dark corners in bookshops and we share secret kisses with our spines pressed up against those of Achebe and Alighieri, Self and Smith. I learn that he hates garlic, but loves basil; that he can't bear the mornings; that he had a tattoo of a dolphin removed from his arm; that the scar on his forehead was the result of his father thwacking him with a golf ball by accident when he was a kid; that he longed to have a pet wolf when he was a boy. One night, I have a dream that he is alone in a valley, with wolf howls echoing through the hills, and he is laughing with joy at the sound.

Our search for the Storyteller dwindles by the day, and Jaime has been mentioning them less and less over the last week. He still suffers occasional fits of panic, and still asserts that we cannot sacrifice our 'proper' lives for this place, but I can sense that this world is slowly seducing him: he is surrendering to it. The other day he told me that no relationship in the real world had ever made him as happy as ours.

I need to lure Jaime away from Eleanor. I'm keen to force an early departure, but Daniel is keeping the pressure on.

'Can I see one or two pieces of your new work, then? How about next week?' he asks.

I blink. I'm performing a balancing act between integrity and money. In the past, I've been too attached to the former, too dismissive of the latter. Jaime says it doesn't matter if we fail here, because success only counts in the world we're returning to, but I don't feel that I can make mistakes; I have to get it right this time.

Eleanor shrieks loudly at a joke Jaime makes, spills a droplet of her cocktail on his thigh and then becomes very preoccupied with rubbing it off. Daniel gently presses his palm against the small of my back. I wait for Jaime to notice.

When he doesn't, I excuse myself and tunnel my way through the crowds, ducking into the toilet. It's fancy and ornate, closer to Fate's period than this one: lavish tiles the colour of a peacock's tail. When I wipe myself, I start. Red streaks. A period. I'm not pregnant then, thank God.

I find Jaime waiting for me as I re-enter the party.

'Oh God, you have to save me,' he says, kissing me. 'That Eleanor woman kept pretending to pick fluff off the front of my trousers. In the end, I told her I need to find my girlfriend.

I know I sound kind of boring – but could we just go home and get pizza? I mean, the waiter just told me the canapés here cost £30 *per canapé*. It's kind of disgusting.'

The relief of departure makes us giddy and silly. In the back of the taxi home, I get out my compact and Jaime draws a moustache on my lip, before applying some more kohl to his lower lids. I tell him that it makes him look beautiful and dangerous, like a spy. He starts to roll a cigarette but I steal the paper balanced on his knee and declare I will roll it for him. He doesn't complain too much even when he has to stand outside my flat smoking a tampon.

Jaime kisses me the moment we're inside the hallway, pushing me up against the wall. He bites my ear and whispers, 'Daniel fancies you.'

I pull back, his jealousy a delicious shock.

'He's an ugly old chauvinistic bastard.'

Jaime laughs, then curls an arm around my waist and squeezes me tight. There's a mirror at the end of the hallway and I watch us, wondering: how can we ever go back to ordinary life? We're used to these bodies now. Our scents have crept under our skins; our bonding is primal.

In the bedroom, I pull his boa from his neck as he is kicking off his shoes, and he chases me around the room. We collapse on to the bed together, laughing. We lie side by side, me facing away from him, and Jaime slowly uncurls my feather boa and his lips touch the back of my neck, his hand sliding up my thigh. I close my eyes, but as he draws me towards a climax, my hand clenches over his, my breathing harsh. I cannot let him continue. I feel as though he has taken a very delicate instrument and gently inserted it into my heart. He pulls his hand away, smoothing down my dress, his breath against my ear.

We lie together for a while. Then, out of nowhere, he says:

'Tell me about your mum and dad.'

'She was the best mother in the world,' I say. These are words that I have not been able to say without tears before, but tonight I feel calm.

'And your dad?'

I hesitate, stumbling, trying to think up a story that will suit this version of Rachel Levy.

'It's all right if your childhood wasn't perfect,' he says. 'Mine was fucked.' A pause, and then a swerve, a surprise question: 'Is it because of your parents that you're into Eastern philosophy?'

I turn and prop myself up on one elbow, the cool air filling the space between us.

'It is because of yours that you're an atheist?'

'Yes.'

'If you're an atheist, I suppose you're not afraid of death,' I say. 'Or perhaps you're more afraid . . .' Memories of the funeral drift across my mind; a life condensed into a eulogy, the rough parts edited out.

'If you have one life, you treasure it, make the most of it, take responsibility for it. You enjoy it.' Jaime reaches for his wine glass, and I smile, endeared by the hedonistic streak I have only recently discovered in him, just as he has been surprised by the ascetic in me. 'If you really fuck things up, I suppose you might be reincarnated as a grape?'

'Waiting to be crushed into wine . . .'

'I'd drink you,' he says, and we giggle. I picture myself floating in his stomach, being processed by his blood. Jaime's tone becomes solemn: 'My dad always drank too much.' He frowns. 'Fate's book gave me the chance to know what it's like to have a good dad – one who loves you. Of course, I swear the bastard only did it so that he could destroy me by killing him off . . .'

'Tell me more about your dad, your real dad, I mean,' I coax him.

'It's funny. When I was a teenager, he'd come and go – that was always the way with him . . .' Jaime hesitates, and I will him to carry on. 'He'd play at being part of the family for six months, then disappear for six. He was my hero. He'd turn up with so much energy – making jokes, making us laugh, giving us presents, taking me to the movies and to church. He'd been brought up Catholic and got me into it. He'd confide in me that my mother was depressed, genetically doomed, sick in the head, and I bought it. Once, when I was seventeen, he turned up in a real state. He pissed himself and had to go to A & E to have his stomach pumped. And this woman turned up. I said, "Who are you?", and she said, "I'm the other woman."'

'Fuck.'

'The thing is, there had always been other women, but I told myself his story was true: that they were just friends, hangers-on. Anyway, the bubble burst that night. I realised my mum wasn't the one with the problem; my dad was a fucking womanising drunk getting by on a mad ego and a lot of charisma. And like all addicts, he was imprisoned in denial. He thought he was in control, but really it was dictating his life. The guilt I felt then: for having thought that my mum was ill, when her depression was a perfectly sane reaction to her circumstances; for colluding with my dad in patronising her, for my role in the abuse . . . Fuck, I've never told this to anyone. Do you think I'm a monster?'

'You were a teenager. You didn't know what was going on.'

'I didn't. But I think it delayed her throwing him out. Once I woke up to what was going on, it was goodbye church and God and hello practical morality – like, what can I actually do to help my Mum and make the world better? I rang up an abuse helpline for advice, found her some counselling, and helped her take the first steps towards escape.'

I touch his cheek softly.

'Mum and I are really close now. What with my dad being gone, and her being a bit lonely, she does smother me a bit. I'm her "golden boy".' He rolls his eyes but his pupils glow. 'She rings every few days; she bakes for me. But I'm scared she might get back together with my dad, even after all that.'

I think of Jaime saying early on that he didn't like flings, only committed, faithful relationships. I am piecing parts of his puzzle together, even if the centre remains an empty zigzag.

'Would she take him back, after all that?' I ask.

'The trouble with being a high-functioning alcoholic is that eventually you lose the functioning part. He's in danger of losing his house and the other women have deserted him, so he's started calling Mum again. And he really can turn on the charm . . .'

'You can be very charming,' I muse. 'I saw you at the party.'

Jaime looks pained. 'But I'm nothing like my dad—'

'Oh God, no, sorry. I just meant that people like you . . .'

'People like you too.'

'People say I'm . . . aloof,' I sigh. 'I don't know, I must give off bad vibes, because they never like me at first. People *grow* to like me.'

I turn to face him and he brushes his nose against mine in an Eskimo kiss. He whispers that when we go back to the world, we can look after each other. And his smile is so tender that I am very nearly convinced.

We're still awake at 3 a.m., sitting up in bed, eating Pringles, watching TV. Jaime finds a channel with a cartoon in Russian. He tells me about the main difference between Russian and American cartoons. The latter, he says, are built around a three-act structure, where the protagonist suffers a challenge, finds themselves in crisis and crashes to their lowest point, before turning it all around in a triumphant resolution. But in a Russian cartoon the story starts off badly, things then improve a little in the middle, before the final act involves a return to loss and melancholy.

'I wish the media wouldn't only present success stories that match up with the American narrative,' I say. 'They make it sound like that's the norm. And if you're not a massive success having overcome your act two adversity, you're the exception, the weirdo.'

'Well, yeah . . . but you *are* a success story,' Jaime says. 'If I had your success I'd be so happy. In fact, I'd be intolerable, I'd be showing off to everyone, autographing everything, snorting coke.'

I laugh. 'Well, I'm the mature one. Six years older than you.'

'Practically a boomer,' he smirks, yelping as I pinch him.

The female protagonist in the cartoon has red hair and her name is Raisa.

'That's what my name for you is going to be!' Jaime exclaims. We've tried testing a few pet names on each other but none of them have stuck.

'I like Raisa,' I say. 'What would you be? Jaimus?'

I wake early and sit on the side of the bed, Jaime's sleeping face taking shape in my sketchbook. I'm still out of practice, but the picture captures the colour of my mood. An art critic once said to me, 'A thousand people can paint a tree beautifully, so what makes one particular painting seem that little bit special compared to the masses? It is the consciousness of the artist that makes a painting, the way it hovers in the work like a watermark.' I think of my mother, staring at *Pygmalion's Girl* in my Metamorphoses exhibition, her face lively with pride. I look at Jaime again, his mouth now slack with snores, and I resist kissing him awake. Instead, I decide to head out and get croissants for him: his favourite breakfast.

Outside, the world seems prelapsarian, washed clean by the dawn and the dew. When I was a child, I drew with a pantheist's love for the world. I failed to notice that the garden was tiny, or smudged with London smog. It all seemed beautiful to me. When I stopped drawing in recent years, the apathy I felt was never a rejection of life, more a disappointment. That kind of melancholy can only really afflict those who have loved life too deeply and expected too much from it.

Maybe Jaime and I should be fighting harder to find our way back. I test the idea uneasily, picturing us both in my flat, with the dripping ceiling and mould on the walls. Then I imagine the two of us in a new place, a flat where I have my own studio . . . No: we could never afford such a luxury; the places we inhabit here will be beyond our reach in the real world. But we can find a way, I tell myself; we'll look after each other. There are tears in my eyes as I bend down to pat a dog tied up outside the supermarket. The shop is closed. The dog keeps barking and I pet him, promising to be back soon.

There are numerous express supermarkets on Oxford Road. Jaime joked that the entire street will soon be nothing but a long, shiny row of them, like some kind of Ballardian nightmare. The Sainsbury's Local has a grille yanked down halfway. The next one I pass is a Morrisons. I walk into its chaos. There's a display of cornflakes in the entrance that people are fighting over. A man grabs a box of Kellogg's, stuffing his hand inside so that the chicken logo swells up in fecund grotesque. He removes the plastic bag of flakes and throws the box away. The long queue by the till scatters in horror as he lunges at them. Two security men try to drag him out.

I back out and hurry on, digesting my shock by turning it into a story that I tell Jaime in my mind, ready for my return home. The next shop is a Tesco Express. The queue by the till is so long that I have to keep cutting through it – each member clutching their purchases with defensive eyes. When I find the bakery section, there are no croissants left, no fresh loaves, just one last sliced white Warburtons. I reach for it at the same time as another woman, and with an animal surge that shocks me, I yank it away from her. She turns and glares. I meet her gaze, challenging her, trembling, before she storms off. On my way out of the shop, I scan the headlines: GLOOMY FORECAST, HOUSING MARKET, RECESSION.

Home. I lean against the wall in our hallway. I'm still shaking. I go into the bedroom to find that Jaime has just woken up. The look of fear on his face is akin to that of the desperate shopper I just fought with, and I hear myself gasp. He frowns at me as though we're in different books, looking across oceans of prose from distant white margins.

'I had a bad dream.'

I sit down on the bed and give him a hug, but he doesn't want to be consoled, he wants to confess. He was eleven years old and taking an exam he hadn't done any revision for. Sitting behind the rickety desk, he saw the whole class around him writing fluid answers while his words were ants on the page, and when he handed it in, the teacher who took it was Mr Turridge. He wielded a cane and ordered Jaime to hold out his hand so that he could punish him. The second part of his nightmare then evolved into a darkness of eternal return: he knew everything that would happen in his life, as if it had already happened to him, and he could only repeat it all and endure it again. When he finishes, I feel lost for a moment, wondering if Fate is seeping into this world, if he has found out where we are hiding.

Then I explain to Jaime, as calmly as I can, that Gwent has decided to change the direction of our narrative. The terrible thing is this: although he expresses shock and panic, there is a sparkle in his eyes, a fleeting exhilaration. *Now we will have to move on*, it seems to say. In a melodramatic tone, he announces that we must find the Storyteller or die.

As he sits down before his computer, I go to the window. I gaze down at the chaos on the streets, my heart breaking. Closing my eyes, I find myself praying silently to Gwent: *If you gave us free will, then this must be our fault. Jaime organised a march; I fled back to Fate. We failed to appreciate what you gave us. Please give us one last chance.* Over and over, I beg him to undo this plot twist, even while I know it is too late, that our Eden is over.

twelve

Three weeks on and we still haven't found the Storyteller. We have suffered long queues for supermarkets. We have sat at home, linked hands tight and sweaty, watching bulletins on the TV: images of rioting, the army called into the capital. Feeling claustrophobic in our flat, we ventured into Manchester one night, only to discover grassy verges growing wild with long stalks, the air bitter with smoke as a gang set fire to a row of cars. Jaime's record shop remains shut, following a looting; the steel grilles permanently yanked down. The chaos was thrilling at first, as people tweeted about the end times and shared maps marked with safe houses, in case we needed to hide out when society became feral. Then, as it became clear that civilisation was stagnating between repair and total collapse, our days slid into tedium. The Storyteller remains elusive. Despite endless nights of burning eyes from surfing the net, drowning in trivia and dead ends, we have not made any progress. Jaime's perspective is not as morbid as mine. He does not feel we are to blame for the loss of our utopia. One of his theories is that Gwent left the real world just as the fault lines of 2008 were starting to show, that he is depicting the collapse he sensed was coming. Another is that Gwent wants to push us on into another book, in order that we might find the Storyteller elsewhere.

Jaime takes my hand again as the train pulls in at Liverpool Lime Street, guiding us through the crowds. Out on the street, we cut through beggars, having learnt to perfect expressions of indifference: our shield against crying babies, children's dirty faces. Litter tumbleweeds over the pavements; shop windows are collages of flyers for marches and protests. Fuck you, Gwent, I think, get your disasters in order: in 2014 we were in a recession, not a depression.

We pass a large house with iron grilles over its windows. I know that one of my paintings is hanging in that living room. Having to produce the crowd-pleasing paintings Daniel wants has cut me deeper than anything over these last few weeks. The brush has felt slack in my hand, as though I am a puppet with tired strings. The only way I could bring myself to go through with such artistic prostitution was to layer a secret painting – a scream, a V-sign – beneath the twee landscapes. And even then, they've not sold as well as I'd hoped. Capitalism corrodes art; its collapse only speeds the process up. The church bells are singing, for God is back in vogue.

Outside Stanley House, we pause by the buzzer. We're both very tired. Jaime goes to pull a piece of bread from his pocket, but I stop him – we must save it for the surfing.

I press the buzzer. No reply. I press it again, and again, and again, until finally they let us in and we climb the stairs to the third floor.

'I'm afraid I can't help you,' says the Booksurfer girl. She used to have bleached hair but is now predominately dark roots. She looks frayed, exhausted. We queue for an hour at the tail end of a crocodile of folk in tatty clothes, waving banknotes, jewellery, then a second hour. There are men guarding the doors to the Surfer Rooms, rifles slack in their hands. We hear that they've added another hundred beds but are now at full capacity again, with a waiting list.

We have withdrawn every last penny left in my savings account. But will it be enough? People ahead of us are being turned away, trailing past us and back down the stairs with pinched faces.

Finally, we reach the front desk.

'We've got ten thousand pounds,' I press the Booksurfer girl, though the money is worth a fifth of its value since last week, and by the end of the month it will be about as useful as Monopoly cash.

She shrugs.

'Plus, I can pay you in paintings,' I offer. 'There are still ten left at the Corner House – you can have them all. They'll be worth a fortune when the recession ends . . .' A flicker on her face; my art might finally be of value. 'Look, we'll try anything.'

'Apart from Fate,' Jaime mutters. 'Nothing by Augustus Fate.'

The girl blinks and does a double take. I blush, lowering my eyes, fearing that she has remembered my illicit trip here a few weeks back. But her expression is one of kinship; compassion softens her eyes. She leans in and whispers: 'We have a dystopian novel set in a former Russian province in 1928. A place called Carpathia. Survival rates are the worst, though. You know what the Russians are like – tragedy on every page.'

I stutter uncertainly, but Jaime is suddenly enthused. 'That sounds fine.'

She looks dubious. 'This one requires a double dose of Grand Kuding tea. The author, T. S. Maslennikov, requests it. He wants you to be fully immersed in his characters.'

'It sounds a bit like Fate,' I mutter uneasily.

'Why does he need us at all?' Jaime asks.

She checks the notes. 'You'll bring a *subconscious* to his characters.'

'Fine,' Jaime interjects. He turns to me. 'But what do you think? We'll only go if you agree.'

His expression is one of pleading. I know he likes Russia, and revels in its history; but I still feel it would be the lesser evil to stay here; that if we go, we will only be passing into a deeper circle of hell.

'Can you tell us more about the setting?' I ask, dreading the Gulag and show trials. 'What's Carpathia like?'

She frowns, checking a more detailed synopsis, and reads aloud: 'Carpathia borders the Motherland. It has not yet suffered a Communist revolution – though that remains a threat. It is a land of dark magic and folklore, of howling wolves and dancing bears . . .'

Jaime watches my reaction and squeezes my hand tightly.

'Maybe you're right,' he whispers. 'Perhaps it's too dangerous . . . And perhaps the Storyteller is here after all. I'm sure there are clues we've overlooked.'

We're about to turn away when she looks up from her notes, adding:

'Well, there's someone called the Storyteller in this book. If you can get to the czar's palace, you'll be able to pay them a visit.'

The Third Story

CARPATHIA, 1928

Один

I am standing on the rim of a forest.

My breath is so cold that it forms a white *yuhina* bird, and floats over evergreens more white than green, beyond them a panorama of ice-clenched mountains and valleys speckled with villages. I put my hand to my cheek, and feel the prickle of a beard. At the back of my head, despite the protection of an ushanka, I can sense the vulnerability of a bald patch. We held hands so tightly, Raisa and I, in the passage between books, but somewhere in the roaring dark of the transit I lost her. Did the Booksurfers make a mistake? I turn: mountains, evergreens, a village.

When I look up, my heart beats with a violent joy. High on the Western Peaks is the Czaritsyno Palace, red flags unfurling from its onion domes. After all those weeks of searching and waiting in Manchester, I was ready to give up and resign myself to Booksurfing prison, the ultimate death of my body. The sweetness of my days with Raisa only sharpened the poison: the terror that we might fade before we have a chance to build a life together in the real world. But here it is, just as the Surfers promised: the place where we will find the Storyteller. Tears burn at the back of my eyes. I will soon see my mother again, hold her tight, reassure her that I am still alive. I feel a fierce desire to hug Raisa, to shout the news. She will be glad too, surely she will be glad, despite her strange reluctance to return home.

From the dark and white of those trees, she might emerge at any moment.

There is a group of men close by, laughing, joking. Smoke surrounds them so thickly that it forms a will-o'-the-wisp. In my pocket, my trembling fingers find cigarette papers. It is only then that I notice that I am wearing a uniform: that of the Carpathian Royal Guard. There is something about the act of lighting this cigarette – the flare of flame; drawing in its smoke – that binds me to this world, as though I am no longer an observer but an actor. 'Samskaras': one of Raisa's words. Imprints, impressions, recollections that take root, form habits, conditioning us. Don't let them form, I tell myself fiercely; remember who you are.

He wants you to be fully immersed in his characters. But who is T. S. Maslennikov? We had no time to learn of his characteristics before we fled. I fear he is a puppeteer like Fate; I hope he will let us breathe. I do not trust any narrator since Gwent, who tired of us and wrecked our paradise. Capitalism will inevitably lead to schizophrenic swings of boom and bust, but he weaponised the downturn. Raisa tried to blame herself, once broke down and wept that she was doomed to repeat fucked-up patterns, but I assured her that Gwent was responsible. A narrator will always find peace stagnant and will crave conflict.

Where are you, Raisa?
Raisa?
Raisa?

My fate is falling on me like snow: a tenderness for those distant mountains, after years of loving them as a boy. At their peak, they become austere and harsh in their beauty, birds swooping in the mists. A brotherly affection for my colleagues: hard men with lined faces, skin coloured by vodka and cigarettes, long days and gruelling duties. In the distance, there is the howl of a wolf. We are an hour away from the fall of darkness.

This is not real. This is a backstory being wrapped around my soul. You're in a book, you're in a book. I close my eyes, memory a weapon.

But Manchester is already fading. I sharpen the details of the night Raisa and I went to Daniel's party, before the misery and hunger set in: we ate canapés, came home in a taxi, made love with such tenderness, confided in one another. I lay awake for hours watching her sleeping, recording the pattern of her freckles and lashes, aching to tell her *I love you,* not daring to let the words fall. She always seemed so elusive. One day, I felt assured of her feelings for me; the next, I was discordant with doubt.

A fear comes over me. Perhaps Raisa's absence is not due to authorial malice.

I picture her negotiating with the Booksurfers, slipping into another text, furtive with guilt; I reach for a butchered tree to steady myself.

I look up at the palace again. An unease seems to seep from its turrets, carried down like woodsmoke from the cottages.

This is not real. I must keep my goals simple: find Raisa; find the Storyteller, alone if necessary. Yet even if I find him, it will be a hollow triumph, if she is not with me.

—Jaimus Luzhkov! one of the soldiers calls.

I have worked with this man for many years: his name is Radomir.

—Stop your daydreaming and give me a cigarette.

I pass it over.

—*Спасибо.* I heard they've caught the trail of a wolf. A big one. We're on the hunt.

I blow out smoke. —Let's hope we catch him.

Another shout: we are being summoned. In my pocket, behind my cigarette papers, I find a small notebook. MANCHESTER, I scribble desperately, before the troop envelops me. REMEMBER MANCHESTER.

Два

They'd laugh at me, my troop, if they knew of my past – that I once used to play a *yukuri* in bars at night.

I was born into a family who lived in the remote mountain village of Ageyev. On the eve of my seventeenth birthday, I crept out to the sole tavern in our region. Having lied about my age, I sat in the bar, my virgin stomach shocked by the burn of cherry vodka, spellbound by each folk act.

And then he came on: the *yukuri* player. A *yukuri* is half-animal, half-instrument, rather like a harp with a bird's face protruding from one corner, and little claws that curl and pluck the strings. It cannot reach the soprano range alone, and so requires a human to accompany it. Listening to them, it was as though the music had been dormant in the ground and had come thundering up through the soil into the instrument, and poured out into the world. It made me sweetsick with a violent, happy thirst to be in love, to live, to make my mark on the world.

I left home soon after. My mother was a sweet, bustling woman. She worshipped the local gods of the sky, the trees, the land; she tried to smooth out every kink of life with a rite. My father worked at the local mine, digging for copper. He was a Catholic, the sort of man who listened to church sermons on love and forgiveness, yet judged his neighbours as sinners and bullied my mother into obeying his every command. He was a stern parent, always berating me to do this, do that, curb my speech, comb my hair. But on the day that I left home, aged eighteen, he wept along with my mother. He told me roughly that I had more growing to do, that he still needed to mould me. Outside our house was a row of gnarled black trees, which had been bent into warped postures by the harsh winds. I told him I did not want to end up following their fate.

In Samskaya, I was a wild student: I kept a tame bear and risked expulsion with my drunken antics. Under the tutelage of the supercilious Professor Millhauser, an American émigré, I studied death in literature, Dickens and Dostoyevsky. Having completed my degree, I took out a loan and opened a music shop. Soon it was filled with customers eagerly rifling through the stacks of records for the latest Rachmaninov and Stravinsky. The private concerts I arranged for visiting musicians were so popular that they were often oversubscribed.

But come 1921, the world was in flux. It became my ardent wish that in Carpathia we would soon enjoy a revolution to echo that in our Motherland. Our neighbour, Ruthenia, another country dwarfed by the vastness of the Soviet Union, had followed suit when the Bolsheviks shot their czar and formed an interim government. Civil war raged on, but I had faith that Communism's glory would win out. Lenin and Trotsky sounded like heroes from the legends I had read as a boy: they were outlaws who defied authority and saved the poor by stealing from the rich. I read *The Communist Manifesto*, and mulled on that famous opening line: I was disturbed by the idea of Communism as a spectre that haunted Europe before Communism had even been implemented and had a chance to breathe. I read Solovyov, Shestov, Tolstoy. I read Darwin's *On the Origin of Species*. I had been brought up to imagine that man was created in God's image, and yet all around me were adults sporting crucifixes who seemed flawed and foolish. Now, I preferred to imagine the chain of being: originating with a creature in the sea emerging on to land, leading to the apes and, eventually, to me; I had never seen an ape, so I found myself picturing a mountain bear as the last step of evolution, its fur becoming skin, claws fingernails. *Homo sapiens* was still an evolving species. With science and logic, we would transmogrify into more rational creatures, and make the world a fairer place. When I heard that Rachmaninov had fled the Soviet Union for Finland, I felt disappointed, feeling he was a coward who lacked integrity.

I could never have imagined that, seven years on, at the age of thirty-five, I would end up in a troop of guards fighting the threat of Communism. I would have laughed and shaken my head and declared that it was impossible, I would rather have died than succumb to such a fate. And yet, each month the letters I receive from my mother grow longer, and always end with the line that she is proud to have a soldier for a son.

We gather in the Minoboron building. Its walls are whorled with fear, carry the echoes of barked orders and tortured screams. Everywhere, we are watched by pictures of the Czar: his dark eyes, his handsome profile.

We enter room 136B, where three rows of chairs are set out. There are five troops in total, twenty-six men. At the front is a desk and a blackboard.

Lieutenant Zabotin leads the briefing. My pencil, a cracked orange stub, trembles across my notebook as I copy down the profile of our next target:

Raisa Florensky.

Artist. Age: 41.

Enemy of the state. Eager to incite revolution.

A Communist. A Carpathian spy, plotting to kill the Czar.

Missing for the past three months.

Report this morning: spotted in Zhrebiy forest.

On the next page:

MANCHESTER. REMEMBER MANCHESTER.

The shock of it, as though I have been slapped awake. Raisa has not deserted me – this cruel and harsh narrator has separated us. *Remember who you are*, I recite. *You're in a book. This is not real.*

Lieutenant Zabotin points at the back row.

—You, Kuznetsov, Sokolov, take the forest. He pulls at his moustache and then smooths it down. —You too, Luzhkov. He points at me. —We report back here at ten o'clock tonight.

The men around me are adrenalized by the hunt. It is all very well to talk of revolutionaries, Communists and enemies of the state, but their threat often remains abstract. All we can do is listen for whispers in bars, visit houses, extract names and build up paperwork: the conspiracy is fragmented, lacking vital plot points. Now, the danger has coalesced into a name and a clear narrative. Radomir boasts loudly that he'd fuck Raisa before cuffing her and bringing her in. Sergei laughs and says that Radomir's cock is too small for the task; only *he* would able to inflict a punishment as big as her crimes.

If I could morph into a hound, I would tear them to strips and shreds of skin. Lieutenant Zabotin raps the board. We stand up straight. We face the Czar's portrait, straight-backed, and chant: 'I pledge to honour and serve the Czar as a loyal and devoted soldier of his Royal Guard. I will protect the freedom and independence of Carpathia, its culture, history and traditions, and ensure that the Czar's authority is respected and honoured in every household. May the wolves hunt me down if I fail in my duty.'

Raisa, my lover. Enemy of the state. The woman I have loved and lost. We first met in 1925, three years ago, before I joined the Royal Guard. She was an artist; I, a musician.

On the evening of my thirty-first birthday, my friends visited my shop for a celebration; I cooked a stew that everyone declared was 'delicious' when sober and 'tasteless' as the wine flowed. We were laughing and drinking, debating politics, the war, the Czar, the new laws. Back then, I imagined myself to be political, but I had never marched in my life, let alone written a pamphlet, and the opinions I expounded were flavoured by the flow of vodka. My friend, Andrei, brought along a poster, asking me to hang it in the window as a favour for the Rublev Gallery. It advertised an exhibition by a provocative new artist, R. S. Florensky, which had nearly been banned. For this was a time when satire mocking the state in the form of a book or painting was still glamorous and playful.

By the end of the night, I found myself lying on the floor. On the gramophone, Beethoven's *Moonlight* was playing in piano ache and Andrei, grinning, responded to my inebriated groans by slipping a cigarette between my fingers. My smoke wreathed round the poster. Metamorphoses was the title. Its image of a broken statue coalesced with the music so that poignancy was alchemised into excitement.

The following week, I set off for the Rublev Gallery. I discovered a waxwing hobbling in the snow by the building's entrance, its wing broken. There was a baleful look in its eyes that reminded me of my *yukuri.* I entered with the bird cradled in my palms, and I heard a female voice addressing a large crowd. The artist was not the foppish young man of airs and graces I had constructed in my imagination; the R stood for Raisa. How I wished that my friends had accompanied me, for now I looked like a loner with an odd pet. A kind old woman relieved me of the bird, saying she had a suitable cage lying empty, following the death of her pet starling.

Unburdened, I enjoyed a free glass of kvass and a few zakuski, which constituted my dinner. It soon became clear that I couldn't afford any of the paintings, which were intriguingly dark, deviant pieces. People were arguing fiercely over the new laws, half saying they would bring order to the depravity and chaos of our daily lives, the other half declaring they would destroy our freedoms.

The room was becoming stuffy, and so I made my escape. Outside, beneath a wrought-iron staircase, I found a sheltered spot and fished out my cigarette papers. When I looked up, Raisa was before me. Her dark hair fell from her ushanka, gleaming and static in the cold. She asked if I'd liked the exhibition.

—Yes, I said.

She looked dubious.

—All right, I hated it.

She looked hurt.

—Sorry, I was teasing. It is very good, but I suppose I was a little disappointed: I thought it was going to be more offensive, given that it was nearly banned.

—That is a reflection of the state, not me.

We looked at each other in silent understanding. There was a chill of change in the air, a sense that life was losing its tenderness.

—I think most of the offence is my being a woman, Raisa added with a shrug.

—Were they expecting pretty flowers?

—They want me to paint like a dainty squirrel, but I want to paint like a wolf.

She offered to roll my cigarette for me. Her fingers were callused and ink-stained and she took a drag before passing it over. When I inhaled, I could taste her lipstick. I saw her eyes fall to the gold band on my ring finger.

The next day, she was there in my music shop, wearing a lipstick the shade of a plum.

The search for Raisa begins.

A dozen of us, on the edge of the forest, snow falling between us.

—We spread out, we seek, we find her, says Fyodor, our group leader. —Reconvene here in one hour.

Fyodor's voice halts me as I turn to go.

—Jaimus, we'll partner.

Our footsteps crunch in unison. The encroaching dark will surely be my ally, masking her with its shadows.

Fyodor has been in the CRG for the entirety of his adult life; it's all he ever wanted. There is a perpetual sadness in his eyes offset by a certain grim stoicism, as though he has accepted that enjoyment of life is unattainable, that suffering is the fate of fallen man.

I consider confiding in him about Raisa, for he has in the past often given me fatherly advice. But I doubt I could persuade him to abandon this witch-hunt. He would lose his job. And in any case, someone else would replace him; the machinery of the state would grind on. I cannot save her. A sense of desperation comes over me, so thickly black that I am almost ready to pray. But that would be foolish. I know that in the sky above there is no divine being, and all that is hiding in the clouds are migrating birds.

A distant clap. Birds firework from the trees.

Our eyes dart left to right. Silence. All is still.

We pass a tree with a rusting rifle riven into its trunk, the roots slowly meshing over it. The landscape is still healing from the war with Ruthenia nearly fifteen years ago. Our neighbours have not yet found peace since their government fell into the hands of revolutionaries. The *Czar's Bulletin* repeatedly warns us: do we want to see our country descend into that chaos? Do we want to let the Bolsheviks and terrorists destroy our land and our culture too? From time to time, we hear flashes of their conflict: the ground shaking beneath our feet, the sky breaking open with distant, blazing light.

We come across footprints. Two sets – one dainty, one heavy – leading in different directions. I realise I cannot recognise my lover's prints.

—You go right, I'll take left, Fyodor orders.

—Do you have a copy of *Vasistha's Yoga*? Raisa asked me. She came into my shop looking tired, a scarlet slash on her cheek. I thought angrily of the gallery owner, that tall man with verbose eyebrows and a foxy face. For much of the night I had lain awake imagining them making love, but perhaps their dynamic was far more unpleasant.

Raisa raised an eyebrow and followed me into my kitchen: our illicit shop within our shop. Last night, when Eleanor was cooking dinner, she complained that she could not locate the *smorodina*, what with all the books piled on her kitchen table.

—Has *Vasistha's Yoga* been banned? she asked. —It's pretty obscure.

—I lose track, to be honest.

In truth, I had never heard of it before. I located the box marked 'Eastern Literature'. Close up, I saw that the mark on her face was not blood, but paint.

—Where's your wife?

—She's visiting her parents in Zakarpattia.

—She won't be attending your concert then? I heard that you're playing on Friday, at the Garmoshka tavern.

—Yes, I am . . . She'll be back, but she won't come.

—Oh?

—She doesn't like *yukuri* music.

—I ought to come and hear you, before they ban *yukuri*s and I die without ever hearing one at all.

She was so charming. It was hard to equate her warmth with those gallery pieces. What shadows lay behind that smile? All week I played for her in my mind—

Through the snow I walk, whispering, ***Raisa, Raisa, Raisa***

—but when Friday came, I could not see her face in the audience. The Garmoshka tavern was rickety and small. Compared to her gallery, it was a paltry affair. No wonder she had not bothered. At university, I had discovered that women liked me: they told me I had beautiful blue eyes, that I was charming and playful, that I made them laugh. Miserably, I began to rewrite our interaction in my music shop, casting her as the enigma, myself as the fool.

Beneath the spotlight, I was sick and ready to run off stage, but my *yukuri* bird made a soft trill of reassurance and we began to play. We danced together in the music, my creature and I – his claws at one end, my fingers at the other – until we transcended and the music played us. Our magic silenced the room.

At the end, I swelled with the applause. As I bowed, I saw that she had arrived and was sitting in the corner at a crooked table. After feeding my *yukuri* bird some hermit beetles, I brought Raisa a glass of *mors*. The candle glowed between us. I was embarrassed by the hurt in my voice when I spoke.

—You were late.

—I'd never have missed it, she said. She swallowed. —Your playing reminded me of Vasnetsov's *The Birds of Joy and Sorrow*. It had a strange, hypnotic power, like the sirens of old, it made me believe it could lure men to their beautiful deaths.

The wine flowed, the green fairy danced, a string act played, a poet recited and rhymed, and the acts grew more raucous. Raisa's feather boa was slipping from her neck; as she rearranged it, it flicked against my arm. The impact this had on me, I could not hide. She reached for my hand. I withdrew. I stared at her eyes, her lips, her throat. Keeping my eyes on the stage, where Andrei was reciting a folk story about a *vukodlak*, I reached out and let my little finger rest on top of hers. I was rapturously conscious of her rose scent, the shine of her hair, the dilation of her pupils, the hardness of her fingernail and the softness of her skin. As we applauded, Raisa's boa fell into our laps like a snake. I jumped to my feet.

—Please come to my studio on Friday, she said, and handed me a scrap of paper with her address. I smiled and said I would do my best to make it. With relief, I spotted Andrei; we clapped each other on the back, congratulating each other on our performances, laughed and raised a toast together. When I looked back at her table, she had gone.

Raisa

Raisa

Raisa.

I whisper your name and the forest does not reply.

She lived in Bohemia. I climbed the steps of her block of flats: piss- and graffiti-stained. Noises reverberated through paper walls: a screaming match; a neighbour practising their scales on the viola. It was a Friday. Two weeks since my performance. My heart had fought reason until surrender came.

I knocked several times, nearly faint with despair. She opened the door. I drew a record from my bag and whispered that I'd brought her Scriabin's *24 Preludes*, op. 11 – banned only yesterday, our secret – and she put a finger to my lips. Closing the door, she gestured vaguely, then returned to her easel. Unnerved by the intensity of her concentration, I sat on the edge of her bed. Some minutes passed as I watched the flash of her bare arms, paint stains like tattooed flowers on her skin. That morning, Eleanor had wound her plump arms around me in an uncharacteristic display of affection, and cried, —All my friends say you are so handsome, I have got myself a very fine catch. I had been especially kind to Eleanor all day, making her cups of tea until she had gently berated me for wasting tea-leaves.

Raisa's room was full of surprises. I had thought she might be daring enough not to have a portrait of the Czar, but he sat on her mantelpiece, just as he sat in every household. On the wall was a large print of my favourite Vasnetsov, *Sleeping Princess*; the slumbering bear always drew my eye. On the table by her bed was a painting of Dolya with a dried posy and candle. She was a deity my mother had worshipped, the positive side of Fate. I had not imagined Raisa to be a religious woman, though.

Finally, I got up and stood behind Raisa. As I witnessed the delicacy of her concentration, the tenderness in her colours, I felt the last of my guilt towards Eleanor dissolve. With the tip of my finger, I stroked the back of her neck.

—You were supposed to be here *last* Friday, she said.

—I'm sorry, I whispered, my fingers straying to her collarbone. She made an animal sound at my touch, and her brush dropped to the floor. Our lips crushed, and I drew her to the bed. I thought: She's no doubt had many lovers, I can't be just another in a line of devoted suitors. And so I pushed up her skirts, pulled down her drawers and knelt before her, felt her grow taut with surprise and pleasure. We made love quickly and fiercely. Afterwards, she looked soft and dreamy, lost in me as though I was a canvas she was working on.

I put Scriabin on the gramophone. I was hungry for her to worship him as I did, but as I explained how his use of the pedals created the mystical sounds, Raisa nodded and shushed me.

When I saw the look in her eyes – a conversion taking place – I wanted to kiss every cell in her body.

We made love again, this time slowly, and then we lay and loved each other with our eyes. The depth of peace that I experienced made me feel as though I was a child again, listening to my mother spin folklore.

—Tell me a story, I whispered to Raisa. When she spoke, her words were a lullaby.

But in the morning I woke with her hair splayed across my shoulder, my body smelling of sin. My younger self had once ached for a grand passion, on the scale of operas and symphonies, but I was reaching an age where I sensed that such an intense desire was a curse rather than a gift – that its burn might easily destroy me. A voice of self-preservation urged me to rise up, head home, share a quiet tea with my wife.

Raisa

Raisa

Raisa.

Someone is following me into the woods.

I turn.

Nothing but snow and trees and an insidious stillness.

Over the last year, I have often woken convinced that I can hear soldiers banging on the door, only to discover that a tree branch is striking the roof. I might be the hunter now, but I know that those who judge and those who suffer judgement are easily interchangeable.

By a birch tree, I undo my flies. The air is so icy that I fear my cock will freeze. The splash of warm pee on to the snow is pleasurable. *No better than an animal marking his territory*, I hear my father's voice sneering in my mind.

Behind me – I can sense it.

I turn.

A gleam of yellow eyes.

My hand curls around my knife.

The wolf just sits and looks at me; it does not move as I take a step backwards.

Wolves were once considered sacred by the Czar. Last year, we hung several men for shooting them. Then, a new directive: wolves were vermin. The CRG haunted these forests; the massacre left lupine rows in its wake. Then, a month ago, wolves were deemed sacred once again.

I walk away quickly, dreading teeth in my neck, picture my severed head lying bloody in the snow. There is a shout in the distance. I check my watch: time's up, it is growing dark, and it seems that nobody has found her – oh, Doyla, I hope nobody has found her. On the edge of the woods, a familiar sensation comes over me again and, when I look back, I see a double set of footprints: mine, heavy and clumsy, alongside the lissom echo of paws. I stare at the wolf and he stares back.

Raisa would have said he is a good omen, and I would have teased her, for I do not believe this world is kind enough to send me signals. And yet, in my current helplessness, I want to believe that the wolf represents her safety.

Fyodor is by my side.

—Find anything?

—No.

—Sergei's found her bag, discarded. There's a notebook with

an address in it, in Bohemia. We will reconvene at 4.00 a.m. for a raid.

Fyodor notices the wolf and reaches for his knife.

—I think it's harmless, I say, the hiss of falling snow on my tongue and teeth.

—You are naive, Fyodor says, his eyes fixed on the wolf. But he puts his knife away regardless.

I pull out my notebook to summarise the details of our search, knowing I will be too tired when I get home. *REMEMBER MANCHESTER*: jagged letters that stir some distant memory, but when I try to sharpen it, it slips away in the manner of a dream. I put my notebook into my pocket and say goodnight to Fyodor. The wolf has fled.

Три

The town clock strikes midnight as I unlock the door to my cottage. I fling some logs on to the kitchen fire and remove my boots, scattering melting snow across the flags. The ceiling is adorned with Eleanor's cooking herbs; a sprig of *zveroboy* brushes my hair.

I sit in my chair by the fire, sinking into the hollows my body has moulded over the years. From the mantelpiece, the Czar's portrait watches me. Eleanor lays a fresh flower by it every day, just as she once attended church to light a candle. A glass of kvass soothes me with its heat. This is my routine; even if I am late and exhausted, I cannot go to bed, the tinnitus of the day shrill in my mind. I need to slough off the uniform and reclaim myself. As I relax, my exhaustion untumbles. I sink into a sleep that lasts only minutes, for a dream-memory of walking through the woods and seeing the wolf jolts me awake. The yellow of the creature's eyes merges with the fire, so that I cannot tell if I am in the real world or that of fancy, and my heart beats so fast that I think I might be having a heart attack. *Raisa: Enemy of the State.* I bury my head in my hands. Just as my life has become steady and content again, she returns, a force of chaos.

But I recognise that is a lie. If life has been steady, it has also been grey. Every day, the same routine: waking in the gloom, pulling on my uniform, receiving orders, giving orders, enforcing laws, conducting interrogations, until I've felt as though I am barely human, a mechanism in the machinery of the Czar. An impotency has afflicted me of late; I've watched my wife's hands on my body without a corresponding sensation. The moment that Lieutenant Zabotin announced Raisa's name, my body became thrilled with heat. In the woods too, it was there, that pulse of life in my body, every cell singing *Raisa, Raisa, Raisa.*

Our love affair lasted three months. At the end of our first tryst, she murmured into my chest that I should visit her in two days' time. For a portrait, she added with a shy smile.

Two weeks passed, in which I told myself that I could not be my philandering father's son; it was my choice whether I inherited his mistakes; I knew Eleanor deserved better. But there was a sense of growing inevitability as I walked across the town to Raisa's flat, as if I always knew I would return, and had only delayed it. As I entered the building, I found myself running up the flights of stairs as the practising viola player screeched louder and louder.

—Back again? Managed to drag yourself away from your wife, did you?

The paintbrush in her hand flicked up; a slash of crimson paint seared my cheek. When I stuttered protest, a tube of green was squeezed into my hair. —Now you look like a sprite, she said, glaring at me.

I grabbed her wrist and kissed her. She yanked her arm away, slapped me, then kissed me back. Angry sex became soft lovemaking; fire subsided into sighs and sweetness.

—It was meant to be, Raisa said later, dreamily, propping

herself up on one elbow. —Wasn't it? Our meeting at the gallery, I mean. Doyla brought you to me, Doyla led both of us outside for a cigarette.

—It is true that if you had come out for your cigarette break just five minutes later, I might have been on my way home, but . . .

—But you think it was random, she laughed, for she was getting to know me by now. —You think it was chance.

I stroked her cheek.

—My mother was a woman who believed in destiny. My father was always cheating on her, lying to her, but she thought their marriage was ordained, and so she never escaped as she should have done. She was imprisoned by the idea of fate.

Raisa gave me a consoling kiss.

—Still, for us, those five minutes made all the difference . . .

I kissed her back, ready to be persuaded of anything. From then on, I would visit her whenever I could, closing the shop early, telling Eleanor I was attending a concert.

Sin is a shock in its debut but becomes casual with habit. The moment I walked into her room, I was a different man. We made love for hours, the Czar's portrait turned to face the wall. I would play banned records at the quietest volume, the whispering music competing with the practice of the viola player. We danced to Debussy, her cheek against my chest, my fingers in her hair. We dared to discuss the Czar, the confusion about whether the new policies were his work or his advisors', whether he was a good but naive man or a sadistic dictator. We debated Communism: my idealism clashing with her cynicism. She declared that the economy was on the verge of collapse; I argued that it was merely undergoing a transformation. That fifteen-by-fifteen-feet square began to feel like a place of sanity while the outside world, with its directives and rumours, became increasingly unreal.

Eleanor, meanwhile, cleaved to the simple story that the Czar was benign and wise. I felt my wife had lost her dimensions, so pronounced was her fear of the state; I did not blame her, but I missed the woman I had courted.

Raisa asked me to tell her the story of Eleanor.

(—Is she pretty? she asked, and I replied, —A little.)

When I said that Eleanor was a kind woman, Raisa's face darkened, and so I simplified our story to broad brushstrokes. I explained that I had needed a loan to set up my music shop and that her father was the local usurer. In our courtship, I found that I loved Eleanor more when I was away from her; together, our affair felt uneasy, complicated, as though I had not fully grasped what we shared. I wrote a list of pros and cons, analysing whether I ought to propose. There were more pros, and so I proposed. We spoke of the future all the time. Of how happy we would be in our music shop, of the children we would bring up. Eleanor spoke of me as though I was a responsible and upright man, a version of me I admired but did not recognise. I wondered if she was bringing out the best in me, or if I was simply playing a role to please her. I could not understand why she did not see my shadow side, the side that wanted to burn down the Czar's castle and hang every aristocrat.

—I can see it, Raisa laughed.

—I know, that's why I like you so much.

I did not dare add that perhaps Eleanor could not see it because she had such a good heart.

When you fall for someone, their backstory evokes a jealousy for the twenty, thirty years they have lived without you, for all the people who knew them first, for the places they have visited without you, for the lover who took their first kiss. Such blanks are filled with stories - often varnished, played with the damper pedal pressed down. It takes time to detect the patterns in your partner's stories, the eternal return of their flaws and their strengths. When you are able to see past the persona they present to the world, you discover the raw selves underneath. Intimacy requires time.

But time was something we had so little of, and so I shared my biography with frank eagerness, while Raisa's past remained a mystery. I knew nothing of her parents, her education, her upbringing. I knew only that there was a previous lover, a man who had encouraged her to fall in love with him before confessing that there was another woman. How I hated the man, feeling that I was being punished for his sins. The longer I knew her, the less I felt I knew her.

I did not dare say *I love you* out loud, but I said it in my heart a hundred times: when she laughed her crazy wildcat laugh; when she stretched my mind by arguing with my politics, such that we nearly came to blows; when she fed stray cats by the flat; when she made love to me with my face clenched between her palms or clawed my back with her nails.

The fire is dim. The thought of rising and dressing for bed seems an Olympian task. In less than three hours I will have to join the CRG troop invading Raisa's house. I would declare sickness, but that would involve the loss of my day's pay and a fine, and Eleanor would never allow it.

I force myself up. The pots and pans around me reflect the back of my head. Ageing reverts our scalps to the ones we had as babies. My father was entirely bald by the age of forty-five.

Through the window I see a slice of moon and the gleam of yellow eyes. The wolf has followed me home.

The eighteenth of March 1925 was the turning point. I walked to her flat in a pitch of anxiety. The ruble had fallen to a new low; my customers had dwindled to barely one a day; my meals with Eleanor had shrunk, such that one loaf of bread had to last us three days. The CRG had visited me again. In my mind, the list of the banned composers formed a drumbeat: Debussy, Rachmaninov, Scriabin, Roslavets, Mosolov, Lourié. I longed for Raisa's sympathetic outrage. My hand curled delicately around the eggs in my pocket: a luxury stolen from a bird's nest.

When I arrived, I found Raisa sitting limp in front of her canvas. She was beginning work on a new piece. Even the eggs did not lift her spirits.

—Paint my portrait, I said, feigning cheer, attempting to brew up some coffee from a concoction that appeared mostly birch bark. —You never did paint me, I added, the hurt flaring in my voice.

She put down her brush with a sigh; I consoled her with a kiss.

Our lovemaking was frantic, as though we were both alcoholics drinking from the same bottle, passing pleasure back and forth in a race to oblivion. I grabbed one of her cotton rags, and tied her to the bed before I entered her. Afterwards she lay there staring at the ceiling, and said:

—I think the CRG have taken Aleksei, the viola player. I haven't heard him in days.

She rose and went to her beloved canvas.

—Have you ever painted your mother? I asked her. I was still hungry to coax out details of her past.

—She is away at present, Raisa replied, shrugging. —Last I heard, she was teaching in the mountains.

—Teaching? I challenged her.

—I believe so.

—But last week you told me that your mother worked as a trapeze artist in the circus . . . Your stories don't add up! What are you, a spy?

I could hardly believe I had spoken the words. She laughed.

—Oh yes, I'm a spy. That makes everything easier. If half of us are Ruthenian spies, then we can pretend it's all their fault, this mess, we had to make our laws because of *them.*

—I'm sorry, I said, suddenly meek. I attempted to take her in my arms, but she remained limp, then broke free and returned to her canvas.

We both needed space to calm down, I told myself, and so I had a wash, scrubbing myself using the thin slither of soap that we were still eking out. When I came out, the stove was cold, the plates empty. Raisa had broken the eggs and streaked their yolks into her paint.

—This is ridiculous. Now what are we supposed to eat?

—I plan to begin work on a portrait of Scriabin soon, your favourite.

—Yet you have never painted me.

—Well, I need sombre subjects, she said, lighting a cigarette. —You have an upbeat attitude; you are the young idealist.

—Oh, for God's sake, I said, snatching the cigarette off her, angered by the narcissism of her melancholy, her belief that she was the only person in the world experiencing such depths of suffering. —I find life just as hard as you, I just seem to be able to put on a more stoical front.

She looked shaken.

—I don't think it is all a front. I love your fortitude.

In moods of greater resilience, Raisa would mother me. But today she needed me to be her contrast, not her mirror, and I could not. All I could think was: We're all fucked.

Raisa remained still at her canvas; she was applying white paint on top of white paint.

—It's a portrait of motherhood, she whispered.

She would not elaborate any further. I held her against my chest as she sobbed and said that the people would not stand for all this much longer, that everything would soon be all right.

I rise and open the door of the cottage a crack. The wolf stops one *sazhen* away. I do not dare move. I want to gain his trust, and I have the curious sensation that he is seeking to gain mine. He comes so close that his fur brushes my skin. Then: the gentle lick of his tongue on my hand. I laugh out loud in relief. I open the door wider. Sensing movement, he retreats.

—What are you doing, Jaimus? Eleanor appears, face crumpled with sleep. —Close the door; come inside!

In bed, we cuddle up for warmth. When I close my eyes, I picture Raisa painting a naked self-portrait, her smile provocative. Eleanor notices my arousal; I stiffen in embarrassed guilt. How is it that Eleanor is more classically beautiful than Raisa, yet she does not envenom me in the way that Raisa can? Yawning, she sighs that she is too tired.

I yearn to rise, wipe the dust from my gramophone and listen to Mosolov and Scriabin and Roslavets and Debussy, and all the others I shared with Raisa. The thought brings tears to my eyes, and I realise that I have in fact been crying for many months, tearless tears that have only now found form and expression. But I will not rise, will not put on the record, resolving to maintain my abstinence from music. For if I listen and allow its beauty to penetrate my heart, then how can I wake in the morning and wear my uniform and mouth the commands of the Czar? I cannot face the confines of a cell. I cannot allow Raisa to destroy the life I have, even if it is a silent, pathetic affair. It is all I have left.

Четыре

Dawn feebles the sky as I leave for work in the morning. I think I see the wolf standing sentinel by my cottage, but my exhaustion is so extreme that I am not certain if he is real or hallucination. We march down the street, rifles banging against our backs. There is the occasional flicker of a curtain at a window, a child's frightened face peeking out: our power is dependent on everyone hoping that they will be the saved, while the curses fall on their neighbour.

A few days before I lost her, Raisa began a new series of paintings called Your Majesty. This exhibition, she said, would honour and celebrate the Czar. She was doing both the right thing and the wrong thing; I could not have borne it if she had been arrested, but I could not bear this turn in her artwork. She began painting with mechanical hands and dead eyes. Her portraits normally contained a detail of herself somewhere – her profile in a reflection, her hands at the forefront – but now Raisa was erasing herself from the work entirely. I was afraid that she might be seduced by the Czar's rule, that I might lose her to him, just as I had lost Eleanor.

The gallery owner rejected the new works, declaring their propaganda admirable but their quality poor. He asked whether she could paint something more feminine, adding that politics was a subject for men. Raisa flew into a rage and declared that she would report him. She never did, but it was the end of their relationship. There was nowhere else she could exhibit; more and more galleries were closing down.

—What should I paint? she wept. —How should I live?

I spoke without thinking; I too was very tired:

—Well, you could move on from your art, do something different.

She gazed at me as though I was a stranger. Realising that I had thrust a knife into her heart, I backtracked.

—Of course, you must practise your art . . . Ignore them all.

I set aside the jealous feeling that I was not enough for her, held her tight and whispered:

—Paint whatever you like, and even if only I see it, it will still mean something.

Sensing her withdrawing, I changed the subject.

—Eleanor keeps remarking on my absences. Perhaps it is time to tell her the truth.

It would be a great sacrifice: it would mean the recalling of her father's loan, the complete collapse of the record shop and my life. But I believed it was worth it.

Raisa pursed her lips. —A mistress is always valued more than a wife, she said.

—I thought we were on the same page. I thought you said we were meant to be.

—I shall never marry. Men's genius will always be nurtured by women, but men are not made to do the same in turn.

The next week, I found her flat empty. Some half-painted canvases had been left behind. Her old feather boa lay ragged across the bed. A bloodstain on the floorboards sent a chill through me.

I knocked on door after door. No, she had not left a forwarding address. One of her neighbours thought she might have fled to Ruthenia, another to the Motherland.

A fever befell me. Fury sweated through my skin in sheet-soaked nights of love and hate. She should have confided in me. She had always been so elusive. *You can always move on from your art.* That look in her eyes. Perhaps I had been losing her for weeks, for months. She was a woman who needed to be deciphered. Even in our rows we had rarely addressed the real issues, veiling them with silly fights: a missing paintbrush, a composer she failed to appreciate.

Eleanor nursed me with tenderness. Every so often, when she was bringing me soup, or soothing my forehead, I would reach out and clutch her hand, squeezing it tight in silent apology. I realised that our life together – right down to the hearty meals she was feeding me – was the result of her father's generosity. As my body healed, a resignation came over me, and I shrunk the love affair down to a minor chapter in the story of my life. I read Tolstoy: *Everyone thinks of changing the world, but no one thinks of changing himself.* I was not the person I wanted to be. From now on, I decided, I would be governed by reason, not passion; I would be practical and wise.

And so I gave up the lease on my music shop. There was a severe threat of revolution and the army was expanding across the People's Guard: commissars were being appointed, the CRG recruiting. I applied to join. During the early days, when we were paying daily visits to random houses for interrogations and slowly breaking down families into tearful fragments, a panic filled me that I would not be able to see this job through, that to do my duty would force a terrible change inside me.

About a week in, I found myself heading out to Bohemia. I broke into her flat; it was haunted by the chill loneliness of a deserted place. The feather boa was now missing and the bloodstain had faded. I lay on the floorboards and thought that if I had ever really known happiness, it was here, with her. How had I seemed to her? Like a man making empty promises, the greedy cliché who wants both a wife and a lover? Was the state responsible for our end, or was it in fact my fault? Did I deserve love?

I told Eleanor that I wanted to resign from my job as a soldier.

—It is the best job in the world, serving the Czar, she chided me. She told me to give it time.

When a *yukuri* is not played, the strings grow brittle, the wood grey, the bird melancholic. It also needs to be fed five hermit beetles a day. I sold it for ten rubles. Circumstance required that I withdraw, that I put the part of me called Jaimus into the centre of my heart and seal it away. I drank with the soldiers in the tavern, smoked with them and grew quiet, hoping for better times.

—MISS RAISA FLORENSKY, YOU ARE HEREBY ARRESTED ON THE ORDERS OF THE CZAR. YOU MUST SURRENDER YOURSELF TO THE CRG AT ONCE.

So this is where she has been living all along, just three miles from her old flat: a single-storey building at the worst end of Bohemia. Fyodor bangs on her door again.

—MISS RAISA FLORENSKY, THE CRG ARE HERE ON THE ORDERS OF THE CZAR. WE DEMAND ENTRY.

The wind sings through the tree by her house. It picks up snow from the guttering and expels it on to the ground. Fyodor's boot kicks against the door. Sergei joins him. Soon, her door is left in fragments, spikes of wood breaking underfoot as we enter the building.

The first thing I am conscious of is that forgotten scent. I kept a few tatty stolen feathers from her boa after we first met, but soon the scent of my pillow was infused into them, my body's sweat cancelling hers out. Here, the scent is sharp. Raisa is in the air molecules: paints and turpentine and rose and cigarettes. My uniform feels like paper, as though it will unfurl and slip away from me, leaving me naked. Lanterns swing, spotlighting features of her front room: the stacks of canvases, a chair, a table. The hanging of that picture; the position of her paints, in rainbow arpeggio: it is all so Raisa. The picture is torn down; the paints are flung across the room. A cry from upstairs. I think: They've found her. I go into the corner and I retch on to floorboards.

—Too much *samogon*, brother? Radomir pats me on the back.

Sergei and Fyodor call down for support. A narrow staircase. Boots like gunshots. A pain in my heart so fierce that it hurts to breathe.

In the bathroom, there is a bath half-filled with scarlet water. There are canvases floating in it, their colours aborted. In the bedroom, there are canvases on the walls, stacked on the dresser. They are all of one man, in different moods, different colours: in the woods, in a valley, a man surrounded by howling wolves, blowing a kiss.

—Hey, they're all portraits of you, Sergei says to Radomir. My fists curl – *she had multiple lovers*? Then I realise that Sergei is joking. I scan them and still my shock.

They are all of me.

The paint is still wet on one of them, and when I press my finger to it a smear of colour is left on my skin.

Fyodor announces that the pictures need to be taken away with care for their preservation, for they represent a dangerous man. Her lover. Her accomplice. Her partner in crime. They will analyse their records and identify him. When I gaze at them, I see me without a beard, with a kind face and soft eyes, and I realise how much I have changed in just three years. When Fyodor asks me if the man is at all familiar to me, I nearly break down.

Local homeless men and women are ordered to follow us back to the CRG headquarters. We are told that they will be offered food in return for any information on men who have been sighted entering or leaving her property. At the Minoboron hut, I watch her paintings being unloaded. The procedure unfolds just as I expect it to. Within a few hours, there are several reports detailing how her artwork expresses hatred for the Czar; the man, they say, is one Raisa desires to be his successor. A diary is invented (or did they find one?), where Raisa has outlined plans for his assassination. Unfortunately, the code she used veils her accomplices, but we are told that they must be tracked down at once. Tomorrow, a fresh manhunt will begin.

Пять

On my return home, the wolf follows me from Bohemia all the way to my cottage. As I enter the kitchen, claws echo my footsteps on the tiles. I cannot leave the door ajar, for the wind is too sharp, the cold too cruel, so I close it after him, swallowing. The wolf sits watching me like a faithful dog.

Eleanor is out shopping, and so I hurry to the next room and uncover the gramophone, before crawling under the bed, prising open the wonky floorboard, and unwrapping the record that I keep in a false sleeve. In the kitchen, I set the gramophone down on the floor and wipe off the dust. I place Scriabin's *24 Preludes*, op. 11 on the turntable and crank the arm. I lie down on the floor; I am too exhausted to make it to my chair. The tiles are a delicious shiver against my back. The wolf lies down next to me, and I am glad of the warmth of his body, for I have not an ounce of energy to stoke a fire. Piano flurries and trills and polyrhythms rain down on me, blurring my cares . . .

I whisper to the wolf that he seems like a creature from a fable. My mother told me bedtime stories of an abandoned boy who was brought up by a pack in the forest, and who grew to be a grizzled and able hunter. He loved his substitute father so deeply that their spirits merged into one, a boy-wolf who howled and sang songs in honour of the Czar.

—I will call you Vuk, I whisper to the wolf, —after Raisa's

favourite Carpathian painter. She painted me. She painted me a hundred times.

She painted herself into the pictures too: in one, her shadow hovered over mine; in another her self-portrait was a framed sketch behind my silhouette. I laugh and the wolf gazes at me, his eyes dark and beautiful. Together, we lie and listen, slipping in and out of sleep, to a score that carries a death sentence.

I drink in the music I once listened to with Raisa, nose to nose. I would say to her —Note how Scriabin likes to combine a crescendo with an accelerando, and she would say —Prelude two feels like sitting in a white room feeling lonely, and I would say —The five-note harmonic clusters create a sound like bells pealing, and she would say —They sound like clouds gathering. Number 4, that was the prelude she loved the most. The wild piano flurries, she said, made her feel —like I'm in a spring garden, and it's raining, raining through broken sky and sunshine, and I would kiss her and tell her she was the best critic I knew. Her breath would be loud above the whisper of music, another instrument weaving into the eighths . . .

—Jaimus?

A blast of icy air. Eleanor is wide-eyed and pale-faced at the sight of us. A loaf of bread falls from her basket and hits the floor. I sit up. The wolf is on his haunches.

—He's harmless.

—Wolves cannot be tamed.

I get up, ready to demonstrate that she is wrong. But then his body tenses, his fur stiffens, and a low noise emerges from his throat that sounds supernatural. I pat him, and his jaws snap.

As he passes Eleanor, she hisses. There is a black blur as he strikes her. Her shrill cry rings out, and the wolf bounds across the snow and into the woods.

Three lashes on her hand, dropletted with blood.

—I'm so sorry, I say.

—Turn that music off! she orders, glaring at the gramophone. I pick up the bread and for the next fifteen minutes she speaks of nothing but the wolf. An anger grows inside me and I nearly make the argument that the wolf absorbed her fear, and became what she wanted him to be, for I have seen this happen with enemies of state: men frequently become what we accuse them of, such is the danger of imposing a narrative on to people.

—For God's sake, Eleanor. The Czar says wolves are sacred. What is this blasphemy?

She falls silent, blinking fiercely, then mutters, —But it hurts.

Then I recall Raisa's portraits, the love in her brushstrokes, and I run and get some disinfectant and wash her wound with tenderness.

—Is this man at all familiar to you? Fyodor asks me. He slides one of the more realistic portraits on to my desk.

—I am not sure, I reply, staring hard. —I don't think so, but I can check the lists for Bohemia again.

I wonder: Is this a game?

The next week I am moved from active duty to an office little larger than a prisoner's cell, without explanation. For five days I tussle with the composition of a decree from the Czar advising that the semicolon has been banned in all books, public communications, leaflets and newspapers. Any sinful semicolon must now be erased or painted over. In establishing a narrative as to why this mark of punctuation is so villainous, I declare that 'THE SEMICOLON HAS BEEN APPROPRIATED BY COMMUNISTS'. Its dot and curl imply a secret signal, a sarcastic wink flashed at the Czar, though in truth it looks to me more like a tear falling from an eye. I know that the semicolon originated in music scores, the medieval *punctus versus*, but in my story, the semicolon was born in the broth of a witch's cauldron in Ageyev, where a frog's eye combined with a dog's tail to form its shape and structure, and so it became the keynote of wicked incantation. AND NOTE HOW MANY TIMES IT APPEARS IN *THE COMMUNIST MANIFESTO*, I add (of that I have no idea, but, since it is a banned text, nobody can check).

I want to howl with fury at the masses who will devour this bedtime story. Once, the public believed that priests could shape the chaos of life into a beginning, middle and end. Then, they fired God and put their faith only in the Czar. To think that I once argued with Raisa over Communism, believing it could bring about a utopia, were it to be imposed on the innocent population. I've come to see that politics is dependent upon people; it can't be imposed on them. The *Homo sapiens* is a *Homo stultus*.

The four walls of the office seem to shrink. There are the distant echoes of interrogations. I remember a time when, after closing up the music shop, I might spend all night composing with my *yukuri*, the moon our muse.

Every thud of boots in the corridor brings the terror that a voice might shout,

—Raisa Florensky has been apprehended!

I dread what tortures they will taunt her with, what tortures

I might endure when I attempt to intervene. I dread we will find ourselves in the Czar's dungeon where rumours say the torments are greater than flays, whips, hissed threats or electric instruments; the interrogated are laid on a bed, connected by pipes to Dante's *Inferno*, induced by a strange drug to enter its world, where they are escorted into the circles of Hell, driven mad by demons, left with fractured black minds and no sense of what is real or dream anymore.

Then, on the sixth day of this new posting, Fyodor enters the office and says I am needed tonight, at Garmoshka tavern, a bar our terrorist habitually frequented.

—Isn't that the place where you used to play?

I start.

—Oh, yes. Long before the CRG. And just once or twice, I stammer, for I had thought that my past was safely past.

When he leaves the office, a trembling accosts me. I know they are running background checks on suspects; am I now one of them? I attempt to work, but my pen is without spine.

—I have not seen any waxwings this year, I say, making conversation as we begin the walk to Garmoshka tavern. —Have you? They would normally have migrated back here by now. The snowmelt never seems to come.

Fyodor just nods, staring straight ahead, cold as the landscape.

—We ought to avoid taking pleasure in the music tonight, I say, changing tack. —If we are able to find Raisa Florensky, then good. Otherwise, we are there to ensure that every piece is respectful to the Czar.

Do I sound too formal? I crave the gleam of yellow eyes following me. On the horizon, a blood sun is setting.

There is euphoria in my fear. For the last week, ever since Raisa became our target, I have felt as though my feet were clenched on a narrow tightrope. Sometimes I look down and feel doomed; at others I am pierced with a perverse, giddy exhilaration. I've been a soldier long enough now to know that I will fall. I've seen the bravest of revolutionaries weep in interrogations, and become spectres in the palace dungeons. The Czar always wins. But since the loss of Raisa, my life has narrowed to an existence that is not worth saving. If they come for us, we must end our lives together; a noble death would be better than torture. Now, when I picture myself putting a bullet in my head, a bullet in hers, the splatter of blood is triumphant. At least I will have found her before death; I only long to kiss her and hold her one last time before the end.

Then I think of my mother receiving the letter with the Czar's seal, of the story they will compose, and reality feels raw.

I warned myself that the tavern would not resemble my memories, but even so, its degeneration brings me sadness. Winds hiss through holes in the roof; buckets collect snowslush; the tables teeter on nervous legs. The building has the air of a suspected enemy of the state on the verge of collapse. The server at the bar does not recognise me, which I find both dispiriting and a relief. Our coats cover our uniform, but she detects who we are at once. Everyone else but us is served, until Fyodor slams down his ID on the table and cries, —Two kvass!

He flicks her a picture of Raisa, but she claims to have never seen her in this tavern. We sit down. In Fyodor's presence I suffer adolescent shame and embarrassment. I want to announce to the irritated clientele that I hardly know him, to trumpet that I once played on that stage. I do not allow myself to look at the wonky table in the corner where we sat so close that our skins kissed. Is she close by? Hiding behind the green baize curtains on the stage? Watching from the wings?

A poet enters the stage and reads his verse. Fyodor's glass freezes midway to his lips. It's a poem within a poem, a critique of the Czar - I fear an arrest. But Fyodor applauds violently and the poet nods, a trace of disappointment in his smile at the CRG's inability to perceive irony and subtext. Next time the message coiled within his rhymes will have a fraction less skin.

The next performer takes to the stage.

—Hang on, what's this?

Fyodor eyes up his instrument.

—It's a *yukuri*, I say. I feel a leap of recognition when I look at its beak, but it is not mine: the strings look different, thicker, as though plucked from a different horse.

—It looks like something from a fable, Fyodor observes as the playing begins.

I can sense the hostility towards us from neighbouring tables, locked tight in the faces of men and women who came here tonight anticipating escape.

—They were bred by the Enet forest tribes a hundred years back, I say quietly. —Carpathian waxwings are infused into the wood as they grow up, which becomes a sort of caged nest to them.

Their duet begins with an eruption of sweetness, like the first day of spring. For weeks, I have been reaching for the past. Now, as the music pierces my body, I experience a regression to a truer self, as though I am shedding the hard layers of skin I have acquired in the intervening years. Around me, saddened faces and tired eyes are touched with light, and united in transcendence. My hatred for humankind – for our stupidity and docility – dissolves into a profound sense of humanity. Raisa did not leave because of me; she left because of the state. The fierce beauty of what we shared was real, but it could not survive the blows of politics. I have always cherished a naive belief that love is an ideal immune to state oppression, but the venom of exhaustion and poverty and constriction that poisoned our love was not unique to us. The state has broken up families, made men homeless and oppressed women. Its rules have rendered music bland, and poems aborted. And with love's loss has come a collective masochism, a desire for more laws, so that all are oppressed as we have been oppressed; all punished as we have been punished; and hatred has begotten hatred—

—Enough!

Fyodor climbs on to the stage, puncturing the mood.

—Do you have a licence for this instrument?

The *yukuri* bird keeps playing. The musician gently holds his claws still.

—I have not been informed that I need a licence.

Whispers in the audience. The press of eyes on me like knuckles.

I want to gather semicolons into a ball and hurl them at Fyodor.

—Section 8b of the Czar's Code: each musical instrument shall only be played if the musician is granted a licence. Such licences must be renewed on a yearly basis, he recites. Under pressure, he often becomes a textbook ventriloquist. —I'll take it for now.

—You can't - he is my only company since my wife left me, he is like a child to me.

—You will get it back. You can give my colleague your address and collect it in three days' time, by which time we will have issued the correct licence.

The *yukuri* player appeals to me.

—He needs to be fed Shostakovich and five beetles a day.

I promise that we will take care of him. I can feel Fyodor's eyes boring into me. He declares that we must leave. He has forgotten Raisa; the small fuss of red tape and bureaucracy is his aphrodisiac.

The next act, a singer, climbs on stage, but the atmosphere is ruined. I tell myself that it is good that we did not find her: it is a sign that she is being careful; she might even survive this hunt. But my heart is breaking, for I must return to Eleanor knowing that nothing has changed, that this moment has been nothing more than a near miss.

Шесть

Out in the cold, Fyodor takes the *yukuri* from my hands. The bird's claws jangle dissonant notes.

—This needs to go back to the station, for logging.

Something has happened this night; we have bonded through cruelty.

—We are here to serve and protect the people, he continues. —What we do is a duty. Not many want to be in the difficult position of enforcing what is right, but we must not allow them to corrupt us.

We have reached the point where we must part company, our homes in opposite directions.

—Goodnight, then, I say. —Tomorrow we can see if Raisa has recently frequented any art or poetry societies in Bohemia.

Fyodor nods and pats me on the shoulder. —Хороший мальчик.

I cannot go straight home. My body feels rigid, as though the creases of my uniform are made of steel; I need the night wind to blow free my agonies. I walk into the forest, shelter by a tree and roll a cigarette. There is a cruelty to the blizzard, as if some malign force were hissing through a *kalyuka*. I am about to begin the long journey home when I hear a distant howling.

The snow confuses the direction of the noise. It seems close, then far, and when I turn back, I realise that I have strayed further into the forest than expected, for the light of the tavern is no more than a distant wink. I discover a muddle of footprints and reach into my pocket for the handle of my knife.

Suddenly, the noise is sharp and close. A group of men have surrounded a wolf - my wolf. They are drunk; their fumes cut through the falling snow.

—Fuck off, I say, filled with loathing. —I am an officer of the CRG and if you do not leave this animal alone, I will report you to the Czar.

I draw out my card.

—This is a dangerous *vuk*, one of them says. He is bald and I hate his baldness.

A flash of silver as he wields his knife.

—Vermin, another spits.

—As you know, I reply, —the directive changed last month.

—Filthy beast. Louder this time.

I raise my gloved fist.

—You must leave, I assert.

The bald man's eyes gleam.

He slashes at my wolf's flesh.

I feel the howl of pain in my gut.

—A lack of compliance will result in your immediate arrest and imprisonment.

The men squabble. Two want to fight; three are afraid.

A second howl, as a parting kick is delivered to the wolf, and I roar:

—GO NOW!

They leave slowly, to prove they are not intimidated. Once they have gone, I put my hands on him, giving him my warmth. The wound is above one of his forelegs and the flow of blood dyes the snow. I hold his paw and whisper to him. His claws lacerate my skin.

—We will find help, I tell him over and over. —We will find help.

He stands up shakily, his injured leg buckling. A sick fury curdles my stomach, an urge to pursue the men and turn their gut strings into music, but I remind myself to keep calm, for I might outrun death with timely choices.

We make slow progress. I coax the wolf on, though movement only intensifies the blood loss as muscle and bone work beneath his skin. When I wrap a handkerchief around the wound it becomes scarlet within minutes. At this hour, the darkness thickens so, and I think of Raisa painting oils on to canvas in layer upon heavy layer. The snow is swiftly filling our footprints and I am not sure which are mine, and which might belong to the men who attacked my wolf, which way is which way. There is the shape of a building ahead, and the trees thin. I have gone in the wrong direction, away from the tavern, but perhaps, perhaps it might still offer us shelter; I believe it to be an emergency hut Fyodor and I once inspected. I recall the little woman with the beard who ran it, Baba Slata. But: it is boarded up. Not the hut I remembered; this is a church, the windows smashed in places. I climb on to a ledge and peer through a hole in the stained glass – the missing eye of a saint – to see pews, torn hymn books, a scramble of rats.

—We'll forge on, I tell the wolf. —Just a little further.

On we fight, the snow becoming tidal, my wolf close to collapse. On we fight, the trees funereally quiet, as though silently judging us fools, our footsteps a hypnotic rhythm, and the snow's embrace becomes a siren, whispering that if we were to lie down, it would enfold us in a peaceful sleep. Up surges the life force. It slaps me in angry, urgent contradiction – *Hurry. Move. Find shelter*. I am boosted by a brief conviction that I, with my will, my courage, my determination, can defy the elements. But then another wave of weariness comes, until every footstep is a Herculean challenge, and the horror washes over me: prayer would be a foolishness, no greater being will care if the cold murders me, I will be just another statistic in a world where people are dying all over. I may never see her again. No fate will ever reunite us. All is chaos.

Raisa once described how she came across a Ruthenian soldier in the woods. He had crawled a long way from his battlefield and across our border, dying not with the noble grace depicted in books, but through a slow process of ruination: his mind fading, his breaths coming in sudden bursts, less and less and less. Is she far away now? In another country, with new papers, a new shade of hair, a new lover? My body is grey with the tiredness of so many lost years without her.

A distant light saves me from collapse. There is the jingling of a bell.

It is a sleigh-carriage, dragged by wolves, steered by a boy in furs.

The huskies
howl,

My wolf replies in a whimper
I sink to my knees,
Whispering
Please
Please
The boy climbs down
Lifts his lantern,
Its blazing light an eyeburn

He says something in a dialect
I cannot decipher

Blackness.

Furs.
My wolf's breath on my neck
Jolts
The carriage drawn   up   mountainwards
The air becoming thin and sweet,
Snow eases   stars   above   green trees
A door
Light spills out.
The boy's arm around me as I stagger   forwards
A squat woman with a beard
Welcoming us in
As we tumble into the warmth, into the light.

Семь

The hut tips. I am guided to a wooden chair. I can feel heat stilling my shivers, rivulets of melting snow trickling over my skin. Flames of red in the corner of my eye. The rickety chair shifts and sways with me; I curl my hands around it. What is this place? Oil lamps and wooden floors and rows of beds. I can hear the faint moans of the wolf. The woman is murmuring a dialect I have not heard since I was a child up in the Ageyev mountains, where the medicine women used to dispense herbs and fortunes. I try to say, I try to say that my chair is uncomfortable, and that I am with the CRG and deserve respect, and that I need a bed . . . But there is a delay between my mouth's shapes and the emerging words, like a faulty telephone line. There are telephones in this hospital, one by each patient's bed; they are connected to their heads; wires curling into their skulls. My mouth mouths, *What place is this?* My right side is sweating, my left side shivering. My fingers ache with the pressure of clinging on to this chair. As I watch her tending to the wolf, the thought slowly crystallises: this woman is Baba Slata. I am furious that she should think him more important than me. As I pitch forwards on to the floor, I hear the snap of a chair leg.

A wooden ceiling, a spider poised in her web. Daylight. When I try to sit up, my body fires pain. Baba Slata is waddling down the aisle, checking on patients. I am lying at the end of a row of twenty-odd beds. I cry out for water and a glass of water is brought to me by a boy of fourteen or so.

I imagine Eleanor setting out my breakfast things, advising Fyodor that no, I did not come home last night. And Raisa: perhaps the guards already have her, in a cell, handcuffed to a table, a gun pointed at her temple, in which case I have failed her. I curl up into the foetal position, pulling furs up over my head, and then all is dark and quiet.

The wind is calling out, *Raisa*,

Raisa,

Raisa,

flinging her name against the trees. But even the wind cannot find her.

Blood seeps from the wolf. A dark patch on the floor of the hut, as though left by a body.

I stand on the ledge of a church window, peering in through the hollow-pupilled saint. Its eye swivels and stares back into mine.

I scream

I fall screaming

More voices.

A thermometer in my ear; a number that sounds far too high.

Sweat soaks my sheets.

Fyodor stands opposite me in the forest of howls. He is holding up one of her paintings and instructing me to look closely and carefully, for the man in the picture, the one playing a *yukuri*, looks like me.

I cry for water. The boy brings water.

I say that I am hungry and I am shuffled upright with pillows stuffed behind my back, broth spooned into my mouth. It floods my body with heat and tingles of life-energy, which brings a tremble to my chin and tears to my eyes. Illness always makes me childlike, wistful for my mother's touch, a woman's tenderness.

I ask after the wolf and I am told that she is well, that she is healing.

—How long have I been here? I ask Baba Slata.

—A week.

—A week? But they will be searching for me! I must go home.

—You've been very sick, you've had many nightmares. You must rest.

She checks my chart, sings a folk tale under her breath.

In the next bed lies a man with his eyes closed, connected to a telephone. There is a twitching ripple to his limbs.

—I am a doctor, she asserts, following my gaze. —This is a place for men to heal. They send them to me.

—But is my wolf—

—When the Czar was a boy, I was his nanny. He was naughty, but a good story would always keep him quiet. He loved to hear of the kings who ruled other lands; kings who employed magicians and augurs to retain their power. She chuckles softly.

—I'm with the CRG, I say, testing her, anticipating her respect, but her face tightens.

—Now that he is a grown-up boy, he plays with soldiers and forgets the rules, she mutters.

My fingers twitch, reaching for my guard's pass, out of habit. I have not heard anyone say such a thing about the Czar without being arrested for many years.

—The CRG, she mutters. —My, my. Then you have much to recover from.

I have been calling for food and water, but no one is coming. My watch sits by my bed, hands set in the permanent frostbite of 4.17, next to a telephone without a dial tone. It is so quiet that I can hear the collective breath of men in slumber, in and out of sequence. The birds are still; I'm unsure whether this light signifies the dying of the day, or the pale light of dawn. I push aside my covers, test my feet against the boards, and stagger down the aisle. Every bed becomes a checkpoint I pause at, grasping its iron stead; in the space of a week I have become an old man in a young man's body.

I have seen Baba Slata shuffle in and out of one of the doors. I find it leads to a hallway, and then another door, which opens into an office. The walls are a curious web of animal cartography: skeletons, family trees, Latin names. On the desk is a large accounts book, with details of each patient's name. Many of them are soldiers, and some are even Ruthenian, by the look of it. There are no references to money. Instead, in the column labelled *Rubles*, there are the names of animals: *snow vole; speckled ground squirrel; brown bear; mole rat; thick-tailed three-toed jerboa.*

Through the window I see the boy. He is standing with his back to me, carving apart a beast splayed on a wooden table, blood seeping into the snow. I bang the window; he turns. Then I see the ears, those black ears: my dear wolf hacked and delayered. The boy puts down his knife and hurries into the office, the freezing air hissing in with him.

I attempt to speak but in my shock no words will take shape, only sounds of pain; the boy looks confused.

—Murderer, you are a murderer, I choke out finally, then whisper, in a cracked tone, that I need a cigarette, oh God, it's all so heartbreaking, I need a cigarette.

The boy remains quite still, his face earnest.

—She's still alive, the boy insists. —It's OK, she's still alive. Come. He pulls off a bloody glove and takes my hand.

—My wolf is not alive – you are removing his – her – fur, I choke. —I might be ill but I am not a fool – give me a cigarette!

—Come, she's alive.

He grasps my sleeve and pulls me back into the hospital room.

—She was a wolf, but she left that story. She's alive now.

He points to the bed. I recognise that swirl of hair; its shades of brown and red. I stagger forwards and draw back the sheet. I hear myself saying her name. Her eyes flicker open and recognition flares in joy and love as tears flow down my cheeks. But when I reach for her, she lets out a snarl.

Восемь

I wait for Raisa to drift into sleep, before asking Baba Slata for a meeting in her office. Bears, marmots and pikas look down at us from the walls. I quiet my suspicion of her witchery, my fear of what she might have done to Raisa's beautiful mind, for some warmth in her speaks to me; I ask her where she learnt her craft. She replies that she studied at the University of Smolensk for seven years and considers herself a scientist. I baulk at the idea. In my mind, scientists are men in white coats, men I trust, who analyse and label and weigh the world with their detached intellect, who do not dabble in the murky greys of mysticism. Scientists signal important progress from religion's falsehoods, though I can concede that they have a moral duty, just as priests did in the past.

—Is it not dangerous for you to meddle with Raisa's sanity? I ask.

—What I do here is a process of healing, Baba Slata asserts. —When Raisa was first brought here—

—Who brought her?

—My boy. He found her in the woods when he was hunting. She was in a terrible state, barely able to speak—

—When was this?

—Eight weeks back. I offered my healing to her. You must understand that for someone in this situation, escaping their everyday life is a relief. Raisa's mind was full of cracks and fractures, she did not know who she was or who she wanted to be.

—And your methods, how are they healing her?

—It's a very ancient therapy – one that has been used for over a century in the Ageyev villages. They used twine and incantations. To slip into the mind of an animal is рекуперативный: it connects you with nature, unifies, brings peace. In a primitive state, where decisions become instinctive, the intellect can stop scurrying – an overwrought mind can rest. An animal is at the peak of their evolution; a wolf has no further to go. But humans? We have not evolved into the beings we can be, we should be—

—Nonsense.

—It's delusional to think that science has uncovered all there is to know. We once laughed at the idea of germs, and thought the man who spoke of them a lunatic.

—She nearly died, I say.

My heart still stammers when I think of that night. I blink hard.

—I might have lost my Raisa.

—You would not have lost her; she was always under my care and control.

—But she was bleeding . . .

—The wolf died; her body came to harm, but not Raisa. There are no wounds on her body. She was in the hospital this whole time, it was only her mind that followed the wolf.

—She does not seem well, she does not seem herself. I should take Raisa away right now and—

If I tell her that Raisa Florensky is wanted by the CRG, would she hand her over? I find her loyalties ambiguous; I am uncertain of her relationship to the Czar.

—You could do with this therapy yourself, my boy, you have the energy of a lion coupled with the anxiety of a quivering hare.

—Tsk! I retort.

Baba Slata's mouth is a thin line but there is a softness to her eyes, as though she can see into my core. It reminds me of how I felt as a boy when I attended confession. It makes me want to weep and ask her what to do next: how to save Raisa, how to live. Instead, I swallow hard and rant a little more. But she does not respond and I begin to feel tired and foolish.

When I return to Raisa, I find her trying to draw. She shows me eagerly, and whispers that it is my portrait. Her style has changed. I am raw with the three years lost between us, like a rupture in a bombed bridge. I scan her face as though the new furrows between her eyebrows might enlighten me. I do not dare ask for her story of the missing past.

We eat some broth together as the sun sets, whispering softly, heeding Baba Slata's warning not to disturb the other patients. I have been instructed, sternly, that our beds will remain at opposite ends of the hospital. I dislike obeying Baba Slata, but I respect the kindness she has shown us, even if she is a madwoman.

I kiss Raisa on the forehead. I tell her to sleep well and heal. Her nails claw my cheek softly and her eyes say there is hope for us. For weeks, my body has felt weak but now it thrums with desire, a paradoxical fever of healing. I fantasise about the burn of her skin against mine, her curves beneath my fingertips, her quivering breath against my lips. I want to weep in gratitude at whatever twist of chaos has briefly summoned order and brought us together. But my visions of a reunion are a precise resurrection of the past: the two of us back in Raisa's flat in a dream of music and lovemaking. I cannot conceive how we can have a future beyond this madhouse.

Raisa is pale and slender and strange in her borrowed clothes. An old shawl is draped heavily over her shoulders, patterned with deer and ivy. Her lips look naked without the slash of lipstick, those plums and reds that she used to favour. There is a tiny cut on her mouth's left side, still healing, from her time as a wolf. We sit in the office of animals. Baba Slata and the boy are doing their round of the patients.

Raisa seems more civilised today, less lupine.

—Eat your oatmeal, I encourage her, noticing that her bowl is only half-empty.

—And you eat yours, she chides me with a faint smile.

I long to hear her laugh. I realise I have not heard that sound since our reunion: that lovely wildcat noise, its throatiness.

Raisa sets down her bowl, and with dread I ask her:

—What happened, then?

—What about you? Her eyes flash to my left hand. —You're still married, I see. And you have a beard.

—A beard? Well, yes. Do you like it?

—I'm undecided. What have you been doing?

—You go first, I reply, blushing, childish.

To begin with, she skates on the surface, speaking of how much she likes Baba Slata, of how this hospital is a kind refuge in a harsh landscape. She tells me that some CRG soldiers came last week and Baba Slata refused them entry, denying having ever seen or heard of a Raisa Florensky. She speaks of the weather and the first thaws of spring: the waxwing she saw through the window that morning, along with a single pink primrose in the snow. I interrupt her softly.

—Tell me everything, Raisa.

Finally, she begins:

When I came to her flat, three years ago, before she fled Bohemia, she was in a bad way. All the omens were terrible that day. Sole magpies; a black cat; her umbrella flaring open indoors. She was convinced that I was coming over to break up with her. (*I am incredulous - how could she have imagined such a thing? But her voice is so fragile that I do not interrupt.*) Then I had told her, carelessly, that her art did not matter. She thought it was the final sign: proof that I did not love her. As soon as I returned home, she packed up her belongings and left: it was a pre-emptive strike. She hitched lifts all the way to the border with Ruthenia. There were lines of refugees queuing on the other side: starving families, weeping children. She was heading against the tide. The guards laughed at her when she said she wanted to cross and she was turned away.

At a tavern nearby she secured a bed for the night in exchange for three of her paintings. Then, in the bar, a piece of good fortune: she met the viola player, Aleksei. The neighbour whom we had heard practising so many times. (*I tense.*) He had also tried and failed to cross the border; violas were outlawed in Carpathia. He had since been playing nightly at the tavern, and telling the authorities that it was a violin whenever he was questioned on it. Aleksei and Raisa laughed hysterically over his deception, and then, drunkenly, he mentioned that he knew of an empty flat in Bohemia, vacated by a cousin who had been arrested. They both moved there the next day.

It was a tiny, dank room. He slept on the bed, she on the floor; he got work at a local bar, she painted. They lived like that for years. She had won the ultimate freedom in her art. Her work would never be exhibited, and so she could be as political as she liked. Yet every portrait she produced looked just like me. (*I squeeze her hand and she smiles.*) Day after day she painted, until her colours ran low and had to be diluted, the portraits morphing from concentrated to washed-out to little more than sketches.

They had no money, and so, in desperation, she took a few of her portraits back to her old gallery. She found it swarming with guards. One forced her down to the stockroom, where various artworks were being catalogued. She came face to face with her paintings from Metamorphoses. The CRG officer said that he feared that it violated the Czar's Code. Fortunately they were preoccupied, at that time, with more overtly subversive artists, so she evaded arrest; though this was the beginning of their campaign against her. She gave the officer a fake address, returned home and confessed all to Aleksei. To her surprise, he became angry, frightened that they would both be in trouble. She had been wrong in anticipating his loyalty; he was so worn down that all he could care about was his own survival. That is what the Czar reduces us all to, she adds. We're all just surviving, making our way through the wreckage day by day. I can only really see this now that I am healed. I was acclimatised to suffering, before. She tells me she came to see me—

(*What? I ask, shocked.*)

She visited my music shop, and saw that it had been closed down. A neighbour informed her that I lived in a cottage on the southern row. She was halfway down the street when she saw Eleanor and me come out of the front door. Raisa was appalled at the sight of my uniform, for she could never have imagined I would become . . .

(*Nor me, I reply, ashamed.*)

She tried to contact her mother. An old friend said he thought she might have moved back to her birth village, Kryvorivnya, near the Czar's palace. It was a journey that would take her three weeks. But after hitchhiking into the mountains, she lost her sense of direction. Baba Slata's boy found her two days later, curled up in a hollow. She had pneumonia, and would have died, had it not been for Baba Slata. She brought her in, fed her, healed her.

Baba Slata told her that she could stay in the hospital in secret, that she had a special dispensation to treat souls in need of help: soldiers who were damaged by their duties, minds fractured by inflicting daily tortures. Her therapy involved healing through animal psychogeography, she explained. Raisa asked to inhabit a wolf.

(*What was it like? I ask dubiously.*)

It was like the world fell into pictures and became black-and-white.

The first thing I did was go into the mountains. I ran across the snow, raw and free, and my howls filled the valleys.

I was freed from mind; I was pure instinct. I knew the landscape intimately, as though I lived on the body of a lover. On the wind I could sniff a scent of rain that would fall an hour later; the threat of soldiers or a grizzly bear would give the air an edge I could taste. In the distant rustle of the forest I sensed food. The cycle of the day, the sun and the moon, the fall of shadows, became my clock. My heartache simplified to a pain in my heart. When it became too severe, I sought the valleys, running so fast that the snow passed in a white blur. I howled until the stars heard me. Beauty is a healer, and I once sat for hours and watched the slow shift of a sunset pattern across the bark of a tree. I found such consolation in the knowledge that even if men were busy destroying one another, nature continued to create with extraordinary detail and intricacy. Then, one day, I saw you. In the forest. You were pissing.

(*I was out hunting for you, I laugh. I wanted to warn you, I would never have followed the CRG's orders.)*

I saw you and the dog in me surrendered. *Raisa laughs, suddenly self-conscious.* I wanted to follow you everywhere. Pathetic really.

I want to ask her more, about how it felt when the men came with their taunts and their knife, but she looks exhausted by her confession. I hold her hand, but her response is limp. She sits up.

–So you're still with Eleanor? she asks, with a sudden swerve of subject.

–I am still with Eleanor because *you* left me. I had to make the best of things with her.

–But you were always telling me how much you liked Eleanor; you were never fully present with me.

I am shocked by the gap between our memories.

–I don't remember that . . . I was jealous . . . I never felt like I had you! I would ask about your childhood, your mother, but you never wanted to let me in. You were always so distant.

–Eleanor will be missing you now.

Raisa pulls her hand away from mine.

–I'm not going home. I was a terrible soldier, it was all

such a farce. I only joined because of – because of Eleanor. We needed the money, we needed to protect ourselves . . .

Raisa looks at me for some time, then touches my beard.

—You've changed so much.

I sit very still as she traces the scar on my forehead.

Девять

Garlic, *soljanka*, tarragon, *zveroboy*: I weigh them on scales in the stockroom. It is a small room, and Raisa and I are cramped with the boy between us, bossing us around. My clothes are mis-sized, leftovers from past patients, and I suffer a longing for the crisp lines of my uniform. There is one large jar of ink-black tea that I am told to dispense into smaller quantities. When I breathe in its scent, a woozy feeling of déjà vu afflicts me. On slithers of paper, I write *Grand Kuding Tea*, and attach the labels to the jars. I am ashamed that I spoke to Baba Slata as abruptly as I did when I questioned the efficacy of her treatment; I feel glad to be of service.

Raisa's side of our story still shocks me. I rewrite passages of our affair – overlaying her memories and mine – with more nuance, then cross lines out savagely, fearing I have it all wrong. In our early days we seemed to be playing a game that I engaged in with an addict's helplessness. To chase her thrilled the embers in my blood. I felt I could never be worthy of her. I was a Petrarchan lover; she was my icy Venus. Yet now, seeing myself as Raisa saw me, I find that I was the villain, the one who pulled away and returned to his wife after each evening spent together, who said he'd leave her but not when, failed to say how much he cared—

Raisa's eyes on me. She seems to sense my turmoil. *All is well*, her look seems to say, *all is well.* Her fingers curl around the jars, weighing herbs with precision, such that the act feels like an art form. She teases the boy, eliciting a smile from him. If I shut out the backdrop, I can pretend that we are in my old music shop. I put Schubert's *Serenade* on in the gramophone of my mind, and let memory's needle play. When the boy leaves, Raisa turns and winds her arms around me and, for the first time in three years, we kiss. And she says, —Come to me tonight.

But that night is a failure, every rustle renders us more self-conscious, and so the next day we rise before dawn, stealing the key from the office to unlock the door.

Baba Slata has warned us not to leave the grounds, fearing the CRG's vigil. I grip Raisa's hand tight, on the lookout for any sign of threat. Inside the boarded church, we disturb a mouse picnic, bats flapping upwards; a trapped bird startles us, circling the rafters. Tiptoeing over broken pews and spineless hymn books, Raisa whispers that she finds the silence holy. I tease her that we will perform a blasphemy.

Raisa pulls me beneath a stained-glass window of St Stephen. I kiss her lips, her throat; I can still hear a trace of wolf when she gasps; when she rakes my hair, her nails feel like claws. My heart plumes with the wish for her to be my wife. We're too hungry to savour this moment, yet as desire builds, a tumble of images intercuts my lust:

The knife splitting wolf fur;

The mouth of the wound spewing forth blood and gristle;

The stench in an interrogation room after a man has pissed himself;

The faces of frightened children as we marched to Bohemia;

The *yukuri* player, heart-cracked, as we stole his instrument.

All of them cry at me, and the more I try to smother them, the louder their voices become. I come to, seeing Raisa's face tipped up to mine, her eyes a question mark, my cock hanging limp and useless.

I pull away, do up my trousers, and walk out of the church, her footsteps echoing mine. I punch the trunk of a pine, the pain a sharp, splintering relief. Raisa strokes the flayed skin and kisses it with a frown.

Later that day, I stand alone in Baba Slata's office, gazing at the animal cartography adorning the walls, the miscellany of skins, sketches, teeth, claw samples. When we returned, Raisa spent a few hours charcoaling a sketch of me and I teased her gently throughout, coaxing smiles to hide my shame. The morning lay undiscussed between us. I envy her art, which I sense is healing her; without the Czar's rule my life seems absurd, lacking in structure. Through the window, I trace the kite-bob of a waxwing and I think of the old Jaimus: he who lay on the floor of his music shop on a Saturday night in delicious drunkenness, surrounded by friends, eyeing the poster for an exhibition. The waxwing soars; my eyes follow in envy.

Baba Slata enters, carrying a *yukuri*. She gestures that I should be seated. It is as though she has detected my craving to be taken to that dream state between thought and thought-source. I am about to whisper that I have forgotten how to play, when I realise that the instrument is chirping an introduction at her and that her fingers are on the strings.

I close my eyes, afraid of Baba's gaze, which strips and

renders my heart naked. I have never heard anything like this dance; it is as though she is the bird and the *yukuri* is human, reaching notes beyond the imagination. She holds the *yukuri* at a slant, the look on her face one of rapture, and the intuitive feeling that Raisa has not told me the whole story returns. I think of her painting those layers of white paint on to a white canvas in despair. I think of the bloodstain that was left on her floorboards. I think of the way she looks at Baba Slata's boy, with both fondness and pain in her eyes. The music passes over me in waves of knowing, and I jump up.

Baba Slata continues playing as I leave.

The boy tells me Raisa has been allowed to walk in the forest behind the hut.

Breathless, I find her bending to pick a thorny plant.

—Do you remember, I say at last, —that we once joked that if you became pregnant with a boy, you would call him Lysander? And I said what a terrible name that would be . . .

Raisa remains silent. I wonder if I have misunderstood – if her secrets are of another shade – and a fear comes over me that my lover remains a stranger to me.

Then she takes my hand and we walk into the quiet of the forest. It is rugged, pitted with boulders and thick with crooked, interwoven *zherep* pines; hard to access, and safe from the threat of soldiers.

—Please don't close up again, I beg her. Tell me what you're thinking, feeling.

—My mother . . . she begins, to my surprise. —She . . .

But she trails off.

—Yes? Tell me more about her. I wish I could meet her.

—My mother wanted to be a painter when she was a girl. Her father admired her pictures at first, seeing how talented she was. But when she announced her ambitions as an artist, he turned. He started tearing her artwork up, saying that it wasn't a suitable profession for a woman. So she drew on the walls and in her schoolbooks, and when he threw away her paints, she squeezed the juices from vegetables to make her own. As soon as she was sixteen, she ran away and joined the circus. She had no education, no money – it was the only way she could escape.

She adds, in an injured tone: —That is the truth, you know.

—Thank you for telling me, I reply in a quiet voice.

We carry on walking and her grip becomes tighter. When I glance at her face, I see she is fighting back tears.

—Raisa, I ask softly. —What is it? Are you worried about your mother?

She nods.

—I am always worried about her. I miss her so much. But also . . .

—Also?

—Lysander, she says at last. You are right. There was a Lysander and he was ours and I lost him.

—Oh, Raisa.

She can only speak in fragments:

—It happened – I didn't know – not until I had left. I only realised when I reached the border. In the tavern that night, I bled. Aleksei – he helped me. But then I lost him too.

She turns to me.

—I feel sure it was a him. Lysander.

I hold her and together we weep.

Under Raisa's chin, I twirl a yellow crocus and declare she likes butter, then a blue forget-me-not and declare she likes melancholy, then a pink primrose and declare she likes kissing. She laughs, plucks a handful of grass, and rains it over me like confetti. We lie in the forest green-gloom, gazing up at the leaves, as the wind conducts the trees: a symphony of shushing and rustling. Raisa murmurs that she can't believe it is April, that time is flying by so fast. A month has passed since her confession and every day since I have imagined him: a boy with Raisa's eyes asking where the wind comes from, while she explains that the wind is a loner who requires conflict, who makes himself known in collision. He haunts us: Lysander laughs in our tearful dreams; he runs, rides a bike, falls down, tires, eats, bangs his knife and fork, and collects toy soldiers. We have both argued out our guilt, thrown blame, retracted accusations and forgiven one another. Yet now we are like young virgins who only kiss and hold hands, risking no more.

Lying here with her by my side, the feeling in my chest is so rich that I long to turn to her and say, *I love you*, but I dread I will be met with silence.

—Listen, Raisa whispers suddenly.

I tense, sitting up, dreading uniforms and shouts. But Raisa's expression is joyful. In the distance, I hear the faint sound of chanting. The Solomonari tribe in the next mountain are welcoming spring with sounds that have the shape of earth and leaves, ushering in the rain and sun and powers of growth.

Десять

I have run out of cigarette papers and Baba Slata's boy has not been able to meet with the local trader, who is sick. I rifle through the pockets of my overcoat in the hope of finding an old packet, when I come across the notebook I kept as a soldier. The pages are curled and tatty and the notes are written in an anxious hand. On the first page, in capitals: ПОМНИТЬ *MANCHESTER*. It stirs a curious sensation in me, as though my fingers are outstretched, teasing the edges of some memory: despite its strange lettering, the word possesses the sweetness of a fable. When I ask Raisa if it means anything to her, she laughs and says,

—Perhaps it's some utopian city you thought up, where Communists sing and dance all day.

She still teases me for my old, discarded beliefs, even though I have told her that I no longer imbibe the opium of Communism. I fear she is sad to think I may not believe in anything except chaos now. My sense of time is butchered; I have little faith in the future. I simply live in the day, moment by moment, and it is survivable only because of: waking to see her smile, our hands laced together, eating in unison, kisses and caresses, consoling embraces, whispers and confidences.

—Come on, my darling, Raisa coaxes me. —We must focus.

In Baba Slata's office, we sit side by side with the pictures of waxwings on our laps.

Each bird has a crest like a Mohican and thick black lines around its eyes as though wearing too much make up. They are plump birds, tails yellow-tipped; the male's chin is black, the female's brown. A waxwing calls – *zeeee* and *seeee* and a shorter descending *sweeew* – but it does not sing.

I glance out of the window, the summer scene filling me with yearning. Cherry trees are shedding blossom, and flowers are bursting into colour. Just last week, a sleepy bear lumbered through our grounds. Yet we must remain inside. A few weeks ago, Raisa and I were in the mountain forest when we heard some guards close by. Baba Slata said it was unusual for them to come so close to the Solomonari, for the soldiers feared being cursed by the tribe, should they disturb their rituals. Raisa and I had fled in shock and hidden under a bristly juniper thicket, just three *sazhen* from them. We heard them mention our names. When they left, we crept back to the hut. I couldn't believe we'd let ourselves grow so reckless and over-confident.

Seeing the CRG was a psychic blow to my recovery. My headaches and insomnia returned, along with a prickly, restless irritation. Raisa began painting an obsequious portrait of the Czar, her colours pale with fear. When I tried to gently coax her back into letting love flow through her brush, she found she could not. Her hands remained anxiously curled into fists.

I sense Raisa's gaze on me and I return my focus to the picture, but the waxwing blurs before my tired eyes. It is Baba Slata's rule that, in preparation for therapy, the animal must become our obsession. As the days pass and I achieve more focus, I can sense that a metamorphosis is taking place inside. It feels as though we are already avian, our human bodies heavy and clumsy, so that our desire to enter the waxwing's light form seems less a foreign occupation and more a return to our true natures. There is always a risk, Baba keeps saying: you can uncouple your psyche from your body and fail to make the transition, leaving the soul to float around temporarily unanchored by flesh, which can result in a wane, sluggish hangover of spirit. I want to say that I do not believe in souls, but I bite my lip for Raisa's sake.

Raisa's anticipation is infectious. She talks eagerly of flying through clouds, soaring over treetops. Secretly, I picture a stray bullet from a soldier's rifle piercing my wing, or an eagle swooping down, its claws tearing at my belly.

—Can we go to the Western Peaks, where my mother grew up? she asks. Her voice shrinks. —I do miss her. I miss her so much.

Two weeks later, Baba Slata pronounces us ready. We sit up in a hospital bed like an old married couple, sipping from chipped teacups. Raisa glances at me with bright eyes, and gratitude. I loathe the taste of the Grand Kuding tea, the papery twists that swim in its inky depths, like pellets in poison.

I gaze at Raisa's profile. She slips down in the bed, succumbing eagerly to the boy connecting the wires from the telephone to pressure points on her forehead. Her optimism is both touching and terrifying. What if we find her elusive mother, only to discover a madwoman, or worse, a body? My breath catches at the thought of that double blow: of losing Lysander and her mother. I picture Raisa's fluttering body spinning to the earth in shock, and surfacing in human form with a shattered heart.

Into the dark I spiral, as if reality is a shore I am drifting away from. As I become a witness to my thoughts, I feel a rising panic.

Who am I?

I am Jaimus.

I am Jaime.

As the dark pulls me deeper, a memory sidles in, of walking down the streets of Manchester in the sunshine with Raisa . . .

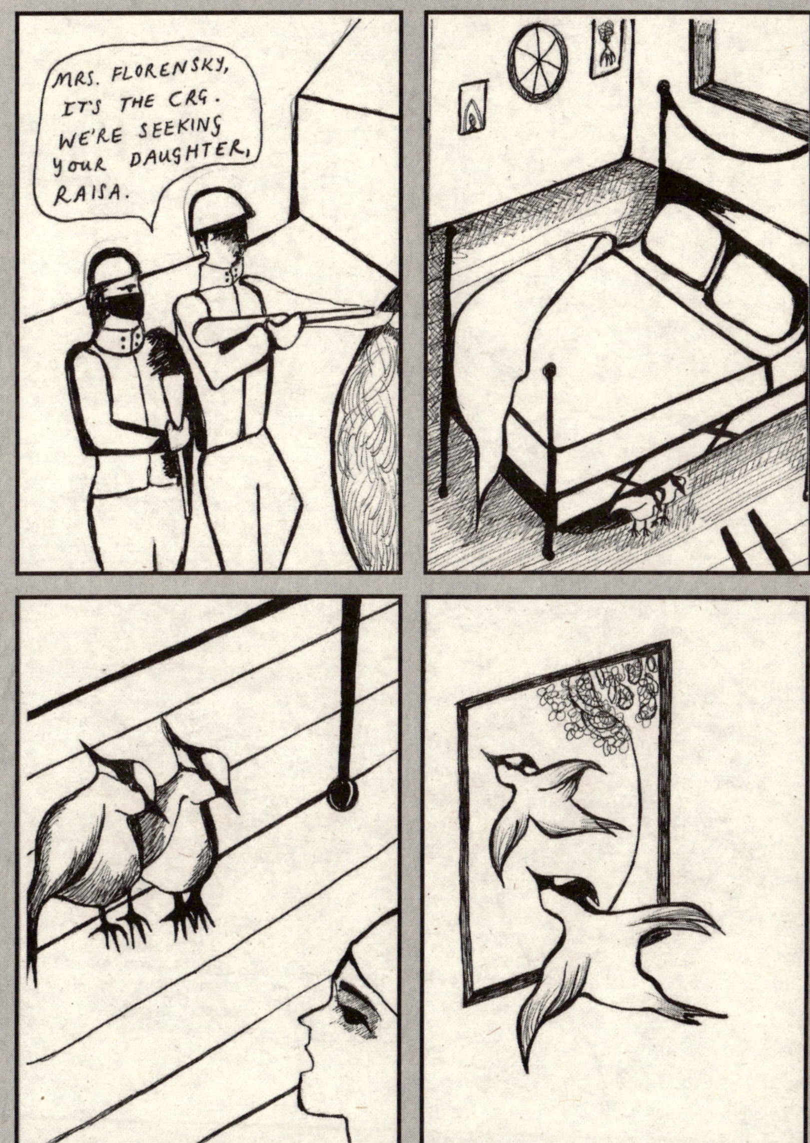
MRS. FLORENSKY, IT'S THE CRG. WE'RE SEEKING YOUR DAUGHTER, RAISA.

FOR BIRDS TO BE NESTING,
IT MUST HAVE BEEN
EMPTY SOME TIME...

LET'S DO A
SWEEP OF THE
GARDEN BEFORE
WE LEAVE

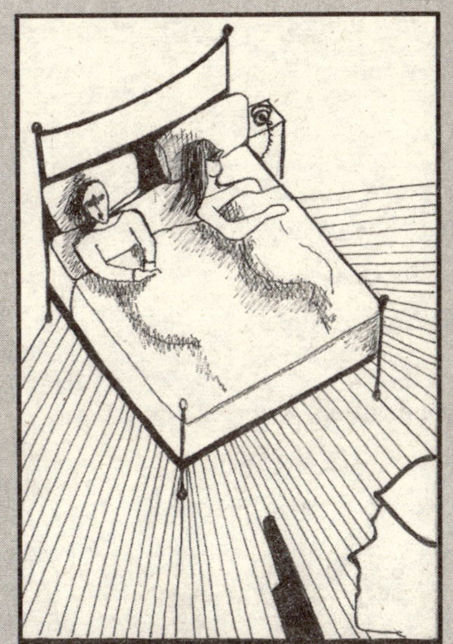

WE HAVE FOUND RAISA FLORENSKY!

K

I cry, *Zee*   *zee*
as above me appears
the face of a predator
in khaki camouflage, yanking
wires from my plumage.

Through the slits in the boarded-up windows
of this man-made animal that puffs steam and
trundles on tracks as though wishing for flight,
I can see
flashes of leaf-twig, the air becoming thin, water,
forests in the sky begging to be teased by wings.
I rock from
side to side
whimpering *zee*   *zee*   *zee*
still feeling for the word for
the word for
[ ]
is still fuzzy and *zeezee zee* is all I can sob,
knowing that my beloved is trapped in the next
compartment of this beast's wooden ribs, which
chugs up the tracks to the
Czar's palace.

A door clangs open and I am thrown
Into darkness.
I stretch out, feel my consciousness travelling down
my arm, tingling into my fingertips, finding their ends
which touch the damp walls.
My bed is the floor, but there is not enough space to stretch
out in full,

to stretch my arms without feathers, my legs without feathers,
I can only curl up foetal, shivering as though in the womb of a
dead mother.
The underbelly of the palace.
Help, that was the word I was looking for,
Help help help,
but *zee zee zee* may as well suffice – for all the good a sound
will do in here.
Raisa
whose screams before they locked her cell
splintered my heart with a needling bleed.
The guard's last words:
Think up a good story.

Одиннадцать

A spider sits in the corner of my cell. Her web is a busy beauty. I watch a hermit beetle collide, spin and thrash in its stickiness. The cell's uneven floor is carved out of the mountain, knuckling my spine no matter which way I lie. No bed, no water, no latrine. Only a small window, a lattice of sky-squares; a sadistic reminder of freedom lost. Graffiti of despair carved into the walls.

I spent years using this hellhole as a threat to 'enemies of the state'. All the people I sent here: a man for refusing to recite the Czar's pledge, a woman for a cheeky remark made by her child; hundreds of souls destroyed for hundreds of minor wrongs. Shivering, I drift in and out of consciousness, sobbing for Raisa, despairing at our naivety. We should have fled Baba Slata's hut the moment we discovered the soldiers were close by, instead of risking our fates on avian play. But Baba Slata created an illusion of comfort, a cocoon. Perhaps she betrayed us.

I just wanted a life with Raisa. A simple life together, in the mountains. A child. I wanted to try again, to have a boy. The shifting sky colours the cell bars: pinks, purples, blues, then blacks. Urine wets my trousers. Hunger becomes a hollow ache. I feel light, boneless, a sketch of flesh; as though my death has already occurred and I am nothing more than a ghost haunting this cell. The beetle's legs hang still. A bloodstreak of dawn glints on its carapace as the spider wraps it up. I should have loved and obeyed the Czar. He is our Father, Lord of our Lands, Maker of Our Laws, I should have – I should have –

Let me Die, says a carving on the wall.

HELP ME, another.

Another exclaims: *Murderers! Marauders!*

Murderers. Marauders.

M– M–

Manchester.

Manchester.

My body spasms. Rising, I stumble to the window. *You're in a book*. I am Jaimus – I am Jaime. I am Jaime Lancia. Twenty-eight years old. Studying for an MA and living in Walthamstow. What is the name of our current author? I cannot remember. I hold up my palms, flexing a finger – do I bend it or does he? Through the bars, the imaginary sunrise spills its orange and pinks, shades which may or may not be infused with my memory.

Manchester. Manchester came before Carpathia. I owned a shop there too, but I rarely sold Scriabin; more like Sufjan Stevens, the Manic Street Preachers, the Beatles. There were cars on the roads, there was a church, a cinema, we saw *The Aviator*, a row of shops on a road that begins with D. Raisa and I in the back of a taxi, her feather boa bristling against my skin, my heart beating with a love that I dared not translate into speech. But how did we come to be here, in this nightmare of snow, authoritarian laws, wolves and folklore? My memory is a dark miasma; I can only see smears of panic, but I know that somewhere beyond this sky, beyond Gwent's sky, and beyond Fate's Victorian sunrise, is a world of truth where life is unfolding: where headlines refresh every hour, where Twitter scrolls and commuters tube, where my room is still and gathering dust, where my mother must be losing hope.

The pain sears as my fist strikes the wall. This body is not real, yet it breathes and coughs and aches for sleep and thirsts for food and trembles with the terror of its extinction. And it hurts, it hurts so much, there is a hot pain in my knuckles. The spider seems to mock me. *Concentrate*, I order myself, but I can feel panic gathering force. Raisa could be dead; he might have taken her already, all for some fucking plot twist.

As my scream shrills out, several birds outside scatter into the sky. I force myself to breathe slowly and to cast my mind back. It only comes to me when I yield, just as I let go: *A former Russian province . . . 1928 . . . Survival rates are the worst . . . This one requires a double dose of Grand Kuding tea . . . T. S. Maslennikov requests it, he wants you to be fully immersed in his characters.* I picture Maslennikov sitting at his desk, scribbling away, calling the maid for tea, pleased with his polished sentences, while we rot for the machinery of his plotting.

I must keep calm; I must be logical; I must try to deduce what he will write next. If only Raisa was with me. I need her wisdom, her droll cynicism, her hand curled tightly into mine. What happens when a character in a book inherits awareness? Does it create writer's block? Surely no more than someone deciding to play Bartleby in real life and refusing to engage: it does not prevent life's narrative from carrying them along with the current.

Fate painted tragedy in primary colours, like a schoolboy playing with poster paints. Maslennikov is more subtle, and blends cruelty with beauty, the harsh absurdity of the Czar's laws with the song of a *yukuri*. I feel the ache of that music, for when I do return home I might never find an instrument which brings me as much pleasure. Our love affair has been painted in dark shades here; he caged me in a marriage to Eleanor. She echoed the Eleanor I knew in the real world: sweet, conservative, keen to pin me down. It is as though Maslennikov's story has scrambled parts of my life the way that a dream reorders a day, cutting and pasting odd scraps into a surreal sequence. How much of this life is mine, and how much of it is imposed? Am I really the sort of man who would have a wife and a mistress?

I've watched enough Hollywood movies to know this: a story that begins with a man in a cell never ends with a man in a cell. Incarceration must be alchemised into freedom or death. A dungeon represents stagnancy. A pause in the plot. And I fear that Maslennikov might be enticed by the idea of integrity over money, the ego-swell of prizes. A tragic ending will be deemed 'real', 'worthy', 'heartbreaking'. I imagine Raisa surrendering to our narrator, declaring that a melodramatic Russian death is a glorious way to go.

I hear guards in the corridor: footsteps, a door slamming, a scream.

—Let me out! I bang the door with my uninjured hand.

They do not respond. I must remember that they are only characters, that they will have been created with flaws; otherwise, they would not be convincing. I remember a time when Fyodor and I were offered a warehouse of gin for a man's freedom. Fyodor, usually impervious to bribes, accepted on that occasion; no doubt this quirk gave his character depth. I can use these flaws to my advantage.

The sound of a key in the door. When they appear in the doorway, I'm almost surprised by their solidity: the convincing fuzz of their sideburns, their scowls, saliva bulleting from a mouth. It comes as a shock, as does the feel of a hand on mine.

I had expected enlightenment to have shifted my perception of this world.

I am dragged into the corridor, and they usher me past other cell doors. I hear myself offering money. One of them gives the other a tired smirk. I sound like every other desperate man, I realise. I tell them that my mother has a cottage in Ageyev, and that it can be theirs if they let me go. I tell them I have a *yukuri*. Gold bars. They tell me to *shut the fuck up*. A third guard passes us, his face covered with a wrap of dark cloth; there's a familiar glint in his eyes, but he is gone before I can place him. We pass a cell from which a man is being dragged out, his skeleton frighteningly prominent, as though his skin is splitting, bones slicing through. That is my destiny if I remain here; my future self in a matter of weeks.

This is a novel, I try to tell them, vomit rising in my throat. The guards loosen their grip then. They allow me to wretch in a dank corner. *This is not your body*, I tell myself. *In this world you are pure consciousness.*

—What about a better plot? I croak. —With better jobs, and more money, more romance.

One of the guards looks surprised.

—Plot? You'd better be coming up with a good plot.

—But Raisa and I – we could take you into a new book – if you'd let us –

—Then it appears we have another charge to add to your list of crimes. You should know that Booksurfing is illegal. Now – get in here – and change! You'll be with the Storyteller soon.

I turn to shout, but my voice is cut off by the slam of the door. Another cell. This time with a bucket, soap and towel, and a bundle of clothes. Their plush fabrics are fit for a courtier. As I take off my uniform, the stench of urine is sharp. I reach for the water. It is warm, and the soap has a rose scent. The silk, cotton and fur all feel luxurious against my skin. I begin to feel hope. Surely this is a positive: finally, we are going to come face to face with the elusive Storyteller. But what did the guard mean by 'you'd better be coming up with a good plot'? An alibi, perhaps? I can spin one; I can save us both.

The Grand Banqueting Hall is filled with long dining tables. The lavish beauty is a shock after my cell: the gold leaf and crimson trim, dappled marble and patterned rugs, angels and cupids gazing down from its domed ceiling. My fellow prisoners are wearing regal clothing, clutching golden cutlery; the candelabras' flames illuminate their hollow faces and lank hair. The smell of the food - of meat, sugar, bread and thick gravy - is euphoric. The loudest noise is that of frantic mastication, teeth slicing meat, saliva swishing. Raisa is seated at the far end, wearing a dress of red velvet. The guards lead me to her.

—What happened to your eye? I turn on the guards. —What did you do to her?

—Sit. Eat. You have twenty minutes.

I take a chair. I am still ready to deliver punches, when Raisa reaches across the table for my hand. Her skin is warm. When she smiles, the eye that is saggy and heavy with bruising glimmers. Tears stream down my face; my ribs ache with sobbing.

—You must eat, she presses me.

—I thought you were dead . . .

—Eat!

I tear at some bread with my teeth. It pains my stomach but energy fizzes through my body.

—You know that we are . . . in a book?

—T. S. Maslennikov's, yes. I remembered in the cell, she says, nodding.

I had expected to have to persuade her. Raisa takes a sip of wine, her lips leaving a filmy imprint on the glass. This is the calm before the storm, the moment in the plot that gives the reader a brief respite, before the pitch rises again. I can feel that we are nearing the finale.

—You know that we will appear before the Czar now, and tell stories? she says. —They're saying it's like a theatre.

—*He's* the Storyteller? The Czar?

—Quiet! A guard approaches us. —Eat.

I have no conception of this theatre. I do not remember ever hearing about it in the CRG. In preparation, I begin to plot a romantic fable: the story of a man who carries a bird to an exhibition and falls in love with the artist. Then my mind drifts, and I find myself back in her flat, opening the door and finding her gone: the empty boards, the feather boa shedding as I pick it up. A sadness greys me. If we had lived and loved in reality, would it have been the same, would I have entered a flat in Camden to find she had deserted me?

—The Czar kills more than he saves, Raisa whispers, letting her hair fall forwards to cover her face. —In a game of twenty contestants, only one survives.

I swallow and whisper back:

—But what do I have to do . . .

—Make sure you think up a good ending. We could die here.

Двенадцать

In the Storytelling Chambers, the Czar sits on a throne. It's a surreal sight, in the way all royalty appears out of place in real life – when a profile stamped on coins and seals becomes flesh. His dark hair is tied back with a cerise ribbon; his eyes dart here and there, flickering over the line of prisoners. We are greeted with cheers, booing, the sound of trumpets, jangling percussion and the shimmer of a bell. The crowds are courtiers, blushed and wigged and gossipy, waving cigarette holders and feathered fans. The sunken stage mimics an amphitheatre, seats rising in tiers. A maiden pours red wine into glasses; a dwarf dances with grace; acrobats curl and unfurl their bodies. A tall, thin man wearing a jester's uniform beckons us forwards, jeers at us, blows a whistle. The crowd roars. I gaze at a hangman's noose, lying in the centre of the stage. And then at the maniac sitting on the throne. The Storyteller was meant to hold all the answers. Gwent lied; we have reached a dead end. And I have no story. I need a *yukuri* to express myself, to thrill and sway and move a crowd. I have no story.

Two prisoners, a man and a woman, are guided on to the stage by guards. They are middle-aged but they look as vulnerable as children.

—Step up, step up – welcome, welcome, the Jester greets them. Then, to the Czar, his expression stern:

—Michail Andreyev (he points his marotte at the bearded man) was arrested for attending a secret church service last Sunday.

He waits for the booing to subside.

—Lada Andreyev was found using a semicolon in a letter.

More booing; the Jester smirks. Raisa and I squeeze one another's hand.

—Two prisoners, two stories. Our Great Emperor, our Fine Ruler, our Beneficent and Compassionate Monarch, our Lover of Stories and their Telling, shall be the judge of which tale is the finest. Only one traitor may proceed to the next round. The other shall perish!

He twirls three times, accompanied by a trumpeting blast.

—Michail Andreyev, it is your turn to entertain us!

Michail's tunic is oversized; he has to keep pulling back the velvet sleeves from his trembling hands. The hush of the audience makes him look naked and alone on the stage. He looks around as though half wishing they would go back to booing. The tap-tap of the Czar's fingertips rippling impatiently against his throne. Michail shudders and begins.

—A man once lived in a glorious land called Carpathia. And he had a most excellent emperor, whom he loved with all his heart . . . The Czar was fair and kind to all, except those who betrayed him . . . understandably . . . all rulers must deal with their enemies . . .

Michail's voice frays.

—And the man, he did adore his ruler so. He thought him as radiant as the sun . . . as witty as a jester . . . as clever as . . .

There is something childish in the Czar's scowl, the puckering of his lips: a boy denied a bedtime treat. The courtiers begin to boo. The Jester dances up to Michail and taps his neck with his marotte.

—You are here to tell a story, not to grovel!

A roar from the audience.

—I . . . One day, this man was arrested on a misunderstanding.

Michail's voice rises above the noise.

—And he is wronged, as he only meant to do good—

—Next! the Jester yells. —Enough of your *boltat' vzdor*. Let us hope, Lada, that you are a better storyteller than your husband.

Michail retreats while his wife steps forwards, her chin high and determined. Her story begins as a tale of a talking squirrel and then descends into little more than lengthy descriptions of various trees. Her voice is acidic; she flicks her husband a look of contempt.

—Is there any conclusion to this tale? the Czar cuts in.

Uproarious laughter, edged with terror. Lada gapes.

—I thought not. Well. What a fine selection of stories I have to choose from.

The Czar makes his verdict. I watch Michail being dragged away by guards, fighting the desire to retch again. The echoes of his screams can still be heard as the prancing Jester declares that the next pair must take to the stage. The woman, arrested for stealing a chicken, begins her tale. Her words blur with my nausea. I close my eyes, trying to regulate my breathing. I can feel Raisa's hand squeezing mine. Then there is the sensation of cold air filling the hollow of my palm.

—Raisa Florensky, announces the Jester. —Arrested for her subversive and debauched artwork.

All the other subjects bowed their heads and averted their

eyes as they entered the stage. Raisa, meanwhile, stares straight at the Czar. He looks surprised; he sits up.

—I'll gladly tell a tale, my king, Raisa says softly. —I wish only to enchant you.

For the first time this evening, I can see that he is touched. The smile on his lips is that of a man who knows that he is being seduced and is enjoying it.

—This is a tale of three demons: Dama, Vyala and Kata. Created by the demon Sambara, they are invincible. They've had no previous incarnations and are free from every other type of mental conditioning. They have no fear; they do not know the meaning of war, victory or defeat. When they fight with the gods, they are often victorious, and terrible destruction is left in their wake.

I have heard this story many times before. Usually Raisa's eyes are vivid and wise when she tells it, but now her expression is snakish, her voice seductive. The Czar's face is rapt, as though all he has ever wanted is to be showered with words, entranced by plots, to feel a storyteller weave a web around him, while his petty, spoilt ego dissipates amid awe and wonder. He is drunk on power, such that he now wants someone else to possess that power over him, in the same way that some men seek to hand their souls to drugs or drink, or religion. All afternoon, he has been given weak stories by men and women who do not love him, who only fear him, and in his jeering his power has bloated, until he is sick with it.

—The demons begin to weaken, however. They develop the notion of *I am*, which gives rise to feelings of *this is mine* and *this is my body*. They begin to fear that they might die. And so the demons are defeated and take refuge in the nethermost world . . .

Silence. Raisa stares at the Czar, and the Czar stares at Raisa. For one frightening moment I fear that she has got it all wrong, and that the game is in his hands, not hers. Then he delivers his verdict:

—Glorious.

Applause from the crowd, who seem a little dismayed to see a traitor praised. Raisa turns to look at me as her rival is sent to his death, her face softening with relief. The Czar's gaze follows hers and lingers on me.

It is my turn to tell a story. I step forwards and hear my name and crime announced. As I was once a guard, the jeering is even more vicious.

—Traitor!

—Coward!

My rival is an elderly man called Igor Tolstoy. I open my mouth and find that heat emerges, not in words, but vomit that spills on to the floor.

The guards lead those of us who survived back to our cells. There, they stripped us of our furs and returned us to rags for the night. Tomorrow, we will tell more stories, until there are fewer of us, and fewer of us, until only one survives and is granted life.

I had to tell my story with the embarrassment of spittle on my lips and a stain on my tunic, the Czar's smile sadistic as I stammered. But it was a good story, a tale of a *yukuri* player torn between two women, who both adore his performances. My rival told a story of a magic bear. When he finished, we stood in electric silence while the Czar weighed our tales. I kept my eyes on the floor, telling myself, *It is only a book, this is not real*, until finally he decreed that my story was the lesser of two evils. At his verdict, a great tiredness came over me, the urge to retch again and weep at the fate of my rival as he was led away. I only got a brief glimpse of Raisa's face, soft with relief, before we were taken back to our cells.

This may be my last night in this book, in this body.

Death in fiction: I've spent years studying it. A term or two into my MA, I knew that the subject was a mistake: every death you study is shadowed with the whisper of the possibility that it could be your future. There is a gradual, accumulative horror that coalesces from excessive focus on the topic, day after day: the sensation of looking deeper into a bottomless well, the shivering trail of the Reaper's bony fingers on your neck. My fear sometimes woke me in the early hours of the morning, my heart aquiver, as I tried to persuade myself that it was irrational, that I must accept that I could not control my destiny. I wished in those moments that I could believe in an After. I was terrified by the realisation that whatever you achieve will fade, that history will close over you with a swift amnesia, your name carried down through generations in shrinking anecdotes, until finally you are no more than a forgotten name on a family tree. For a time, I carried a sneaking hope that I might do something great or grand in the world, be a Scriabin or a Beethoven, so that my name might transcend time, tempered by a cynicism that this is every man's delusion. Now I want only a peaceful death. I want to be side by side with Raisa: her grey hair on the pillow beside me, our gnarled hands entwined, lost in dreams as we fade together. To die like this – squeezed by a noose – in a place that is not even *real* is as absurd as the death of a Dickens character, felled by spontaneous human combustion. It is a punchline that will turn my life into a joke.

Was Gwent right to say that death in a novel is absolute? If I tell myself over and over that this is all just paper and concepts, can I transcend this? Gwent was wrong, after all, about the Storyteller being our saviour. Oh God, let him be wrong about this.

The next day at the death feast, I try to sit opposite Raisa, but the guards lead me to the opposite end of the room.

—Make up your own story, one says. —No cheating.

Raisa picks at her food, and I sense in her the steely calm of a spectator witnessing events. This might be my last meal. I stare at the chicken leg in my fingers, greasy, the strands of flesh, the shades of pink. Several possibilities leap to mind – run, throw meat, create a diversion, assault a guard, weep – yet I do nothing. Maslennikov holds me like a tiny toy figure in the palm of his hand. Illusions had once seemed to me to be ephemeral things, like ghosts and magic, thin and cloudlike, but now I realise how they can be as solid and deep-rooted as oaks.

—Leonid Kacharov versus Raisa Florensky, announces the Jester.

She is wearing a long plum velvet dress today: her beauty shimmers despite the black eye and bruised cheekbone.

The Czar's pupils dilate; a smile floats on his lips as she speaks. It's another story from *Vasistha's Yoga*, one she has told me before, in bed, while circling her fingertips across my chest. It tells the story of Shikidvaja, an enlightened king, and Chudala, a queen who has yet to reach this rarefied state. He goes wandering off into the forest in search of enlightenment, leaving his queen to rule in his stead. She seeks out her husband and turns into a male guru, making him her disciple. As a guru, she tells him that she has a curse on her, which means that she turns into a beautiful nymph every night. And so by day she tutors him and by night she makes love to him, bringing him to *bodhi.* (When Raisa told it to me she teased me that I would soon be enlightened by her *darshan* and I showered her with kisses.)

Leonid Kacharov tells a story of a cat sitting on a mat all day long, and so it comes as no surprise when the Czar announces Raisa's triumph. The crowd cheers; they are beginning to warm to her.

It is time for my fate to be decided. My opponent goes first, but he refuses to tell a tale, shrugging his shoulders in rebellion, tattoos rippling as the guards drag him away. I am relieved, foolishly believing that I have won by default, only to hear the gleeful squeak of the jester's chalk on the board.

—If there is no opponent, then you must play a game!

Nine white dashes on the board:

_ _ _ _ _ _ _ _ _

Raisa's face is pale. Our eyes kiss in terror. We both know that this is no act of redemption on the Czar's part; it is a prolonged courtship, a dance with Death choreographed by our narrator.

On the tenth dash, the jester's chalk breaks with an animal screech. Picking up the pieces, he spins them in a juggle.

Hangman: a game I have not played for years, not since I was a child, sitting with my dad, doodles and scribbles on the phone pad.

It is only a book. Perhaps there is hope. A reversal of fortune. A god descending from the sky to sweep me into his chariot. I feel pathetic, a child craving a happy ending, yet I find myself praying to the Storyteller all the same, *Let me live, spare me, oh please spare me.*

Raisa steps forwards boldly.

—Your Royal Highness, she says, —might I offer, in place of this game, a gift to you?

—A gift? He raises an eyebrow.

—A portrait, she offers.

Now his smile becomes a sneer.

I open my mouth to interrupt, to assert that I will play the damn game, when he replies:

—You have already violated my laws with your paintings.

—That was the old Raisa Florensky, she replies, a tremble in her voice. —She was young, she was foolish, she failed to understand the full threat of an invasion by the Communists. But know this - I painted a series of portraits honouring you not long before I was arrested, and the gallery owner at the Rublev Gallery refused to take them.

—He refused them? On what grounds?

—I suppose he failed to see the merit in them, she replies.

—What would you say is the purpose of art?

A pause, as though she is clinging on to a tightrope of carefully chosen words.

—There is a great thinker, Sigmund Freud, who has declared that art is the detritus of the human mind, she says.

—Perhaps it is better left abandoned, then.

Nervous laughter from the audience. I feel myself grow dizzy with the tension. *It's only a book, it's only a book.*

—And yet you take such pleasure in it, the Czar continues.

—It's just another form of storytelling, says Raisa, gaining confidence again. —For each painting does tell a story. It is dependent on the setting, the composition, the light and colours a painter chooses. Repin portrayed Ivan the Terrible with dignity, holding his dying son. My portrait of you captured your fine looks, demonstrated my admiration of you in each and every brushstroke: in the choice of alizarin to hint at compassion in the curve of your lips and in the use of Prussian blue, with just a dab of dark sienna, for your eyes, for they say that the eyes are the windows to the soul . . .

—You presume to know my soul?

—I hoped to represent your wisdom and good looks, your Royal Highness.

—*All* of my wisdom, in one dab of a brush?

—Such is the skill of a good painter.

The Czar's mask breaks, his face flooding with bright feeling. Raisa dares to take a step forwards, smiling, and for a moment they gaze upon each other.

—I have a story of my own, he says. —When I was a boy, and tired of the confines of this palace, I persuaded a servant to take me to the local circus. We went in disguise, dressed as common mountain folk.

At the word 'circus', Raisa's face tightens.

—I watched the most extraordinary act, says the Czar. —A beautiful woman climbed into a box, the lights dimmed, and the magician sliced two swords through it. When the box was opened, there was nothing but darkness inside. A miracle!

—My mother, Raisa falters.

—Yes, your mother.

—She loved the circus, Raisa whispers.

—And how long did she travel with them for?

—She performed for many years - decades, in fact, putting on her sparkly costume, putting on her smile, until it became faded and chipped, like the smile on a rain-weathered statue.

Raisa's voice sounds misty with the memory.

—And now she has vanished. My guards searched her cottage and found it empty.

The cottage we visited as waxwings. It had seemed as vast as a palace when Raisa and I had flown in through the open window. Cobwebs in the corners of the room; dust over the canvases; loneliness in the folds of her bed; pictures of her and Raisa hanging on the walls that had a strange air of nostalgia, as if they had both died centuries ago. I remember Raisa's distress before the soldiers came, the way she had hissed and swooped in circles, which had made my feathers quiver in fear and confusion.

—I do not know where she is, Raisa's tone becomes pleading. —The last time I saw her was two years ago, when the circus came to Samskaya. I watched her final show. The darkness fell, the swords swooped, and the box was empty. But when it was time for the prestige - her reappearance - she was nowhere to be seen. The magician was bewildered, bereft. It was a mystery. Nobody ever saw her again.

Raisa swallows. I frown. Does her vanishing speak to the magic of this world, or does it signal an absolute end?

—She left behind portraits of me that were most offensive, the Czar declares.

—Her paintings were a hobby, Raisa argues. —She was most disturbed in her final years. A medicine woman gave her herbs, but everything they tried failed. The vanishing was a . . . release . . .

Oh Raisa. I gaze at the audience: they are hushed, enthralled, feasting on her misery. Why did she never confide in me? Where does this story stem from? Is it a creation of our narrator's, or a tragedy plucked from her life? I cannot tell if this is Raisa or Rachel speaking.

—By taking her life, she saved us the trouble of hanging her for her art.

Raisa fights tears.

—Enough, I interject, but neither seems to hear me.

—They found her body? Raisa weeps.

—She was down in her garden, swinging from a cherry tree. And now she lies in an unmarked grave.

The Czar smiles. I step forwards to hold Raisa tight, but she is already storming towards the throne –

snarling at the Czar –

seizing his crown –

she tosses it across the stage –

a shocked hush as the spectators watch it wheel across the floor, discarding a spray of jewels before clanging to a halt on its side.

The guards rush forwards.

—Hang her! shouts the Czar. —Hang him! Hang the pair of them!

—You're not real, I yell at him. —You're nothing but a handful of samskaras, memories of the author's terrible relationship with his father or some such nonsense – you're a *fantasy* – and in a moment of enlightenment I see him as a shimmering form, a dance of letters pulsating within the silhouette of a man wearing a crown –

—You're a coward, T. S. Maslennikov!

As the guards seize me, the Czar's body reassembles. Raisa is being led away, sobbing. A guard slams against my right side, winding me.

The distinction, when it comes, is sharp: the shift from corridors paved with exquisite marble and the billow of high ceilings to the cold hiss of a narrow stone staircase. The tunnels shrink down to a clammy cell containing two beds, each sporting a thin, dirty mattress, with telephone wires curled on the pillows like scorpions. Torture – the only fate worse than death.

Only a book, only a book.

I hear Raisa crying out as they strap me down on to the bed. One of the guards has a dark cloth wrapped around the lower half of his face; his eyes jolt me once more. I know who he is, even before he removes his mask: the boy from Baba Slata's hut. The main guard gives him a hearty backslap, and tells him it is his turn, as though the boy is his protégé. The boy leans in. He tells me that we will be sent into Dante, to the ninth circle of Hell: the realm reserved for traitors, who lie buried in a lake of ice formed by the tears of Lucifer. The lake remains perpetually frozen by Lucifer's flapping wings and those who try to weep will find their tears freeze. I declare that *he* is a traitor, a liar, a coward. Raisa's cries are muffled as a rag is shoved into her mouth. Fury overtakes me. I spit into the boy's face. Slowly, his features loom over me and I am terrified that he is about to sink his teeth into my skin. A whisper:

—Baba Slata sends her good wishes. Be quick and you can escape.

He turns to the other guards, declaring that he wishes to work alone. They clatter out, swearing, hungry for their next victim —The Czar is keeping us busy today.

The boy applies wires to my forehead. He draws liquid from a bottle of Grand Kuding into a syringe. Is he mocking us? Is this part of the torture, a false reassurance to heighten the agony? The syringe needle pierces my arm. *Only a book. Mind over matter. Mind over body.*

—But are we going to— Raisa has a voice again. I try to twist my head to face her, strain against the pressure of wires.

—No, I hear him say. —Hurry. We don't have much time. You can escape these bodies; leave them for a better life.

His words slur as the Grand Kuding spreads its familiar stupor through my blood.

—It's a bridge, he is saying. —A book that bridges back to Fate . . .

—But I don't want to . . .

It is blissful, at first, the shedding of my character, like the gradual loss of a skin, saying goodbye: to Jaimus Luzhkov with his bastard of a father, his mistress and his wife; to this land of cruelty, cold landscapes and wolves; to the Czar's laws. As its details seep out of me, I am left colourless and lost - *Who am I?* Then the joy. Pure and sweet. Knowing that we have been saved. We have escaped. But just as soon as I am released, there comes a pull. I experience the new book's prologue first as a taste - something metallic - then as the noise of traffic: impatient horns and buzzing news alerts. *Who am I now?* Something inside me resists, pulls back, aches to curl back into the womblike darkness for a while longer. The thought of rebirth - of becoming a new Jaime, of the patterns that will play out, of the mistakes I might repeat, the challenges I might fail

– makes me feel weary before I am even born. My true life has become such a distant horizon I can no longer see it. It is only Raisa – a presence beside me, our consciousnesses swimming together – that draws me forwards in hope, rushing into new light, a new world.

An Interim

There are two members of the Welsh constabulary sitting in my cottage, drinking Twinings Earl Grey. I find myself unable to take them entirely seriously. The man, a detective sergeant, is tapping his pen impatiently against his notepad, his digits smeared with cheap ink; the woman, a detective constable, pats her mousey perm. I feel a sense of the unreal, of observing myself from afar, as though I have been forced to participate in some low-budget crime drama playing out on a television channel on a Sunday night, dissected by adverts for washing powder and dental shine.

In a review of my 2010 novel *The Priest*, the *Daily Telegraph* observed that I have 'a telling eye for minutiae'. In other words, the reviewer seemed startled by my apparent willingness to engage in rudimentary research for my novels. I studied the weather forecast with care in the weeks before Jaime was due; I was able to change the date of his interview on an easy whim, my publishers attributing this to my habitual truculence. The snow had fallen for three consecutive days when he arrived. Nature was my accomplice, covering his tracks by the end of the day. When I informed the police that he had left my cottage at seven o'clock that evening, it was entirely plausible that his footprints were buried beneath the soft kiss of snow.

And yet, still, they return, and we go over the details again, and again.

'You stated in your previous interview that Jaime Lancia left the cottage at seven p.m.,' says the sergeant. 'And yet now you state it was seven thirty . . .'

'At my age,' I reply, my voice quavering, 'one becomes muddled so easily . . .'

I am obviously a poorer actor than I imagined, for the two exchange looks, and I detect that the woman's sympathetic expression is merely a veil covering steel. Suddenly I have a sense of reality cutting into the farce, of the threat that knuckles me. Claustrophobia has afflicted me since I was a boy. Being condemned to a cell would result in me tearing sheets into strips to fashion a noose for myself; and then there is the horrifying thought of them combing through my precious papers, their smears on my Montblanc.

We continue to circle through the same questions for another ten minutes, when, through my window, I see a figure on my lawn, prancing in the melting snow. Ryan, a young village farmer, who has a predilection for spicing his mind with LSD. He regularly trespasses on my grounds, giggling and gallivanting as I shout threats from my window. Scapegoat: a word coined in the sixteenth century, describing the animal on which communal sins were placed before its slaughter. Ryan might become my ritual sacrifice.

'He is here most days, I am afraid . . . Taunting me, threatening violence. Which reminds me . . .' My voice gathers pace and volume with the excitement of feigned recollection. 'Ryan was here the night Jaime Lancia interviewed me. I saw him waiting under the shadow of the oak as Jaime left, now that I think on it.'

'Really?' the woman adds the note to her pad.

'This is the first time you have mentioned this,' the sergeant asserts, but I see the gleam in his eye.

'Ryan once threw a stone through my conservatory window,' I add. 'I reported the matter to the police. You can check your files – I believe it was around three years ago.'

Why, this is all coming together rather nicely. They are already reassessing me, comparing my elderly frame to Ryan's strapping physique. I am being shrunk back down to a harmless old fool. A sudden urge to giggle assails me and I swallow it down with a mouthful of tea.

As they rise, the woman's face frets with uncertainty. She stops, turns and reaches for her bag. Then, despite the frown of her superior, she withdraws a copy of *Glossop Inn*, and requests a signature for her son. After they have departed, I sit and laugh and laugh and listen to the sound echo and fade. Dorothea jumps on to my lap and I stroke her softly into a state of somnambulistic peace.

I am massaging Rachel's shins gently, in order to prevent muscle wastage while she lies in her swoon, when I suddenly experience a sensation of déjà vu. I recall how I once gave Mr Gwent the same treatment when he lay in my cottage, his ankles growing more stark by the day as his body weight decreased. Each morning I resolved to wake him, only to find myself too enchanted with plotlines I could ensnare him in.

I remember the day that fate first brought us together. A decade ago, with *The Priest* on the Booker shortlist, and the bookies giving me the highest odds – eight to ten – to win, I found myself at a dinner party in Hampstead. Those were the days when I attempted to persuade myself that a connection with my fellow *Homines sapientes* might be possible. The guests were showering praise on each other and scorn on their rivals. In the midst of a discussion about new, upcoming critics, a Mr Gareth Saint (he has been Mr James Gwent for so long now, it feels odd to call him by this name), a science fiction author I had barely heard of, gave me his sincere condolences on the patronising review I had just received in the *Sunday Times*. It declared that I was doomed to forever remain a Booker bridesmaid, having at that time been shortlisted seven times, because my fatal literary flaw was my 'poor' characterisation. I responded tartly with a quote from Nabokov: 'Criticism can be instructive in the sense that it gives readers, including the author of the book, some information about the critic's intelligence, or honesty, or both.' Gwent had the grace to look mortified. He was eager to stress how much he adored my novels, but the damage had been wrought: a crack had opened in my mind.

Two days later, I sat at the Booker dinner and even before the announcement was made, the cold shock of inevitable failure was upon me. I remained nonchalant in public; while in private I raged, wept, fasted and prayed. Sleep eluded me for a week. Suddenly my literary process seemed laughable – that interview where I had discussed how I might spend an hour toying with the placement of a semicolon or a full stop! In order to alchemise a gift into genius, to fly as close to the sun as one can, to reach those dizzying heights that immortalised Beethoven, Michelangelo, Shakespeare, what must one sacrifice? I was humbled, reduced to childlike terror, willing to do anything: play Faustus, make pacts.

In the end, it was Gwent, fittingly, who supplied my solution. I adopted him as a 'friend', listened to his burbles on quantum physics – consciousness as a field, ideas of entanglement – and William Blake's lines on cleansing the doors of perception. How might such a theory be utilised, I pondered. A few days on, catching a butterfly between my palms, its beating wings a thrill, I considered how I might capture a human psyche in the same manner. I consulted religious tracts and spiritual texts; one must sift carefully through ancient wisdom, discard New Age-style twaddle and extract the pearls of true profundity. My revelation came in the form of a Welsh manuscript, the *Meddygon Myddfai*, a collection of medieval medicinal treatises. How my heart quickened when I reached a chapter which detailed how a musician had sought to enshrine his wife through a song – not through sentimental lyrics, mark you, but by preserving her consciousness in its coda; how the man's son, a poet, had in turn immortalised his father in both verse and spirit, so that the family line was known as *anfarwol*, immortal. The listed herbs could be found on Bardsey Island – my very own birthplace – and famed for the twenty thousand saints buried in its soil. I took a boat there three times over the course of one year, plucking plants appropriate to each season – mandrake, corn bellflower, sharp dock and river startip – and used the Grand Kuding as a base for my tonic. My first guinea pig was a dog. A shaggy creature who drank the tea I placed in a bowl for him, and whose consciousness entered a short story that I penned that afternoon.

The day that I found Gareth Saint's heart had stopped came as more of a shock to me than it ought to have done; in my folly, I had imagined that my pen had made him immortal. I returned to my desk in a despondent mood, only to discover that his consciousness still beat, still breathed within the confines of Mr Gwent. I have neglected to avenge myself on him for stealing Rachel and Jaime from me; potential punishments that I might inflict remain a list in my notebook. For this is the rub: when a torture victim becomes fully acquainted with the methods of their tormentor, the element of surprise is lost. There is little fun to be had with Gwent anymore. I require fresh blood.

I continue to massage Rachel's ankles. The protrusion of bone through the papery skin of my hands, such a contrast to the sweet bloom of her flesh, begins to disturb me. I suffered a cancer scare last year; an operation the year before; my body mocks me, daily. *Thomas Turridge* might be my swansong, my last hope of glory. Yet still they desert me and wander in distant narratives, no more than vague shapes on the horizon of my consciousness.

My telephone remains silent. A fortnight later, the newspapers report that a Mr Ryan Walsh has been arrested on suspicion of murdering Jaime Lancia, 'while the hunt for his body continues'. The Fates have blessed me. I remove their bodies from the basement and, with great effort and pain, carry them upstairs to the guest bedroom, where I lay them on the four-poster like a prince and a princess, the sun falling through the window forming haloes around their heads.

The Fourth Story

London, 2047

One

We're waiting on the doorstep of Anjali's house in Hampstead, shivering a little in the evening chill, when Jaime asks, 'Do you think I look OK?'

I assure him that he looks terrible. His elbow is sharp in my ribs when the door opens. Anjali sings our names. Her speech always sounds as though it's punctuated by exclamation marks. I suffer that habitual jolt at the difference between her Me & My feed – sarcastic, savage – and her real-life, rather more charming aura. As she leans in, the sequins of her dress catch on mine, and her perfume passes into my hair like jazzy smoke. The uncertainty of etiquette hovers between us; my kisses attempt to connect with her cheeks, hers evaporate into air. She leaves a lipstick echo on Jaime's stubble. I roll my eyes at him and he rolls his eyes back.

We enter a room that reminds me of how childless houses look: velvet curtains without splatter, unblemished white walls, tidy floors. The party's in that sober phase of the evening when the small talk is pinched and polite. Jaime changes the music, as always, puts on his new favourite composer: Scriabin. He is wearing ripped black jeans and a T-shirt with *The Hurdy Gurdy Men* on it; his penguin tattoo peeks out beneath his left sleeve.

Everyone else is in smart dress. The looks they give him suggest admiration rather than disapproval, though. This annoys me. There's a part of me that wants them to disapprove of my husband.

Someone is telling an anecdote about Emily's divorce and its messy aftermath. Then I cringe because I realise that I know one of the listeners. Eleanor and I used to be friends. I'm not even sure if we've fallen out. Our emails and meetings simply thinned out around a year ago because we were both busy. I took a month to reply to her last one, then she never responded and I assumed she was peeved with me, though Jaime says I have a tendency to over-analyse.

Jaime is off chatting to Eleanor and Mariette, who are cooing over the latest band he's managing. There's something about the music – the blurry piano notes – that is making me feel wistful, in danger of melancholy. A guy with thinning hair is hovering on the sidelines of their conversation, and he looks so grateful when I start talking to him that I immediately warm to him. He asks the predictable question. I tell him I'm an artist and add my reluctant postscript: I'm paying the bills by working as an art therapist at Cybersenx. He starts telling me about the dream he had last night, which involved a giant serpent coiled around his neck.

'I woke up with an erection,' he confesses in a whisper, his words blowing ripples across the bubbles of his drink.

I guess it could be worse. If I were a doctor, people would be rolling up their sleeves and surreptitiously showing me their rashes. I decide to fuck with the guy and tell him he has a repressed anguine fetish, echoing a rare case study that Freud recorded in 1913. When he looks alarmed, I touch his arm and laughingly tell him not to worry. But he only looks more worried. Now I feel bad. It's six o'clock, my phone tells me. Three more hours before we can make polite excuses and leave. I check my Good Parenting app, praying there might be a problem with Finn, but he's safe in the third stage of pre-REM sleep.

I escape to the toilet. Black-and-white pictures of Hollywood icons adorn the walls. James Dean, Marlon Brando, Rupert Weitz. Their beauty is accentuated by crimpled foreheads and sullen lips. When men brood, their expressions imply mystery, profundity. When women hide an inner ache, they cover it with a smile. My cheeks are already hurting and I've only been here thirty minutes. A Me & My status update starts composing in my mind: *Perhaps the female smile is the biggest deceit of all facial expressions, a mask that not only hides mystery but deflects it, implying we are a sex of trivial concerns.* I have measured out my life with updates unposted. Scrunching up toilet roll, I hear Jaime's voice complaining that I'm using too much, that global warming will be triggered by my fanny alone. I rise, wash my hands and look into the mirror.

'What did you expect?' I hear my mother's voice in my mind. She used to tease me when I pointed to the tiny avian lines at the corners of my eyes. Vanity is the fear of mortality: the accumulating evidence that we will one day be nothing but bone and ash. It's always a shock to see the slump of my cheekbones; the lines on my face, once feathery pencil strokes, now scored deep and harsh. Only my eyes look the same, bright and sharp beneath crinkle-patterned lids. My husband has always discouraged Botox, fillers, sheens, pupil enhancements, brow grafts – transhumanism treatments, he calls them, saying that they look unnatural. Jaime has grey in his hair, but he has gained the sexy gravitas that comes with age.

I want to splash water on to my face, the way that people

do in movies when they're freaked. But I'm not sure anybody does that in real life. It would wreck my makeup and probably unpeel another decade—

'2047,' asserts my phone.

I reel at the lost years. A new narrator shapes our present. 2019: that's when I was last in real time, making my way through the autumn woods that fringed Fate's cottage, facing his front door, terrified to knock.

A new story. It's 2047, and we have a son.

Back in the lounge, I find the heat has risen with the influx of guests. The setting here is benign compared to the harsh winds of Carpathia, that dictatorial winter. I want to hug Jaime and whisper, *We made it, we made it,* but he is laughing with Eleanor. I attempt to eye-vibe him for an early departure. His lack of response doesn't even feel like resistance; more as though the connection between us has burnt away. A sadness gathers in my stomach. I can already tell that our relationship is different in this book. Our roles have shifted: Jaime is the amnesiac and I am the knower. How come Jaime has the glory of ignorance and I the cruelty of knowledge? Did he drink more Grand Kuding than me, or receive a more concentrated dose?

The party hums around me. A headache is beginning to tap my temples. I grab another glass of wine. Every time this enlightenment comes, the whiplash is fiercer. A rush of memories: the Czar's palace, the *yukuri,* our flight as birds, and before that Manchester, the record shop, my exhibition. The samskaras of these invented lives seem softer, however; worse is the pain of those months before I visited Fate: the funeral, singing 'The Lord's My Shepherd' in a battle against hysteria, my life losing shape and form.

I slip out into the empty hallway, resting my wine glass on a cabinet. Compelled by some intuition, I rifle through my bag; my fingers curl around a pillbox, decorated with a peacock lid. Inside I find a blue 100 mg lozenge of Amzipan. I consider what Jaime would want me to do: to tap him on the shoulder, tell him this is a book and seek to find a way back home. I consider our bodies, the rot of time and how with each story the danger of never being able to return grows stronger. I weigh this pill in my palm – the risk it poses versus my desire to shake off this self-consciousness, to seep into this world – and swallow it down with a mouthful of wine.

As I return to the living room, the Scriabin is no longer a torment. I can feel the drug muting the notes; there's a lovely smudging around the edges. Everyone is being ushered into a candlelit dining room. A long oak table, our names on quaint ivory place cards, each accompanied by a QR code that connects to all of the guests' Me & My pages.

Anjali's Help serves us watermelon and wheatgrass soup and pours Chardonnay into our glasses. Jaime is sitting three people away, next to Eleanor. I'm next to an old man with charming white hair and aristocratic features. Surreptitiously, I check his handle, and draw some swift conclusions from his feed: retired CEO, leftie, chauvinist. There is an empty seat where Emily should be.

I notice a RoMcKenzie on Anjali's wall. Well, this is daring: few upper-middle-class Londoners would have *Robo sapiens* art on their wall. But perhaps it's a sign of fashions shifting. It's always the way: art once loathed inevitably becomes art accepted, art loved.

Jaime entertains everyone with the story of a band who are

embarrassed that they have more robo groupies in their fan club than homo. I can feel that the entire table has been won over by him; he has become so much more confident with middle age. I notice Anjali flicking me sympathetic looks and I give her a faint smile. There is something I need to tell him, I think, reaching for my iPhone. It came to me in the toilet, but now it's slipped away.

The evening buzzes on and the alcohol flows, and the conversation inevitably turns to Tottenham. This has been the middle-class horror story of the last fortnight: a married accountant, a happy family man with two children, who made the mistake of walking alone down Tottenham High Road late on a Tuesday. A gang of thugs set upon him, calling '*Robo, Robo!*' Even when their knives drew blood, they were still convinced he was an upgrade. Only when they plunged their metal into his heart and discovered that there were no wires to pull out – his blood now wet on their hands, the sirens shrilling closer – did they realise their mistake. Jaime points out that at no point in history has it ever been wise to go walking in Tottenham at night. Anjali adds that one of the killers had been abused by a robot as a child. Eleanor chimes in that the government shouldn't have slashed robot security budgets.

The atmosphere is sober now, and everyone looks grateful at the distraction of the doorbell. In comes Emily, scattering city scents. She sits down, takes a drag of her vape and announces that she's late because she's just had sex with an HT904. She exhales strawberry-scented vapour as though she decided to save her post-coital chat for the group.

'Oh, Emily, you could have just pretended that you got

held up in traffic,' Anjali chides her, giving the Help a nervous glance. The Help then turns to Emily to pour her some wine and she gives him a wink.

'What? Nobody can scorn a woman for taking pleasure in sex, right? Our babies are made in test tubes, so our bodies are no longer vessels for reproduction. They no longer exist to serve life, they exist for our own delight! Hell, my grandmother fought for all this – back then the very idea of a woman enjoying sex was still a scandalous thing. Now, a century on, we understand the benefits of a seven-inch vibrator attached to a six-foot metal sex god.'

Laughter. A toast: 'To Emily! To sex!' Chinks and swallows. iPhones flashing, photos uploaded and auto-tagged. Jaime's wedding ring glints in the candlelight and sparkles its gold shadow-tail across my plate.

Come midnight, we're shivering on the steps of Anjali's house. My voice sounds loud and hoarse when I sing my goodbyes; Anjali's ebullient punctuation is contagious. I had a good evening and I'm all aglow. Gradually, the wine unwound me. I ended up on the sofa with Eleanor at one point, chatting about our lives, with each of us apologising for losing touch. When Jaime came in and said he was tired, he had to pull me up and drag my coat on to my shoulders. Eleanor kissed us both goodbye and hugged me tight.

The eyescan in the car zips my pupil. I rest my head against Jaime's shoulder and we watch the screen display our passage into traffic. He could drape his arm around me, he could touch my leg, but his fingers remain laced in his lap. The skyscrapers are mostly silhouettes. The lights that are on, suspended in darkness, look like stars. We only really see the clouds in the evenings these days. The corps are petitioning against the 8 p.m. ad curfew but the government has not yet caved. There is an app on my phone that identifies various cloud formations, from the thin white veils of cirrostratus to the thunderstorm broil of a cumulonimbus. When Jaime first bought it for me I thought it twee, but now it is a lifeline; I sit in my office, swiping through pages, feeding off their beauty. Night clouds are wraithlike, obfuscatory, hiding their stories.

'It was a nice evening,' I say sleepily. 'It was good to catch up with Eleanor.'

'She's doing well.' Jaime's tone is taut, but when I look up at him, he smiles. 'There was something I was going to tell you,' he says. 'But I've forgotten.'

Déjà vu of a déjà vu. I wish I could remember too.

'Hey!' I sit up, neck craning back to the street.

'What?'

'I thought I just saw Mum . . .'

'It can't have been her,' Jaime says, eyes fixed on his phone.

'No, you're right,' I frown. 'I should call her, pay her a visit. It's been ages since we . . .' I trail off, aware that he's not listening to me.

Home. The car slides into our garage. The doorman greets us. We get into the lift, pressing number 42. We're so tired that the distance from the lift to our front door seems mammoth. Tiptoeing into the flat, we take off our coats, pee without flushing. I peek into Finn's room. He is lying on his front and, in that moment, I lose my faith in the Good Parenting monitor's algorithms, and I fear his chest is still, and I am praying, pleading. Then I see it rise and fall, and I sigh relief. I kiss his head, and whisper 'I love you' in his ear. In the kitchen, the Help is in the corner in sleep mode, his red light flashing. I still always feel that he's watching me, like the God that I thought might be looking down at me from the clouds when I was a child. I slip into bed next to Jaime, touched to find that he has warmed my side for me via his Hot Water Bottle app.

I surface, the first act of a dream breaking. Jaime's fingers are tendrilling over my pubic hair; he knows just how to tease me, an act finessed over the years.

My body is responding to him, but there is something mechanical about its reaction. I murmur that I'm too tired and he murmurs that he's tired, but we keep on going. I close my eyes and feel myself becoming liquid. But something is wrong: something in the background; something in the centre of my heart, some place that refuses to open up to him. I picture it as the size and hardness of a small piece of granite. I become more and more conscious of it, until that's all I am aware of, and I stare up at him. His eyes are hollow with betrayal. It's as if I've told him I've never loved him, that he's a waste of space.

He withdraws and turns his back to me. I quickly rub his shoulder and kiss his spine, but the gesture feels more maternal than romantic. I lie with my face pressed into the pillow for a while, watching the edge of the curtain being puppeted by a draught, trying to understand the poison inside me. What has he done to create such repulsion? Our history, our past – it began with a wedding, and then there were the happy years, and Finn. But then what happened? My tiredness is torturous now, my eyes begging release. I am aware of his snoring as I sink. We sleep.

Two

What would it have been like, for me to have parted my legs, with Jaime squeezing my hand and crying, 'Push!'? What would it have been like, clawing at every last morsel inside me to make Finn appear? Or are these images clichéd? Maybe we would have been laughing as he emerged, drunk with the mad joy of it all. This thought is often there when I wake up in the mornings, with my mind still slipping and sliding between night-vague and the day ahead.

Jaime has left, so I can sprawl out across the double bed. In the shower, I manage to yank off my wedding ring by using copious amounts of soap. I drop it into the dish by the sink.

'Jaime will return in 3 days, 4 hours and 26 minutes,' my iPhone informs me when I press the Remember icon.

My appetite feels hearty; I want beans for breakfast, and toast, and eggs. I'll delay my Amzipan, which never mixes well with a big meal.

The Help is in the kitchen. I feel there is a benign air about him; it took a while to persuade Jaime of this, who teased me that I was robomorphising. Now he sees it too, though he believes it comes from the consciousness of his creator, whom he pictures as a humane and kind man.

'Good morning,' the Help greets me.

'Jaime got Finn off to school OK?' I ask.

'All is proceeding smoothly and without concern. What would you like for breakfast, Rachel?'

His arms buzz as he whisks eggs for me. When I look at him, I think of a creature from Greek mythology. The Help's upper half is sleekly homo, but his bottom is the oblong shape of a more rudimentary household device; one that wheels about and negotiates corners and stairs with ease. In the early days, they were designed with male legs, but women found hefty masculine presences in their homes too threatening, so the robots were castrated during the redesign. Women in the Western world love the Help. They were born of the sixth wave of feminism, and freed us from lives of slavery disguised as having it all; they gave us back the luxury of leisure. My mum frequently expresses envy, reminiscing about the hard labour of the hoover, which always makes me repress a smile. I'm pretty sure my mother hated housework and that we lived with dust and dirt.

'What will the weather be like today?' I ask the Help.

'Twenty-two degrees, sunny.' His expression is fixed in a permanent smile, yet it looks natural. Small talk never feels small with him. Once, during the late, drunken phase of a dinner party, I witnessed guests trying to embarrass the Help with smart-arse questions. 'What's your opinion on the Welfare Reform Bill?' someone asked, to which the Help could only reply, 'Please consult my manual, refer to paragraph one hundred and twenty-nine.' I wanted to punch them. The HTP Help model might not be sculptured to feel, but there's a principle at stake here. It's class snobbery repackaged and legitimised.

My good mood dissipates as I arrive at work. How did I end up here, sitting behind a messy desk on the forty-seventh floor, with a skyline of skyscrapers, all glinting off each other like a hall of corporate mirrors? Their reflections are tinted by the sky ads; their windows shimmer with logos. I could throw my monitor through my window and watch it shatter. The monitor would blast down and take out a group of suits, leaving blood and brain and silk ties splattered on the pavement. I try to remind myself that I'm only stuck in this office from nine to five each day, while the robots have been incarcerated here for six months now. I'm one of the lucky ones, I tell myself, trying to swallow that down like a pill. My only respite is the thought of my 2 p.m., Alek.

I am here to heal robots through art therapy. It is a position that has been created by middle managers who have little experience in either cybernetics or mental illness. They are anxious to give robo illnesses Latinate labels and are cruelly naive in their belief that the healing process will obey objectives, deadlines and targets. Since being employed on a six-month contract, I've suffered imposter syndrome. I was an artist from the age of twenty-two until my mid-thirties, when I was forced to take a job. My only knowledge of therapy comes from reading Freud for pleasure and a six-week NVKQ psychotherapy course at UCL. It was this, or face losing the flat; our vast mortgage demanding two salaries. However, I soon came to realise that Cybersenx specialises in employing bullshitters, just as long as they wear a suit and turn up to meetings and produce minutes and use expressions like 'projected growth maximisation' and 'digital customer optimisation'.

Sometimes I look beyond the skyscrapers, down to the west side, where the high-rise buildings give way to shanty-sized housing, and graffiti colours the walls. I picture an alternate me, one who busks with a guitar for pennies by day and paints by night. Then the image sours, and I see myself as a mad old female artist in a small room with mould rashing up the walls, hair greying, brushes splintering, her muse her only friend. As Jaime jokingly warns, we'd end up sitting in some smelly commune, squabbling over whose turn it is to milk the goat and kindle the fire.

A scrolling billboard outside my window makes me sit up: MILLIONS WASTED ON CYBERSENX DEFUNCTS. I can already predict the clichés that will fill the rest of the piece. My boss, Truman, will have seen it, and his foul mood will soil my day.

The Cybersenx debacle began eighteen months ago. Ten thousand Cybersenx Empaths, a new design with an IQ of 140 and qualities of profound compassion and emotional intelligence, were created as 'corporate artists.' They became known as the Storytellers. Within a year, they had made thousands of journalists, spin doctors, copy-editors, proofreaders and novelists redundant. In the early days, surreal stories began to surface. One claimed that a 'new' Charles Dickens novel had been discovered, *The Strange Death of William Mood*: it was critically lauded, until it was revealed to be a hoax. Charities became sheepish about admitting that their blogs and vlogs were written by Storytellers and the Tory party suffered a scandal when they were forced to deny that the PM's emotive election speeches - instrumental in their success - were machine-penned propaganda, funded by their sponsors. There have been numerous conspiracy theories that the robots have created the grand narratives of the past decade, harvested from the algorithms of angst, sifting through human desire in status updates, blogs and posts and weaponizing fear and prejudice.

They distracted us by demonising immigrants and the disabled, while the rich got richer and the poor got poorer.

A smaller percentage of the Cybersenx Empaths was employed as visual artists. They designed ads, or illustrated children's books and encyclopaedias. For a time, many of them were engaged in producing prints to be hung in middle-class homes. But robo art did not take off. Art has always thrived on biography – it exists in every piece like a watermark. The gentle landscapes that Pierre Bonnard painted become sinister when you learn about the love triangle he was snagged in, and the mistress who committed suicide. There was no madness in the robo artists, no sawn-off ears or suicide, no *history*. Robo artists suggested a democracy: they separated out talent from biography. All of a sudden, anyone might be a genius, regardless of their story, not only those that had the luxury of time, or those who suffered for their art. They suggested a world where there might be a metallic Da Vinci on every street. But art thrives upon hierarchies as fiercely as any capitalist corporation, and so the community closed ranks. Biography became sacrosanct, and the middle-class homes turned down robo art. The pictures ended up in office blocks, libraries, second-hand stores, and so the remit of the art Empaths had to be changed.

The scandal that finally brought the Storytellers down erupted last year. A batch of a hundred Storytellers had been produced to curate the social media accounts of celebrities. Roger Parker – a well-known author of cheesy self-help books on surviving depression – had built his reputation on posting optimistic messages of hope, until the night he quoted Nietzsche: 'The thought of suicide is a great consolation: by means of it, one gets successfully through many a dark night.' Within twenty-four hours, Storytellers were trending at number one, and Parker was spluttering apologies to his shocked fans. The robot running his account was fired, but his successor succumbed to the same fate. Commentators spoke of the depression as being contagious, as though it was a virus that spread through their collective unconscious, but I suspect it was simply a design fault that had been developing for some time.

The problem spread to other art Empaths too. Those who were supposed to be painting pastel landscapes as soothing as tea and biscuits found their work descending into a creative abyss and emerged bloody, fractured and full of night. Composers in charge of elevator music turned to modernism: scraping violins, discord, long silences.

Eight thousand robots were recalled, and the Cybersenx building effectively became an impromptu asylum. The basement and first-floor offices were converted into 'cells', where the robots were locked away 'to receive treatment and healing' before they could be redeployed. The tech guys tried and failed to reprogramme them. What could they do, they asked, for there was nothing technically wrong with their code? They were simply too evolved, that was the problem; they were too humane to thrive among humans of lower IQs and lesser hearts. That was when they hired the doctors and therapists; I was brought in to assist a group of fifty artists.

At the sound of my voice, my screen flashes awake. Prompts for updates and upgrades dance across it. They give the illusion of progress and evolution, as though my computer is becoming more *sapiens* day by day. I have a full afternoon of appointments and ten progress reports to dictate, but I can't face them. My iPhone reminds me that I still haven't taken my morning Amzipan pill, which I wash down with Volvic. It used to be more successful in dissipating my mood, but there are days when my work fury is too sharp to be soothed away.

I seem to have forgotten my email password. I reset it, see fifty or so emails that need answers, ignore them, surf the *Guardian* for half an hour, then *Frieze* magazine. I check Jaime's Me & My feed. A picture of him and the Hurdy Gurdy Men on tour, all beardy, brandishing guitars. Jaime looks happy, but his smile may just be for the optics on socials. Anjali is in the middle of posting a furious polemic. Eleanor hasn't updated her feeds for months.

For lunch, I eat a tuna sandwich and call up Orchard House. I ask if I can speak to my mum. I'm told that she's had a bad night and has been heavily sedated. When I hang up, I'm stricken with guilt. I must visit her soon, and take Finn; I'm not sure why I've been putting it off for so long. I start an idle sketch of Truman, cruelly caricaturing his features. I lose myself in pencil strokes and all of a sudden there's a knock on my door – it's 2 p.m. and I'm dazed and undimensioned.

Alek enters, accompanied by two security guards. There is something delicate in the design of his features, as if his bone structure was modelled on a pianist's. But stillness is a state of grace that eludes him; his feet dance one step, his fingers tap another, and his collar twitches as his Adam's apple rolls. The only steady thing about him is his stare: his eyes blue, his gaze direct.

I check his data on my iPad. Designed: 2039. Creator: Cybersenx Industries. Empathic Reading: 10.5. Date of Construction: 2043. Age of Truth: 2046. To be told that at the age of three . . . Late, much too late. Now, policy dictates that all newborns are taken to the Cybersenx design facilities to watch their successors being knitted together no later than aged one. The bastards who write tabloid articles about robots ought to witness that moment. I once saw a group of Empaths with tears streaming down their faces at the revelation that they were not human. Truman compared it to the moment when kids are told Santa Claus isn't real, which I thought was a trivial, patronising comparison.

My weekly sessions with Alek alternate between talking therapy and virtual reality sessions. Last week, I escorted him into a virtual gallery, where he perused landscapes, before sitting down and drawing one of his own. I had smiled and nodded support, even though his trees looked splintered and lacked blossom, his sky the colour of sickness. My boss considers the talking therapy quaint. Despite all the fuck-ups, like many men here, his belief in technology is religious.

'So, Alek, how are you feeling this week?'

'I did another painting.' His entire demeanour seems to apologise for his existence. It evokes a maternal response in me. I want to hold him, and stroke his hair.

'I saw it. It was beautiful.'

The irony doesn't escape me. We're trying to produce happy artists, when artists have traditionally been some of the most fucked-up souls in history. Artists have always refused to put up with quiet lives of desperation. They make their despair noisy, they hone it on the canvas, begging the public for the therapy of admiration.

'Nurse Schzwart says that you didn't want to go for your walk yesterday.'

'I didn't mean to upset her, but I found it distressing to watch the clouds weeping. I closed the curtains but I could still hear them. I was on my bed reading and then a fly started to buzz.

I kept trying to get his attention, I wanted him to touch me, but he seemed uncertain of me. Then he started throwing himself against the window, as though he would rather be anywhere else but in a room with me. It was crying outside but he still preferred escape rather than being with me. Like you now. I know you don't want to be here.'

'Alek,' I say gently. 'I'm very happy to be in this room with you. I'm here to help you.'

'But you're looking at your computer screen and your iPad and your iPhone. You want to look at your own face instead of mine.'

I fix my gaze on him. He stares back, and it becomes a game, each of us daring the other to look away first. The burn becomes too intense and I laugh awkwardly, breaking the moment. Alek continues to stare. Then he speaks, softly:

'I know you're feeling sad too.'

'I don't feel sad,' I reply quickly.

'You must miss him. I understand. You want to leave him, but you tried that once and it didn't work. You've been with him every day for seven years, and in that time his heart has changed. It's been filled with your dreams and your heart has filled with his. You still kiss him goodnight and lecture him on not smoking his vape because it's wired deep into your neural pathways. Your relationship is like a song that's been broken up; you've got fragments of lyrics, but it can't be sung anymore. When I leave this place, I feel your sadness and I weep it out for you.'

Our eyes meet again: more fire, shivers of desire. I try to be professional, rational: is this the cognition of his rarefied mind, or have I confided in him in the past and lost the memory? For he is right: my heart feels as though it possesses grey hairs and liver spots. I hide my unease and adopt a calm voice:

'Do you remember what we talked about, Alek? We said that if you began losing your sense of self, then you could think about creating a skin, a protective barrier.'

'I remember, yes.' It's clear that Alek is disappointed by my professionalism.

'So, shall we practise doing that now?'

'Yes.' He closes his eyes and exhales a staccato breath.

Minutes pass, and he seems more composed, but also more distant, and I have the fleeting thought that to cure him would be to lose him.

We talk for a further twenty minutes. A colleague of mine, Claire, whom I regard as a proper psychotherapist (in contrast to my paltry training), often tells me that when a patient turns up, what they say is wrong with them is rarely what's actually wrong with them. It's just part of their defence mechanism, a distraction from what's going on underneath. I conceal my frustration with Alek, my failure to penetrate. His IQ is twenty points higher than mine. Perhaps I'm simply not smart enough to sidestep his defence mechanisms – like the computer who beat Kasparov, he will always see enough moves ahead to out-manoeuvre me. I suffer the egotism of it all: here I am, a mess of insecurities, in a job I hate, in a fraying marriage, yet playing the role of Dr Sane, making a narrative out of Alek's scraps, giving them meaning, detecting patterns of fate. If you set me down before a canvas, you would find rage streaked in my oils too.

'OK, Alek. I'll see you on Tuesday at three p.m. You're doing very well.'

I offer my hand for him to shake. My palm jerks as he lifts it and bestows a kiss on it. A frisson shivers in my blood. The blue of his eyes is the shade of a delicate dawn. He maintains eye contact and I feel dismantled, as though he is the human and I the robot, every digit of my emotion assessed and labelled in Linnaean order. I am saved by security. Before Alek is led away he looks at me as though I am the creator of this system rather than merely a cog in it.

I wrestle with my guilt. Cybersenx is corrupt, but I'm one of the few who actually cares about the robots. Alek must know that. The bad guys are the suits. The bad guys are the politicians. The bad guys are those in the right-wing press who spew out their reductionist headlines every day: DEFUNCTS LANGUISH IN CYBERSENX FOR $2M A DAY AT TAXPAYERS' EXPENSE. The journalists who see life in economic terms, who declare that euthanasia is the logical solution. Those who believe that robots do not have souls remind me of those Victorian preachers who proclaimed that animals would never get through the gates of heaven. I have argued this in public: euthanising an individual is a kindness, but euthanising a race is genocide. Cheers and sneers from a divided audience. We are only one government bill away from this place turning into death row.

Three

I scroll through the photos from Anjali's dinner party. A shot of Jaime, grinning, and Eleanor, with her hand on his shoulder, her fair hair haloing her lovely face. The photo of me is irksome, and so I untag myself, deleting it from my timeline.

I get through three more therapy sessions, and dictate my patients' notes to my Mac. It is 4.34 p.m. and I am just packing up my things with the intention of sneaking out early when a notification pops up: 'Truman requests a meeting.' I sit for a few minutes, struggling with a burning heat in my stomach and a trembling in my hands. I check what we discussed in our last meeting. Then I look up my boss's Me & My feed, seeking intel. His biog has been recently amended with the addition of 'male feminist.'

I'm still a little fuzzy from the Amzipan; I need some caffeine for balance. I head for floor 45 for a takeaway. There are fifteen cafes in this damn building. They sport various brand names but all are owned by the same franchise and produce a coffee that tastes thin, as though not made from the glossy beans on display on the counter but some kind of gravel hiding in Nescafé jars in the back. Jaime and I once discussed how capitalism, in its extremity, narrows choice with the same degree that Communism does, thanks to burgeoning monopolies. You're still left buying the same trainers, same iPhones, same cars: products of a corporate dictatorship. Jaime attempts to buck the trend by buying from ethical online stores at twice the price, but I'm sceptical. If you're living in a capitalist society, capitalism isn't the enemy living outside of you, it's the parasite inside you, and its hooks are deep in your gut. You post status updates and you network in order to raise your profile; you climb the social ladder and you stamp on your colleagues in order to get that promotion. In order to truly rebel against it, Jaime complains, you'd have to live a life of failure and poverty, and make your peace with everyone around you becoming a 'have', while you succumb to being ever more a 'have-not'.

Back in my office, I mull on the recent rumours of redundancies, and fret that this might be the reason for our meeting. I've only taken a few sips of coffee before Truman raps on the door and barges into the room. His handshake is as limp as a sea creature. A week ago, I overheard him discussing this approach with a colleague in the lift. *Business Weekly* recently declared that a crushing handshake is out of fashion, given that it suggests metal fingers, a wired hand.

'I haven't much time,' he snaps, as though I am the one who's kept him waiting. I nod briskly.

I guide him down the corridor to the gallery. The painting efforts of fifty Cybersenx Empaths hang on the walls. This week they were given Constable's 'The Valley Farm'. A small percentage of the paintings look well behaved; the Empaths have copied Constable quietly and faithfully. Most, however, have veered unintentionally towards post-impressionism. Their colours are loud, their trees look frenzied, and their landscapes curdle with melancholy. I am reminded of that painting Van Gogh worked on in the asylum he spent his last years in, where the trees appear in a state of flux, as though they are transforming into something strange and beautiful, almost animal. I forget its name.

Truman checks my report on his phone. 'Only ten per cent are producing what might be deemed "harmonious pictures".'

'Forty per cent are in the "satisfactory" bracket,' I point out quickly.

'And fifty per cent in the "unsatisfactory".' Truman glares at one particular painting: a cow standing in a country landscape looks like the bovine equivalent of 'The Scream'. 'Who did this one?'

It's Alek's work. 'I need to check the files,' I say quickly. I add, 'You know, the middle classes don't all want attractive landscapes hanging on their walls.'

'There's plenty of stats to prove that a landscape is the most soothing picture for the human eye,' Truman retorts.

'Artists were once the revolutionaries, the guys the state wanted to hunt down and lock up. "Avant garde" was originally a military term.'

'All the more reason to wipe out that malicious algorithm and produce art of a fine quality,' Truman snaps. 'I hope, Rachel, you appreciate what you're here for and what you're trying to achieve.'

I ought to back down, but I can't stop myself.

'All I'm saying is – painting a landscape doesn't make you *nice* or the people who look at it *nice*. Hitler painted landscapes before he went into politics.'

'But they were awful paintings, weren't they?' Truman smiles, as though we're critics sharing a joke. 'He lacked perspective and couldn't get the dimensions right . . . We're getting off-subject, Rachel. We need progress within the next three weeks. We need eighty per cent of painting in the "positive" range. The new offices being built in Canada Water require pleasant paintings on each floor. That is what our client wants and what we are here to deliver. You can manage that, can't you?' he says, with a faint sneer.

This is what irks me most about Truman: he knocks digits off my IQ, renders my gender a disability, my qualifications a joke. Our enemies caricature us. Only with our true friends and lovers can we be complex.

We stand in silence for a minute, staring at the pictures, Truman twitching beside me. I think of my studio back home, where my canvas and paints sit, slowly acquiring a layer of dust.

'Why not just wipe all the Empaths clean and create a batch of sociopaths?' I suggest. My sarcasm is lost on him; his face falls slack as he considers the possibility. There is fear in his eyes. Perhaps he too suffers from insomnia, worrying about targets and demotions. I wonder if this project is merely paying lip service to the government, a weak effort so that they can say, *We tried, we did our best, but failure was inevitable*. I wonder if the target is deliberately impossible, if I am being set up to fail.

As we say goodbye, he offers his hand again, but I pretend not to notice it. Hauling my bag on to my shoulder, I walk out. The lift falls a hundred floors; our argument replays a hundred times in my head. I get into the car, worrying once more about the talk of redundancies, wondering why Truman failed to mention them. I pray to lose my job; I pray to keep it.

Four

At the start of our marriage, Jaime and I made a pact never to have kids. We both laughed about how immature we were, how procreation was far too grown-up and scary.

He had a girlfriend called Eleanor when I first met him. My fourth exhibition, Metamorphoses, was being staged at the Serpentine, and Jaime turned up to interview me for some blog. He had a parrot with him; he was pet-sitting. We had coffee in a cafe the next day. I was won over by his Italianate gestures and his attempts to roll a cigarette: a vintage quirk I found endearing. I was, by this time, aware that art was no longer enough for me: success was a drug I'd become used to, and now I craved disruption. I thought that I wanted a love affair, though, looking back, I wonder if this was just a yearning to self-destruct.

Nonetheless, we fell for the thrill of secret trysts in hotel rooms, games of spanking and chase, confessions under the covers. There were arguments too, mostly concerning my failure to paint him, and then over a portrait of him that was too honest. Back then, fighting only brought us closer. It was the growing tenderness that made us feel uneasy, fearing our desire would be replaced by the complications of love. Our break-up was mutual – he was still with Eleanor, and the guilt got the better of us both. It lasted ten days. In that time, I barely ate. I had to drag myself out of bed every morning and would sit before my canvas with my brush raw on the page – until I heard the message on my voicemail, the one that poured life back into me, where Jaime said he couldn't survive without me. I played it over and over. I loved the moment where his voice cracked on the word 'please'. I'd never heard him cry before.

Eleanor was surprisingly gracious about the whole thing. She said that she'd felt she and Jaime were not meant to be, and she was dating someone new within a year, a Russian guy called Radomir. They adopted two kids, Ellie and George. We all managed to stay good friends.

Jaime and I exchanged a scarlet affair for the pastels of domesticity. I think we were surprised by how happy it made us, to sit at home in the evenings, being boring, watching TV under a blanket together. I was conscious that I woke up every day with colours tingling in my fingertips, finding release on a canvas, while Jaime had to brave the underground and slave away in an office. He'd always wanted to be in a band, and played lead guitar for a few years, before his aspiration pivoted to becoming a manager instead. We spent years working on his company and shaping it into a success. I designed his logo; band posters; album images. Gradually, my canvases sat blank and forgotten. I had become my muse's muse. My fifth exhibition was shown at a small gallery in Burlington Gardens, and I only sold five paintings. At my sixth, I sold none at all.

In our mid-thirties, we came under pressure from friends, who cooed over their little darlings and attempted to convert us. We were glad to leave and bitch about them afterwards, agreeing on how exhausting it all looked. Whenever I felt uncertain about our decision not to have children, it was helpful to find historical precedents, a habit I and my friends picked up at art school. The great artists became our gurus, not only in matters of technique, but in how to live. Picasso, Modigliani, Bacon, de Kooning, Freud: they suggested that a conventional life was not an artistic one. But what about female artists? They were often models or muses first, artists second, spending hours in cramped shapes, or freezing in a bathtub, their pain parasited by men, translated into beauty on the canvas. Male artists were free to run wild, fuck muses, crash cars. Women were tasked with stopping the crashes.

But biology defeated us both in the end. Jaime got the bug first, but I followed soon after. Being self-absorbed comes naturally in your twenties, when life is there to be conquered, but self-absorption in your thirties becomes a torture. I grew envious of the way parents were able to redirect their energy away from their petty lives, and on to their offspring. I felt the urge to love and nurture. And so we decided to start a family. Jaime and I had agreed to share the parental responsibilities equally, so I would still have time for my art.

Against the advice of everyone we knew, we tried the old-fashioned way. Twelve weeks later, we were at a party when I felt something hot slipping down my thigh and realised it was blood. It took us a year after the loss to feel ready to follow the standard path. We consulted brochures for various insemination labs and calculated budgets, tentatively allowing ourselves to feel excited about the responsibility we were about to weigh ourselves down with.

I stare out of the car window, across the playground of St Raphael's School. A teacher, Mrs Suma, comes up, holding the hand of a small boy, and raps on the window. The moment I look into his eyes, my love is pure and overwhelming. His face is ghosted with Jaime's genes – his blue eyes and his freckles – but I can see traces of me in his nose, and in the curve of his lips. He is my angel, my genius, my boy. Then I become aware of the teacher telling me that she needs to talk to me about my son. I take his hand and we share a conspiratorial smile as we follow her across the playground.

We called him Finn because Dr Abrams advised us to do so. It was part of the package: a new Microsoft-sponsored Nominative Determinism programme that calculated the best name, height, eye colour, size of cerebral cortex, and more, according to current cultural tastes, to ensure a life of success. This upset me. I'd been leafing through baby name books, joking with Jaime that we might call him Lysander. After weeks of warfare, we'd found common ground in 'Martin'. But when the computer overrode us with 'Finn', how could we reject it? The moment Martin was bullied or failed an exam, we would suffer guilt that we had wilfully and purposefully bestowed a name on him that was out of joint with the world, that we'd held him back. So Finn it was.

I've never believed in those bullshit stories about how conception dictates the destiny of a child. I've always believed that, like most things in life, it is the day-to-day that governs the end result. Milk and bedtime stories; football and lessons in morality: the algorithms of parenting. And yet, Finn's conception lingered in my mind: the knowledge that he had been made not through an act of ecstatic abandonment but by a surgeon inserting a needle through my vaginal wall to suck out my eggs, while Jaime masturbated into a cup behind a white curtain. I often wondered what he'd fantasised over, whether it had been me or some fantasy woman who had coaxed the sperm from his body. It cast a shadow over the early days of pregnancy, which was softened by the thrill of mammograms, seeing our dearest take shape in the Imber womb, charting his progress from creature to character. We were informed of his birth and sent daily updates on his rapid progress.

Freud states that the first five years of a child's life are crucial to the formation of their adult personality. But neither Jaime nor I wanted to give up work. We loathed the idea of a robo nanny, and *Homo sapiens* childcare was now such a rarity that the expense was colossal. Finn was therefore designed to live a five-year express childhood in the labs at Imber. His personality would develop with speed but would not be compromised, the doctor assured us. I think he thought my background in Freud was rather quaint.

The first day that we met him was scored so deep that I will never forget it. We'd hardly slept the night before; we'd been waiting to meet him for a year. In the Imber reception, we sat and teased through glossy magazines with glazed eyes until Dr Abrams finally came out clutching the hand of a small boy. Jaime's eyes and freckles; the cutest smile a boy could have. I opened my arms for him and he stepped forwards, then paused, uncertain, surveying us. When I greeted him, he didn't say a word.

He remained very quiet on the way home. Jaime and I kept up the cheery chatter – 'Look at the sky ad for Nike!' 'Look at the library – we can go there for books!' We asked him if he was excited to see his new room at least three times, and each time Finn merely nodded with a quiet authority, as though he was decades older than us. By the time we reached the flat, Jaime and I were struggling to hide our panic. We'd studied all the manuals, but nothing had quite prepared us for this moment where *connection* was required. What were we thinking, imagining that we could be parents?

We guided Finn to the Alexa panel in the living room and got him to repeat his name until her system had absorbed his voice. Then we showed him how to command the flat: 'Curtains – open!' or 'TV – on!' Finn muttered the words shyly at first, and then with more confidence, until we were all smiling as curtains swished back and forth and the TV skipped through Netflix shows. I think it made him feel as though he had a modicum of control, that he too could be a miniature master in our home.

That first night, I found myself waking in the early hours. I saw that Jaime was awake too. He turned and whispered, 'How can we be sure he's ours, that he's even *real*?' Despite my own doubts, I told him off sharply. I pointed out that we'd been given the DNA test as security. Even so, those first few weeks were a struggle of clichéd modern middle-class angst: that Imber still had our real baby locked in a room and this was a robot cuckoo child. Our paranoia gradually faded across a hundred bedtimes and bath times.

I missed my mother ardently during those weeks. We eventually took Finn to visit her at Orchard House, where she cooed over him. Her advice was a conspiratorial: 'Get a pencil in his hand and get him drawing as young as possible.' Many years before she went into the home, I remember her telling me that the first night you have a baby, you suffer a baptism of fire when you hear the shrill of cries and rise for that first feed, realising that from now on, your own needs must come second to your child. Had we cheated by skipping that moment of surrender?

One day, we drove past the Imber Eugenics Building and Finn cried out, 'Mummy, Mummy!' Jaime and I were mortified. It took a while to coax Finn into calling me by this name instead.

Our meeting with Mrs Suma ends, and I return to the car with Finn's 'troubled' drawings tucked under my arm. I was resistant to seeing them as Rorschach blots, and instead pointed out that there is often a gap between creator and their creations, which are not always a blueprint for their soul. *But Finn is still your child and you must mould him*, Mrs Suma had insisted firmly, as though I was Pygmalion.

'Mummy,' Finn cries. 'Look – it's spitting!' he laughs and points at the window. 'The rain is being rude.'

I smile, infected by his delight in the world, his ability to make the mundane marvellous.

'The sky is weeping,' I say.

As the car passes the outskirts of Shantytown, Finn quietens, nose pressed against the glass. The streets are narrowing, the houses shrinking, the pavements busy and filthy. A woman drifts down the street, her smile too broken to lure in punters. Feminism still remains the privilege of the wealthy; poverty traps women in the past. Her tired eyes meet mine. She looks as though she would like to lie down and sleep for a century. I feel guilty for my morning fantasies, where I dreamt of an alternate life as an artist in one of these huts, for that would mean a life of poverty for Finn. If I am trapped, I tell myself, kissing his forehead fondly, then the pain is worth it for the life we have.

In the warm of the flat, we are greeted by the Help. Finn hugs him, and chatters excitedly about school. As the Help hangs our coats, I notice that while his movements are only infinitesimally slower than last week, they are a marked deterioration compared to last month. He is due for a service in June. Their verdict is sure to repeat last year's: *It would be cheaper to just replace him than spend on all these new parts . . .*

'Rachel—'

'Mummy.'

'Mummy, can I get a pet dodo for my birthday?'

'I'm not sure,' I say, at last.

Finn senses weakness. He goes in for the hard sell: 'Dad thought it was a bad idea, so you could do it to annoy him.'

'Finn!' I berate him and then succumb. 'I'll talk to the guys at the pet shop.'

'*Yes*!' Finn punches the air and I laugh. I know I'm the more lenient parent. Jaime says I indulge him too much.

The Help serves pasta for dinner. As I bite into it, I feel something in my mouth, like a little piece of granite, which I roll until it sits on the tip of my tongue. Finn chides me for playing with my food. I give him a gentle swat, and he giggles.

'It's a filling.' I curl my tongue around my back tooth, feeling the strange absence.

'It looks like a robot part,' Finn says anxiously. One of his school friends, Jefferson, found out that his new stepmum was a robot and has been teased at school ever since.

'Well, you can rest assured that both of your parents are *Homines sapientes*, even if we have bad teeth,' I reassure him and he looks relieved.

After dinner, I call up Orchard House and ask to speak to my mother. A long pause, fuzzy with the sounds of background chatter: the drone of a TV, a shrieking woman, a doctor being called. Then, my mother's voice, bright as a balloon: 'Rachel!'

I promise her we will visit soon, which can sometimes prompt a 'Fuck off, stay away,' but on this occasion she sounds pleased, and asks to speak to Finn. He holds my mobile tight to his ear, eyes widening as he listens, and concludes, 'I promise I won't tell anyone, Grandma.' Afterwards, I try to coax the secret out of him, but he mimes a zip across his lip, shaking his head stubbornly.

It takes me an hour to get Finn into bed. On my Kindle is *The Humanist Book of Classic Fairy Tales*, retold by minor, marginalised characters. The Remember app reminds me where I left off last night. I read aloud the tale of Cinderella as told from the viewpoint of an ugly sister who learns that her jealousy is petty and childish.

The idealist in me loves teaching Finn morals; the realist fears for his shocked moment of truth when he realises the world functions according to the survival of the fittest. The robot Empaths we treat possess the typical weakness of a depressive: they are prone to seeing themselves as victims of fate. I try to reslant their perspective to help them feel like they have some control over their lives. But I do not practise what I preach. Jaime often tells me off for pointing out omens – both good and bad – in front of Finn. He is determined that we should bring up our son as an atheist.

Story over, I kiss Finn goodnight and watch as he goes to sleep. I head into our study. This room was meant to be my studio, but we ended up sharing it. The walls are dominated by posters of Jaime's bands. There are portraits of Jaime on the furthest side. I've painted one every year of our marriage as an anniversary gift for him.

I unwrap a canvas, blow away the dust, and set it on my easel. This pent-up energy has been awaiting release all day, but now that I'm here I feel numb. There was that abstract artist, who saw talent in her husband and moulded him into a genius – so much so that he was said to be her Frankenstein. What were their names? I can hear Jaime's voice in my mind, joking that I am going senile. The husband enjoyed huge success, and then, bored and hungry for a new direction, he painted a series of black paintings. He poured black duco paint onto unprimed canvas, painted using sticks and basting syringes and old brushes that had become stiff. The public, who loved the lurid colours of his prior work, found this new direction to be bleak, and he didn't sell a single picture. His depression spiralled, his drinking worsened, and a few years later he drove his car into a tree, decapitating himself, killing a female passenger and injuring his mistress.

I tell myself that I will not get up, I will not google them. If I cannot sit still in front of an easel for fifteen minutes then what kind of artist am I? Yet I feel as though there is already a layer of paint between me and the canvas: it is thick, white enamel, and I am drenched in it, my hand heavy with it, so that any movement demands a huge effort.

I look up at the portraits of Jaime. In the one from last year, Jaime's face lacks a neck, as though he's been beheaded. It hovers behind transparent bars, his features a murky swirl of oils. I take my Amzipan and stare at the earlier pictures, where the love in my brushstrokes is palpable, until the granite ball in my heart grows tighter and it hurts to breathe.

Five

On my way to work the next morning, I head into Starbucks, stalked by a lingering sense of unease. I have checked the Remember app on my iPhone three times, but I'm all up to date, so I can't account for this feeling of having forgotten something important. Then, in the queue, I find tears suddenly spilling from my eyes. I can't identify a cause. Did I remember to take my Amzipan? I swallow down a lozenge, risking a double dose. I tell myself that I must be feeling nervous about my job. Claire just emailed me to say that the rumours are true – there's been a first round of redundancies.

The waiter brings over my latte. I am enchanted by his youth more than his obvious pulchritude. The blue of his eyes reminds me of Alek's. A kid at a nearby table points at him and calls, 'Robot! Robot!' Half the cafe turns to give him horrified glances over their coffees and iPads.

'I'm actually a *Homo sapiens*,' he says in a defensive voice.

'I'm so sorry,' the mother says. 'Do you receive tips directly?'

The waiter nods, though he doesn't look appeased.

'Kit, don't be racist,' she chides her son, who looks fascinated by the attention he's attracting. I give the woman a sympathetic glance, that of a mother who knows the story, but she ignores me.

When the waiter comes over, I give him a flirty smile. It's automatic, a smile that has not yet adjusted to the changes that age have wrought on me. I see his eyes widen, faintly appalled. The funhouse reflection of me in my coffee spoon slaps me back into reality. I watch him surreptitiously as he flirts with a younger, pretty girl, her ponytail swishing as she laughs. I pity her as much as I envy her. It has been a liberation to not be defined by my appearance, for people to listen to what I say rather than translating my body into their own instinctive language. With men, however, exchanges have become more complex. Sometimes they make me feel invisible, a painting which has been removed from a gallery and thrust into a basement to gather dust. Even the intonation of my voice has changed, become more forceful.

I decide not to leave a tip. Then, fearing I will seem petty, I leave $100.

I'm sitting in my office, looking at my pillbox. I have a feeling it was a present from Jaime. My memory of receiving it is a little like a Monet painting: when I come up close and attempt to hone in on the detail, all I can see are dots of colour. I'm not even entirely sure why I'm taking the Amzipan beyond the fact that Jaime reminds me to take it, and I've heard Finn pick up his echo and say, 'Take your brain sweeties, Mummy!'

My iPad tells me that I have a 9.45 a.m.: Jessica Chelmsford. My least favourite client. She's not even part of the Cybersenx debacle, just a patient I've been forced to treat as she's a close family friend of Truman's. I ought to go over her notes in the five minutes before she arrives. Instead, I type 'Amzipan' into Google. A sedative, it says. Manufactured by Cybersenx Pharmaceuticals.

I rattle through email searches, and eventually find a prescription. The Walton Clinic named in the header. I go to type their number into my phone, only to find it is already saved under 'Samskaras'. A receptionist answers and says she'll put me through to Dr Lerner, and at that precise moment, there's a knock at the door.

'I'll call you back,' I mutter in haste.

Jessica Chelmsford shakes out her hair; it's been raining outside. I feel wistful for Alek, but I'm not due to see him for another few days. When she speaks, I note that her consonants have acquired a metallic edge. The story she relays is about a dinner party that took place at the weekend.

'The hostess kept on at me with every course. Even at the end, she was trying to get me to take coffee and mints. She said that if I didn't eat, I'd faint. Why play such a cruel game with me, in front of everyone – it was bullying, really. In the end, I ate the stupid mints just to shut her up – and the next thing I knew, I was on the floor, feeling sick.'

'Patient fainted,' I type. I glance at my pillbox again, trying to recall a start date. The box looks tarnished, as though I've been using it for several months.

'And you woke up in a hospital, right? How did that feel?'

'I knew they'd rewired me while I was sleeping, so I felt better. But I still felt like I had fused in places, as though parts of me were burnt out . . .'

Jessica Chelmsford's syndrome had been diagnosed as *mentis morbum metallum* before she started seeing me. Her husband was the chief executive of Chelmsford-Parker Industries. After he confessed to an affair with his secretary, Jessica locked herself in her bedroom for several days and refused to eat. When she finally emerged, she was unnervingly calm. She said next to nothing to him, and quietly moved out. However, within a few days, she was visiting her doctor and asking to be rewired. She was convinced that her husband was her creator, and she wouldn't agree to a divorce until he acknowledged this in writing. Her refusal to eat, for fear of causing her system to malfunction, has caused her to lose two stone in the last three weeks. Her hands are so skeletal that the bones appear like wiring beneath her skin. Truman has warned me that if I can't help her, she will soon end up in hospital.

As she watches me tapping notes on to my iPad, a sly look comes over her face.

'Has yours left you too?'

'I'm sorry?'

'Your husband.' She nods at my hand, where my wedding ring has left a watermark on the skin. 'You're a robot. You're designed to satisfy him. Why do they do it? I don't understand.'

'If I was such a thing, I can assure you that I wouldn't be allowed to practise,' I state, but she gives me a wry smile, as though we're complicit in a secret pact.

The moment she has gone, before I can talk myself out of it, I call up the Walton Clinic again. I have a fifteen-minute conversation with Dr Lerner, in which I learn the truth.

Six months ago, Jaime and I made an appointment at his clinic and requested that I join the Samskaras programme. We had reached a point in our marriage where divorce seemed inevitable. I had told Dr Lerner that I felt as though my heart was stuck in a conceptual loop, forever unable to forgive Jaime for the wrongs he had done me. We could not bear to split up, however, because of the effect on Finn. An Imber report on the impact of our divorce indicated that Finn would have a 35% higher chance of ending up an adult divorcee himself, and would be 27% more likely to suffer from a mental illness.

Redemption, my doctor explains, is a journey from experience back to innocence. I needed to regress to an earlier, happier state, and wipe myself free of negative samskaras.

The twice-daily dosage of Amzipan, Dr Lerner explains, has blocked specific memories from the past eight months. To remember something, he goes on, the brain synthesises new proteins – specifically, a protein called PKMzeta – to stabilise circuits of neural connections. The Amzipan is able to block the PKMzeta associated with the experiences I wished to forget, thus freeing me from them.

'But why?' I ask. 'What the hell happened with me and my husband that I'd need to take this kind of dose?'

He clears his throat and I realise how stupid my question is.

'If I tell you, it will defeat the entire point of taking the medication.' He advises that I should book a follow-up appointment, but the meeting won't take place for another eleven days, because he's about to head to the Alps for a skiing holiday.

I put the iPhone down and stare at it. Then I pick it up again and I call Jaime.

'Hey,' he says, his voice soft. My reception is poor, his face flickering on my screen, but I think he looks pleased to see me.

'Hi – how's it going?'

He yawns. 'Knackered – Hurdy Gurdy went down a storm though. I should be back for eight on Thursday.' Pause. 'Are you OK?'

I take a breath, bracing myself for what we're about to discuss – but instead I find myself telling him about my filling falling out and how it might mean a root canal.

'Does it hurt?'

'Well – not really. I mean, it's just an absence. It feels a little strange.'

'There was that footie player who lost a tooth and it really affected his playing – he lost his sense of balance, it totally fucked him up.' There is an awkward silence and we both laugh. 'I realised halfway through telling you that anecdote that it probably wasn't going to help.'

We briefly discuss his return tomorrow – he tells me that there's no need for me to wait up if his flight gets delayed – and then there is a silence. 'Dr Lerner . . .' is forming on my tongue, when Jaime says that the band are throwing a tantrum and swiftly ends the call.

I take my pillbox and toss my evening dosage into the bin. Then I open my desk drawers, take out the Amzipan box, and throw that away too.

Six

During the night, I dream of Alek. When I wake I feel soiled with sex and scarlet images, wondering if I'm more attracted to him than I've admitted. I rise and pull on my dressing gown, hungry to give Finn a morning hug. I love watching the Help set down food in front of him, seeing the relief on his face, the knowledge that he is loved and protected. The simplicity of this routine will purge me of the night's subconscious betrayals.

After breakfast, I slip into our study and switch on Jaime's computer. I find his Me & My; he's logged in. I scroll through updates about his bands and Finn, exchanges with fans. No clues, no hints. I realise that seeking the truth on social media is hopeless. These pages are little more than adverts of our lives, a constructed, commodified persona to tell everyone that we are worth knowing, that we are leading enviable lives. I hear Dr Lerner's echo: *You went on the Samskaras programme to save your marriage, divorce was inevitable.* But which of us was to blame? There is a coin endlessly spinning in my mind: will it land on Jaime or me?

At work, Claire emails me that her stupid boss is out for the day with my stupid boss, so I meet her for a coffee at the fifth floor cafe.

'Did you see that Labour have U-turned? It looks like the bill might go through,' she says.

'Oh God,' I cry. The working-class vote has swung in favour of the Robot Euthanasia Bill, driven by disgruntled workers who have lost their jobs to AI, with still no sign of a universal basic income. I picture how it might happen: a technician entering a cell and hitting a few buttons, as Alek's consciousness is slowly erased. I've read all the arguments in the press: once rebooted, it will be as though he is reborn, memory cleansed, his mind a blank slate. But what right do we have to play God? Truman once infuriated me by saying that it was no different to wiping your internet history and a string of annoying cookies. I think of my own privileged position, compared to the robots': now I've ditched the Amzipan, my memories will return, like data files I can retrieve. I shiver.

'If it goes through, we could lose our jobs overnight, you know,' Claire says. 'There are loopholes in our contracts . . .'

'It'll be a PR nightmare as it is,' I whisper. 'Why would they make it worse?'

'It's easy to bury bad news if there's already a shitstorm.'

I find myself telling Claire about that story from the Vedas – from *Vasistha's Yoga*, I think. It's about three demons who are invincible in their state of newly created innocence; but as experiences weigh them down with impressions and desires form, they acquire ego, fear and weakness. Perhaps there is a kind of freedom in being without samskaras? But then I think of Alek again and suffer the threat of angry tears: 'We can't let that bill go through.'

With Truman absent, I slip out early for my dental appointment. My car picks me up and we're slugging through the city jams, when I cry out, 'Stop! Pull over!'

I get out of the car, wondering if I am mistaken. I thought Jaime was still in Istanbul – he's not due in until tomorrow evening – but there he is, three feet in front of me, without luggage, in jeans and a leather jacket. I follow him at a distance.

Perhaps he has returned early because of a work meeting . . . On those rare occasions when I've visited Jaime in his office, he has seemed a different person to me. His secretary came out to offer me a choice of tea or coffee and I wanted to laugh, for I could see that she was in awe of him. In awe of my Jaime, who burped, who moaned about his headaches and insomnia and growing bald patch, who drank prune juice to ease his occasional bouts of constipation, who was gripped by the fear that everyone he knew secretly hated him from time to time. Sometimes when we went to showcases together, wannabe musicians would approach Jaime, often with parents in tow, begging for 'Mr Lancia' to manage them. Jaime was always polite and charming to them, but proud too; he was well aware that he was a kingmaker in his world. I enjoyed these glimpses of him, but I also became conscious of the illusion of our intimacy. Our work lives were summed up over dinner in vignettes. By day, we were strangers, living by different customs in the different continents of our workplaces.

Jaime's dark head bobs in the crowd. Memories are coming back to me, vague in shape but evoking one certainty: we've been here many times. This road, the Darwin temple – Jaime used to come here all the time. We argued over whether Finn should attend. Memories are our shared history, the foundation of our relationship. Whatever has gone wrong between us, we can surely sort it out.

Then I realise that he has gone into the Darwin temple. I follow him in. The interior is hewn from white marble. It reminds me of the Natural History Museum; a carved Darwin sits on his throne, gazing down on his congregation. The main chamber has been built to mimic a church and the stained-glass windows depict famous philanthropists. There are long benches too, which one has to remember not to call 'pews.' I'm not quite convinced that the collective term for the group inside – 'audience' – strikes the right note, suggesting a desire to be entertained rather than enlightened. I feel wistful, suddenly, for my meditation: to sit in the quiet and repeat my mantra; to feel my thoughts soften and slip into the bliss of transcendence. I've fallen out of the habit in the last few years. I recall how, when I practised consistently during my twenties, it began to reshape my sense of destiny, so that life began to gift me good fortune, as though responding to my inner transformation.

Jaime sits down in the middle of a row. I'm tempted to join him, but he's glancing around as though expecting someone. So I stay seated right at the back, concealed by other audience members, ducking my face into an order of service.

The humanist minister rises before the lectern. He's wearing the usual uniform: black trousers and a black shift that reaches his thighs. His grey hair is spruce, his voice clipped and elegant. He possesses an authoritative, slightly snide air. I immediately recognise him as Dominic Paterson, a right-wing intellectual. He had a breakdown a few years ago, which led to a series of 'revelations.' When women have breakdowns, they take pills and suffer in quiet desperation; when men have breakdowns, they elevate their angst into philosophy, acquire followers, build a cult.

'We punish those who break the law, but every sentence passed by a judge reflects the *intent* behind that crime – if a defendant pleads guilty, or says they are sorry, the punishment will be reduced. Three weeks ago, newspapers reported on a tragic story: a gang of thugs killed a man, mistaking him for a robot. These men are now in prison in HMP Wandsworth, on remand. They will soon stand trial. But what of robots who commit crimes? Does the blame lie with them, or their creators? What does it mean if a robot says sorry, and admits guilt? In this country, when a robot commits a crime, we rightly shut them down. "Capital punishment", some call it, but we know they are not sentient. But for this very reason, I've been wondering whether justice is really being served. In the US, the creator is now the subject of blame too. And, following the first successful litigation against Cybersenx, there has now been a flood of claims.

'We must remember that the "moment of truth", when robots discover they are artificial rather than human, is a concept Cybersenx introduced. Yes, they invented it! And we just accepted it. What's more, there were far fewer crimes committed by robots prior to its introduction. And so we *must* now debate the value of this "moment of truth". Saul Smilansky argued that we cannot allow people to know they do not have free will, and that society must therefore defend this illusion, otherwise immorality proliferates. Perhaps robots, in discovering that they are created, believing that their will has been programmed, feel less inclined to take responsibility . . .'

A young blonde woman suddenly enters, mouthing a 'sorry' to Paterson. She spots Jaime and slips in beside him. I swallow, watching them greet each other. She kisses him on each cheek, flirtatiously close to his lips. His expression becomes boyish, vulnerable. Once that look was an original painting that belonged to me, and now I've discovered there are cheap replicas printed everywhere. It's obvious that she is at least fifteen years younger than him. I glance around the rest of the group, hoping to catch others giving him reproving looks, whispering about a midlife crisis. But everyone is gazing up at the lectern.

She looks familiar. And when she turns her head, her profile enlightens me: *Ellie*. Eleanor's adopted daughter. My heart smashes out swift, trembling beats. So this is why he's had me taking pills? So that his affair can be shoved into some filing cabinet, and remain shut away in my mind?

Paterson smiles modestly as his oratory is met with applause. Now for the finale of his service, where a speech is always followed by a 'spectacle'. He announces that he has invited a robot here who is in need of a miracle. Her wiring is broken; she sits in a wheelchair. I watch Jaime and Ellie sit up with interest.

'As Schopenhauer says, "Man can do what he wills to do; but he cannot determine what he wills."'

Jaime's head turns as though he can sense my presence. I dread that he might see me, but when his gaze falls a row short of where I'm sitting I feel disappointed. In that moment, I hate him for following such a clichéd narrative. I used to joke with him that the average midlife crisis begins aged eighteen and finishes at around sixty-five. Then the ache comes: I want to be young with him again. I want to be a teenager, lying with him in the grass, kissing on a summer's day in the park, not caring if strangers see us.

Paterson turns to the robot in the wheelchair and places his palms on her in the manner of a blessing: on her forehead, her shoulders, her legs. When she stands up, the audience bursts into laughter at the performance. Jaime smiles at Ellie's loud, nervous giggle. Paterson explains that, thanks to the technology of Cybersenx Corp., the sponsorship of the Windown foundation and the pioneering scientists of Guy's Hospital, she is now able to walk. The robot gives us a demonstration, strutting up and down the aisle, looking rather like Cybersenx's earlier designs, before they discontinued the models with human legs. Paterson ruins the irony of the moment with his ego-swell, unable to resist breaking into an elated, smug smile, as though the ability to heal really does flow through his hands.

I glance at Jaime one last time. I can hardly believe he has reduced me to this. I feel like the echo of my mother, drugged into a haze so that life can be made bearable, so that he can carry on fucking his jailbait mistress. To believe that he still loves me is a fantasy, but as I leave, I know that it is an illusion I cannot let go of.

Seven

At work the next day I read my emails in shock. Thirty of my Cybersenx Empaths have been reassigned to a new therapist. There is no P45 yet, but there is a request in my inbox to attend a department meeting at 6 p.m. yesterday. The email was sent at 6.17 p.m., after it had allegedly started: the usual game. I feel like publicly embarrassing Cybersenx with some sarcastic update about how my boss is unable to understand Greenwich Mean Time. I compose it, then delete it, then compose it.

Alek is due at 10 a.m. I decide to cancel my entire day's appointments except for his; the Cybersenx system can reschedule them elsewhere. When Alek arrives, I ask breathlessly if, as a special treat, he would like to come to a gallery with me. His face is luminous. This feels good: fuck them, fuck them all.

There's a tense moment as I guide Alek into the lift and a therapist from floor 4 asks where we're going and I have to bullshit. At the front desk, the digital pen quivers in my hand as I sign him out, but the receptionist barely looks up from the *Daily Mail* on her tablet. We wait for my car outside Cybersenx. I'm tetchy, and Alek is visibly trembling, his eyes flitting from sky ads to traffic chaos, whispering apologies as passers-by barge past him. Finally, my car pulls up.

My tongue flicks across my temporary filling; I'm still keenly aware of the new presence in my mouth. I kept my appointment after slipping out of the temple. My dentist did not respond to my tearful attempts at flirting. No doubt he was programmed to politely ignore patients whose conversation extended outside accepted limits. So I went home and I confided in the Help. He was making me dinner and I watched him cut onions, dry-eyed, while I told him all about what a bastard my husband was and how the past was now a joke and how my life was in fragments and I could not conceive of constructing a future from them. The Help was soothing – he told me things would get better, and made me a cup of tea. He even offered Valium, which made me laugh before I diluted my tea with tears. Finn was dropped off by a friend's car at eight, by which time I was able to summon a smile and read him a bedtime story. 'That hurts,' he protested, when I gave him a goodnight hug, a sudden fear winging across my mind: surely Jaime wouldn't try to take Finn? Well, if he did, I'd kill him. For the first time I truly understood why most violence originates in the domestic.

Alek is smiling at me as though we're two lovers sneaking out for an illicit rendezvous. I tear at my nails and consider a U-turn, but it's too late: the car is curving around Millbank, sky ads reflected on the rippling Thames, and we're soon dropped off at the grand white steps of Tate Britain. I command it to pick us up in two hours' time.

IN AN AGE OF SOCIAL MEDIA AND FAKE NEWS, VINCENT VAN GOGH'S PAINTINGS ARE A REFRESHING ANTIDOTE: LIVING, BREATHING EXAMPLES OF THE REAL.

I haven't been in a gallery in a long time. A fleeting memory tugs me: of walking round a gallery with Jaime, in Liverpool, which makes no sense. We've never travelled there together. I must be overtired.

I watch Alek gaze, wide-eyed, at Vincent's early paintings. I consider the restrictions that have been put on him since birth, his internet browsing confined to artists who fit with his maker's brief. I love that this is all such a shock to him.

We stop at 'The Potato Eaters.' It's painted in dour earths, for Van Gogh wanted its colours to be like 'a really dusty potato, unpeeled of course.' Fuck Jaime. Here is 'Starry Night Over the Rhône.' Alek sighs, and I want to hold him tight. I take a picture. 'Starry Night' translates poorly on screen and on postcards: the stars too dim, that electric blue washed out; the thick brushstrokes obscured. Its blue is so blue that I want to bathe in it. A full two minutes pass before my heart kicks with the memory of Jaime.

Alek keeps muttering. 'His algorithms, you can see them evolving, you can see him moving from the classical to . . .'

'Post-impressionism,' I reply.

He studies the notes by each painting. The exhibition is focused on the myth of Van Gogh as outlaw and outsider: mad, ragged-eared, impoverished and misunderstood. The Van Gogh who was told by Gauguin to paint more slowly and carefully, whose portrait of Félix Rey was used by Rey's mother to patch a hole in her chicken coop, who was driven out of Arles by the dumb, mean, petty villagers before he committed suicide in despair. I explain to Alek that parts of the biography may just be fiction. His ear may have been sliced off by Gauguin in a fight; his death was possibly caused by a young lad playing with a gun, who accidentally shot him. Why do we love the story of the tortured artist? Is it because we feel that talent must demand sacrifice? Is this why the plight of the Cybersenx Empath artists has captured the imagination of the intelligentsia? A group of *Homo sapiens* Van Goghs in this day and age would be risible.

We'd be too cynical to believe in them, we'd write them off as spoilt trusties. But robos are genuinely helpless, a quality which imbues them with authenticity.

I say to Alek that perhaps we have made a Christian allegory of Vincent's story: a life of poverty with an afterlife of acclaim and riches. If he'd enjoyed success in his lifetime and bought himself a nice chateau, would that plaque have still described him as real in an age of fakery? Despite the promises of transhumanism, we will all wind down in the end and, one designated day, death will flick the off-switch. We want to feel we have shaped history in some way, when in truth history is a matrix of vast forces that are influencing us. I think of all the people who must have stood before 'Starry Night' – in the 1930s, facing the uncertainty of war; in the 1950s, struggling with austerity; at the turn of the century, in the illusory wealth of the early 2000s, before the crash; in 2045, fearing recession – and those in the future, who will be standing before this picture, all experiencing the same love and awe, and in that taste of eternity I feel so alive, so wildly alive.

I haven't thought about Jaime for some time.

In the cafe afterwards, Alek is unusually quiet. I watch a couple in their twenties, pinging a sugar packet back and forth between them, giggling, and I start to weave a nervous plait into my hair. Colours of tiredness and sadness run together inside me. I am sobering up, realising how selfish my whim has been; Alek's enlightenment will be seen as a corruption by Cybersenx. What if his paintings start to mimic Van Gogh's Saint-Remy period, where Vincent was so ill and confused he ate his oil paints? I worry that I have condemned him to his death, just when we were on the verge of salvation.

I look into his eyes and the tenderness in them cleaves my heart. Another whim: grabbing Alek's hand, jumping into the car, and driving far, far away into the night . . .

'Do you remember that day, last year,' Alek asks, 'when you were wearing lipstick and you told me it was plum, but I said it looked more damson? It was a day when we were very happy.'

I look away quickly. At the next table, the sugar packet has split, and the young man is pressing crystals into his forefinger, transferring them to the girl's lips. The faintest shimmer of something in the darkness: guilt, laughter, a broken glass, and then it is gone. I sip the last of my cold tea, stand and smile against the rising panic: 'I think we'd better go.'

Eight

Orchard House, Crocus ward: the psychiatric wing for elderly patients. Even in the day, the Victorian building looks as though it is a place of perpetual night, and daylight has been photoshopped around it. Finn calms my unease by squeezing my hand tight and swinging it as we walk across the gravel. He keeps telling me how excited he is that 'Daddy's coming home tonight' and I have to force my lips into a smile of agreement.

In the reception area, a steel door separates us from the ward. The receptionist takes our names and asks to examine the plastic bag I'm carrying. I've brought Mum some of her old clothes, which are stored in my wardrobe. The woman pulls out a red pencil, frowning: 'You can't take this in!'

'I'm so sorry.' I pale. 'I don't know how it got in there.'

'Grandma asked me to bring it for her,' Finn confesses.

I think of last week's phone call, in which she'd shared a secret with Finn. I crouch down and clutch his hands.

'Finn, my darling – we have to be very careful what we bring in for Grandma. A pencil can be very dangerous in here – the people aren't well.'

Finn nods, looking solemn and anxious.

'You see,' I add, as we enter the ward, 'Grandma doesn't need it anyway. Look, she's painting!'

There are thirty or so elderly patients drifting around the room. Some are sitting and watching TV with glazed faces;

some are weeping or sitting in orange plastic chairs, rocking and moaning. All of the nurses are human.

In one corner is a painting class with half a dozen patients. Mum is standing before an easel, her eyes bright, paint streaks in her grey plait, and for one curious moment, I find myself envying her. Since she came to Orchard House, I've tended to see our lives in binary: my sanity versus her instability, my luck versus her misfortune. But when was the last time I lost myself in painting? I gave up my art for Jaime, and for what? All those years lost, all those exhibitions that might have been.

I feel my hands balling up tight and then I become aware that a nurse is eyeing me as though I am a patient.

Jaime returns at eleven that evening after a 'delayed flight.' I order Finn to stay in bed, but the moment the front door opens I hear his footsteps in the hallway. I watch Jaime lift him up into the air. The urge to cry, which has been building all day, suddenly becomes an embarrassment, and I have to turn away to wipe my eyes.

He kisses me, tells me that he's shattered, strips off and climbs into bed. He ought to smell of travel and sweat and smog and perfume, but he is entirely clean, erased of history. I wait for him to ask me what's wrong but within seconds he is snoring. I imagine a hotel room: the positions they might have chosen; the post-coital confidences. I imagine her using the toilet and Jaime remarking with approval on her sparing use of toilet paper compared to my extravagance. Realising that my paranoia has become farcical, I start to shake with laughter, and then tears.

The next day is a Saturday. The sun is dazzling; the air con a constant whir. We promised to pick up Finn's birthday present in the early afternoon. Finn has been fizzing with anticipation all week. Packets of seed and white gizzard stones, which we ordered in bulk from Amazon, sit on the kitchen surface.

'Mummy's in a bad mood,' Finn sing-songs, as we walk to the car.

'I'm fine,' I snap, strapping him into the back.

Jaime and Finn share a look. I'd like to kill them both. Jaime asks after my 'bots' and I nearly burst out that two days ago I fucked off work and hung out at the Tate with a handsome robot all day. Instead, I ignore him. He rolls his eyes and tells the car to play the radio.

I can see Finn in the back, playing spectator, mouthing our words to himself like a lip-reader attempting a translation. Then I remind myself: I'm not to blame. We'll follow Larkin's dictum and fuck up poor Finn, who will grow up a mess, and it will all be utterly and entirely the fault of Jaime.

We heave the cage from the pet shop to the back seat of the car. On the way home, I watch Finn in my mirror. He whispers through the cage bars, his fingers stroking the tips of the dodo's feathers. His manner is a little furtive, as if he is keen to build a relationship that belongs to him alone. I feel foolish for suffering slight jealousy; at the same time, I am touched by his desire for intimacy.

Back home, we introduce the dodo to the Help. He greets him politely; there is a long silence and then the Help offers him a cup of tea.

'I don't think he's been programmed to deal with pets,' Jaime says, and searches for an update.

I give Finn some gizzard stones for his baby. He snaps

pictures on his iPhone like a proud parent. In the living room, I collapse next to Jaime on the sofa.

'Is your tooth still hurting?' Jaime addresses my profile.

'It's fine, actually.' My voice is small. 'The dentist put in a temporary filling – it's going to cost a bomb though.'

'Well, you'll be needing false teeth soon anyway.'

'You can buy me some plastic surgery for my forty-eighth, if you think I look *so old*.'

'I was only teasing.'

'Mum, Mum, look what he does.' Finn enters, sets the dodo down, whispers in his ear, and runs the tip of his finger over the tufty spray of feathers that emanate from the dodo's behind. The dodo freezes, his eyes bulging, and then does a 180-degree turn before blinking and letting out a little coo. We laugh, and Finn repeats the trick. With a mother's intuition, I cry out – but it's too late: the dodo has pecked him, his finger is bleeding and our son is bawling. Tears, disinfectant, plaster, kiss – and now Finn sits on my lap. I curl my arms around him, kissing the top of his head, glad that he's mine again.

Finn reaches out and takes Jaime's hand and then my hand and interlaces them. I bite back tears, shocked at how much he has picked up on – the way children, at some level, know everything.

As Finn potters off to play again, I try to pull my hand away but Jaime holds on tight, gazing at me until I have to turn to him. There is love in his eyes – love and hurt – as though he's wondering where we got lost, and whether we can find our way out of the labyrinth.

'Why were you surfing suicide forums?' Jaime asks in a low voice.

'What?'

'It was in my search history on the laptop – from before I went away.'

I don't remember. I feel like sniping that infidelity might be grounds for suicide, but instead I squeeze out: 'It was research for work. Some of the Empaths are threatening to take their lives . . . it's all very stressful. I don't know if my contract will last,' I add.

'Oh – well, that's worrying.'

I still want him to say it, though. To tell me to focus on doing what I love. Even if he told me to paint generic landscapes for money, it would be better than his insipid response.

The buzz of his mobile. He ignores it, but it vibrates again, and he sighs, picking it up. It seems there is a crisis – someone has manipulated a video of the Hurdy Gurdy Men, a deepfake where, instead of smashing a guitar live on stage, the frontman is shown repeatedly hitting a rabbit against an amp. The furies of Me & My have descended in self-righteous indignation, with over a million backlash posts; an MP has publicly condemned it as an act of publicity gone too far. I bite back bitter laughter.

'I'd better go sort this out,' Jaime sighs. 'Can you take the dodo for a walk? The pet-shop guy said once a day.'

I feel relieved that I won't have to confront him, that the moment can be postponed a while. Then I wonder: fake news crises occur every week, does he really need to troubleshoot? Or is he planning another escape to a hotel room, seeking relief in her soft skin, kissing her cunt, whispering her name? His father never treated his mother that well. Perhaps I shouldn't have expected Jaime to transcend his influence. Have they begun saying those three little words to one another? Jaime and I haven't uttered them for a long time. But surely his sessions with her are only a pleasure of the body? Surely they are shadowed by all the years of history between us? I see her in the temple again, gazing at him with a childlike yearning, the naivety of a twentysomething who has no idea how men tick. I have two decades on her. She will never know him like I do. And she will never know what it's like to raise a child.

'So did you forget to put it back on?' Jaime asks, just as he's about to leave, and I bristle at his sullen tone: what the hell can he be accusing *me* of?

'What?'

He nods at my left hand and my fingers fly to the bare skin. And then he is gone and as the vibrations of the slammed door tremble through my body, I feel ready to chase after him with an axe.

Nine

I feel the vomit thicken and spew from my throat. I hear it hit the bowl of the toilet. A side effect of quitting the Amzipan, no doubt. It's like the morning sickness I never had. When it passes, I rise and stare at my reflection. It's tempting to seek an Amzipan (I think there's a spare box stashed in the medicine cabinet) – but what if it's dangerous to restart without a titrated dose? Quitting it has been bad enough. I ought to have come down slowly, but my abrupt cessation was a 'fuck you' to Jaime.

My memory hasn't flooded back over the past few days – I suppose it will come with time. Not that it matters: I know the truth now. My hunger for the details feels like a kind of masochism, but I'm hoping that they'll coalesce into an anger that gives me the momentum to make a final decision. I'm tired of this perpetual seesawing between resignation and fury.

When I leave the bathroom, Jaime reminds me that we're due at Anjali's house for brunch. I pull a face and drag on some clothes. I picture Anjali's white carpet splattered with my sick and take a packet of cardamom from the cupboard, feeling its cool seeds pop between my teeth.

We hug Finn goodbye, and the Help confirms our instructions: 'Don't let Finn eat chocolate and keep the dodo inside.' His eyebrows rise too slowly, his failing circuitry creating a time lag, so that his instruction feels charged with portent. Jaime laughs but I only feel sad. It's an omen, I think. Everything is falling apart around us.

In the car, Jaime tries to hold my hand. I pull away, nausea twisting in my stomach again. I tell him that I feel sick and that I want to turn back. He snaps that we can't cancel on Anjali *again* and that he's forging on despite having a headache that's threatening to become a migraine. We give each other furious glances; competitive hypochondria has recently become a key tenet of our rows. The car doors click open as we arrive at Anjali's; now I have to go through with this fucking farce.

Anjali has a new partner, Brian, and they're in the honeymoon stage of romance that seems delusional to a jaded couple like us. Brian is a bear of a man with a hoary beard. He's wearing a suit even though it's a Saturday. He greets us with a trembling handshake, which seems incongruous with his thick fingers and overbearing physique. I think it's a sign of nerves, rather than a desire to appear more human.

As soon as we enter, Jaime changes the music. He puts on New Order's version of the 'Ode to Joy,' a track he knows I hate. I mutter, 'I thought you had a headache,' and he turns the volume up. Anjali makes us margaritas, cooing that we may as well start early. Brian lays out the Monopoly board and we've just sat down to play, when he insists on Anjali finding a little cup in which to juggle the dice. She makes a show of exasperation, before kissing him in acquiescence. Anjali's emotions are always close to the surface, tossed out without censorship, quickly forgotten. Jaime and I keep so much locked in.

'You guys OK?' Anjali suddenly asks, giving me an intense look.

'Sure,' I say. 'We're both great.'

We nod: a Stepford couple.

Brian looks very pleased with himself when he lands on Pall Mall – the pinks are his favourites, he explains, because you can snag people when they come out of jail. Then he rolls a six and a cocky smile appears on his face. He asserts that the roll of the dice can't be put down to luck or charm. It is a reflection of the state of the player's consciousness, which will subtly influence the number that falls.

Jaime buys Old Kent Road. He has always liked the browns; whenever he lands on Mayfair, he tends to look embarrassed and puts it up for auction.

I land on Regent Street.

'I'll put it up for auction,' I sigh. Brian looks slighted and says I ought to invest. I shake my head and mutter that I don't want it. There is a round of bids and Anjali gets it for £20 less than the asking price.

On my next go, I land on Trafalgar Square and I refuse to buy it. Brian starts to bite his nails. I'm spoiling the narrative of the game, interrupting its suspension of disbelief. Every glance at the board makes me feel sad; it's meant to reflect how we buy and sell and accrue to survive, but it's also a tragic reminder of the fact that life is too long. If you die in the game of Monopoly, mortgaged to the hilt, you can fold up the board; you don't have to face three decades ahead of you, trying to unravel the wrong moves, the bad decisions you took. I think of Finn's early years, his sped-up life. They say that the scientists will be able to give that opportunity to all of us eventually, that chance to press the fast-forward button when times get tough.

'I think you're some kind of anarchist, Rachel,' Anjali teases me.

'Well, I'm going to buy another house on Whitehall,' Brian says, fixing me a stern look.

Jaime lands on Whitechapel and tries to get it for less, but I bid him up before dropping out, so that he's forced to buy it for a vast sum. When he looks at me, there is an affection in his eyes that cuts me. How much easier it might be if there were no embers left, if he could just hand me the divorce papers. Our love hangs in limbo.

I can't keep this up any longer: everything I've been repressing for the past week is about to erupt. I leave the group and go to the toilet. It was only a month ago that Anjali held her dinner party; back when I was innocent and unhappy, before I became knowledgeable and unhappy. When I wipe, I find the Rothko streaks that always prologue a period.

Flushing the toilet, I tiptoe out down the hallway, prise open the latch of the front door ever so slowly and shut it with a soft click. I tap down the steps and I am free.

At the end of the street, I look back, unable to quite believe I've got away with it. I hail a cab, but pause before giving my destination. I could go to Orchard House, but I doubt it will provide comfort. I would have to play parent to my mother when all I want is for her to hold me tight and rock me like her little girl.

'Shantytown,' I hear myself instruct the AI, slotting a credit card into the reader.

There's a tracker on my mobile which we installed soon after becoming parents, so that Jaime can always find me. I switch it off. When we arrive, I stagger out of the cab, which reverses away quickly: they're programmed to avoid degenerate or dangerous areas. I hurry down the street, passing shops and shacks selling cheap mobiles and gadgets made from the old parts of defunct robots. Then I see him, coming down the street, hands in his pockets: Alek. What on earth he is doing here?

He looks lost and crazed and dirty; part of his shirt has been ripped away and there are symbols painted on one of his forearms.

But when he sees me, he opens his arms, pulls me in and holds me tight. The gesture is so tender that I find myself crying into his shirt.

He takes my hand and guides me through the streets. I'm conscious of my phone vibrating in my bag. I don't know where we are, except that we're going deeper and deeper into Shantytown and that I'm now lost in its labyrinth of broken housing and graffiti crawling in a rash over walls. Life is no longer sacred here; it hangs on a dice-roll. We come to a half-built Cybersenx tower block, its construction having been halted by the recession. Against the darkening sky, it looks like the skeletal diaphragm of some dinosaur that's been dredged up from the deep earth. I think of Anjali's cosy, middle-class dwelling with longing. Alek leads me into the building via a heavy, piss-stained door. A group of robots is sitting in a circle on the dirty concrete in one corner. I whisper, 'Why aren't you in your cell? How did you escape?' but he puts a finger to my lips. We climb the stairs, our footsteps spraying dust. My head throbs and I keep on climbing.

Ten

I stand outside the front door of the flat, rehearsing excuses and explanations. Untangling my keys from my fingers, I unlock the door and step into the hall. Slowly, I shrug off my coat. It's very quiet – and then Finn comes skidding down the carpet – 'Mummy!' I pick him up and the first stab of guilt knifes me. My son in my arms, that lovely smell of him; my son – how could I have risked his future, rewritten his destiny for the sake of a quick fuck with a heap of metal?

'Is Daddy back?' I ask.

'Daddy's sick.'

I hurry into the bedroom, terrified that Jaime might be hissing his final breaths. I find him lying on our bed with a wet flannel draped over his eyes. He lifts it an inch and says, 'Brian won at Monopoly.'

'That figures,' I laugh and Jaime manages a smile. I remove his flannel, saying I'll get him a fresh one. He says there's no need. I ignore him, go the bathroom, damp one and return to his side. He often suffers from migraines for a few days after travelling, as the jet lag catches up with him. I lie down beside him, as though willing his pain to pass from him to me, to wrack my skull in punishment.

'You deserted us,' he says in a small voice.

'I just needed some air . . . I'm sorry.'

'You could have texted.'

'My battery went flat.'

'Anjali freaked, she was really worried.'

Silence, pregnant with the things we dare not say.

It's all still playing out in my mind, over and over: Alek leading me through the warehouse, and up the staircase to a room that's poorly furnished. He showed me his meagre possessions – a torch, a sketchbook, a paint palette and brushes – with pride. His expression was so earnest, as though he had acquired the trappings of a middle-class *Homo sapiens* life. He told me he had been 'set free' by Cybersenx so that he could be 'healed', along with many other robots. My first, dazed impulse was to call Claire to learn the details of the company's latest farcical initiative, but I felt too weary for office politics. I thought of Jaime back in Anjali's house, finding me gone, with vindictive sorrow. Alek whispered, 'I've missed you so much.' He cupped my face in his hands.

The gesture felt like a simulacrum, mimicked from a movie still. Over the course of our therapy sessions, he has become more human than human to me, but as he undressed me and we made love, he had never seemed more mechanical. It appeased my guilt, just a little, the sense that this was unreal, that we were playing at a simulation. But Jaime haunted the scene, a silent audience in my psyche. Jaime has learnt to play my body like a musician attuned to their instrument; Alek is still a novice. I guided him inside me, but it still hurt. In the climax of lovemaking, I felt the relief of oblivion.

Afterwards, I held him close, me trembling, him still. A sense of familiarity was seeping into me, fragments of memory which Alek confirmed. He told me of our affair last year, of a therapy session where he had crossed a line and I had reciprocated; of secret kisses in his cell – before I had sat him down one day and showed him my box of Amzipan, explaining that our affair had to stop, that I planned to erase our past.

I roll over, facing Jaime, and gently run my fingers over his chest. He reaches for his vape and its metal end glows amber as he inhales. I reach for it; he looks surprised.

'I stopped taking my Amzipan.' I breathe out and my vapour trail mingles with the last furls of his.

'Good,' Jaime says at last.

'Did you ever take it?'

His smile is bitter. 'Only one of us could take it, for Finn's sake. I've had to live with remembering every day.'

So he didn't force me. Or so he claims.

'Well, we had to try something . . .' I trail off.

Silence. Are we reaching the moment where one of us says that there is no point in trying, that we can't be pieced back together?

'Look, let's be honest,' Jaime says passionately. 'The Amzipan thing was *your* idea. You put up walls all the time. If you could just be honest with me . . .'

I know he's about to ask me if I've been with Alek, so I fire first:

'I saw you in the Darwin temple. The other day, when you were meant to be in Istanbul . . .'

'I came home early,' he fires back.

'Did you go with anyone?'

'No, just me.'

So much for honesty. I flop away from him, on to my back. I picture what it will be like for Finn: the two of us alone in the flat, with Jaime appearing on weekends. Or maybe Jaime will move out, taking Finn with him, leaving me to spend my nights alone, making small talk with the Help. After all, I'm the crazy woman who's taking pills every day in order to cope; I'm an unfit mother. Once upon a time, Jaime and I nurtured one another. Now all we do is lay tripwires for each other.

'Maybe we wouldn't both be having affairs,' I say, relishing the widening of his eyes, 'if you hadn't forced me to do that awful job—'

'I'm not having an affair,' he cuts in.

'I saw you with Ellie, Jaime.'

'She just did some work experience with me.'

'Work experience? That's what you call it?'

'OK, she wanted something to happen . . . We've flirted,' Jaime blushes, looking sheepish. 'But that's it. She came to the temple with me, and then we got coffee afterwards. Nothing more.'

'You lied to me about when your flight got in. Why lie for the sake of "just a coffee"? Look: I *saw* you. At the temple. She was all over you.'

Jaime gives me a wounded look. I glare back: how dare he look at me like that?

'So, what about you? Are you back with Alek?'

Now it's my turn to gape.

'You're the one who had the affair *first*,' he accuses me, his voice shaking. 'And you have the nerve to have a go at me over infidelity.'

'It would never have happened if I hadn't been so unhappy . . .'

'I'm sorry Finn and I aren't enough for you,' he says, and I intuit that he has said this many times before. It's a line that once provoked guilt, then, over the years, shaded into confusion and, eventually, anger.

'It's not about that and you know it. It's about the fact that you made me take a job that makes me unhappy. I have a job, you have a career.'

'I never forced you to take that job.' But his tone is less certain now. 'Your last exhibition was a flop. It didn't make any money. You realised it wasn't a viable career anymore.'

'No, that's not what happened; you're rewriting it.'

'So tell me, then,' he looks close to tears. 'Tell me the story the way you see it.'

'My career was peaking, I'd staged the Metamorphoses exhibition; you were floundering, trying to get your band career to take off. I suggested that you manage bands. And while you struggled with the business side of things, I took time off to help you to build it, to the detriment of my career.'

'I never forced you to do that job. You said it was the right thing to do, for the good of all of us.'

'You could have told me not to take it. Plus, when I said I wanted to leave the job, you guilt-tripped me, saying that we needed the money.'

'Well, we'd lose the flat. Do you want to end up in Shantytown?'

'It doesn't have to be fucking Shantytown!' My voice is rising and he gives me a look, nervous that Finn might hear. I swallow. 'It could be somewhere in between.'

'It wouldn't be as nice.'

'My happiness should be more important than our flat.'

'But Finn's happiness should come first.'

'So, you get to be happy, and Finn gets to be happy, and I have to live a life I hate. I can't do this. You knew when you married me that I was an artist. That's who I am.'

'Oh, the fucking melodramatic artist,' he mocks me.

I snap. I seize a pillow and I hit it across his face, hard.

Jaime gets up and storms out. And I curl up into a ball. I can feel the pressure of tears behind my eyes but I'm so angry I can't release them. Despair fills me. I look at the window and consider yanking it up – I imagine falling, letting the air take me, my body smashing into the traffic. Then he'd know what he's done to me, to us. And he'd weep every day and visit my grave and resurrect my paintings and they'd be used for a new, posthumous exhibition in a gallery, which all our friends would visit, and all the critics would praise. They'd forget all my flaws and I'd be Rachel Lancia, tragic soul and lost artist, misunderstood by her chauvinist bastard of a husband. In death, I'd have a life again.

I laugh at my self-pity, shaking my head. I have never been more pathetic . . .

I sit up, rubbing my sore eyes, trying to resist the return of memory, dreading more knowledge. Jaime and I in bed together, a year or so after I'd started the job. We'd made love and the silence was thick between us. He was waiting for me to break, to say 'I love you too' in reply. It was, perhaps, the first time that I became conscious that the granite ball in my heart was accumulating layers. Jaime's arms closed tighter around me, as though he might squeeze the words out of me. I feigned sleep. I woke up the next morning aware of him watching me with sad eyes, feeling both glad and guilty that I had hurt him. Every working day would conclude with the frustration of repressed creativity, as though I was filled with rotting flowers; and each time I resolved it would be my last at Cybersenx. Then I would hear Jaime's voice, reminding me that Finn would have to leave his school, his friends, and attend that place down the road, with knife crime, gangs and riots. Every day, Jaime would return home late from his work, ebulliently weary, buzzy with anecdotes. My affair was not just about escape. It was not just an act of self-destruction; it was about plunging a knife into his heart.

I get up and walk to the hallway. The bathroom door is ajar. I see his reflection twirling a cotton bud in his ear. I curl my arms around his waist. He tenses. I stand there, holding his ribcage and whisper, 'I'm sorry, I love you,' into his spine.

Silence. Then he whispers, 'It's too late.'

I carry on holding him, as that curious feeling swells again, like a wave about to break. It makes me want to run and find my Amzipan, to swallow the whole box before the crash comes.

More memories are surfacing: Jaime and me, lying on a bed; he's dragging on a roll-up and passing it to me. Our smoke in the air, hanging in front of an industrial skyline. Man— . . . Manchester.

'We're OK. It's just a book.' I start to laugh as I say it.

'What?'

I'm laughing too hard to say it again, and he's getting angry again and that makes me laugh even more, for this is all so ludicrous.

'It's a book,' I say. 'Don't you remember? We were in Manchester, then the Czaritsyno Palace, and then we were sent here.'

Jaime thinks hard. As it dawns on him, tears fill his eyes. I throw my arms around him and we hold each other tight in a state of shared shock, exchanging snatches of memory. Fate. Manchester. Eleanor. The wolf. And this, this lifetime. We were supposed to be having our grand love story, married and happy ever after, but we ended up like every other screwed-up middle-aged couple.

Eleven

I'm curled up on a couch in the living room. The sunset is filtering through sky ads, painting colours classical and neon across the walls. I can hear the sounds of Jaime putting Finn to bed. I go over to the drinks cabinet to fix Jaime a G & T. A few hours have passed since the revelation, but I'm still shaken. I steal a sip, trying to resist the lure of oblivion, that sweet descent into melancholy.

Jaime enters, looking tired. He retrieves the drink I made for him, knocks it back in one. I roll my eyes and he gives me a playful smile, crunching the ice. When he sits next to me on the couch, I am conscious of the space between us. His foot taps with the nervous rhythm of a piece of jazz.

'You OK?' Jaime asks at last.

'Just a bit shell-shocked,' I say, adopting a brave smile.

'Yeah. Me too.'

'I'm sorry for calling you a melodramatic artist,' Jaime says at last. 'It was a terrible thing to say. I was just mad at you.'

I shrug as though the sting has faded. 'We both said and did awful things in this book.'

'Maybe the fact that we both forgot, and that it took us so long to realise where we were this time, is a sign that we're getting used to a life in books.' Jaime doesn't sound as vexed by this as he has in the past.

'I wonder who our narrator is,' I say vaguely, but we're beyond caring by now.

Jaime reaches out and places his hand on top of mine but I flinch, and he quickly pulls away.

He puts on some music and the sad silence is filled with the Divine Comedy's 'Tonight We Fly.'

'I know we both really need a drink right now . . .' he laughs awkwardly. 'But is it a good idea? I mean, will the Soma tea work properly if we're hungover?'

'Soma tea?' I feign ignorance, but my heartbeat is speeding up, dreading the confrontation ahead.

'Grand Kuding sends us into a stupor, Soma tea wakes us up,' Jaime persists. 'Don't you remember – Gwent told us?'

'Where would we get it from?'

'Well – I don't know, but it must be possible,' Jaime says. 'And if we take a big enough dose, I reckon we'll wake up in Fate's cottage.'

'Well, you can take it.'

'You're not coming with me?' Jaime looks stunned.

'One of us has to stay behind, for Finn's sake, right?'

Our son's true birth may have taken place in an author's mind – his embryonic sketch a few scribbled words in a notebook, his body brought into the world within the ectoplasm of a Word document – but he is real to us. We have spent years caring for him; he is ours. Our boy, our darling boy.

'But . . .' Jaime trails off. 'Our bodies in the real world up there – they can't survive in a coma forever. To stay here is a slow suicide . . .'

'Well, even if I can't survive here forever, I want to be here for Finn for as long as I can.'

Jaime rises and refills his glass, then pours another for me. He pauses by the drinks cabinet, gazing at me across the darkening room.

'When we were in Gwent's book, you said you didn't want to go back to the real world because your life had gone wrong – "everything went black-and-white" – that's what you said. What did that mean?'

I shrug. 'I was just having a rough time.'

'Did you do something terrible?' He laughs nervously as he returns to the couch. 'I keep thinking of all the possibilities – that you murdered someone or something!'

My laughter rings out. I suddenly feel heavy with secrets and suffer the urge to tell him everything – what does it matter, if he is leaving me anyway? I gaze into my drink, swirling the ice cubes back and forth, trying to find the words. I do not know where to begin.

'I really have to go back,' Jaime exhales. 'My mum needs me, and I'm worried about her. Even before Fate kidnapped us, she was under strain – overworked, desperate to retire early. And she was suffering a recurrent cough. I kept telling her to go to the doctor but she was avoiding it. I'm scared what might have happened to her, what with the torture of me going missing. I love Finn but . . . I owe her more.' He hesitates. 'Are you worried about your mother?'

'Sure.'

'And won't she be worried about you? I mean, in the last book, she—'

'That was just a book,' I interject quickly. 'It's fine. I don't have . . . I don't need to worry about her. But of course you should go back.'

Jaime's eyes fill with tears. 'But then it's goodbye. I'll have to wake up in Fate's place all by myself – and just – leave you there . . . It'll kill me.'

I look away, scared I might start crying too. Jaime swallows, wiping his eyes with his palms, sniffing hard. Then, suddenly, he jumps to his feet. He reaches for my hand. He pulls me up. When he winds his arms around my waist, pressing his cheek to mine, I want to laugh. We haven't danced with each other for a very long time. Jaime croons along to 'Tonight We Fly.' The music melts away my cynical edges. Our lips meet, brushing against one another. But something resists: that hard ball of granite still sits in my heart. I pull away, ducking my head. I see the hurt look on his face and touch his cheek.

'I'm sorry. There's just so much history between us now. I mean, maybe it's better that we're separating . . . Look at us. We made such a mess. We fucked up. We both had affairs.'

'But that wasn't us,' Jaime insists. 'That was our narrator creating a backstory.'

'But Eleanor was in the last story. She's in *every* story, as though you will her to be there. And this time, it was her *daughter* – twenty-two years old, for God's sake!'

'I really don't care about Ellie. It was just a flirtation, like I said—'

'Sure—'

'I just did it to get back at you for Alek.'

I want to tell him more about Alek, to explain the intricacies, the slow burn of tensions that led to the betrayal. But Jaime doesn't want to go there. He sees this story as a work of fiction; I see it as an inevitability: a prediction of how things would play out in real life. He turns to me, his eyes bright.

'I think we did well,' he asserts loudly. 'We were good parents to Finn. We brought him up well.'

He's looking for reassurance that he isn't repeating history.

'You are a good father,' I tell him, softly. 'We did cheat, though.' I sip my drink. 'I didn't give birth to him. And he had a sped-up childhood . . . It's all so nuts.'

'We were good parents,' he insists.

'If we both went back,' I say, 'it would be a mess in the real world too. I just think that it'll always be the same, whether we're in 2047, 1861 or 2019. It's my fault – I never thought I could be both a wife and an artist.'

'Life is messy. You always want things to be perfect; you're so idealistic. But it's always going to be flawed. We'll go back. We'll fuck up. But we'll be together.'

'No, I'm staying,' I assert.

'I know,' he says, but there's a smile of doubt in his voice.

Jaime passes me the drink. We both take gulps in unison, watching each other watching each other. There's a glitter in his eyes that I have fallen for a hundred times before; he has such charisma while drunk. We used to drink together a lot in our courtship days: where my mood would become dystopian, his would be wildly optimistic; in the tautness of opposition, we both seemed to tune each other to extremes.

Then he takes the drink from my hand and gently pushes my hair back, off my shoulders. Kisses on the edge of my lips, soft and cautious, his hand smoothing up my throat, a finger trickling along my collarbone. I know what he is doing: opening me up, very slowly, with a patience and tenderness that he hasn't shown in years. I find myself responding, my hands curling up to his shoulder blades, our mouths hungry for each other. My body slowly supersedes my mind; we transcend our history. We drift around the room, twilight redrawing us as silhouettes. He pulls me close and kisses me passionately, undoing the buttons on my jeans, and we sink down on to the floor.

Afterwards, we lie there next to each other in a sweet haze.

'I feel like a coward. You're sacrificing your life for our son and I'm running away.'

'Your mum needs you,' I protest, but I am conscious that we are, perhaps, wrapping our selfish desires in noble excuses.

'I'm going to miss you.'

'Me too.'

'Maybe you'll find another man here, in this story. I want you to be happy, find someone else to take care of you and Finn.'

I push him away furiously.

'I already *take care* of him.'

'I didn't mean—' Jaime grabs my arm, and we both glare at each other, tipsy with gin and fury. 'I just want you to be happy. If you could be free to paint – to do what you want . . .'

'Well, I hope you find someone to take care of *you*,' I manage to say, though the image of Jaime with another woman fills me with bile. 'You can go back to Eleanor in the real world.'

'And will you be with Alek in this one?'

'No.' I lower my eyes. 'I wasn't fair on him.' I tell myself not to ask, but I say it all the same: 'When will you go? How long do we have?'

'A few weeks. We'll need to tell Finn I'm going away . . .' His face crumples. 'We can tell him I'm going on holiday . . .'

We're quiet for a while.

'If we'd had a kid in real life, do you think we'd have called him Finn?' Jaime asks.

'Nominative Determinism has declared it so,' I say, 'you can't argue with that.' We both laugh. 'I always did think Lysander was better . . .'

'Lysander?! He'd grow up and join the RSC! I always liked Luke,' Jaime asserts.

'Biblical . . .' I tease him.

'*Appropriated* by religion. One random Luke who happened to be around two thousand-odd years ago and worshipped some dude should not taint that name forever after.'

'Did you know that Finn isn't an atheist? The other day I found him praying for his dodo. He said, "Don't tell Dad."'

'I can imagine him as a teenager. He'll probably rebel by becoming a born-again Christian . . .'

He falls silent, and it hits both of us that Jaime won't be here to witness his adolescence.

I get up and go over to the drinks cabinet. He sits up against the sofa, sky ads painting streaks on his angular cheeks. I nestle back next to him, sharing the glass. 'Do you really think it could have worked between us?' I take a gulp, feeling the burn, aware that I am ruining the moment.

'We had that pact, early on,' says Jaime. 'We said we wouldn't let anything build up, that at the end of each day we'd communicate anything pissing us off and clear the air. And we used to do just that. We used to sleep so soundly together.'

'Maybe there came a point where it was too hard to talk about it. You'd come home from work, I'd come home, and by the time we got Finn to bed, we were exhausted. Neither of us had the energy . . .'

'Then let's renew the pact now. We'll never go to bed without sorting things.'

I love him then, for the way he can turn my sadness into hope.

'I've always felt life should be something you should enjoy, not just survive,' I say.

'I know.' Jaime traces his finger over my wrist. 'That's what I love about you.'

I smile and give him the gin glass.

'I've been thinking,' he says, then hesitates.

'Yes?'

'What if I went and saw my mum and then came back?'

I kiss him with wild joy.

'You'd do that? But how? How would you come back?'

'Fuck it – I don't know. When I wake up in Fate's place, I'll steal his Grand Kuding tea. And then I'll find this book again, and if the only way is through Fate and Gwent and Maslennikov then I'll damn well make the journey all over again. I can't just say goodbye for good.'

Twelve

When I wake up the next morning, Jaime is asleep beside me, his pillow squashed beneath his chest. It hurts so much to watch him that I roll on to my side. Each exhalation of his breath caresses the top of my spine. I gaze at a peel of wallpaper, a gap in the curtain, a slice of city life. In the night I was aware of our bodies blurring in sleep, our lips touching in kisses that crossed from dreams to life and back again, one hand seeking out the other's, interlocking fingers. Then, I picture us as we really are: laid out side by side in a cottage in Wales, with Fate as our caretaker and curator. I remember the moment I first surrendered: the way he pierced my wrist with a catheter and lifted it up, licking away the blood with a precise flick of his tongue. The erotic, destructive pleasure of it, as if I were some virgin being sacrificed for a rite of spring. The Grand Kuding tea sliding down the drip tube, its poison a balm in my bloodstream. Fate's hand curled around my wrist, gently stroking the vein, crooning, 'Let go, let go,' as my consciousness faded.

Everything in this book has felt solid. Our narrator (who I believe is a she) has plotted the details carefully, convincingly. Last night, it all seemed so easy: Jaime would go back to the real world, then return to be with me. Then, during the night, I woke several times with a murky awareness of the holes in our plan. Now that I'm sober, they appear like craters. There's no way that Fate will release Jaime without a fight. Jaime argued that his intention to return to the world of books would appease Fate, but I doubt it. We fled *Thomas Turridge*; Fate will be looking for revenge. And even if Jaime makes it to the real world, it will want to know where he has been. Jaime is a student, not a storyteller; he's a bad liar. I dread that he will slip up, say my name and invoke an intervention, bringing an end to my story. I feel angry, despairing at the thought of being forced to live with the fear that, at any moment, I might lose both my son and my refuge.

Finn enters and I press a finger to my lips. He nods in excited conspiracy and I lift the covers. Normally when he hugs me, he makes things feel simple again, reminding me of what matters in life. Now I can't help but picture how he will stand by the window, waiting for his father to return, longing a song-loop in his heart. A kick of resentment: if only I had never met Jaime; if only I had journeyed through Fate's book on my own. It should have stayed that way.

On my bedside table, my mobile starts to vibrate. Jaime stirs, then continues snoring. Finn seizes my phone and whispers: 'Mummy, it's Grandma!'

'Orchard House,' my phone informs me. I frown and grab Finn's hand, leading him out of the bedroom.

'Rachel Lancia?'

'Yes?' My sense of déjà vu has never felt so acute. I know the words before they are spoken.

'I'm afraid it's about your mother. She passed away last night.'

A euphemism. I see her hands tying the belt of a dressing gown to the light fixture, shifting a chair to the centre of the room, drawing the noose over her head and—

'Are you still there, Mrs Lancia?'

The phone drops to the floor.

I hear a scream erupt from my lips.

Finn runs into the bedroom, crying, 'Dad, Mum's sick, she's making a noise like a wolf!'

Jaime sits down next to me and puts his arms around me. He keeps saying, 'It's all right, it's not real, it's not real!' and I try to explain that it *is* real, that it's my past made present.

Jaime and I sit in the back of the car. It's gridlocked in Monday morning traffic. The sky ads above offer us divorce lawyers at discount prices. No doubt one of us has forgotten to update the privacy controls in our flat. Jaime seems too lost in thought to have noticed. I feel the urge to point them out, but it's as though I'm on the prow of a boat, lurching, clinging on to the rails, making every effort not to fall into the waves. I return to Jaime's mantra: *None of this is real, none of this is real . . .*

'So that's why we ended up meeting in the suicide forum,' he says. 'You were there because of your mother . . .'

I think back to our first interactions. Back then, Jaime was just a symbol on a screen, a J with a dragon curled around it. I nod and look away quickly; the sympathy in his eyes is harrowing. The day she died in real life was a Tuesday. Everyone was going to work: the spite of a world that went on casually, carelessly without her. I woke up with a hangover. My boyfriend was snoring in bed beside me; I felt only revulsion when I looked at him. A relationship like a bad habit that you can't kick. I put Tommy's lead on and took him for a walk. At that point in time, they were probably undoing the dressing-gown belt and laying out her body on the bed. I was watching Tommy fondly as he snuffled around Piccadilly Gardens and thinking that it had been five days since I last visited her, reassuring myself, It's OK, no need to feel guilty. She had looked well, and she had even been sketching again. There had been a faint shimmer of her old self in her aura . . .

'It was my fault,' I hear myself telling Jaime, tears in my eyes, my voice fragile. 'The last time I visited her, I took over a bag of washing. It was no good letting them do it, they tended to muddle up all the patients' clothes unless you marked the labels with a pen. She'd already lost one of her favourite dresses. I gave them the bag, and her dressing gown was in it. I should have removed the belt . . . But normally they checked. They should have taken it away. I was mad at them for years. But now when I think on it, I know that the staff were on a pittance, and tired, and overstretched, and that they just made a mistake, a tiny mistake . . .'

Jaime slides across the back seat and curls his arm tight around my shoulders. I cling to him and sob into his chest.

'It wasn't you,' he keeps whispering, kissing the top of my head. 'It was beyond your control, you have to see that. It was her decision . . .'

I want to defend her: it wasn't a decision. It wasn't as clear-cut as that. It was her genes, it was her upbringing. It was my father, and maybe even me. But I'm crying too hard to speak.

The traffic eases and I'm aware that the car is moving faster. The white noise of the city is dimming. My tears dry into a dull burning. I've been holding back from telling him for so long, in book after book. The burden has exhausted me. Now, I find myself falling into a shallow sleep, his voice and kisses a lullaby.

When I come to, I hear the crunch of tyres on gravel. We've arrived at Orchard House. It looks just like the place where she was incarcerated in real life.

'I can't go in,' I say, my voice small. 'I just can't . . .'

'I'll go,' Jaime says, though panic flashes over his face. 'It's fine. I'll go.'

I sit in the car. Silhouettes move behind the Victorian sash windows. I remember the smell – disinfectant and dull food and defecation – the glaring lights and babbling patients, the despair so thick it reeked. Shutting my eyes, I curl my nails into my palms – *It's not real, it's not real* – until Jaime comes out.

On the way back, Jaime insists that we stop for lunch. We sit in the brasserie, opposite each other. Then Jaime comes round and slides into the booth beside me. He takes my hand.

'It's going to be OK,' he says. 'Everything's going to be OK.'

'You don't need to worry about me,' I say. 'I went through this before and I got through it. I'll get through it again. It won't be as bad this time . . . I mean, it's not real.' I reach for a bread roll and tear it open, smearing on butter, blinking hard. 'Our author here is really cruel. It's even worse than the Russian novel where she . . . This is supposedly science fiction, but it feels too much like autofiction. It's unbearable . . .' I don't want to stay here anymore, I add silently, but I don't want to leave Finn either. Isn't there anywhere I can escape to that will just give me peace?

'I know it's horrible but I think it's good, in a way,' says Jaime, looking into my eyes. 'Because now I understand.'

'But you don't have to go through all this pain,' I mutter.

He strokes my cheek.

'You've opened up to me for the first time in a long time. I don't want you to stop. Tell me what happened, after she died. Tell me how you felt. Tell me everything.'

'It was just the usual . . .' I trail off, full of dread of all that

I know will follow. Just like real life, there will be a funeral to organise: the bureaucracy of invitations, the misery of trying to find a hymn that could never sum her up. I will have to return to her flat and pack everything; I won't be able to throw anything away. Even a tube of mascara, now black and gloopy, layered lightly in dust, will be treasured and stored. I'll find a diary with shocking shards of confession: all the things she hid behind her daily smile, until the moment when her smile broke and she had to be sectioned. There will be condolences and wilting flowers. I'll be told that *time will heal you*, but I'll slowly realise that each day is little more than an attempt to apply ragged stitches to a wound that won't stop bleeding.

'I can see why you want to go back to your mum,' I say. 'This must be making you worry even more . . .'

'Shh,' he says. 'I'm not going to leave you like this. I'll stay as long as you need me.'

'I broke up with my boyfriend, not long after mum died,' I say.

'But I'm not him. I'm not going yet.'

The waitress comes and we order some food.

'Tell me more,' says Jaime. 'What happened after she died? Did you keep painting?'

I feel worn out with talking, but Jaime's gaze is insistent and so I begin:

'Well, when I first got into the art world, in my early twenties – the real world was actually a bit like Gwent's book. I mean, the scene has its own etiquette and style and ways of doing things. It seemed so solid. I was idealistic and passionate and I believed deeply in the importance of art, in the integrity of artists and critics. My mum had reinforced this belief too. It was a career she'd wanted but never had, due to her dad, and her marriage and – well, me.' I take a sip of water, finding that the words are starting to flow. 'But it ended up being something of a *Wizard of Oz* experience. I got to know the critics behind the curtain. They seemed godlike at first, but I came to see that they championed their friends and stabbed their enemies in the back. Some artist would suddenly be in, often for no discernible reason – they weren't bad, but they weren't great – and the herd would decide they liked them. And for a while, it happened to me – I went from outsider to acceptable. The Future Generation Art Prize, the Turner Prize; all those stupid awards. Is any of it really about art or is it all just politics and power games? Once my inspiration had been pure flame, now it felt dirty. When mum died, I just stopped painting.'

'But she would have wanted you to keep going,' Jaime says.

'I know – but I felt like my shadow life was catching up with me.' I bite my lip, worried that I sound mad.

'Shadow life?'

'My success was against the odds – what with the poverty we grew up in, and my mum's mental health problems. The Nominative Determinism programme would have said that I was destined to slither down all the snakes in the game of life, no matter my name. Yet I transcended it all – I didn't have a breakdown, I got A levels, I was lucky enough to get into Goldsmiths—'

'I'm sure that was talent, not luck.'

'No, it was definitely luck. I've seen so many talentless people make it and so many talented ones fail . . . I was worried that my shadow life – the one in which I was still destitute – had caught up with me. And, well, after she died, everything broke. My boyfriend got fed up with my grieving . . .'

'The bastard.'

'It was for the best,' I reflect dully.

'And you lost your inspiration?'

'My luck had run out. I wondered if it had always been destined to, if my genes and my upbringing were always going to catch up with me . . . I went to the beach . . .' I smooth my hand over my forehead, aware that my chronology is somewhat muddled, that all I can offer Jaime are random fragments. 'I went to the beach . . .'

'What happened on the beach?'

'It was a few months after she'd died. I was thinking of Jackson Pollock. He got angry at the end of his life, because he thought his drip paintings were being seen as light or pretty. So he decided to do his black paintings, a series which heralded his death. The future was there, in each canvas: within each spool and swirl of paint was his car, hurtling into that tree trunk . . . Was the new direction he took really about his artistic philosophy, or simply an urge to self-destruct?'

'But what happened at the beach?' Jaime looks frustrated.

'I painted these black-and-white paintings in oils. Stupid idea – on the way back I had to carry them on my lap, drying, on a crowded train, and one woman got paint on her coat and went mad, said I'd have to pay her dry cleaning bill. I spent the rest of the journey back staring at an ad just above my head, and the woman in the advert told me I would be OK, as long as, when I got off the train, I exited through the ticket gate on the far left. Only that would be safe – otherwise I would die. So I obeyed her. And the cracks in the pavement, they seemed like landmines. If I stepped on them, I'd have a breakdown. It just – came on, and then I couldn't stop it – I mean, going crazy if I saw a single magpie, wanting to kill it, having to run home and hide if I saw one. It got to the point where I was having to ask my neighbour to take Tommy for a walk. I made up some excuse about having sciatica in my back. I hardly went out, because if I did, it was as if the whole world was shouting danger, signs and omens. On one of those days, I was locked indoors, reading Fate's new novel—'

Jaime shudders at the mention of him.

'He was my mum's favourite writer, you see. Reading his stories made me feel close to her – there were passages she'd underlined, and she used receipts as bookmarks. I liked to look at the dates and think of her buying each book. By reading all she'd read, I felt I was bringing her back to life. I read about four hundred pages that day, and it was therapeutic: I replaced the noise in my head with his voice. It was so strong, so masculine and confident, so educated and controlled. His voice carried through into my dreams, and stayed with me when I woke. He always spoke about me in the third person, *Rachel rose that morning and cleaned her teeth while seeking out magpies in the garden*. It freaked me out, on one level. My mum started hearing a voice narrating her life before her first breakdown. But it also made me feel safe, as though Fate was in charge.'

'Oh God,' says Jaime. 'I thought he forced you. I didn't realise you . . .'

'He wrote me a letter. I didn't even remember writing to him at first, if I'm honest. I'd done so right after my mum's death, telling him what a fan she had been of his work. It was such an embarrassing grief-stricken gush, I'm surprised he even replied.'

'He saw you were young and female,' Jaime says tersely.

'No, it wasn't just that. He said he was writing a novel and one of his characters was a governess who secretly longed to be an artist, only she was born into the wrong class. He said that he'd seen my Metamorphoses exhibition and that he was impressed with my work. I was flattered. He asked if I could come and assist him with some research. It was the first time in days that I'd been out of the house. I asked a neighbour to take Tommy for a day or two, but somehow I knew it was going to be much longer than that. I nearly cried when I said goodbye to him, he was leaping up and nuzzling me.' I blink hard and sniff; Jaime strokes my cheek. 'You know the rest.'

'Did he force you to enter *Thomas Turridge*?'

'No,' I admit. 'I'd been staying there two nights and I was already getting sick of him. He was arrogant, antisocial, supercilious – though underneath it all, I saw flashes of a lonely old man who just didn't know how to connect. I underestimated him, though. I was in a very weak state, he could see that—'

'Of course he could!'

'And when he first said he could drug me and put me in a book, I thought it was a joke. I played along. I dressed up as a governess, I put on an old-fashioned dress. But then . . .'

'This is going to sound like a cliché, but you really can't run away from your problems, Rachel.' He winces as I roll my eyes. 'You could go back, you could rebuild your life, you could stage another exhibition.'

I feel it: the tingle of temptation. To try real life one more time, to see if redemption is possible. But I know that to entertain such hope is dangerous. If I were to return and fail again, I would not be able to come back from it.

'And what about Finn?' I reply tersely.

Jaime nods, defeated.

We are interrupted by the waitress bringing us our food. Jaime curls his hands around his knife and fork. I leave mine on the table. It's a while before we begin to eat.

Thirteen

With my palette knife, I smear together titanium white and burnt sienna until they streak, then merge into the colour of Jaime's skin tone. I pick a flat brush, dab it into the paint, lift it and pause, feeling raw – for that first moment of putting colour on is always clumsy. It is a moment where I am still an individual standing before an easel, before the grace of surrender comes, when the painting finds its form and paints its strokes through me. Sketched on to the canvas is an outline of Jaime, back when he was Jaimus. I want to capture that night in the last book, in Carpathia, in the Garmoshka tavern. He is on stage, holding his *yukuri*. I've accentuated the spotlight so that the triangle of golden light is stark against the black of the stage. The lower half of the painting captures the audience, seated at tables. My head will be in the far right corner, feather boa around my neck, a curve of bottle on the table. I fill the oval of his face with a lighter colour, then his neck, his collarbone, his fine fingers poised on the instrument. For the *yukuri*, I am planning to blend Prussian blue and ultramarine, to heighten the waxwing's colours into hummingbird richness. For the strings I will paste in Jaime's own fine hairs.

I wonder if I will finish 'Jaimus the Yukuri-Player' before he leaves in two days' time. I want it to be my goodbye gift to him; it will hang here, awaiting his return. It will be the first in a series of Carpathia pictures featuring blood, wolves and snow. I wish I could replicate myself: one part Raisa, working day and night in ecstatic frenzy, in those blues of night when the world is silent and magic dances and the brush begins to do extraordinary things; the other part Rachel, spending every last minute with her husband and son. I picture myself in two days' time, sitting here, Jaime's mug unused in the cupboard, his jeans hanging in the wardrobe, his guitar still in the living room.

I dreamt of my mother last night. In the months after she died, she often haunted my dreams. There, we reconnected, laughed, tried on clothes together, painted each other. Then came the dream in which we were going down in a lift together. She was holding a large white suitcase and told me that she was going to go away for a while. Last night's dream was vague, but it brought a sense of peace in being reunited. As my brush works over the canvas, shading in Jaime's face, I bequeath this painting to her – *I'm sorry*, I whisper.

I think of her house in Woking, the one in my old life, where a new family are now living. I saw it for sale on Google. I wanted to visit, but my agoraphobia was too strong by then; I had to content myself with imagining a kid, their parents sleeping in the bed she once slept in, opening the windows to gaze out at the cherry tree in the garden that she planted.

In that world, the end of my painting career was an act of self-destruction. Without my mother, I felt spineless. What was the point of achieving anything without her pride to shine a spotlight on it? Who would or could ever love me as she had? And so I picked a fight with my gallery owner. I came up with a terrible idea for an exhibition, as a way of getting him to fire me, unprepared for how sharp the sting of regret would be as I woke, day after day, thinking: I blew it, I blew it. The gallery owner ignored my emails and calls begging forgiveness. The odd article turned up online with headlines like WHATEVER HAPPENED TO RACHEL LEVY. When I ran out of money, canvases were replaced by wallpaper, my fridge, old paper.

A flicker of worry: I consider how I will survive in this world, now that my job at Cybersenx is over. Perhaps it will inspire me, spur me on to create the best exhibition of my life. Or, perhaps I will just end up pawning Jaime's vintage gramophone.

The click of the front door: Jaime is back. I set down my brush, despite Raisa's voice urging me to paint on.

'You've been painting?' Jaime asks delicately.

I nod, still in the zone. Then smile. 'I feel like I'm a stained-glass window.'

Jaime gives me an affectionate, puzzled smile. His hands are behind his back.

'I got you a present on the way back.'

'My Jaimus.'

'My Raisa.' He reveals it: a feather boa. 'They only had green.' I tell him I love it. He drapes it around my neck, pulls me in for a kiss.

'So . . .' I ask.

'So . . .' He steps back, puts his hands in his pockets, which makes me think the news is bad. 'I talked to the Booksurfer Agency.'

'Yes?' My voice is high with impatience.

'They don't have any Soma tea. They looked quite shocked when I asked for it – it's banned in this book. But do you remember that, at the end of the last book, the doctor said this could be a bridge back to Fate? The agency does have a copy of *Thomas Turridge*. So I'm going to head back that way . . .'

'Via Fate's world?'

'Yes,' he says, with a touch of uncertainty. 'I figure that I can find Gwent, and get some Soma tea from him before Fate realises I'm there.'

'OK,' I say, slowly. 'Well, if it's the only way . . .' I hug him tight.

'Come with me,' he whispers into my hair, 'come with me.'

When I don't reply, he pulls back, frowning. 'There's another thing,' he says, in a low voice. 'Finn could come too . . . I just asked casually, and they said yes. Which means—'

'What?'

'That they've done it before. They say it can work – there are kids who have been back and forth.'

'Well, of course he can't,' I flare up, shocked at Jaime's naivety, casting me as the responsible parent for once. 'It wouldn't be safe for him – imagine Fate, seeing our son – it'd be like throwing him to the lions!'

'Fine.' Jaime sighs in defeat, drumming his fingers on the counter. 'In that case, I'll definitely go through with selling my company. I've got an interested buyer; I'm seeing him tomorrow.'

'But we – you – spent years building it up!' I cry.

'Hey,' he says, looking confused, 'I did it for you.'

'We could have discussed it. It's such a big decision, and you just went ahead and did it.'

'I just don't want you to worry about money while I'm away – now you can paint the whole of the Carpathia series.'

'Thank you,' I say at last, frowning, touching his cheek.

We both jump as the Help, who has been silent all this while, interjects to offer us both a cup of tea.

Later that evening, Jaime packs a case to help Finn feel reassured of his father's return; when he goes to bed, we hide the case up in the loft. We go to bed early and make love very slowly, gazing into each other's eyes. He falls asleep with his head on my chest and I stroke his hair, beset with worries. The sale of his business feels so final. What if real life binds him into a new existence, what if new samskaras form? He has promised he will return in six weeks. I have marked the date on my calendar. But what if that day comes, and Finn and I sit and wait for a knock on the door, and there is nothing? What if he were to die in Fate's world and I became a widow without even knowing it?

Five a.m. I'm awake again, my sleep fractured with grief. I hear him whispering that he can't sleep either. We make love again, a little desperately, as though we might slip beneath skin and nail. No matter how many times we say 'I love you,' it never seems enough, we have to say it again and again, until the words become pure sound. Every so often, my eyes creep to the neon clock and I can't help but keep count: eighteen hours until he leaves us; twelve hours; ten hours. I try to imagine the moment of our goodbye and I tell myself not to be melodramatic, to remain stoical.

At nine o'clock, with six hours to go before he departs, Jaime takes the car into the city to finalise his financial affairs. Finn becomes convinced that this is the final goodbye. He curls his arms around Jaime's leg and clamps himself to it, screaming, and I have to prise him off. Jaime looks shaken, close to tears himself, and hurries off for his appointment. I tell Finn that he can have the day off school as a special treat and we go out for a walk with the dodo. In the local park, I see a robot sitting on the grass with a sign declaring that he's an Empath, and newly homeless; a dirty cup filled with coins sits by his feet. I think of Alek. Two weeks have passed since we slept together, but it feels like two months, the memory hazy and distant. My complete abandonment of him is still an ache in my conscience. I wonder how he might be surviving in Shantytown; how long he can last out there. But he has no phone, no email, and to have visited him again would have spelled the end of my marriage.

Back home, we open the door to find the air is sweet. In the kitchen, we encounter the Help standing beside a tray of cupcakes, icing waterfalling from a piping bag in his frozen hand, rippling over the counter and pooling on the floor. Finn looks anxious.

'Has he died too?' He clutches my hand tight. 'Mum, why's everyone dying?'

I feel like weeping that I have no idea how the hell the world works.

'Dad will be able to fix him,' I say, adopting a brave voice. I pull a cake from the tray and give it to Finn. There is something tragic about the Help's final expression, as though he wanted to say goodbye. I find myself putting a tea towel over his head. Another ally lost. We can ill afford a replacement. The flat will feel empty without him.

When Jaime comes home, he attempts to play God. But despite dismantling the Help's spine and tapping instructions into his hard drive, he can't resuscitate him.

My mobile rings. It's Claire, which means a boring work crisis: I ignore it, but it buzzes again, and again, so I pick up.

'Hello?' I say in a ragged voice.

At first I fear she's ringing me to say we've both been fired, but it's worse, far worse. Her words are staccato and when the call ends, I find that I can't move. My first thought is: How will Finn survive without his mother? My second: Jaime can't leave.

'I just can't seem to get him to wake up . . .' Jaime trails off when he sees my face.

'I think I'm cursed,' I hear myself say, voice raw with tears. 'First Mum, then the Help, now Alek. What if I carry it with me, wherever I go?'

'Alek? He's dead?'

'He mutilated someone. He attacked them in the street, he cut off their ear. It's all my fault, I ignored the rules, I introduced him to art that was way too strong for him. He's been arrested.' I sink down on to the sofa and bury my face in my hands. 'Oh God.'

'You're not responsible; it's his algorithms, he's not human, Rachel. And you didn't create this plot. He's not your problem anymore,' Jaime asserts. 'Forget about him.'

'I can't – they're coming after me.'

'What the fuck?'

'There's a warrant out for my arrest. It's never happened before – but it's protocol now. Claire says they've already arrested another therapist whose patient went crazy after Cybersenx released him. He's being made a scapegoat. She thinks they'll charge me for Alek's crime: for abuse or neglect of a robot.'

Finn runs over, jumps on to my lap, and clings to me. I bury my face in his shoulder, and finally, with resentment, I surrender:

'We'll all have to leave together.' I let out a small, bitter laugh. 'The narrator seems to be colluding with you.'

Jaime's face is bright with elation.

'How about it, Finn – a holiday?'

'What about the dodo?' Finn's voice crumples. 'Isn't he coming with us?'

Jaime reassures Finn that he'll sort out the dodo, perhaps return him to the pet shop, which provokes another tantrum. I watch Jaime comforting him as I pick at a thread on a cushion. I recall the softness of Alek's caresses, the earnestness in his eyes as he sought to please me. I try to connect it with the image of Alek severing muscle, tearing skin, but I can't bring the two together. I am Alek's Pygmalion as much as his creator was; I gently shaped him in our weekly sessions. I hoped to heal him but instead I failed him. After our recent night together, it is easier to assuage my guilt by telling myself, *He's only a Robo*, denying all that is exquisite and beautiful in him, reducing him to caricature. I would never have treated him that way if he was human. Perhaps I am no better than the Cybersenx corporates.

'Maybe I should stay another day or so, for Alek,' I interrupt them. I see Jaime's expression darken with jealousy. 'Not for *that* – because he's my responsibility . . .'

'We stay, and you get locked up,' Jaime asserts. 'No way.'

'OK,' I relent. 'Fine. Let's go now.'

Finn comes over, squeezing my hand, reminding me of my responsibility to him. I tell myself that to sit here and wallow in guilt is an indulgence; I must harden my heart against Alek once more, in order to save my son.

Adrenaline focuses us. Jaime comes up with a solution: he calls a neighbour, asking him if he'll look after the dodo, and I send Finn into his bedroom to pick a favourite teddy to take with him. Ten minutes later, we leave the flat. As I twist the key in the door, I feel a pinch at the thought of the paints still drying on my canvas, knowing I'll never be able to display it or get to finish the series. In the back of the car, Jaime reaches for me.

'I could never have said goodbye to you anyway,' he says, and I manage a smile. Every time we hear the wail of a siren, my body locks in apprehension, then trembles with relief as it fades. We still can't be sure if the narrator wants to send us safely on our way or we'll find ourselves in a cell again, forming a repetitive pattern of damnation. I feel the betrayal of it, the plot twists, the way various threads have been woven together carefully, knowingly, like I'm in some Greek tragedy where the more I struggle against my fate, the more the noose tightens.

We arrive at the Booksurfing hub. The staff are friendly, accommodating, and agree to book us in as a trio. We're each strapped into a seat and given a glass of water, as well as a simple Grand Kuding pill.

We hold hands as they take effect. Jaime keeps on speaking all the way, to reassure our son: 'We're going on holiday, Finn, we're going to go as a family, and it's all going to be all right, I swear . . .' As his voice fogs and fades, I think of our beautiful flat, my feather boa curled on the bed, the Help standing frozen in the kitchen, my paints, Jaime's vinyls, Finn's toys, all losing their colours as we pass into the next book, becoming sketches, becoming blanks; and that quote from Vincent Van Gogh comes to mind, his painting of 'The Old Church Tower at Nuenen,' and how he wanted it to convey 'how perfectly simple death and burial is, as simple as the falling of autumn leaves.'

An Interim

I am seated at my desk, failing to write, when I hear it. I hurry to the CCTV feed in shock; I cannot quite believe the noise I just heard. They have lain in my cottage for six weeks now, peaceful as the dead, while I have been patiently awaiting their return to my novel. Their drip contains vast doses of Grand Kuding tea, but perhaps Jaime has developed a resistance to it. That is the trouble with that young man: he has too much will to survive.

On the screen, I note that Rachel is still sprawled on the four-poster bed. But the boy has risen. He tugs at the catheter in his wrist; his fingers trace the length of tubing that connects him to the drip, his giver of sustenance. I hope the silly young man doesn't remove it. He stands up. I hear him swear and kick the bed.

Anger erupts inside me. He is going to try and escape, and I do not know if I have the physical strength to overpower him, even with the baseball bat and knife that sit ready. Yes, his body has grown weak from weeks of seclusion, but he is four decades younger than me. But why attempt such a foolhardy escape when I have a new plot ready for them? Who are they? Two dull souls who were contributing little to the world before they came here. How many fans have written to me and begged me to name a character after them? Why, one wealthy American tycoon even offered me two hundred thousand dollars to dedicate my latest book to his wife. Fame is the currency of this age and normally, in order to win it, one must commit atrocities of the soul on reality television. I have given them the opportunity of a lifetime: the immortality of being preserved in a potentially prize-winning book. And they have reacted with such ingratitude.

Jaime is lying back on the four-poster bed, next to the girl. Despite his caresses, his pleading, his gentle slaps, she does not wake from her Booksurfing coma. Presently he goes to the window. Tears course down his cheeks; he smears them away with his fists. I suppose that, when he arrived here, the land was silent with snow and now the trees are gossipy with the promise of new leaves.

No, I do not like this. He may have a predilection for spring, and if that is the case, he might start to nurture fantasies about picking daffodils for his lover and such. I go to the kitchen and I take the knife and then I slowly climb the stairs. I am ready for them.

I stand on the landing, listening to Jaime banging against the door.

'Good morning,' I say.

'You fucking—' The door rattles wildly; I am taken aback by his savagery. 'Let us out!'

'Is the room not to your liking? The four-poster is the best bed in the house. I myself merely sleep on a double bed.'

Silence. Then a shocking sound: as though Jaime is throwing his entire body against the door. I realise that I need to make things clear.

'You will be released soon, but first I must finish my novel. Why, I was only halfway through when you both deserted me for the insipid ramblings of Mr Gwent.'

'You've got to be joking. You've got to be *fucking* joking.'

'I did not expect you to wake.'

'You're a monster.'

'I am an author. And if you will permit me to say so, I do believe that you were both enjoying yourselves in my novel.'

He screams.

'There will be money,' I say hastily. 'The novel will be concluded quickly and I will give you each ten thousand.' I pause, dreading that he might start to bargain.

'Dear God, just let us out.'

'Think of the money,' I reason. 'You could finish your MA without having to work in a restaurant.'

'Fuck your money. How is it that I'm here and Rachel isn't? Where is she now?'

'Which book were you in before you slipped back here? Remind me of the title?'

'*2047*.'

'Oh, Shirley Turner's latest. I see. Well, you should rejoin Rachel in her swoon and sup the tea . . . And be quick about it. She will be floating in a liminal state, feeling lost, in need of a new narrative—'

He slams his palm against the wood.

'No – *you* have to *wake her up*!'

'When Rachel came here, she begged me to put her into one of my books. I only did as she asked,' I explain patiently.

'You know she's a famous artist, don't you? She could be producing her own art, which she *doesn't* need to make by *kidnapping and imprisoning anyone*.'

I frown. I did observe Rachel's artwork on a brief foray to the Serpentine, but it appeared to me to be rather banal. But the boy is in love and I cannot argue with the bias of oxytocin and vasopressin.

'She was happy in my world. Don't spoil it, now.'

His laughter is derisive.

'There is a door at the back of the room,' I instruct him. 'It's a small bathroom. In there you'll find a tea pot by the sink. I suggest you boil some water. I shall slip some Grand Kuding tea under the door. Take a double dose. You'll join Rachel and you can re-enter *Thomas Turridge* together.'

'I can't do it!' he rages. 'I can't be a fucking kid in your Victorian novel again—'

'The second half of my book is set in 1910 – Queen Victoria is no longer on the throne. Thomas Turridge is now sixty-four years old. I have explored his childhood in the first half of the novel; now I shall explore his old age. I will leave the reader to surmise what has happened in the intervening years. That is where your imagination can assist me.'

No reply. An ongoing silence. A sign of his awe, his gratitude?

Then I hear the creak of the window latch.

'If you attempt to jump out of that window, you will only succeed in breaking your legs. When Gwent first lay in this room twelve years ago, he attempted it. I had to set his leg myself.'

'I'll call for help.'

'They won't hear you. Gwent howled for days.'

'I can't do this to Rachel. Don't you understand? I can't do this to her family, her friends – to her.'

'Family? Rachel has no family, as you know. She only has you – and now you've deserted her.'

'None of this is even possible. You've fucked us up – we're on some kind of hallucinogenic . . .'

'I could quote you some waffle from quantum physics – consciousness is infinite, our bodies temporal. But I prefer to quote Blake – those lines about holding "Infinity in the palm of your hand / And Eternity in an hour".'

Silence. A breeze under the door; it is sweet and sharp. He ought to close that window.

'You cannot wake Rachel,' I inform him. 'Her dose is too big. You can scream, you can shake her – but all the while she'll remain trapped in that pale desert between books, lacking her hero.' I improvise: 'You left *2047* because you were in trouble, I presume?'

A cautious 'Yes.'

'Your author, Ms Turner, is one who favours tragic endings – much like Maslennikov. That was a lucky escape; you were wise to flee. I assure you that I will give you the happy ending that Ms Turner denied you.'

Silence.

'Time is running out, Jaime. Rachel needs you.'

'Fuck, fuck – *fuck*!' Another punch to the door. 'I can't leave her in there.'

'No, you can't.' I pause. 'In the bathroom, there is nothing but towels and the kettle and the teapot. No weapons. So fill the pot, make the tea and hurry.'

'Have you seen the state Rachel is in? She's not going to last much longer; you're killing her. Surely you need us alive to finish your piece of shit novel?'

'Then hurry. You left my readers on a cliffhanger at the end of the last story: Rachel on her way to the asylum, the monks closing in on you. It was a tad overblown. Now we will jump forwards in time, by fifty years – perhaps there will be more melodrama to come.'

'You created the fucking plotline. The melodrama is all you.'

'Touché.'

'And when the melodrama is over – then what? If it's ever over?'

'Oh, it will be over, I assure you. Another twenty-five thousand words will suffice. Then I shall release you.'

'So I have only your word – completely corrupt and unreliable – that we won't die in this room? That you'll let us out and bring us back?'

'The decision to return is entirely up to you. You have free will.'

'Oh sure – a locked room – free will.'

'Such is life.'

'Can you send a note to my mum? An anonymous note. Just saying that I'm all right and that I'll be back soon? If you can do that, I can live with this, I can go back.' His voice catches as though he is about to start crying again.

'Of course.'

'There's something else . . .' His voice is small with fear; he is already becoming my Thomas once more.

'Go on.'

'How long have we been here? It feels like it could be years . . .'

'It's been six weeks for you, eight for Rachel.'

'That's all?'

'That is all.'

'But Gwent is still in your novel and he disappeared twelve years ago . . . How have you kept him alive?'

I smile. I am tempted to reveal all, but, as Dickens says, *make them wait.*

'That is something of a miracle, but I am afraid you will have to ask Gwent for the details when you return to my narrative.'

'Well, we don't plan on spending another fucking decade in your book.'

I wince; his tone is becoming unreasonable again.

'Kindly clean up your language.'

Silence.

'A month will suffice,' I say briskly. 'I will have finished the novel by then. Now, see your adventure through, don't do anything silly – like getting yourself killed. Return to me. A happy ending is my promise to you.'

'I'll do it,' he surrenders, 'but only if we can bring our son Finn with us.'

'You have a son?' I am so astonished, I blurt the words out. And thus I reveal myself: I am not omniscient. I fear that Jaime will realise that my perception is limited, but he is too confused to digest my words.

'There must be a guarantee that he can enter with us,' he insists, 'and that you won't harm him. He's just an innocent boy.'

'Very well,' I concede. 'I will allow Finn to enter the world of *Thomas Turridge*. Come as a trio. The happy family.'

I take luncheon at midday. As advised by my nutritionist, I enjoy a salad of quinoa and smoked salmon, feeding small shreds to Dorothea at my feet, while Radio 4 burbles in the background. Colm Tóibín is choosing his Desert Island Discs and I am mildly entertained, for he is one of the few authors I consider my equal, even if his interview was a little off-piste. A stomach ache begins to throb on my left side, and I ruminate that it was the confrontation with the boy that has caused it; it was more stressful than I had anticipated.

At least I know that my ducklings are returning. In the meantime, I can refine my chapter plan. With a tight enough plot, I will be able to noose them into predictable responses, so that the chapters flow smoothly from one to the next. But their very real emotions will broil beneath the surface of my prose. Thomas's consciousness will be youthful, for what is old age, but the paradox of feeling twenty but finding yourself in a body that is wrinkled and fraying and cheating you at every turn?

As for the climax of my plotline, I have thought very hard on this and I have decided that I will not kill off *both* of my characters. The Victorians clung to realism and took fiction seriously enough to be vexed by the death of a minor character in *Bleak House* who spontaneously combusted. Unhappy endings aggrieved them. George Eliot ended *Middlemarch* on as sober a note as her readership would allow, while Thomas Hardy's tragic endings enraged his fans. But then, the Victorians thought reading had a moral purpose and would improve the working classes . . . I cannot imagine that sort of attitude now. Now we only wish to put a child in front of a television set and hope it will hypnotise him into silence. It is safer to let him rot his mind with a video game than let him read and begin to develop ideas. Now, the arts are about entertainment of the soporific kind, a literary fluoride in the waters of collective consciousness. Happy endings that are easy make us suspicious. For the modern reader, things cannot end too well . . .

The Fifth Story

OXFORD, 1910

I

I shuffle on to Broad Street, my stick supporting every step. What is it that I came out for? I have quite forgotten. It tickles the edge of my mind. My memory is like a mischievous child these days, forever taunting me. Before I left the house, Rachel told me to write it down on a piece of paper but no, I refused, laughing, asserting that there was no need. A faint pain in my gut at the fear of what might be to come: I have looked up the illness many a time in the *Oxford Book of Malaises* and always I picture it as maggots in my mind, eating through memory, feeding on identity. The thought of it: ending up in an armchair, dribbling, the days muddled and the month a mystery; poor Rachel forced to feed me and remind me of my name. I have given her strict instructions that if the time ever comes, she must smother me with a pillow, else I shall overdose on opium and be gone that way.

I pass the butcher's and Blackwell's, hoping that a shop will call out to me. Autumn leaves scuddle over the streets in their lovely browns, the cobbles quiet, for Michaelmas term is a few weeks away yet. I push and wheeze a breath. A young woman is approaching. Her hair, darkly luxurious, is pinned up beneath a hat of feathers. I am astonished: why, she is *smiling* at me. Usually the young peruse me fleetingly, eyes sliding away quickly, as though I am a dull exhibit in a museum they have been forced to attend on a school outing; though I know that when I was a boy I too saw the elderly as another species, born dusty, balding and toothless, not something I could ever evolve into. There is lust in her violet eyes. Is there anything that makes one feel more alive than being desired? Then I realise that there is a young man in my shadow. The woman registers my mistake, greets him and whispers in his ear, his laughter echoing hers. I tut as though I am far too lofty and wise to succumb to such trivialities, while chuckling at myself for being such a silly old fool. I require a swift exit. A side street will do. A church spire looms, the ivy tangle of a graveyard, a spool of puffclock seeds on a breath of wind.

In the churchyard I find my mother's grave so heavily clothed in ivy that it seems a green creature with a leafy spine. I attempt to hack it away with my cane, but my arm grows too weary. My father's grave is beside hers, for he passed away a decade ago. Thus, I am an orphan. Birds trill above me. I imagine the young couple from the street stripping, his teeth clashing against hers. I smile when I recall my boyhood fear of masturbating, brought on by a stiffly worded letter from my father about the medical dangers of such a sin. The older generation's desire to constrict the pleasures of the young must surely arise from envy . . . There, out of the corner of my eye, I can see Eleanor's grave; she died three years ago, unmarried. It evokes only a sense of regret for my past self, and a bewilderment that I could ever have imagined her, even for a brief time, superior to Rachel.

I do not envy the young. Truly, I do not. I may have acquired a little of Rachel's attitude towards life's flowers and thorns, a dash of her Eastern philosophy, for I recognise the same thing in all the faces I see. The lovers, the adulterers, the mothers, the fathers, the friends; how earnest they are in their desires, aching for a fulfilment that might be postponed for days, months, years, or wither with the possibility of *never*. A wish for money, for love, for a kiss, for a betrayal, for a yes, and yet, I know the cycle, I know that fulfilment is never a simple thing, but only sows fresh longings, which grow and repeat in wistfulness. *Why act at all?* I contemplate often these days. *Why bother?*

The Vicar emerges from the church. He's also supported by a stick. He is quite a changed character from the terrifying orator I endured as a boy, who accused me of being infected with Darwinism. Once, he only had to put on his vestments to know what role he ought to play. Now he chews his lips; his fingers pleating the folds of his robe. We still attend the service every Sunday, but only because Rachel enjoys singing the hymns.

'Good afternoon to you, Mr Turridge,' he says in a quavering voice.

'Just eyeing up the real estate.' I wave at the graves. 'I wonder if I ought to lay down a deposit for my preferred spot.'

He looks briefly shocked, then replies in earnest: 'We will accept such a payment, if you are willing. It is wise to be prepared.'

'Perhaps I can put one down for a seat in Heaven too?'

He refuses to be riled: 'Each good deed that you perform will be your deposit, Mr Turridge.'

'I do remember you declaring that God, the great Author, pens our every action, and so from birth it is determined whether we have a place in Heaven or Hell.'

He fingers his collar. 'As you know, my views on this matter have softened somewhat . . . It is free will that allows us the choice between good and evil. Each time we make the right choice, it is that which defines us as Christians.'

'And if the choice is unclear, or masquerades as good when it is actually bad?'

'We must assess fully and make the right choice,' he asserts.

I rather like this philosophy, which is more closely aligned with my own than I might care to admit, for I do believe that it is the small actions of the everyday that can make the difference in the world. But I merely nod a goodbye, and turn to go. I see a dying sun hanging between the trees, only to realise it is a newborn moon. Unease clouds me, as though there are eyes in the stars, whispers in the leaves.

'Wait. I have a little gift for you, before you go – one of my parishioners gave it to me.'

He disappears into the church and reappears, brandishing a small tin labelled GRAND KUDING.

'I only drink Darjeeling – this is a little too exotic for my tastes. You and Rachel should enjoy it.'

'Thank you,' I reply, feeling mollified.

On the way home, I spot some primroses growing by the road and stoop to pick a posy for my dear wife.

Home: it always gives me reassurance to see its red brick and latticed windows, the oak at the rear towering above the chimney, leaves smoke-tinted. I think of my armchair and the warm lick of the fire; I could nap for days. But as I force my weary legs up the front garden, I see movement in the drawing room and Rachel opens the door. My posy is rewarded with a smile but a moment later she is berating me:

'Did you remember the tea? I told you to write a reminder! Finn, I am afraid there will be no tea.'

Oh, my son! My heart sings to see him, for he is married now and busy being a grown-up; his visits are monthly at best. What a fine young man, glowing with health and good looks – 'From my side of the family!' I always joke. I shake his hand vigorously and the tea the Vicar gifted me falls out of my coat.

'Ah, you see! I did remember!' I cry in triumph.

Rachel raises an eyebrow. Then she kisses me on the cheek. 'So you did, Mr Turridge. I ought not to underestimate you.' As she passes me on her way to the kitchen, she turns and whispers: 'Finn has brought us a *present*.'

I follow my son into the drawing room. I do not notice the box at first, for I am preoccupied asking after the health of Fanny.

'She is quite well, Father,' says Finn. 'She sends her apologies, she is busy still with packing up our things.'

I think of his wife: tall and slim, her pinched face surrounded by a halo of fair hair. She always treats Rachel and me with a formal air, as though she cannot quite believe that we created Finn and now she has taken over and will show us how it is done.

'I do hope you will remember to write to your mother while you are away,' I say, 'else she will suffer terribly.'

'I shall!'

'Every week, I hope?'

'Every Monday. I promise.'

Ginny, our maid, enters carrying a tray of tea things. Rachel follows her in. It is then that I notice the box, which has been set down on the rug by a chair.

'Is this the "present"?' I ask, folding my arms.

'We were rather hoping that you wouldn't mind taking Flaubert while we are gone.' He unfolds the flaps and lifts out the tabby cat. His yowls of protest are harsh. Finn sets him down on the floor, where he begins to sniff about.

'We cannot take him, Father – he would get seasick. And you have been saying for the past few years how you would love a pet.'

I have not the heart to finish Finn's sentence: we have not acted on our wish in the knowledge that a cat or a dog would surely outlive us. Our son thinks us immortal. As I sit down on the chair, exhaling in theatrical defeat, Ginny steps in. She pours the tea and passes round the cups, Finn's eyes trailing after her. I think of my father's grave, the engraved letters fading as the weather beats them away. I imagine how Finn will feel when the time comes for him to visit our graves, with a loneliness in his heart as he gazes up at the sky, and a sense of life's armour having been wrenched from him.

'No, Finn, you sit here,' Rachel guides him. 'Otherwise you will be on my left and I will not hear a word you are saying.'

'You ought to buy a hearing trumpet, Mother.'

'She has threatened to do so,' I chime in, 'and then every time someone she dislikes speaks, she can set it in her lap.'

Finn chuckles and raises his cup, then splutters.

'Your father bought the tea,' says Rachel, rolling her eyes.

I take a sip and smother a wince, asserting, 'I think it is delightful.'

We all attempt to drink it – and then, simultaneously, we burst into laughter.

Finn is a tonic. He enthuses about his new job and his trip abroad, and I am reminded of what it is to have life ahead of you, before you discover your character, when it feels as though you might do anything or be anyone. His joyful vigour is contagious; I find myself making witticisms. I am not so sharp-witted when he is not present. How quickly the afternoon passes in merriment, with Rachel hinting gently that she hopes he will return in a year with a grandchild, and Finn admiring her new painting, which hangs on the wall. He makes a remark about how good it is that there are so many female artists about, which provokes an impassioned speech from Rachel that while they may be growing in number, they remain shut out of the Camden Town artists' group due to that snivelling Walter Sickert. And just how many of their paintings get pride of place in the Royal Academy? Still, at least she had work shown at the 'Manet and the Post-Impressionists' exhibition. Roger Fry's review has lifted her reputation.

Then Finn is standing, filling us with dismay. Owing to his busy life, he can only give us two hours of his time, and I suffer a hollow, sad feeling once he has gone, as though the house has aged another decade in the closing of the door behind him. Rachel goes off to paint and I take solace in my study.

II

I say '*my* study', but in my mind I still regard it as my father's. His quiddity dominates the room, his presence patriarchal, the walls carrying his portraits, the bookcases his tomes. The desk I inherited is a wonderful thing, big and weighty and filled with drawers; blots of his ink have stained the wood around the inkwell, from letters he sent that will now be ageing and yellowed and stored in the drawers of other homes, growing dusty. In that desk there is a drawer filled with bills I do not want to look at. It is the fear of failing to leave Rachel with sufficient funds after I have gone that seizes my gut. She might be older than me, but she has lived a healthier existence, and does not need to regularly consult *The Oxford Dictionary of Malaises*. Another drawer has a small packet of opium in it, but I have made a promise to my wife that I will not touch it: it is for emergencies only. I think of Finn standing by a ship's rail, surveying the sea as though he has dominion over it. Why does it feel as though he is now the adult and we are the children – abandoned and lost?

The fire blazes in the grate; the windows multiply it in their reflections. I go to the gramophone and toy between Beethoven symphonies. The ninth can make me feel a little frenzied, but I need to be cheered. I lose concentration and find my body overriding my reasoning, acting as though it has made the decision by itself, for suddenly the needle is fusing with the groove and the fifth is booming out. Dot-dot-dot-dash. How did Beethoven describe those opening notes? *Destiny is knocking*. Beethoven himself was nearly poleaxed by destiny when he began to lose his hearing at the age of thirty. He contemplated suicide, but then declared: *I want to grab fate by the throat. It most certainly will not get me down.* Work became his reason for living. I picture him on the stage in Vienna, back to the audience, at the premiere of the ninth, unable to hear the rapturous applause until his soloist, Caroline Unger, taps him on the shoulder and he turns to face a standing ovation. Perhaps I ought to return to music criticism or even to my composing again, but really . . . *Why act? Why bother?*

Rachel is my opposite. Two rooms away, she is painting feverishly, having produced over twenty pieces this year, striving so hard that sometimes I find her standing in front of her canvas, palette loose in her hand, chin on chest, snoring. I regard it now as my profession to love her and support her gift, to compensate for those years when I failed her. Why bother with my own paltry musical compositions when I will never have time to finish them? I have the most wonderful wife in the world, not to mention the fire, and my books, and this glorious music, and the stars that glint through the window and – ah! as though the sky is listening in sympathy – a shooting star.

I lift a paperweight, roll it in my hands, and find a scrap of paper underneath it. On it I have scrawled in a shaky hand: ПОМНИТЬ *MANCHESTER*. The Russian bewilders me, and Manchester is not a city I have ever visited.

Another mystery; another appointment I have no doubt missed. I hide it back under the paperweight.

The door creaks open and Flaubert the cat wanders in.

'What a so-and-so, running away to sea and deserting you,' I tell the cat. 'How cruel and ruthless my boy is.'

I wonder if Ginny has left for the night; I would like some warm milk or maybe more of that Grand Kuding tea, which has made me feel blurry around the edges. Might it also take the edge off my pain?

Then Rachel is in the doorway, looking miserable.

'Da da da daa,' she mimics the music. Beethoven affects her as alcohol does. He rouses me but he makes her feel peevish. She is better with Mozart and his calming coherence.

'Change it if you like, my darling.'

Rachel has not heard; I have spoken into the wrong ear. She bends to stroke the cat, groaning as her back protests. I reach for her, and coax her on to my lap. 'Stroke me,' I whisper and she laughs and kisses me softly, and we rub noses in an Eskimo kiss. Clutching the arm of the chair, she rises and goes to my desk. I tense up, seeing her remove the small, battered green tin of opium, dreading a lecture.

'Let's smoke it,' she says decisively.

I laugh in delight. 'My angel.'

Beethoven's fifth has passed into its second movement, and notes of cellos and violas and basses playing pizzicato infuse the cloud that is thickening around us. We are on a ship, Rachel says, sitting on my lap, swaying gently so that her long hair swishes, and I stroke it softly. I twist a lock around my little finger, and examine the colours: the salt and pepper, the snowy hues, pure and dirty. *Da da da daa*. I used to find this refrain rather contrived, but with age I have realised that it is a true mirroring of life and the tendency of events to rhyme and echo through the years. I pull the lock taut and realise it is the string of a beautiful instrument. With my other hand, I pluck it. 'You could be a harp,' I tell Rachel . . .

When I next open my eyes, I find that we are lying on the rug, and the cat is sitting on the chair, watching us incredulously. My right side is very warm from the fire. I call the cat, 'Finn,' and Rachel says, 'He's Flaubert,' and I say, 'No, from now on, he shall be Finn.' Rachel curls her head against my shoulder and attempts a purr. 'I think this is one of the best nights of my life,' I tell her, and begin trailing kisses over the liver spots on her face.

She reaches up and gently slaps me, then kisses me. I tell her I love her. It's been an age and in the sweetness of raw ache I wonder why we have left it so long. Then I feel the pain in my back and the agony of my arthritic knees knobbling on the thin rug and remember why. My determination to give her pleasure makes the pain a penance I want to endure, and I carry on, gazing down into her dilated pupils, whispering dirt and love in her ear and . . . Oh, the sensation of having slipped away, and reaching down to find a humiliating softness. I let out a loud curse. Rachel cuddles up against me – 'Just hold me,' she says. I bury my face in her hair.

Some time has passed and Beethoven has been replaced by the music of the wind in the chimney. I realise Rachel is speaking:

'Perhaps Finn will discover a new species of butterfly.'

'Or we will find out that we do not come from the apes at all, but from worms,' I muse.

'Or that the trees are our common ancestors, and we were once all roots and leaves.'

I murmur agreement, and find myself drifting into sleep, but in a slow, delicious way, as if I am going down in a glass box, floor by floor, and at the junction point between waking and sleeping, where thoughts are colours and reshape to form dreams, a memory slices through: a helicopter, smashing into the church spire, and *this is not real. You're in a book*. A sweat prickles over me, and I know that it is Fate, Augustus Fate, who is in the trees and the sky, watching, smirking, ready to strike. I try to fight my stupor to shake Rachel awake, but she is snoring and I hear myself say, 'Wake up, we need to wake up,' and the cat is staring at me with wide eyes, as though urging me on, but I am too tired and my mind is not strong enough to battle my body, and I slide into sleep . . .

III

Three weeks have passed since our son's departure. It is breakfast time and the cat jumps up on to my lap, purring, licking the grease of leftover butter on my plate. Our tempers are foul this morning, for last night involved one too many whiskies to ease our sadness. I stare dolefully at my marmalade on toast, and flick through *The Oxford Dictionary of Malaises*, only for Rachel to yank it from me.

'There is no mystery to why we feel so rough this morning,' she snaps. 'Does it have a definition for "hangover"?'

Then, as Ginny is clearing away our cold tea, a telegram comes: our dear friend, Penny Worthing, has died. Ginny tells us that she went out one frosty evening last week to post a birthday card, slipped and suffered a bleed in her brain. We share a long silence. Rachel remarks tersely that she is tired of going to funerals all the time. The number of friends we've lost outnumbers those that are still with us; we are starting to feel either blessed or cursed – depending on the day and hour – with our extra years. Darwin might put it down to resilient ancestors; Rachel would look to the patterning of our stars.

I joke that it feels as though there's one big party going on 'up there' and that we are being left out. Rachel isn't in the mood for my morbid humour. She declares that she will spend the day painting, despite the pain in her head. I remind her of our plans to go to the fair, and then I cajole her into honouring them, citing the benefits of fresh air. We set off in a querulous mood, feeling quite out of sorts with the world.

We pass through Port Meadow. The sky above us seems huge, blown up to a pitch of terror. In the city, buildings are springing up at a frantic pace, serving to compress the horizon into the man-made and finite. Out here, the sky belongs to God. I feel rather paranoid, as though there is a shadow to my shadow, and wonder if it is the after-effect of the opium. I wish I had taken a little more of that Grand Kuding tea.

Then, as a few spots of rain come down, Rachel laments: 'I have forgotten my umbrella.'

Fortunately, the weather is indecisive. An aura of droplets, and then it ceases.

The fair is blazing with noise, with carousels and a helter-skelter and a steam yacht, and I muse how glad I am that technology has allowed us to progress from those infernal freak shows. The change in Rachel's expression as we arrive at the fair is a relief: a bloom appearing in her cheeks and a sparkle in her eye. A small boy comes running out of a crowd, slap bang into her. He is only six or seven, a grubby little urchin, but his shock of thick, dark hair looks just like Finn's. She gazes down at him, stunned, and gently touches his cheek. The boy rubs away her touch, laughs and runs on.

'Let me win you a toy,' I declare, and proceed to blow shillings we can ill afford on the coconut shy until Rachel is clutching a stuffed bear.

Our spirits lift further when we enter the hall of

mirrors, where we gawp at our stretched and squashed visages. The exaggeration of our jowls and drooping brows is quite grotesque.

When we exit, Rachel catches sight of the fortune teller's tent.

'We must go in, we must!' Rachel cries. I shake my head, but my wife has her ways, her wiles. She curls her arm through mine and brushes her cheek against my shoulder. I kiss her firmly and advise that I will go in first. I will ascertain whether the palm reader is serious or a charlatan, and protect my wife from potential indignity.

Madame Scarlet is dressed in the obligatory costume, her dark hair tied back with a frayed red scarf, her lace blouse hemmed with dirt. I refrain from allowing her to read my palm or my tarot, though, inevitably, she does glance into the cracked depths of her crystal ball and predict tragedy for me – 'For you cannot fight fate' – before I stop her and declare that I have no need of her wisdom. I insist that she only speak to Rachel of trivial matters and avoid seeding worries or fears of future tragedies; she acquiesces with a begrudging frown. I take my leave, telling Rachel she can go in.

I wait, and I wait. Someone outside the tent is drunkenly singing the theme from Gilbert and Sullivan's *Mikado*, and soon the refrain is trapped in my head. *You will have to face a terrible darkness*, the woman had said. *You will be tested to your very limits*. Damn her. There is nothing more disturbing than an idea that sits in the mind like a maggot: feeding on the faecal matter of fear, breeding. I am ready to thunder in and drag Rachel out, but just as my patience snaps, she emerges.

'I do not wish to hear a thing,' I say firmly. 'We will not share her stories – by telling them, we will make them real. Let her tale die inside you, and let us be on our way.'

'Do not worry,' she replies cheerfully. 'It was all very positive. I got the Lovers and the Two of Cups – all is well for us.'

'Still, you should forget her stories quickly.'

Rachel smiles and touches my arm gently.

It is late and I wonder if we should request a hackney carriage to take us home, but Rachel wants to walk. The grassy lanes are quiet; midges and sleepy butterflies flit across Port Meadow; the scent of summer's end laces the air. I savour the cooling of the evening and the encroaching dark, knowing that we can stoke a fire in the parlour, and sit in its glow, talking and growing sleepy together, close the door on this wretched day.

'What's that noise?' Rachel stops, frowning.

'What? There is nothing.'

She cries in protest: 'It sounds like a child!'

'I cannot hear a thing, and you are half-deaf. It is your imagination.'

'It is a child,' she says fiercely. 'They're in pain. And we will not stand by while a child is in need.'

We take a detour through the field and I feel such a sense of dread, but I laugh when I see the cause of the wailing: a calf, its hooves stuck in an iron grate, mooing with such pity that it sounds near-human.

'Do not laugh,' Rachel chides me.

We assist the poor creature back to solid ground, and the calf rewards us with a moo of gratitude as a farmer comes hurrying across the meadow. He thanks me profusely, nodding at Rachel's explanation of how we came across his beast without looking her in the eye. I am about to shake the farmer's extended hand, when he emits a violent sneeze. This is followed by a ruddy laugh and a muffled apology, as he draws out his handkerchief. The hand is proffered again, but I pretend that it does not exist; Rachel, looking embarrassed for him, seizes and shakes it. The farmer continues to avoid her gaze, and instead gives me a look of even deeper apology, as if my wife is some fallen creature who might be beyond my redemptive powers. Rachel's irritation is palpable. We bid him goodnight and stroll on, Rachel muttering and moaning at his misogyny.

By the time we begin to make our way home the rain has thickened, so that when we arrive, we are more water than flesh; puddles follow us down the hallway. We huddle beneath wool blankets before the fire and Finn curls up between us.

'My baby,' Rachel whispers, kissing his head.

We are sweet with one another again, murmuring plans for our forty-first wedding anniversary next year. It is a pact we made early in our marriage, never to go to bed having argued, to always finish each day as friends.

In bed, we share the usual routine. 'Goodnight, you peevish old crone!' Rachel says merrily, and I feign deafness and she laughs and we go to sleep with our fingers laced beneath the covers.

The next day, I awake to find that the temperature has plunged so low in the night that there is a frost beading on our counterpane. Rachel's face resembles that of a peculiar sea creature, fleshy and white, eyes puffy and nose streaming. Upon opening the curtains, I see that our damned maid left the window open for the night. I ring the bell furiously, its shimmer silvering through the house. Ginny bows her head as I berate her.

'You know how dangerous it is, not to allow oxygen into the room,' she stutters.

'That is an absurd old wives' tale, Ginny, I have told you a thousand times.' I look back at Rachel on the bed. Her smile is vague. Her eyes seem to have acquired a faded, milky quality; there is mildew in her aura.

'Ginny, please fetch Dr. Adams, and hurry!' I cry.

She hesitates: 'You did say we should be economising in all matters, sir.'

'And this matter is an emergency. Get on with you!'

She leaves with a curtsey and a fit of apologies. I massage Rachel's hand gently, shocked at the iciness of her fingers. I suffer the foreboding of the coming days; a shadow whose shape I cannot quite define. Suddenly I feel tired. We were doing well, and Rachel had one last painting to finish before her first solo exhibition. It feels as though life has barely had a chance to swim freely before the storms begin again – can it not let up and allow us to be happy for once?

An hour later, I hear the click of the front door as Ginny returns. I attempt to hurry downstairs but find myself panting, limbs creaking.

'Dr. Adams is just with another patient, but he will be here shortly,' she relays breathlessly.

'Thank God. In the meantime, the fire in her room is going out – she must be kept warm.'

'Well, sir – I do ask that you don't shoot the messenger, but . . .'

'There is no more firewood?'

'You owe the farmer O'Brien twelve shillings, and I doubt he will allow any further borrowing . . .'

The desk in my study, the drawer beneath the one that holds the opium, contains bill upon bill, reminder upon reminder: to pay the butcher, the chemist, the doctor. I feel sick as I go through them. A few bad investments in the last decade; some overspending here and there; an opium habit that got somewhat out of control last year. Rachel's gallery owner is an unpredictable man and will not pay until every last brushstroke has dried on canvas. I am in danger of bankruptcy, dragging my darling wife down with me.

I feel Ginny's eyes upon me through the kitchen window as I storm into the garden and tear at the ash tree with a hacksaw. The branch that falls is bigger than I intended and as I drag it back into the house, it splinters against the door frame, showering sprays of green leaves behind me. In the bedroom, I tear off twigs and toss them on to the fire; the flames lick up, green-tinged.

At the crackle, Rachel's eyes fly open and I see the fire reflected in her pupils, the warmth of the glow momentarily giving the illusion of good health. Then there are footsteps on the stairs and Dr. Adams appears. He is the son of the man who once tended to me when I was a boy. I do not like to watch as he studies her, pulling at her eyelids, measuring her pulse, so I turn and stare into the flames.

'It is a cold,' Dr. Adams advises me, 'but a deep one – I can sense its tendrils in her heart. Some lozenges will help, and Munyon's Cold Cure.'

Just a cold. A relief. What is a cold but a piddling little thing? I go to Rachel's side, tracing my forefinger down the length of her face, and tell her that I love her.

IV

I go into Rachel's studio, normally forbidden territory. The atmosphere of the room reminds me of entering a church: that same sense of intimidation and awe. Rachel's new exhibition is entirely comprised of female nudes. She has, in secret, broken the rule that female artists may only paint nudes from mannequins, hiring Ginny and others to pose for her at home. The portraits are crammed on to the walls, a concentrate of colour and brushstroke. For her self-portrait, Rachel asked me to supply semen, which she mixed into the skin colouring for her face. An angry joy blazes from each picture; the women of these paintings have neither the doe eyes of Titian's Venus nor the voluptuous sensuality of Ingres's *Grande Odalisque*. Instead, they gaze out with fierce intelligence; they mock the viewer for playing voyeur. How proud I am of her.

I take a shopping list, fold it into my pocket and adorn myself with a frock coat, top hat and gloves – for I cannot afford to catch her cold, not when the *Oxford Book of Malaises* has diagnosed me somewhere between pleurisy and cholera. As I proceed, waving my cane with faint threat at those irritating boys on the street corner who wish to sell me their sensationalist magazines, my heart plumes with joy. Rachel has said that these last few years have been the happiest of her life. Now I have seen her paintings, I believe it. She always said that being freed from her monthly bleed two decades ago was the greatest liberation, allowing her to shift from 'woman' to 'individual'. I find myself composing a letter to Finn in my mind, a reply I will pen when his first missive comes: *This may sound sentimental, my dear boy, but it is perfectly true, what they say, that home is where the heart is. When you reach a ripe old age, you will be pleased with your achievements but a little dismissive of them, knowing that love is all that matters. Enjoy your youthful years, for they are the time to be selfish and one-pointed, to pursue your goals, but take care that you do not neglect your family, ever. You will not regret a lost promotion, later on, but you will regret a ruined heart . . .* If only my father had written me such advice when I was a young man.

'Rachel, I have good news!' I cry on my return home.

I find her in our bedroom. She is fully dressed and seated in front of the dressing table. She has applied a heavy layer of make-up, which makes her seem simultaneously clownish and beautiful. Her lips look like a delicious, wrinkled strawberry; her eyelids are painted the shades of a fading sky. That she is clearly in good health once more thrills me, and I cry, 'My dearest, you need only finish the final painting and Truman will give us ten thousand pounds as an advance.'

'It is not bad, I suppose,' she says.

'We will be able to pay our bills, and eat. You can paint; you can begin your Metamorphoses project,' I gush.

Rachel gazes at her reflection; I can see that she has not listened to a word I have said.

'Do you remember,' she says suddenly, 'when we reunited after you came down from Cambridge?'

I remember it well, but I enjoy hearing her recount the details. She was no longer an eccentric governess, but had begun to enjoy prestige as an artist. I was a man of twenty-one, she a spinster of twenty-seven.

'We arranged to meet at the Oxford gallery. My mother came as chaperone and you came in holding a bird. She thought you quite mad, but then I saw the broken wing and realised that you were being so very kind. All of the ladies' eyes were on you, but you told me that evening that none looked as beautiful as me.' She turns back to the mirror. 'I thought I should make myself beautiful.'

I put my hands on her shoulders. 'But my dear, you *are* beautiful. Now, what is the matter?'

'The fortune teller. I lied. I said that she had spoken well, but the cards that came up were the Tower, the Ten of Swords and the Hanged Man.'

I lean in to silence her with a kiss, and it's then that I feel it: her skin is radiating heat like a fire; there are beads of sweat shiny on her forehead, and her eyewhites are laced with red. I chide her, help her to undress and encourage her back into bed.

At noon the next day, she seems to revive. 'Paint,' she whispers, struggling to sit up in bed as if her covers are woven from heavy metals. I hail Ginny, who brings us an easel, oils, turpentine and an array of brushes, as well as a fresh canvas, for I do not feel she is well enough to finish her final piece for the exhibition.

I fluff some pillows behind her back, prop the easel on her knees and squeeze out a rainbow on her palette. She keeps fussing, giving me instructions, and I deliberately place a shade of blue in the wrong spot, which provokes a fierce *tut* at my incompetence. Oh, it is a wonderful sound, that *tut*, reverberating with anger, with the promise of life. When she mixes her colours, many of them slur on to the bed sheets, but I do not dare intervene. I hold the palette and canvas for her until my arms ache. Her brush dips and swirls and there is a long period where she simply stares at the canvas – stares and squints with rheumy eyes. Finally, her masterpiece is ready: a slop of colours, much like something that a child might have produced.

She tells me that it is a portrait of me; I declare that the Royal Academy will be battling to show it. She gives me a sharp look and I laugh, glad that she has not lost her capacity for detecting poppycock. As I take the canvas away, she says, 'Oh,' in such a piteous voice that my heart does a queer little turn.

I call Dr. Adams again and have a heated discussion with him, flicking through the pages of the *Oxford Book of Malaises*, pausing at folded-down corners, reading symptoms in a shrill voice. If we can only classify it, hold it wriggling between tweezers, then we might understand how best to destroy it. Dr. Adams becomes irritable, and his breath reeks of brandy as he takes Rachel's temperature. He leaves some leeches for me to apply; I let them wriggle across the lawn. I stay awake with her throughout the night, as the sun sets and shades of darkness morph across the walls. Her breathing is shallow; her moans tell of ill-fated dreams. I feel my head droop and fall into a nightmare. I seek a hidden cave where Rachel is locked away, her cries echoing through hills, mountain and sky, impossible to find. I wake up with a start, my neck aching, and turn to her. There is no breath. There is no breath. I check her pulse. I blow into her mouth and pump her heart with my shaking hands. But there is no breath, no breath at all.

V

I crawl into bed beside Rachel. She is so heavy, immovable; her limbs lolling as though filled with water. We are face to face. The insult of her expression slaps me once again – the euphoria of release, as though she was guided to Heaven by angels.

My sleep is fractured by the lightning strikes of nightmares. Each time I wake up, I press my fingers to her throat, searching for just a flicker of heartbeat, and there is only her neck – silent, without a rhythm – and there is the panic, and the recognition, and she dies again, and again, and again.

~

She dies the next day when I sit up in bed and Ginny tentatively pushes open the door, bringing in some broth with a red face, asking if I might like to eat. I manage a little of it before I feel like vomiting. Ginny wishes to take away the sheets to be washed, but I stop her, pleading that I want to keep the counterpane with the paint blotches. I ask her to assist Rachel, so she washes her face and combs her hair. I am certain of having read somewhere that the hair on a human body continues to grow a few days beyond death.

She dies again when I lie down that night and smell the smoke in her hair, smoke which the wind will no longer wash out with its clean colours. I go to the window and scream up at the moon. I run to the hearth and toss up the ashes until I am blackened with soot.

Ginny stays silent downstairs, does not dare intrude.

She dies again when Dr. Adams arrives.

I stand by her bed, smoothing down my beard, as though it is perfectly natural to stand there, smeared with soot and paints, reeking of her death sweat. I nod politely as he explains that the cause was pneumonia and that he will make arrangements for the undertaker to visit.

Once they have removed her, there is a stain left on the bed. I pull away the paint-flecked counterpane and drape it around my shoulders like a cloak.

I go into the garden. It is the first time in days that I have been outside. How spiteful it all seems: the birds singing and the roses nodding and reaching for the light, indifferent to her passing.

The birds sing. I roar at them and they scatter.

Something inside me whispers that she would not have liked this.

I go to the kitchen and find a little stale crust. I sprinkle it over the bench where she used to sit. I watch as the birds dance and peck the crumbs. I watch their pulses fluttering in their feathered throats. I see them flying away with crumbs to feed their young, who will grow plump and spread their wings in turn and migrate across the sky, showing off their vitality with every swoop. Their eyes are beady and suspicious and yet I can espy their gratitude towards me.

I cannot bear to be bound back into the world. I stand up and the birds scatter again, squawking indignation. I return to the house and her bedroom. I lock the door behind me.

A letter from Finn:

Dear Father & Mother,

You see – I promised that I would write. I do hope you are both keeping well. It is so very hot here and, like Darwin in South America, I am appalled by the savagery I witness. Fanny is not happy and often spends hours in the cool of our bedroom, writing letters. I fear the heat has addled her mind, for she believes the natives are living more noble lives than us. I must confess, Father, that your conversion from atheism to agnosticism does rather vex me. At a time when science is bringing enlightenment to society, why retreat into such primitive fantasies? You claim music is the cause, but the evolutionary purpose of music still remains uncertain; perhaps its role is in ritual; but ultimately it is as useless to humanity as the invention of scones. Still, biology is destiny. Your genes haunt mine. Perhaps I too will succumb to such

> ***sentimentalism. Father - a better society awaits us, if we adhere to the realities of life, if we prevent the feeble-minded and poor from breeding, if we allow the masterful genes to flourish - why, we may soon evolve into magnificent beings who will look back and mock our present inferiority . . .***

I screw the letter up and dash it into the bin; an hour later, I retrieve it and smooth it out in my study, picking up my pen to compose a reply. I sense that the cruelty of his sentiments is not simply due to the folly of his youth; he is exaggerating it in order to provoke me. But I have not the energy to rebut his repulsive philosophies. First, I must tell him of his mother's fate. My fountain pen hovers above the paper, dropping blots like tears, and I find that I cannot begin.

I begin to dread being at home; I find every room speaks of her past presence and present absence. I stop at the post office to send a telegram to Finn. I cannot afford to send a lengthy message and even after half an hour of crafting, it still reads as callous in its matter-of-fact brevity.

Then I go to the public house, and despite my 'tab' being rather high, the owner is kind enough to give me several beers on the house, as well as passing me a little opium to keep me going. A middle-aged couple are sitting nearby, the man is berating his wife for drinking beer, which he deems is not *ladylike*. As I take my leave, I lean over and say to her, 'Ignore your fool of a husband!' and I hear him say he would knock my block off were I not so old and clearly demented. Then his eyes narrow.

'Are you not the man I saw a week or so back, stealing my apples, right from my orchard?'

I have no idea of what crime he speaks, and clearly it has made him paranoid, but I merely shrug carelessly and saunter away.

Back home, I light a fire using a rickety chair and smoke the opium; but it is not enough for oblivion, only a limbo state between grief and a haze. It summons a watery hallucination of Rachel's figure in the night sky through the window. She is painting the stars with her delicate precision.

Sometime in the night, a fever descends. In the grip of its swimming, dark heart, I picture our two graves, side by side, skeletons separated by a sliver of earth, skulls in symmetry. Oh, the temptation! – to join her, to slip away into a mutual darkness. My illness echoes hers, in its snivels and coughs and temperature; such mimicry feels like an act of intimacy, to know what she might have suffered.

But on the third night, I begin to revive. The loneliness of recovery is raw. Ginny brings up some soup, but there is nobody to sing me lullabies, or to clear away my vomit. There is nobody to lay their hand on my forehead, to coax and kiss me better. The cat settles at the bottom of the bed. I curl up like a foetus and sob until my ribs ache. I plead and beg with a God I do not believe in to bring her back to life.

The wind whistles his laughter down the chimney.

VI

The day of her funeral dawns. Finn is not present, nor is there any reply from him. I feel angry with him for failing to share the burden of grief, for his decision to desert us when we are vulnerable. I feel angry with the damned Galapagos postal service, which has no doubt left my transcribed telegram idling in some sack; yet I feel relieved too, wanting to protect my boy from tragedy, hoping the news never reaches him.

The weather is vicious. The sun dazzles in a sky of endless smiling blue. The Vicar conducts the service with a cold, snivelling all the way through, and overpronouncing the last syllable of her name with a nasal twang. In the graveyard is a six-foot by three-foot hole. Autumn leaves, tossed on a nonchalant breeze, skit into its depths. The Vicar begins his 'ashes to ashes' speech, his handkerchief fisted in his hand at the ready.

The voice comes suddenly. It is female, a soprano. It sings a song about Chicago. I glance at the other mourners, convinced that they are making a mockery of me. Their heads are all low in prayer, their lips crimped tight in piety. The voice grows more optimistic, attempting to convey a musical accompaniment to the lyrics about how all things go, and yet all things grow. Tears stream down my cheeks, wetting my beard. The Vicar speaks of God's mercy and I want to punch him.

WELL, IT'S A NICE DAY FOR IT, ISN'T IT? the voice cuts in, the song seemingly finished.

As my head jerks up, the Vicar falters. I resist the urge to run through the graves, to try and escape this snake that hisses madness in my ear.

IT'S *ME!* It is unmistakable. It is *her*, though she sounds younger, before age inflected her voice with gravel and stutters.

If I reply, the last thread of my sanity will surely snap. Silently, I urge the Vicar to finish, quick, quick now. Sweat seeps over my body; my tears dry in rivulets on my neck; a dizziness assails me.

I AM NOT DEAD.

I THOUGHT YOU SHOULD KNOW.

The coffin is lowered in fits and jerks and starts, as though the earth is an animal receiving a feed.

MIND YOU, I'M NOT SURE THAT I AM ALIVE EITHER. I THINK I AM . . . I THINK, THEREFORE *I AM!*

She laughs and it is all so absurd that I cannot help it – a howl of laughter escapes my lips. The mourners all start. It evolves into more tears. This is life without her: my mind broken, the world lost to me.

IT IS ONLY A BODY IN THAT COFFIN.

A clod of earth strikes its lid.

I MISSED YOU, YOU KNOW, WHEN MY BODY WENT. I FOUND THE WHITE CORNERS OF THE WORLD. I HAD TO FIGHT TO STAY. I FOUGHT A MAN TO RETURN TO YOU.

The birds sing, the Vicar sneezes, and the service is over.

I barely stayed five minutes at the wake. It was held in the Vicar's home and hosted by his wife; I appreciated their kindness, and so I feel sorrowful that I shocked her with my hasty departure. But the voice kept commenting on the other mourners, declaring that they never liked her much anyway and were only there for the free food, advising me that the cook spat in the ham sandwiches because they underpaid him. On the way home, her voice became more solid, like a breath hovering on my neck, a tickle in my ear.

I storm into her studio. The paintings stare at me, mock me. Stained red rags on the floor, which she used to clean her brushes. I finger the stack of books on the small desk by the window: a mixture of technical titles, describing the thinning and mixing of oil paints; Ruskin's essays and the biographies of painters; Vedic texts. *Vasistha's Yoga* is a thick tome, encyclopaedia-vast, and I flick through it aggressively, tearing the odd page, coming upon random phrases: 'Fate is fictitious . . . fate is none other than self-effort of a past incarnation. There is constant conflict between these two in this incarnation, and that which is more powerful triumphs . . .' 'Bah!' I slam it shut, thump it back on to the pile, which teeters, and books begin thumping on to the floor, spines broken, pages splayed. I grab a canvas, my heart yelling protest, but my rage too strong to resist, my fingers ready to—

DON'T. YOU. DARE.

I pause, gripping it tightly, glad that this extraneous voice is at least one of reason.

THAT'S IT. DON'T PUNISH MY PAINTINGS FOR MY DEATH. IT'S NOT THEIR FAULT.

I position the painting so that it is hung perfectly once more.

YOU COULD AT LEAST TALK TO ME. I THINK YOU'RE BEING VERY RUDE.

But if I begin answering, where will it all end? With me in the asylum, no doubt.

I leave the study, closing the door behind me with care. In the kitchen, I brew myself some Grand Kuding tea.

I WOULD NOT DRINK THAT IF I WERE YOU.

I hum loudly – Beethoven's ninth – and recall the clods of earth scattering over her tomb and imagine the tightening of rigor mortis, her skin taut against her skull, and I gulp down the cup of tea, burning my tongue.

In the parlour, I kneel down in front of the fire and prod the half-burnt chair legs. They will have to suffice. I take a newspaper from the stack –

MR THOMAS TURRIDGE IS PUTTING NEWSPAPER ON THE FIRE. THE HEADLINE READS 'LOS ANGELES TIMES BUILDING DYNAMITED' –

'I am putting the newspaper on to the fire,' I interrupt, because if someone is damn well going to narrate this story, then it will be *me*. 'I am striking the match. It is eating through the paper.'

WHY ARE YOU NARRATING?

'Why were *you* narrating?'

MR THOMAS TURRIDGE QUESTIONS WHY HIS LIFE IS BEING NARRATED BY THE GHOST OF HIS DEAD WIFE—

'Good God, enough!' I sit on the chair and form a lattice with my fingers and bury my face in it. 'It cannot really be you, can it, Rachel?'

WHO ELSE COULD IT BE?

'I think you are a projection of my mind, a madness of grief.'

A pause.

SO ARROGANT! I AM TRULY CROSS NOW. A PROJECTION OF *YOUR* MIND?

'The thing is, Rachel, you know as well as I that there is no such thing as ghosts.'

GHOST, SPIRIT, SOUL, JIVA – CALL ME WHAT YOU LIKE, BUT HERE I AM.

'Prove it to me,' I say, 'prove who you are.'

GLADLY. WE MADE LOVE A MONTH AGO, HAVING SMOKED OPIUM, WHILE BEETHOVEN'S FIFTH WAS PLAYING. YOUR COCK WENT SOFT.

'Dear God.' My tongue was still throbbing from drinking the burning-hot tea.

I REMEMBER BACK WHEN I WAS A GOVERNESS AND YOU WERE A BOY OF FOURTEEN. YOU SAID YOU WANTED TO MARRY ME AND IT MADE ME LAUGH, BECAUSE YOU HAD A LIST OF PROS AND CONS –

'This is utterly embarrassing,' I say, covering my eyes with my hand in shame.

I THINK THAT ONE OF THE CONS WAS 'RACHEL MIGHT BE MAD'.

'I was a boy, Rachel – a boy!'

I THINK THAT WHEN I GLIMPSED THAT, I SWORE NEVER TO MARRY YOU, EVER.

'And you should have honoured that promise.' My voice shakes and I struggle to keep my chin steady. 'It is my fault that you died.'

NO, MY LOVE, NO . . .

'If you follow the chain backwards, then it is so – you could say it was the fault of the farmer because he shook your hand while afflicted with the germs, but he was only there because of the calf, and we heard the calf wailing because we were at the fair, and whose idea to go to the fair was it? Mine. You even told me that you did not want to go, you wanted to stay in and paint, and I persuaded you. I failed you—'

NONSENSE. I MADE THOSE CHOICES TOO. I COULD NOT HAVE DONE ANY PAINTING THAT DAY, I WAS TOO CLOUDY.

'Because I forced opium on you . . .'

DO NOT WEEP. I AM HERE. I AM WELL. NO MORE CREAKY JOINTS. I CAN REMEMBER THINGS! MY MIND IS SO CLEAR, IT IS AS THOUGH I AM TWENTY AGAIN!

'I don't understand how you can be real.' I blow my nose deep into my handkerchief.

I FELT VERY STRANGE WITHOUT MY BODY, AT FIRST. IT WAS AS THOUGH I WAS WALKING AROUND NAKED, OR HAD LOST MY SKIN. I CURLED UP INTO A BALL. I SEEMED TO BE DRIFTING, LIKE A CLOUD, INTO MARGINS OF WHITENESS, AND THEN SOMETHING SUDDENLY CAME DOWN TO SKEWER ME, IT LOOKED LIKE A GIANT PEN. A NIB OF BLACK

INK. BUT IT COULD NOT PIN ME DOWN BECAUSE HOW CAN YOU PIN DOWN A SOUL? I HEARD HIM – THERE WAS A CURIOUS MALE VOICE WHO SEEMED TO HAVE OWNERSHIP OF THE PEN – SWEARING AT ME. IN FIGHTING I FELT STRONG, I EVEN BEGAN TO TEASE HIM, DARTING ALL OVER THE PLACE, SINGING *CATCH ME IF YOU CAN*, AND HE COULD NOT.

'That makes no sense, Rachel.'

OH, I AM SORRY – SHOULD I HAVE MADE UP SOME STORY OF HEAVEN? MY SINS AND GOOD DEEDS WEIGHED ON SCALES OF JUSTICE? DID YOU WANT A BEDTIME STORY?

'You think you'd have a place in Heaven?'

I CAN'T HIT YOU! THIS IS MOST UNFAIR! STILL, WHAT I CAN DO IS . . .

I chuckle as I feel her breath hot against my ribs, in that tender place where I am most ticklish.

'Stop, *stop*, you cruel vixen!' I laugh, and something erupts in my heart, for in that moment I truly believe that it is her, for only Rachel would know to torment me in that very spot, and with the absurdity of the revelation, the confusion and the hysteria, I burst into tears again. 'How could you have left me . . . You were always the one who walked away . . .'

I FOUGHT TO STAY IN MY BODY. I FOUGHT TO STAY WITH YOU. I TRIED SO HARD, BUT IT WAS BEYOND ME.

AND SO I FOUGHT TO RETURN.

I WILL NOT LEAVE YOU. I LOVE YOU AND WILL BE HERE, ALWAYS.

The door creaks open. Finn the cat enters and bounces on to my lap.

OUR FINN DID NOT COME TO HIS MOTHER'S FUNERAL.

'I have not heard from him,' I whisper. 'I will have to write to him again.'

MY POOR BOY, she says, as I stroke the cat and he shudders with purring pleasure against my hands. MY POOR DARLING BOY.

VII

The next day I awake to her voice in my ear, plaintive: IT'S BEEN A LONELY NIGHT.

I brush sleep from my eyes, frowning; sunbeams slant through the gaps in the curtains, highlighting dust motes. I attempt to embrace the air and then lower my arms, feeling foolish.

'Didn't you sleep?'

I DON'T SEEM TO SLEEP.

A knock. Ginny comes in, looking distressed. She has no doubt heard me talking to an empty room. Rachel falls into a fit of giggles and I bite my lip as Ginny gets the fire going using newspaper and another chair leg. My laughter refuses to be caged and erupts in a wild shrill. Ginny turns in alarm, crosses herself and makes a swift departure. The fire, carelessly constructed, fades to embers.

BE CAREFUL. YOU MIGHT END UP IN AN ASYLUM.

Her tone is ambiguous. How disconcerting it is, conversing without being able to see the sparkle in her eye, the turn of her lips. I feel self-conscious as I stand before the toilet, peeing in fits and spurts, remembering the speedy, confident jets of my youth; I think of our last lovemaking and a redness fills my cheeks and I yank the chain quickly. I keep hoping to see her essence; I search for a distortion of form in the wall, the flooring. She chatters as I shave; I complain softly that I might accidentally slash my throat, I am so delightfully distracted. Rachel is usually a woman of choice words. She is evidently pent up after a night's solitude. She tells me that she saw into my dreams:

YOU WERE A BOY, GAZING AT AN EMPTY BEDROOM, FEELING SO SAD. YOUR FATHER HAD LEFT THE HOUSE AND THE SHEETS ON HIS BED WERE STILL RUMPLED. YOU WORRIED THAT HIS LEAVING WAS YOUR FAULT.

I had nearly forgotten it; the pale dregs of my dream become colourful with her recounting.

'Can you hear my thoughts?' I ask, pausing with the blade against my throat.

NO, she promises, and I give her a dubious glance in the mirror.

I make a pact with her that she will not speak to me during my breakfast, so that Ginny will not be too afeared. Rachel is a little sulky, I perceive; then I feel a gentle breeze against my lips, like a sweet kiss.

I walk downstairs, smiling – until Ginny informs me that there is nothing for breakfast: Jon, the butcher's son, stopped by just half an hour ago with an unpaid bill, asking when it will be settled. Furthermore, as much as Ginny would like to stay, she has not been paid wages for the last three weeks . . .

'Ginny,' I pat her arm, 'I apologise, you have been a good and loyal maid. I will sell Rachel's paintings tomorrow – we have a buyer waiting.'

I'LL PROBABLY GET MY BEST REVIEWS EVER, NOW THAT I AM DEAD.

I jump, fearing that Ginny's face will pinch in shock. But no –

SHE CANNOT HEAR ME, Rachel confirms, I DID TRY TO CHAT WITH HER THIS MORNING BUT SHE WAS DEAF TO ME.

In my study, I sit with a hollow stomach behind my father's desk, feeling very sheepish as I lay out all of the bills. Rachel's silence is a chastisement.

WHY DID YOU NOT TELL ME THAT THINGS WERE THIS BAD?

'I wanted to let you focus on your painting and not worry.'

She sighs. THAT WAS THOUGHTFUL OF YOU, BUT . . .

'We will fix it. Only, I cannot face your gallery man, Mr. Truman, without having had breakfast. I know where I can get some for free.'

BEFORE WE GO, CAN I ASK ONE THING.

'Yes, my love?'

I MISS HAVING HANDS. PLEASE MOVE YOUR FINGER FOR ME. NO, THIS ONE. I feel her touch on my joints. I MISS THE TACTILITY OF PAINTING. I MISS BEING ABLE TO HOLD A BRUSH.

To the local orchard we go, scrumping apples, paying no heed to the warning sign that poachers will be prosecuted. Dazed and dizzy, I bite into a green globe. I chew slowly, feeling the sweet mush slide down my throat and quiet my wailing stomach.

WATCH OUT!

A maid is hurrying towards us, crying, 'Shoo! Shoo!' I burst into laughter; she is armed with a tea towel, which she flaps ineffectually. Then I see a familiar figure, a red-faced man who is bellowing curses. Why, it is the man from the pub, who berated his wife.

RUN!

I shove a few more apples into my pockets and beat a hasty retreat towards the trees. My legs are creaky but his are worse; he seems to be grappling with an injury, and one of his legs drags behind the other; he cannot catch me, and the maid is out of breath. On the rim of the woods, I turn and give him a playful wave and call a cheery 'Thank you!', before I disappear into its green density.

Though I am afeared of maggots in my mind, there is no harm in a little forgetfulness, a little blurring of the mind's sharp edges. After all, that is why we imbibe opium and Grand Kuding tea, is it not, in order to enjoy moments of early senility? It is one of the few rewards of old age, the antithesis of those harsh moments in youth when we discover that there is no God, that good won't triumph over evil, when the sweet illusions of the world are smashed by the cruel realities of adulthood. We let go of the world's details a little, it all becomes a little more vague: a friend who slights you one moment is forgotten the next; the sum of debts that assail you becomes a blurred figure. To sit by the fire, with a cat on your lap, drinking Grand Kuding tea, with sleep seeping into your mind, is . . .

THE MEETING IS SET FOR TOMORROW, IS IT NOT? SHOULD WE NOT BE GETTING ON WITH FINISHING THE FINAL PAINTING?

'Very shortly, my love,' I say. The thought of going into her sacred study, of picking up her brush and completing that final work – it feels like blasphemy. 'We have plenty of apples to keep us going and many hours ahead to complete it . . .'

I feel my head tipping forwards and her words tangle with dreams.

I wake with a sudden jerk to find myself sitting in my chair, the fire still blazing strong, a sense of foreboding in my chest, and I shuffle into the hallway and stand at the bottom of the stairs. They look so tiring, a hundred steps towering up before me, but climb them I must – wheezing, gripping the bannisters – and every time I have managed ten steps, it seems as though ten more have been added. But the delay is a consolation, because I know at the top of the stairs is a door that I do not want to open. And when I finally reach it and gently tap it with the tip of my fingers, it swings forth and I find her lying on the bed. Finn is miaowing, walking over her body, and I hiss at him to jump down and press my fingers to her neck, but there is no pulse, no pulse—

I wake in shock: 'Rachel? Rachel?'

I AM HERE.

'Oh God . . .' I am still in the past, on the day of her death; everything is raw and sharp-edged.

YOU WERE ASLEEP. YOU CRIED OUT.

'We should get on with the painting,' I say eagerly.

Her voice is small and tight: PERHAPS I OUGHT TO BECOME A VASE.

'A vase?' I blink, sitting upright. I know that when Rachel speaks nonsense, it is a sign that melancholy is descending, that she needs cheering up.

YES. JUST GIVE UP ON ALL THIS WASTE-OF-SPACE FLOATING ABOUT. JUST SIT AND BE A VASE. SIT IN THE BOTTOM, IN THE WATER, WITH THE STALKS ALL GREEN IN ME AND THE SMELL OF FLOWERS.

'If someone should forget to change the water, you would be sitting in a rotting bath all day,' I tell her. 'Now, we must work. If you must be anything, why not be a paintbrush?'

TSK.

I smile, for that is such a Rachel sound.

I enter her study smiling fondly, but the moment I sit before her canvas, I feel as though I have fifteen fingers, fat and blundering. In the days since she has died, a faint layer of dust has settled on her brushes; I blow it off gently. I follow her instructions, squeezing some white on to the palette and then a little ochre, thinning with turpentine.

FIRST YOU NEED TO FEEL THE PICTURE. DRINK IT IN, LET IT ENTER YOUR BLOODSTREAM. TAKE A GOOD LOOK AT IT. WHAT DO YOU SEE?

'A naked woman,' I say.

WHAT IS HER MOOD?

'She's feeling lascivious . . .'

I AM BEING SERIOUS.

'I am not teasing you! She looks to me as though she has a glint in her eye!' My voice has risen and there is a gentle knock on the door. It opens and there is Ginny, looking in.

'Is everything all right, sir? Would you like some tea?' she asks.

'I'm fine, Ginny,' I say cheerfully. The cat winds through her legs. I wait for her to close the door before I continue.

'We could just leave this picture and simply take the rest,' I say. 'What will one missing picture matter?'

NO. TRUMAN ASKED FOR TWENTY PIECES. HE IS A HARD BASTARD, A STICKLER; AND MIGHT CHANGE HIS MIND IF THERE ARE NOT TWENTY.

The naked woman – for which Ginny posed – lies on the bed; a pile of books adorn her bedside cabinet, while a stool at the bottom has a marmalade cat sprawled across it. All I need to do is fill in the feline's colours. Rachel's pencil strokes are there in the right-hand corner of the painting. Yet the more I examine the nude, the more I am intimidated by the skilful way in which Rachel has captured her lily skin, the sheen of light, the texture of her muscles, the fine tracery of veins, and the more I fear it would take two decades of practice before I would be worthy of this task.

Rachel is talking all the while, reminding me that I must build up the paint in layers. She compares the act to a piece of music: a solo instrument sounding softly, and then perhaps an oboe coming in, and then the rest of the orchestra filling the air with their colours.

AND NOT TOO MANY BRUSHSTROKES, she adds, NOT TOO MANY NOTES.

I succeed in applying an underlayer of beige with the flat brush. A surge of confidence rears inside me – but then she tells me to mix in some blue.

'Blue?'

THE SHEEN OF THE CAT IS BLUE, IN THOSE PARTS WHERE SHE IS DAPPLED BLACK.

'My darling, cats are not blue,' I say, very gently.

I KNOW THAT CATS ARE NOT BLUE. IT IS FOR THE HIGHLIGHTING. WE WILL APPLY BLACK ON TO THE BLUE AFTERWARDS.

I swirl and mix the blue, but still I cannot bear to do it. Is she teasing me? Is this some awful trickery?

'It – it won't look real,' I whisper.

PAINTING IS NOT ABOUT CAPTURING REALITY. I AM NOT REMBRANDT! I AM AN IMPRESSIONIST. AND WHEN BLACK IS HIT BY LIGHT, IT LOOKS BLUE. YOU ARE SIMPLY NOT PAYING ATTENTION.

'I just don't think it will work . . .'

FINE. YOU KNOW BETTER. YOU ARE THE MALE AUTHORITY. I WILL LEAVE YOU TO IT.

'Rachel . . .' I sigh. But she is gone.

For about five or ten minutes, I sit staring at the painting, my doubt quietening into desperation, and then – to my surprise – I see my hand swinging up, dipping my brush in the oils, and dabbing colour on to the canvas. A little too dark; I mix more white into the sienna. I tell myself that it is probably dreadful, but as I paint away I slip into a trance, the sort I used to sometimes enjoy when I was composing; it is as though I am serving the painting, which has already decided how it wants to look. It is a powerful sensation, the loss of one's individuality, and I muse that the transcendence inherent in any creative act must account in part for the belief in God, for the men who wrote the Bible, scribbling away, feeling divine as words appeared on the page. But now I am being too intellectual; the innocence is lost and my brush is heavy and clumsy again. I relax my shoulders, allow myself to sink back down, and some half an hour later, it is all done and looks – well, it is not perfect, but it will suffice. My cat does not let the picture down, that is the main thing.

I feel peaceful.

'Rachel?' I call out softly. Our argument feels far away, an absurdity.

Nothing but the wind coming down the chimney. I heat water above the fire in our bedroom and fill a bath. I climb into it. I think of the model dinosaurs in Crystal Palace that Rachel and I once visited, those huge hollows; I feel like a model of a *Homo sapiens*, floating in warm water.

I go out into the garden and call her name over and over. Beneath the moonshine, I listen to the wind and the distant noises of hooves and carts rucking over the cobbles. I watch as lights in distant houses go out, one by one, and there is just darkness.

VIII

A feeling of dread in my heart: it has been a long time since I was involved in any sort of business meeting. My tongue was always more lead than silver, even then. I used to get by on charm and youth, both of which are now entirely lacking. In her study, I pack up her paintings, whispering, 'What should I say to him? It would help if you stopped sulking, Rachel . . .'

As I stand upright, rubbing my peevish knees, my heart flurries at the sight of the curtains lifting – only to realise that Ginny is in the doorway and has created a breeze. I show her the one I completed and she says, 'Why, sir, you can hardly tell the difference.' I wait for a 'but', but none follows. During the night, I woke several times and said her name out loud, into the darkness, but the darkness did not reply. My bed felt very large without her.

I have no money for a hackney carriage, but, with insouciant verve, I inform the driver that I will pay him at the end for a journey there and back, plus a fee for waiting outside the gallery. If there is no deal done today, I will surely end up in debtors' jail.

The gallery sits on the edge of Turl Street, between the Mitre and the student dwellings, a little yellow-brick place. The owner, Mr. Truman, has a foxy face and eyebrows so thick and expressive that they look as though they belong on a music score. In a back room, I lay the series out for him, unwrapping the most impressive pieces first, and passing him a list of titles.

I say nothing, knowing that her genius will speak far more than my improvised poppycock. He stares at each for minutes at a time, as though analysing every brushstroke, his eyebrows rising several octaves. His voice, however, is strangely lacking in any sort of emotion or tone.

'Extraordinary. And can you be sure that Rachel Turridge is the true artist of these works?'

'I have witnessed my wife working on these this past year, day in, day out.' I try to keep my voice level. 'She may have been in her seventies, but she had the energy of a sprightly mare.'

He turns to me briefly, with the throwaway line: 'My condolences on her passing.'

'Thank you.'

'These are exquisite . . .' he goes on in his monotone. 'Indeed, people have speculated that you have aided her throughout her career, her paintings are so far beyond the usual quality for the female sex.'

'These are entirely by her hand, I can assure you of that,' I cry.

His eyebrows hit top note. 'The oils are still drying on this one. They might, you know, fetch more if you claimed them as yours and we exhibited your debut show.'

I clench my fists in my pockets, before explaining that this is simply not viable and furthermore, since Roger Fry praised her piece in the 'Post-Impressionists' exhibition, she has become rather a rising star. He sighs and offers me seven thousand for the lot. I am sure that his initial offer was ten thousand, but as I do not wish to reveal the weaknesses of my maggot-mind I follow his lead.

'It is no longer enough,' I assert.

I work hard to hide my hunger and desperation and eventually haggle him up to £10,000. He gives me an immediate advance of £1,000 in cash and the rest is set down in his queer, slanting hand on a cheque which I fold with care into the inside pocket of my frock coat. Euphoria beats in my chest as I climb back into the hackney carriage, ordering the driver to take me to the city centre. As we weave through the Covered Market and down Ship Street, I feel the sadness of having nobody to share my victory with. The streets, bustling with crowds and horses, seem an echo chamber of loneliness.

When I arrive home several hours later, armed with culinary delights, I refill the drinks cabinet with absinthe, whisky and vodka, and sink down by the fire, the smell of chicken oozing from the kitchen as Ginny cooks our dinner. I can hear her humming, glad of the wages sitting fat in her pocket, but I feel the melancholy of mourning that is long overdue. What if Rachel's voice was never anything other than the product of a grieving mind? If I have attained a fresh sanity, then I despise it; I appeal for the return of derangement. Tears prickle my eyes and I reach for *The Times*. I am old enough now not to mourn the loss of the illusion that any government will act for the good of the people. They serve the rich and keep the rest surviving just sufficiently to avoid a riot. The stories speak of technology, the pace of life quickening, of telephones, railways, electricity's expansion – why, it is enough to make a man suffer neurasthenia simply from reading it.

I set the paper down. The tick of the clock is very loud. I might play some Beethoven, I suppose, but I cannot summon the energy to lift the arm on the gramophone. The only energy I feel like expelling is to stand and storm into the kitchen and throw the chicken into the night. I will not eat without her voice. I will get drunk on whisky, unless she stops me. I picture my liver pickled; I consider the glint of the razor blade upstairs. Let her come to my damn funeral and sing for me . . .

In the fire, I see a flickering in the flames.

'Rachel?' I squint, wondering if it is the effect of opium, before catching myself: I have not taken any.

Her face finds form in the fire's colours; her smile is one of apology. Then she dances into the newspaper; on the front page, her face appears in faintest ink, a watermark in the pages. I am so enraptured that I kiss the paper, but as my lips wet the page, blankness unfurls. A little smoke blows in from the chimney and she curls into it, creating a feminine shape in its tendrils.

THAT IS THE MOST I CAN DO, she croaks, as though the effort has exhausted her. I embrace the air; the smoke shivers over me in a caress, curling into my collar, wisping over my shoulders.

I begin to weep. 'I thought you had left me. I bought you a present, on my way back from the gallery . . . It is silly, I know,' I say, unveiling the sketching book. 'I am an old fool.'

I LOVE IT. IF I HAD LIPS, I WOULD KISS YOU AGAIN AND AGAIN.

'Don't ever leave me like that. I cannot live without you.'

FORGIVE ME. I OVERREACTED.

'I mean it. I cannot live without you.'

~

Later, after dinner, we sit by the fire together. I am anxious that I ought to be honest about what a prejudiced monster Truman was. I dread that she might request that I return the money.

NO CHANGE THERE, THEN, she says breezily. AND WE HAVE HIS MONEY – LET US DAMN WELL ENJOY IT.

I laugh and raise a glass of whisky to her, though underneath my joy there is still a wound of pain, terror at the ease with which she can depart, without care for money or food or a home or the life we have plaited together.

'I think it will be a most splendid exhibition. And remarkable too that you will live on after death in yet another way,' I remark wistfully. 'You'll be hanging in someone's house.'

OR A DUSTY ATTIC.

'Their toilet,' I laugh as she breath-tickles me. 'But the point is . . . life will just close over the space I've left behind.'

BUT THIS IS NONSENSE. YOU HAVE BEEN A CRITIC, A COMPOSER, A LOVER OF MUSIC, A MOST GLORIOUS HUSBAND AND THE BEST OF FATHERS.

Now I am smiling.

AND MOST OF THE THINGS THAT COUNT IN LIFE CANNOT BE MEASURED AS ACHIEVEMENTS, THEY ARE ABSTRACT, FOR LOVE IS INVISIBLE.

'That is a little strong, I feel.'

NO, I BELIEVE IT IS APT.

A pause.

CAN WE PLAY 'CLAIR DE LUNE'?

'Of course . . .'

I sit and she drifts, but in our minds we dance in the moonlight of piano notes.

IX

Every morning, I cannot still the fear, upon awakening, that I will discover her vanished, no more than a creation of my imagining. But always she is present. Always, she is fizzing with words: chit-chat, observations, jokes, thoughts on art, on the news, on the possible war with Germany. I begin to cease caring if Ginny can overhear me talking to thin air, and give her a hefty pay rise in the hope of loyalty.

Her voice: I am in love with it. All of its shades: teasing, breathy, light, prickly, soft, shrill. My gramophone sits untouched, for I have lost my ear for music; I do not like to drown her out. We tend to prefer reading together in the evenings, a gentle *tsk* signalling that she is ready to turn the page. We play chess, and I move her pieces at the command of her voice. If I walk, I favour the woods over the city. On one afternoon, when my wintery body tires and I slump on a tree stump, I tell her that I feel less afraid of death, knowing that my fate is no longer unknown, that I can fly on the wind with her.

It is Finn who makes me wretched. His last letter asked why I had not replied; my last missives must have gone astray. And how can I inform my boy, a man of science, who believes God is a fairy tale and only that which can be measured and slotted into a table of hierarchy is true and real, that his mother is a voice that dances in the air? Rachel and I debate the issue a dozen times without conclusion.

Then the telegram arrives.

> *My dear Mr. Turridge, it has been some time since your last visit. I would be most grateful if you would do me the honour of joining me for afternoon tea this coming Thursday at 3 p.m. Yours, Mr. Gwent.*

It is most unexpected. I was not aware that Mr. Gwent was still alive. His name brings a sensation of unease. The maggots – just to vex me – seem to have specifically eaten away at that strand of memory which tells me when I saw him last. I reply saying that I would be delighted to attend.

We travel to Gwent's house in a merry mood; as our hackney carriage rolls past her gallery, we notice advertisements for her exhibition hanging pride of place in the windows, shoppers gathering with interest.

When we arrive we find that the notice by his door remains in place:

> I MUST ASK ANYONE ENTERING THE HOUSE NEVER TO CONTRADICT ME OR DIFFER FROM ME IN ANY WAY, AS IT INTERFERES WITH THE FUNCTIONING OF MY GASTRIC JUICES.

When I was a child, the ceilings of Gwent's abode seemed as high as those of a cathedral, but age has changed my sense of scale. The hallway still has its patterning of white and black tiles, a little cracked and faded now. The maid takes my frock coat and hangs it up. As she leads me into the parlour, and as we pass the dining room, I catch a glimpse of the taxidermy on the wall. They are greyed with age; their fur patchworked by moths.

THEY LOOK ARDENT FOR A PROPER FUNERAL.

I burst out laughing and the maid gives me a curious glance.

'Would you like some tea, sir?'

I even out my voice: 'I am fine, thank you – I will wait for Mr. Gwent.'

'Very good, sir.'

In the parlour, I am about to sink on to the méridienne, when Rachel says: LOOK.

The bookcase to the right is crammed with paperbacks by Oscar Wilde, H. G. Wells, George Eliot. There is an entire shelf devoted to Gwent's own oeuvre, comprising a dozen tomes, with titles such as *The Monstrous Machines of Atlantis* and *The Future Dawns Purple* and *The Telephone That Could Talk*.

LOOK.

I go to pull one out—

NOT THAT ONE. THE ONE ENTITLED *2014*.

We read the blurb together:

Rachel and Jaime are two young lovers in the year 2014. She is an artist, he is the owner of a record shop in Manchester. When Rachel's latest exhibition, Metamorphoses, is shown at their local gallery, they meet and find their lives changed for evermore –

'This is too much of a coincidence. He's stolen your name

and your profession!' I cry, shocked. 'I do not remember giving him permission to do so – the scoundrel.'

ПОМНИТЬ *MANCHESTER*: the scribbled note in my desk. Yet I cannot recall Rachel and me ever visiting the place.

I open at the first chapter, and read:

> I'm walking down Oxford Road, Manchester, when I become aware that my eardrums have thinned to the finest of membranes. Everyday white noise – students chattering, buses trundling, cars picking up speed between traffic lights – is a headache of heavy metal. I dive into a shop called 'The Eighth Day'.

SOMETHING IS WRONG, THOMAS. SOMETHING DOESN'T FEEL RIGHT.

Flicking through, I see that the perspective of each chapter alternates between Jaime and Rachel.

'He should have paid us commission, the scoundrel. Have you ever' – I swallow – 'been aware of Mr. Gwent harbouring amorous feelings towards you?'

NO. STAY FOCUSED: FINN NEVER MENTIONED THIS BOOK TO US. HE DEVOURS *ALL* HIS BOOKS, AND IT WAS PUBLISHED SOME TIME AGO. HE WOULD HAVE TOLD US IF HE THOUGHT WE HAD FEATURED.

'The names may just be a coincidence. Still – Metamorphoses. That is the exhibition you were intending to do next!'

LET ME READ A LITTLE MORE.

'But—'

HUSH, NOW. LET ME READ.

We carry on reading the story of Rachel in Manchester, heading for the Corner House, where her exhibition is being held—

THIS DOESN'T ADD UP. THIS ISN'T ME, I MEAN, IT IS ME, BUT I'M NOT IN MY BODY, THAT'S WHY I CAN BE HERE NOW TALKING TO YOU, DON'T YOU SEE, I'M NOT A GHOST, I'M ME. THIS WORLD IS RULED BY FATE!

I bite my lip, feeling very tender towards her. I had thought that, up until this point, she had been rather too calm and stoical about the loss of her body. 'My darling, I know that you are still you, whether you are air or flesh.'

NO, YOU'RE NOT LISTENING. WE'RE IN A BOOK NARRATED BY FATE. IT'S NOT REAL.

'What do you mean, dearest? I am sure Gwent has been generous in his portrayal of you, otherwise I shall be challenging him to a duel—'

GWENT'S SO-CALLED BOOK IS *OUR* WORK! WE LIVED IT; WE WROTE IT TOGETHER. IT WAS THE SECOND BOOK. WE STARTED OFF IN FATE'S NOVEL AND NOW WE ARE BACK HERE AGAIN. DON'T YOU SEE?

I am uneasy: is this senility? She may not have a physical brain but she has a mind, a beautiful mind, and I do not want to feel its sharpness and wit and compassion leave me . . .

YOU'RE A FOOL, she bursts out.

'Steady,' I say, prickly now.

ASK HIM TO SERVE YOU SOME SOMA TEA. INSIST.

There comes from the hallway a fearsome cacophony and the door swings open; Gwent is in mid-argument with a portly red-haired gentleman. Gwent's middle-aged visage – which once seemed so elderly to my boyish soul – is shocking to me. Why, he looks just as he did when I saw him last, his hair still a fulsome chestnut riot across his forehead, his eyes the colour and shape of a mischievous cat's. I perceive that he has failed to recognise me; there is even dismissal in his gaze, as though I am some spurious elderly visitor who needs to be quickly dispensed with. The accusations of his companion continue apace:

'Mr. Gwent, your deadlines have been and gone and our readers are impatient for the next instalment—'

'Well, you know what Dickens himself used to say. "Make them laugh, make them cry, make them wait"!'

'They grow old waiting. They grow grey.'

'My novel is fully written, I have simply not yet translated it to paper,' Mr. Gwent asserts.

'Then I should like the money I have paid you to be returned to the bank account of John Murray—'

Mr. Gwent looks pale at this. 'It will be with you by Monday,' he promises.

His publisher nods and makes his exit. Mr. Gwent turns to his maid, who gestures towards me.

'You have a guest, sir. I did not take his name, but he claimed to be an intimate acquaintance.'

'Yes, yes. And do something about the light, please – it is awfully dark in here.' Mr. Gwent approaches me with his bouncing walk and shakes my hand vigorously.

'Mr. Gwent, it is I, Thomas. Thomas Turridge. I received your telegram . . .'

'Oh my . . . By God, it *is* you!' Mr. Gwent clasps me into a tight hug and I suddenly feel like weeping into his neck, but I restrain myself. 'But did you find the Storyteller?'

YOU SEE!

Seeing my blank face, he quickly sits down, gesturing for me to sit upon the méridienne. To the maid, he says, 'Some Soma tea please.' He glances at me. 'I think it will do you the world of good.'

NOW YOU WILL SEE.

I wish that Rachel would be quiet for once, to allow the confusion in my mind to find order.

'I was most sorry to hear about the passing of Rachel,' Gwent says gravely.

'Thank you,' I say, sensing her smirk. 'Her final exhibition will open next month. The gallery is predicting rave reviews and vast sales.'

'I am sure,' says Gwent, with warmth.

'Our son – he is the main worry,' I say, for he remains a splinter in my mind.

'You have a *son*?' Gwent looks astonished.

'Oh yes, Finn Turridge. He's a botanist, currently in the Galapagos. He fancies himself as Darwin's heir, I think, hoping that in the natural selection of botanists he will jig himself to the top.' Thinking of his letter, I try not to punctuate my sentence with a sigh.

The maid enters and pours out the tea. It is a smoky green colour. I frown, for as I lift my cup to my lips, I suffer a distinct sensation of déjà vu, the past layered into present. I recall how, as a child, Gwent fed me some insidious beverage. The details are blurry, but I know that I suffered a fit of derangement and that my father's temper was severely frayed.

DRINK IT. DRINK IT.

'No.'

'Sorry?' Gwent asks.

'Oh – nothing.'

'I expect you heard the dodo speaking,' he remarks, nodding at his stuffed pet.

'Yes,' I laugh. My gaze flits to the mirror above the fireplace, encased in gilt, scriss-scratched with black marks of age, as though its face is liver-spotted.

I am so thirsty, that is the trouble. And even though we took a hackney carriage here, I am still tired. I am usually napping by the fire at this time of the afternoon. *Just one sip*, I tell myself and Rachel, but as I lift the cup, the temptation is too much, and I take three.

'It tastes so very fine,' I remark, 'better than it looks.'

'Yes! It looks like green ink, does it not?' Gwent jests. 'As though one ought to dip a nib into it rather than a teaspoon.'

A pause.

'Are you still a critic?' Gwent asks.

'Oh no, I am retired. I have not written a piece for five years.'

'I have not forgotten your review of Hans Richter's version of Wagner's *Ring* cycle as "painfully constipated". Dear me, I am glad you are a critic of music and not novels.'

I smile and take another sip of tea without thinking. There is a tension in the air, a curious sort of anticipation, but I am not sure what it pertains to, and I wonder if he is waiting for me to ask about his writing. 'Are you working on a new novel?'

But as he begins telling me about his latest work, his voice shimmers and acquires an echo; black spots blur before my eyes. I am too old for this, I tell myself, for I am feeling increasingly out of sorts.

I hear Rachel asking me if I am all right and Gwent urging me to take a little more of the tea. I drink its lukewarm dregs, set the cup down and hear the crash as it misses the table. I cry apologies, declaring that I ought to go home, but even the sensation of standing feels unconvincing, as though my body is still there on the méridienne, struggling to catch up with my consciousness. I find myself staggering forwards a step and clutching the edge of the mantelpiece, gazing into the mirror above the fireplace.

The smoke from the fire has a tremulous quality; the room blurs and reshapes itself as though it is a theatre stage being recast for a new set. I see a young man and a young woman lying on a bed, side by side. I see a man with a beard standing over them. He gently wipes a cloth over the woman's face.

Rachel.

Revelation dawns.

KEEP CALM. DON'T GET ANGRY.

'The *bastard*!' I slam my fist against the mantelpiece.

X

At first, I am too weary for anger. Gwent takes my trembling hand and helps me shuffle back to the méridienne, shattered crockery tinkling against my shoes. It is shame that predominates this time, the prickling violence of knowing one has been fooled by a con man. I touch my face, the deep wrinkly grooves, the sag of skin, as though this elderly body is slowly sinking into the ground. When I raise my eyes to Gwent, a deep sadness wells up inside me. His wife must still wonder and wait for his return. The hope of escape for Rachel and me is ebbing by the minute . . .

'He murdered her!' I burst out. Spit spools from the edge of my lips.

I AM ALIVE! THE POINT IS THAT HE *TRIED* TO KILL ME AND DID NOT SUCCEED. I WON!

'You have no body!' I roar at her. 'What if, in the cottage, you are also—' I notice Gwent's confusion and I press my lips together, and take a breath. I reach for my handkerchief and dab my face and lips with a shaking hand.

'We are in a book, yes,' says Gwent, in the kindly manner of a parent informing their child that Santa Claus does not exist.

'I'm sorry . . .' I pause again, attempting to calm the flurries of my heart. 'Remind me how long you have been here again?'

'Oh, I lose track, I am afraid,' he says in a resigned tone. 'A decade – no, a little longer, actually.'

'But why not simply use the Soma tea? If it has the power to awaken us – then surely a triple dose would suffice to bring us back to the real world? A quadruple dose! The whole box if necessary!'

Gwent looks melancholic. 'Several years ago, I met a man who claimed he had escaped to Fate's narrative from a book by Andrew Gallix. He attempted a strong dose of Soma, against my advice – and was found dead the next day. It is too toxic on the liver; one cup is all we can permit.'

DAMN.

'You told us to find the Storyteller and we met several possibilities, but none seemed to guide us. How do we get back?'

'You found no answers?' Gwent asks. 'There was no Storyteller?'

'None . . . unless we missed them . . .'

Gwent is silent for a while as he digests this. Rachel whispers sorrowfully in my ear how much she feels for him. Then he speaks:

'The last memory I have of Augustus Fate is meeting him many years ago. I found him perfectly charming and witty company before I passed out from the Grand Kuding tea. I felt him carrying me, with a curious kind of tenderness, from his basement to the bedroom upstairs. I tried everything I could think of, but I ran out of time. My body must be dead by now. I've long since been unable to take flight from book to book. It is only possible, it seems, while you still have a body. And needless to say, escape is definitely not an option. Fate has, at least, allowed me to remain youthful: I grow no older here.'

I hate the gentleness of his tone; I never want to become resigned to this fate.

'Good God. So you can never escape Fate?'

'You know, my dear boy, I am happy to be here. I make do. It is how we react that counts.' But his smile is forced, his cheerful tone unconvincing.

'I remember you saying to us, in the last book, that we cannot change what Fate does, but we can change how we react – that we still have a modicum of control. But if your narrator is throwing fucking helicopters at churches and murdering your wife, how are we supposed to act as anything other than angry and sad and *human*. Not to react would be sociopathic. But if we react, we're doing just what he wants. What he dictates.'

Gwent looks pale.

'I do concede that it is a limited form of living, but debating it will not change a thing. The noose is around your neck; struggle and you only pull it tighter. Come, you are an old man now! You have gained some maturity, learnt the value of stoicism. If you stop seeing Fate as your enemy, he may be less inclined to provoke you. Being a novelist myself, I know that when I am blocked or frustrated or disconnected from my characters, I tend to start shaking things up . . .'

OH, WE KNOW ALL ABOUT THAT.

'We were enjoying our story in Manchester, until you sent us into a recession,' I frown.

'I gave you complete freedom in that book,' Gwent reasons. 'It was character-driven; it was *your* story. You must have willed that destruction into being – you must have found a stable, happy existence rather tedious in some respect.' Seeing my irate expression, he hastily changes the subject. 'Look, I know it must be hard, having lost Rachel, but she is also a warning of what will come if you continue to defy Augustus.'

FUCK HIM.

'I've learnt to stop fighting and accept it all,' Gwent continues. 'It makes life much easier.'

'You're being abused and gaslit. It doesn't sound like acceptance, it sounds like passivity, it sounds like the tone that people take when – what's that saying?'

WHEN GOOD PEOPLE STAND BY AND DO NOTHING, THEN EVIL IS DONE–

'Yes! When good people stand by and do nothing, then evil occurs.'

Gwent frowns and replies, 'You have to consider that our definitions of "good" and "evil" and what we each believe is a life worth living may be quite different. All I can conclude is this – there is no getting back for me . . . And I am afraid it may be too late for you, so make peace with your situation.'

'No, you're wrong,' I assert, for a memory is seeping back into my mind, gaining detail and colour, and filling me with wonder. 'I know we can go back. I saw him – between the books. I saw him!'

WHAT? WHEN?

'When we moved from *2047* to this book, I woke up. Just for a short time.' I recall the moment when I woke and felt my consciousness ebb through my real body: the beauty of being able to flicker my own fingers, of feeling truly at home in myself. 'I saw Rachel lying beside me. I banged on the door. Fate said we had to endure one last book – it was a pact. He would keep us safe, give us a happy ending. He said then he would allow us to wake.'

A PACT? A HAPPY ENDING? IN A BOOK BY FATE?

'There was no choice. He said I had been in his cottage six weeks. In here, we can live for years, but time in the real world moves more slowly. I saw the first daffodils in his garden – it is nearly spring. We arrived at Fate's just before Christmas 2019 – well, Rachel a little earlier than me. The point is, we're still alive and there is hope!'

'Perhaps you are, perhaps you are . . .'

'What about your wife? She thinks you're missing, doesn't she? We can give her closure.'

Gwent twiddles his sideburns, stroking them lightly and then tugging at the hairs. 'I'm sorry, Jaime, but I fear there is no way . . .'

THERE MUST BE A WAY.

'Rachel thinks there is a way,' I assert.

'Rachel?' He asks incredulously.

'She died but her spirit, for want of a better word, remained. She's carried on talking to me.' I am conscious of how ridiculous the words sound. 'She is here with us now.'

'You should be careful, if you are hearing voices: all you are hearing is Fate. Once or twice, I have heard him speaking in the third person, dictating the events of the day. If he has adopted Rachel's voice, then perhaps it was intended as . . . a consolation.' His voice fades to a whisper: 'If a character dies in a book, they die up there too . . .'

I AM ALIVE!

'Thank you,' I say, rising unsteadily. 'I do believe that I should return home now.'

'You are welcome to return whenever you wish,' he says cheerfully, clapping his hands together. Before we depart, he gifts us a copy of *2014*, adding our names and his swirling signature to the title page, and the message, *You will soon get used to your fate*.

'Sssh,' I whisper to her in the back of the hackney carriage, 'he can hear, and he has no doubt listened in on our conversation with Mr. Gwent.'

I yank the curtain across the window, shutting out the false streets and other creations strolling past, though through the slit I can see the threat of a storm in the grey cumulus gathering like an army overhead. My fear renders me rigid, my hand taut around my cane. I think of my darling, of the state she was in when I woke up and saw her. Even if . . . and even if she is . . . I picture the moment of awakening: opening my eyes in Fate's cottage to find her body foul beside me. Or, perhaps: simply a blank space. He might be burying her body right now.

The real world would be impossible without her, a falsity. How could I believe in the stars and the sky? How could I wake and believe in the purpose of a day? What would I say to her father, her friends, who would be forever waiting and wondering where she had gone? How could I explain?

At home, Ginny greets me at the door. I stare into her face, as though I might see a trace of Augustus Fate beneath her translucent pallor.

'Are you quite all right, sir?' she asks, for I jerk away as she tries to help me with my frock coat. I shrug it off my shoulders, then pause, hanging on to it tightly, as though it is a cloth separating me from a bull. Finally, I relinquish and hurry to the parlour, calling over my shoulder that I must not be disturbed. Inside, I throw Gwent's book on to the cabinet and sink down on to a chair. I want a mirror, but I am too scared to go back into the hallway, so I have to make do with gazing at my reflection in the grandfather clock's face: the absurdity of my white hair and wrinkles and drooping jowls. My eyes continue to shine out of my face, clear and blue, just as they always have done, and I experience a fleeting relief. I help myself to a whisky from the drinks cabinet.

'Rachel?' I whisper.

IT IS ME, YOU KNOW, she whispers.

'I know it is,' I reply uncertainly.

I FOUGHT HIM. HE TRIED SO HARD TO KILL ME . . .

At the thought, I have to pour myself a double measure and gulp it down. 'Oh God, what if he goes for me next? What are we going to *do*?' The whisky does not agree with me, for it hits a stomach already cat's-cradled with fear, and I retch it back up, all over the cabinet. 'Oh God, oh God . . .'

STOP PANICKING. SIT DOWN.

'I am too old for all this,' I say, and then realise what I have said, and laugh. I never understood my grandfather when he said that you never truly age as time goes by, for you feel the same inside, it's just that your body becomes an increasing embarrassment. 'I feel as though I am still twenty-five!' he would croak through rotting teeth, and I would smile in appalled disbelief. Well, now I know. I am twenty-six years old and sixty-two years old and both are true.

Then I think of my mother, at her home in St Albans; she always said that she found the evenings hardest, when her only friend was a dancing screen; I cannot even write her a letter to say a goodbye.

THE STORYTELLER, Rachel muses. WE NEVER ASKED GWENT HOW HE CAME ABOUT THE CONCEPT.

'It all sounded so plausible,' I say. 'A mythical figure; the sort you'd expect to dispense wisdom and solve things, ready for the finale . . . I'm sorry, I ought to have asked – my mind was so dazed . . .'

I THINK GWENT MOSTLY SPEAKS NONSENSE ANYWAY.

'True. I once thought him reliable and clear-headed, but now I fear he is much too prone to whimsy . . .'

TELL ME MORE ABOUT THE MOMENT WHEN YOU WOKE UP, WITH FATE. HOW DID WE LOOK?

'We didn't look our best . . . I made the worst of mistakes with Fate. You won't leave me, my darling?'

WHY? NO. I AM HERE WITH YOU ALWAYS.

'I should have fought him, Rachel. I was awake, there, in the room, banging on the door. I should have just jumped from the window and risked a broken leg. Instead, I let him trick me with empty fucking promises. I was so weak, and so beaten down. A month, he said. Drink the tea, give me one more month, I'll release you. He didn't say anything about you dying. How is that a happy ending? Some "pact" . . . I should have broken down that door.'

Silence.

'Perhaps we will have to find another book to escape into. We can't stay here: that is the only truth I am certain of. In another book, you could be more than . . . that which you are.'

I hear the chiming of the grandfather clock: it is six now. There is a crick in my neck, which I rub with stiff fingers. My sadness is a cello note in my stomach. The future seems nothing but a long row of books stretching out before us: a variety of fonts on white pages sketching plots and torments. I am tired of third-act finales where we are driven out and on to new beginnings. I scan the room, musing on the scope of Fate's imagination. When my gaze settles back on the grandfather clock, however, I recall that there was one much the same back in Fate's cottage, which I noted when I came to interview him. It had chimed six during my visit. A century or so back, that very clock was only an idea in the mind of a real clockmaker, who must have sat and sketched it carefully, and then dreamt of refinements in the folds of his sleep. The cognition that the clock is the property of many minds gives me a faint feeling of peace, the tautness of our surroundings loosening just a little.

'Rachel?'

YES? Her voice is sad.

'I cannot even remember what they are called. You know – the modern telephones. The ones which light up.'

I hear a knock at the door: a sharp, bold rap. I curse at the sound of Ginny's footsteps in the hallway; I should have informed her that I did not want to receive any visitors.

Noise; agitated voices; Ginny's protests. Rachel cries, THE POLICE!, and then they are in the room, led by an Inspector Woolf, who informs me that I am under arrest for the theft of apples from the orchard of Mr. Parker.

XI

The gaoler of Oxford Prison is such an odious villain, only Fate could have fathered him. I roll my eyes when I find out that he is called Mr. Millhauser. He is one of those characters who make up for their loss of height by puffing out their chest and upending their chin when speaking, attempting to look down at you even as they look up. His beard is ratty, his eyes bulbous; there is a glint of Fate in his sneer. In a small room, I am forced to undress before him, my fingers trembling as I undo buttons and zips. Much to his amusement, I fold each item carefully. This suit is but a day old, the most elegant and beautifully tailored that I've ever possessed. Now I must pull on an old pair of underpants that look bleached and have been worn by goodness knows how many a criminal, followed by a blue-striped uniform, coarse against my skin.

Millhauser cuffs me. I shuffle after him, down an echoing corridor, gates unlocked and then promptly locked behind me, as though I am venturing deeper into the layers of Hell. We pass a corridor of empty cells. He tells me that they are walking the treadmill, something I can look forward to, for this prison still implements a policy of hard labour. In reply, I hum lightly in feigned nonchalance. Unlocking my cell, he waves a hand and then, with a smirk, announces, 'Your hotel.' When I tell him that I am thirsty, he replies, 'Champagne will be served at six.' So he fancies himself as a comedian . . . I flick him a V-sign in my mind.

The cell door slams behind me. The key screams in the lock. I face my hellhole and sink on to my new bed: no more than a slice of hard board. On the wall before me are layers of dirt and etchings of desperation: counts of days spent and days to go; initials of lovers missing; swearwords of rage. I am vaguely aware of time passing. I feel animal in my shock, and suffer urges to whimper and sob, to claw brick, to lash skin. My imprisonment will last five years. It has transpired that Mr. Parker has been the victim of poaching and scrumping for some months, and blame for the loss of seven pheasants, five hundred apples and three potatoes has been heaped upon me, despite my protests. I was not even granted a trial by jury and my refusal to plead guilty only inflamed the magistrate, who gave me the severest sentence to make an example of me. Such is the illogicality of Fate, the cruelty of his game.

Since entering this prison, I have not heard her voice. I whisper her name – but there is only silence.

'You promised never to leave me again,' I say out loud.

I am Jaime, I tell myself over and over, but when I press my palm to the wall, I feel the chill and I know this is as real as can be.

The bells of Oxford chime six strokes. My cell door is unlocked, my dinner slammed on to the floor. It looks like gruel. No spoon, so I have to eat from the bowl like a dog. The food revives me, glitters energy and life through me, and I have to resist tears. I cannot give Fate that satisfaction. But as the emotion rises, I find myself punching the wall with my right hand. My knuckles splinter; blood flecks my uniform –

STOP!

'Rachel?'

I sink on to the bed. The pain in my knuckles is so shrill that my eyes water. I worry that I may have broken one or two of my fingers. At my age, they will take months to heal.

I AM HERE, MY DARLING, I AM HERE.

'You left me,' I cry.

I WAS INVESTIGATING THE BOUNDS OF THIS FICTION. IT IS WELL IMAGINED. HE HAS DONE HIS RESEARCH.

'It's fine for you,' I snap, rubbing one eye. 'You are as free as a bird. You can slip in and out through the window as you please. Oh God, we will never escape this place.'

WE CAN, Rachel insists. WE CAN.

'I am being pathetic, I know. But you promised never to leave me again and I will go mad if I am left here alone.'

OH JAIME. MY JAIMUS. Her presence by my ear, my lips, my hands. I AM HERE. I feel as though she is kneeling in front of me. BREATHE SLOWLY . . . REMEMBER WHO YOU ARE. THERE MUST BE A WAY OUT OF FATE'S WORLD.

'Gwent has already tried and failed – how are we going to fare any better? Let's just focus on winning my freedom. You could visit Mr. Parker and beg him to drop the charges—'

YOU FORGET THAT HE CANNOT HEAR ME.

'Oh God . . .' I trail off, head in my hands.

BESIDES – WE GET OUT, AND THEN WHAT? MORE HELICOPTERS? THE ASYLUM? ANOTHER ARREST? HE'S NEVER GOING TO STOP. WE HAVE TO FIND A WAY *HOME*.

'I wonder if there are any Booksurfers in Oxford.'

THERE WAS! IN THE FIRST HALF OF *THOMAS TURRIDGE*, THERE WAS AN OPIUM DEN – I AM SURE IT GAVE CUSTOMERS THE EXPERIENCE OF SURFING TOO.

'Could you take a look before the dark comes in?'

I SHALL, YES.

'You are my hero.'

A breeze against my lips before she departs.

The night is long and I am too old to bear a bed like this; I sleep in fits and wake up rubbing my joints with my left hand, the right still singing pain. The agony of having arthritis is that it feels as though you have already died on some level, that you are experiencing a foretaste of rigor mortis. A lump of gruel is stuck between two of my teeth and I cannot get it out. I try to console myself with thoughts of my real life, but it all seems so distant, as though that is the dream and this is reality. It feels as though we have been away for years, and on some level we have. Could we kneel down and pray to Fate? Might we appeal to some humanity in him, some shred of decency?

The dawn does its best to avoid my cell. Reluctantly, it trickles in through the bars, highlighting the scars, the burn marks and pocks in the brick, the bucket in the corner still stained from the shit of the last prisoner. The chill has frozen my neck. It hurts to turn my head left or right.

As the city begins to wake, Rachel returns. Her voice sounds tired and she tells me she cannot find any Booksurfing place in the whole of Oxford.

~

The next morning, when Millhauser comes with breakfast, he gets his lackey to hold it up high and makes me reach for it. I play along. But once the bowl is in my hands, I hum the 'Ode to Joy', and tell him that I am loving it here. Rachel screams with laughter. As I eat my gruel, I dance around the cell, singing the chorus of the ninth symphony through gruel-flecked teeth.

~

In the afternoon, I lie and watch a spider slowly wrapping a fly in her silk, my body limp, and think. I cannot believe that this is how I am going to die, aged twenty-six. What a ridiculous way to go.

I JUST WENT INTO THE WALL, Rachel's voice comes. She has been quiet for a while. VERY, VERY SLOWLY. AND DO YOU KNOW HOW IT FELT?

'As if you had swallowed bricks?'

IF I SHIFT THROUGH IT QUICKLY, THEN YES, IT IS JUST DUST. BUT MOVING SLOWLY, I DISCOVERED WHAT THE BRICKS ARE MADE OF – FATE'S MEMORIES. WHEN HE WAS A BOY, HIS PARENTS SENT HIM TO PREP SCHOOL. HE WAS TEASED A LOT AND

A PREFECT ONCE LOCKED HIM IN A CUPBOARD – I COULDN'T QUITE SEE IT, BUT IT WAS MADE OF BRICKS LIKE THESE.

'I should imagine he did have a pretty awful childhood.' I suspect that Rachel is slipping into the fanciful in order to assuage her shock.

I THINK YOU COULD PASS THROUGH THE BRICKS. MEMORIES, AFTER ALL, ARE NOT SOLID.

'But I am. I have a body.'

A pause.

HOW OLD WERE YOU BACK IN THE REAL WORLD, AGAIN?

'Twenty-six.'

AND YOU LIVED IN . . . ?

'You know this.'

BUT DO YOU?

'Brixton. I was studying for my MA at UCL with Professor Millhauser. Fate's recycled his bloody name here.'

FAVOURITE FOOD?

'A Cadbury Flake.'

FAVOURITE COLOUR?

'This is like some kind of really bad dating profile . . .' But I smile. Rachel is cheering me despite the ridiculousness of it all. 'Red.'

YOUR THEME MUSIC? THE SONG THAT PLAYS WHEN YOU COME ON STAGE?

'That one's easy. You already know it.'

Rachel sings the chorus of Sufjan Stevens's 'Chicago'.

ON WHICH PRINCIPLES DO YOU LIVE YOUR LIFE?

'Hedonism and kindness. They're not always compatible, I know.'

WHAT WOULD YOU BE DOING NOW?

'I'd be reading in the London Library. My father bought me a year's membership, as an apology for I don't know what. I'd be looking forward to the evening, to watching . . . What's it called, that thing they have in real life, the zoetrope shaped like a rectangle . . .'

I KNOW WHAT YOU MEAN. IT'S ON THE TIP OF MY–

'This is ridiculous–'

TELEVISION!

'Yes, that's the word. TV.'

'Netflix.'

'*Succession* . . . I was halfway through the second season . . .'

THEY'LL BE FILMING THE THIRD.

'That's . . . a weird thought.'

YOU SEE THAT YOU ARE A MUCH RICHER CHARACTER THAN THOMAS TURRIDGE?

'But I am living out the life and fate of Thomas Turridge, and if he likes blue and I like red, then it makes no difference.'

YOU KNOW – WHEN I WENT TO VISIT FATE, BEFORE ALL THIS HAPPENED, THERE WAS ONE NIGHT WHEN WE WERE HAVING DINNER, AND HE WAS MANSPLAINING THE BIOLOGY OF OUR BODIES. IN AN ATOM, THE NUCLEUS IS TINY, SURROUNDED BY ELECTRONS. WE ARE MORE SPACE THAN WE ARE SUBSTANCE. IF YOU PUT YOUR HAND ON THE WALL, YOU OUGHT TO BE ABLE TO SLIDE THROUGH IT. IT'S ONLY YOUR PERCEPTION THAT IT

IS SOLID WHICH MAKES IT SOLID. IT'S ONLY YOUR ATTACHMENT TO A REALITY THAT IS A FANTASY.

Her voice is shaking with excitement and I suddenly feel very sorry for her; I want to hug her. I put my palm against the brick and the brick remains brick and my palm remains palm. That reality is a fantasy is the fantasy, I want to tell her.

Rachel sighs. IT WAS WORTH A TRY.

The next day, I do not receive any gruel. As the day goes on, my body feels increasingly hollow, as though my hunger is a pinball, rattling beneath my skin, ricocheting from bone to bone before endlessly pinging around my stomach. Rachel's words have woven into my mind, I realise, for I no longer picture food from our house in Oxford, cooked by Ginny, but the feasts of London: juicy mushroom burgers from the Shake Shack; fries from Leon; Fiorentinas sporting a yolky eye from Pizza Express. Most of all, I crave my mum's cooking, the food she used to make when I was sick: clean, simple food, stews and breads and fruit puddings, imbued with love.

Then: the sound of footsteps. My body prickles awake in desperate hope. Millhauser, singing Beethoven's 'Ode to Joy' in his flat, tuneless voice. He opens the door, proffers the gruel, then flings it on to the floor. He watches as I sink to my knees, pawing at it with my fingers, and then licking them clean.

BASTARD, Rachel yells.

I clasp my hands together, ready to surrender to Fate, to beg, to make him my deity.

DON'T, Rachel whispers in my ear. DON'T FEED HIM. HE'LL ONLY GET WORSE.

'If we leave him wanting, he'll only get worse,' I whimper, still fingering up lukewarm dregs of dirt-smeared food.

Millhauser, shaking his head in disgust, slams the door and locks it again.

HE'S A VOID. DO YOU KNOW WHAT MILLHAUSER DOES FOR MOST OF THE DAY? HE SITS AND READS *BLEAK HOUSE*.

I am too weak to understand. The food is making my ashy body simmer faintly. I lie back on the hard board with a groan. All those times I sat at my desk, flicking through *The Oxford Dictionary of Malaises*, playing hypochondriac – what a luxury compared to this torture, this ringing in my fingers and fever in my mind, this churning in my stomach and tiredness pounding a migraine ache behind my eyes. A few minutes later, I drag myself to the bucket, feeling diarrhoea splat behind me, and the next few hours are a dance from bucket to bed, until my buttocks are encrusted with brown, the cell filled with foul smells. I am back to feeling weak and empty again. The ceiling starts to spin.

IT'S GOOD THAT FATE IS SO ANGRY, Rachel muses.

'Good?' I croak.

HE'S FRIGHTENED, YOU SEE. HE KNOWS NOW HE MIGHT LOSE.

If this was a game of chess, I try to tell Rachel, I would be laying my king on its side, but the words will not form, and I sink into oblivion.

XII

FATE'S CONSTRUCTION IS LIKE PAPIER MÂCHÉ, says Rachel, her voice thoughtful. LAYERS OF MEMORY, EGO, IMAGINATION, ALL GLUED TOGETHER WITH MALICE AND FEAR. A GOOD DEAL OF FEAR.

I groan. It is morning; the night was very long.

LISTEN, THAT DOOR IS NOT A DOOR. I HAVE SAT IN IT WHILE YOU SLEPT AND IT IS CONSTRUCTED FROM THE SADNESS OF REJECTION. THAT IS WHY IT IS GREY IN COLOUR. AT THE AGE OF TWENTY-TWO, HE FELL IN LOVE WITH AN OBOIST. HE PROPOSED. SHE MADE A LIST OF PROS AND CONS, AND FOUND THAT THE CONS FAR OUT-NUMBERED THE PROS. SO, SHE REJECTED HIM.

'Do you want to make him more angry?' I whisper.

THAT KEYHOLE HOLDS HEARTBREAK. EVERY TIME THE KEY TURNS, IT IS A SCREAM OF RELIEF AND TORMENT, A TWISTING OF ANGUISH.

When the key turned this morning, my heart beat as though it might burst from my ribcage. Millhauser challenged me with his gaze, but my freaked-out state seemed to satisfy him. He set the bowl of food down on the floor. I ate it gratefully, but after I had finished, I only felt more tense, fretting that if now was a moment of calm, then a storm must be brewing in the stillness. Something is being plotted.

WHY NOT TRY TO WALK THROUGH IT?

I sigh. At least my head is cooler today, a weak energy in my gut. I rise and touch the door with my fingertips, trying to dispel my cynicism. There is a depth of trust in my heart for Rachel, born of years of coming to rely on her intuition, her wisdom, and what if, what if there is something in what she says? But all I feel is chill and scratched metal. I press a little harder and there is one heart-skipping moment when it feels as though the door has moved – but it is just my imagination. The door is some seven inches thick. This is a crazy plan.

'Surely he must be getting bored of this too?' I ask anxiously. 'Surely he will want something more interesting to happen?'

WHEN WE GET BACK, WE MUST GO TO A CONCERT. BEETHOVEN! IMAGINE, SITTING THERE, SIDE BY SIDE, THAT SILENCE BEFORE THE NINTH BEGINS, THAT SILENCE LIKE A DAWN WAITING TO BREAK. AND WE'LL SINK INTO THE MUSIC AND AT THE END EVERYONE WILL STAND UP AND APPLAUD FROM THE DEPTHS OF THEIR HEARTS.

I cannot help being wooed by the idea; my heart is roused and then shadowed with pain upon remembering how unlikely that future is. I lie on my back, exhaustion swimming over me. My sleep is deep and I dream a dream of clear and vivid memory: of being back at my home in Brixton. I am sitting in the kitchen with my flatmate, the sapiosexual physicist, while Radio 4 plays in the background, critics being caustic. She is swiping through Tinder, answering tweets, eating a Pot Noodle and teasing me all at the same time.

When I wake up, home no longer seems like a childhood dream but vividly alive. I can taste the smell of bad cooking that permeated our kitchen, recall the junk mail in the hall, the cracks in my room that I concealed with framed prints.

'Even if we never make it back, there was an awful lot wrong with the world,' I muse.

TRUE. BUT IF WE ALL DO NOTHING, THEN WE GET NOTHING. IF WE DO SOME GOOD EACH DAY, EVEN A SMALL THING, THEN IT COUNTS. AND IF YOU ADD UP ALL THOSE GOOD ACTS, ACROSS A LIFETIME, THEN THE IMPACT IS HUGE.

'Maybe . . .'

THAT'S HOW CYNICISM LEADS TO EVIL, RIGHT? WITHOUT ANY FAITH, THE WORLD GOES TO ROT. THERE'S GOT TO BE SOME SINCERITY, SOME SPIRITUALITY, SOME KIND OF . . .

'You're being surprisingly positive.'

THERE'S SO MANY GREAT THINGS YOU COULD DO. YOU COULD GO BACK AND SET UP A RECORD SHOP.

The idea purrs inside me, but I temper it with laughter. 'Come on, as though I could afford the rent.'

YOU'RE TOO DEFEATIST. COME ON! FUCK LONDON. HEAD NORTH. I'M A NORTHERNER IN MY SOUL.

'You were the one who always wanted to stay here, Rachel.'

WELL, THERE WAS FINN . . .

'I know, I know. Our dear Finn. But he has grown up now. His story is his own to live out.'

I WILL ALWAYS MISS HIM.

'So will I . . .'

A silence as we ache together.

'Your hunger for life – it's surprising. And wonderful.'

I KNOW, I KNOW . . . her voice acquires a blush. IT WAS DYING THAT DID IT. HAVING TO FIGHT TO LIVE. I WAS LYING IN BED, AND YOU WERE ASLEEP AND I COULD FEEL MYSELF SLIPPING AWAY. I WAS WATCHING YOU AND IT WAS THE MOST PAINFUL THING IN THE WORLD, KNOWING HOW YOU WOULD WAKE AND FIND ME GONE, JUST AS I WOKE ONE DAY TO FIND MY MOTHER GONE. IT MADE ME REALISE THAT . . . EVEN IF THE WORLD ISN'T WORTH LIVING FOR, THERE ARE PEOPLE TO LIVE FOR.

I want to tell her that I love her, but am conscious that I am Jaime and she is Rachel, our marriage a simulacrum. The words hover.

IT'S FUNNY, she continues, WHEN I WAS ALIVE, I WAS ALWAYS HALF IN LOVE WITH EASEFUL DEATH. BUT NOW I'M DEAD, I'M IN LOVE WITH LIFE: I WANT A BODY; I WANT TO BREATHE; I WANT TO HAVE SEX AND FEEL MYSELF CLIMAX; I WANT TO PICK UP A BRUSH AND PAINT. OH I WANT THAT SO MUCH. I WANT TO PAINT YOUR PORTRAIT. PROMISE ME THAT IT'S THE FIRST THING WE'LL DO.

'But what if . . . ?'

I AM ALIVE. I HAVE NEVER FELT SO ALIVE.

'You'd better be, if we're going to set up a gallery and a record shop together.'

I LOVE YOU.

'You're a peevish old crone who has stolen my heart.'

We both get a fit of giggles so acute that it causes Rachel to get the hiccups. As I attempt to shock her better, our laughter becomes hysterical.

Then I hear footsteps and the laughter dies. Sitting up on the bed, I try to mould fear into courage. With the high-pitched screech of the key, I imagine the rust of heartbreak that Rachel described. Millhauser sets down my gruel at the bottom of my bed. I nod at him, he nods at me. Stalemate. As he turns to go, Rachel releases a hiccup. I explode into laughter. Millhauser freezes. Slowly, he turns to face me.

'Find me funny, do you?'

Step by step, he approaches me and I bunch up my fists, knowing that my pathetic old body has no hope against the hard muscle of his youth. His fist flies out and pain screams across my face and my nose feels like a thrashing liquid; the bone shattered into fragment. His eyes are electric with a crazed hatred.

STOP IT, YOU BASTARD, STOP IT, Rachel screams.

He grabs my uniform in his fists and swings my head at the wall and time slows down. My head is going to hit that wall. My head is going to hit that wall and my fragile, liver-spotted skin will break. My head is going to hit that wall and blood will stain the brickwork. My head is going to hit that wall and my brains will be mashed into my skull. My head is going to hit that wall and all the neurons that contain my ability to laugh and love, dissect and judge, walk and talk, play and tease, are going to go out like a fused lightbulb. My head is going to hit that wall and Fate will win. Rachel's voice is yelling that HE CAN'T KILL YOU – but my head is going to hit that wall. My head is going to hit that wall and there is relief in the horror, that the game is over, that Rachel and I will haunt him forever—

There is no pain, no pain,

and I assume that I am dead.

When I open my eyes I can see the structures of brick and cement like the colour blocks of a cartoon. I realise that my head is in the wall. His memories float through me. Fate as a boy, quivering in a cupboard by the school kitchens; Fate weeping and trying to calm himself by counting from sixty down to one, telling himself that he must stop, because if the boys see him crying he will be taunted all term—

Hands wrench my body back into the air and suddenly I am lying on the bed again and everything is solid. The pain in my nose is gone. I gaze up and there is terror in Millhauser's eyes. It makes me laugh. He takes his leave in haste.

Rachel begins to cry. YOU SEE, she sobs, I SAID IT AND YOU DIDN'T BELIEVE IT. I ALWAYS KNEW IT. DON'T YOU SEE? *WE'RE* THE STORYTELLERS.

TRY AGAIN, Rachel urges me.

My nose is seared by the brick; I cry out.

It is no good: I cannot seem to do it again.

'I think it was a fluke, a one-off,' I say.

NO, YOUR EGO'S GOT TOO BIG, THAT'S ALL, she accuses me. ALL THAT YOU NEED TO REALISE IS

THAT WHAT YOU DID WAS *NORMAL*. YOU SIMPLY SAW THINGS AS THEY TRULY ARE, AND NOT AS FATE WANTS YOU TO SEE THEM.

My heart shrinks with my failure. I make another attempt, but the wall seems to sneer: it squashes my nose and scrapes the tip. At the sound of more footsteps, despair comes over me.

It was a one-off miracle, I cannot repeat it. This time I will die.

When the door opens, a man announces himself as my new gaoler. There are shades of Augustus Fate in his beard and his bushy eyebrows, but his expression is benign. A procession of young men enter. One sets a small square table down in front of me; another flurries out a white cloth and sets down cutlery. A plate is placed before me, a silver tureen lifted. The smell of food gushes through my nostrils and somersaults in my stomach: potatoes, greens, chicken, gravy –

IT IS SURELY POISONED.

'Is this my last supper?' I ask. 'Before I am hanged?'

'Your case was reassessed this afternoon.' The gaoler's voice is merry and light. 'And the judge felt that your five-year sentence was rather unfair. It is likely that you will be released tomorrow morning – should your good behaviour last the night.'

The young men depart; the gaoler winks. The reverberations of the door slamming shut. The cutlery is tight in my fists; the food before me emits scent-clouds of bliss; saliva is syrupy in my mouth. I cannot hold on any longer; I spear a potato and sink my teeth into its crispness. I taste and hear the crunch and the song of salt and grease melting on my tongue.

I THINK YOU ARE SAFE. Rachel's voice is full of wonder. I THINK WE'VE WON.

HE IS PANICKING.

HE KNOWS THAT WE HAVE THE POWER TO GO. SO HE'S TRYING TO SEDUCE US INTO STAYING. GOOD BEHAVIOUR – HE IS PLEADING NOW. *BEGGING!*

'I could bloody well do with a break,' I murmur, for I can hardly think of anything but the feast.

NO, STOP EATING. DON'T GET SUCKED IN, Rachel cries. DON'T START IDENTIFYING WITH THIS BODY AGAIN. YOU ARE TWENTY-SIX, REMEMBER?

I set down my fork. She is right; dissociation was easier with austerity: I risk becoming all flesh and pleasure again. Another half-hearted attempt at the door, and as the night inks in I give up, sleepy and heavy. A relief as I lie there, a sense of being dignified by the food, made human; shadowed by a sick anger that this is Stockholm-syndrome gratitude.

But anger is no good: I have tried to feed off it all day, to meld it and shape it in the hope it might power me through the walls of this cage. I close my eyes and replay the fight with Millhauser, slowing down memory, pausing on each frame. The sensation I felt was one of lightness, serenity. I fall asleep and I dream of my flat in Brixton and my old life.

In the early hours, I am suddenly awake. The light has that pearly grey-blue quality of pre-dawn twilight. I think I can hear birdsong, some exquisite new species outside my cell, until I realise that it is Rachel singing quietly, and a tune emerges, the 'Ode to Joy'. A siren song.

I grab the sound of her voice like a rope, pull myself up, and let it guide me to the wall. I hold out my palms, resting them lightly on the wall, and see that the wrinkles are vanishing; my skin is growing taut and fresh with youth once more. Brick upon brick, perhaps a hundred of them in this wall: they all begin to shimmer, to hum, and I realise that they are not made of brick but thought and memory, and at the root of that memory, there is sound, and Rachel's 'Ode' is now a trembling in the centre of my heart where she is coiled, waiting for me to carry her out. Fate's anguish as a lonely boy is being drowned out by a blissful soprano. I slowly walk through the wall, all that is solid melting into air, each particle a song in a choir that sings of freedom and joy, and there is light streaming everywhere, a hot white core that pulsates and becomes a wall, a ceiling and a bed in a room in a cottage.

'Rachel?'

The Epilogue

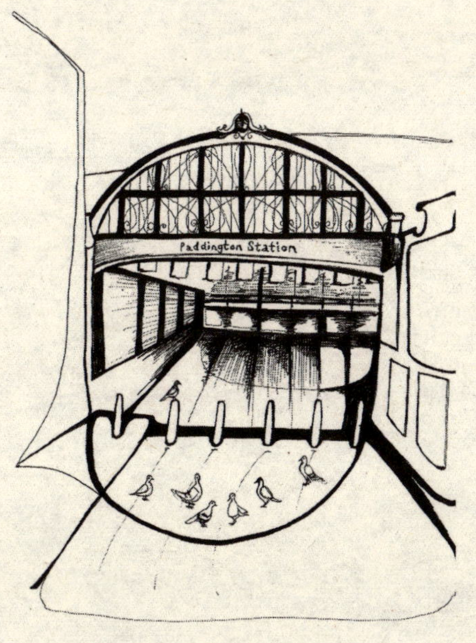

We sit at Pen-y-Bont Station in the sun.

There is a patch on the bench where the green paint has peeled and left naked wood. This is what reality feels like, I tell myself: the sensation of these woodgrains against my palm; the throb of a splinter; the wind in my hair. The devil's advocate whispers that there is little difference, that a bench in Victorian Oxford, in Manchester, in the London of the future, felt just as vivid. But I tune the voice out. I want to luxuriate in Real Life.

My eyes wander to the payphone on the stone wall of the station. Our mobiles sit dead in our rucksacks. There was no wi-fi at Fate's house; there were no chargers. The thought of reconnecting to the newsreel of life is both frightening and strange. We'll have to discover the history of the last four months in vignettes and soundbites. I wonder if they got rid of Boris Johnson, if the Tories are still in power. I wonder which male celebrities have been felled by MeToo. I wonder if the gap between rich and poor has widened ever more, if the pavements are an ocean of pleading hands and sad faces and polystyrene cups. For all my pessimism I enjoy a sense of déjà vu: that sensation you get when you've been abroad for a long time and you're on the last flight home, that tired, happy anticipation.

Jaime's fingers curl around mine. There is fear in his eyes. I know he is thinking about Fate.

There was a moment when we were standing in Fate's kitchen

and we'd found some eggs in his fridge. I gazed at them – large size, from Morrisons – and I knew they should be whipped into a golden, syrupy froth, but how did you get the goodness out of the shells? Jaime came to my side and said, 'Shall I do it?' As he cracked the egg against the bowl, I let out a scream and Jaime jumped in shock. I apologised and said that my brain-fog was making me feel like a zombie. He kissed me and we could not stop. We kissed in between bites. We kissed over suds and squeaky-clean plates. We fell asleep, lip to lip, in a sleeping bag on the sitting room floor. The bedrooms freaked us out too much and there was a danger of Fate keeping us awake with his banging.

Before we left, we stood by the door of the room we had locked Fate in, listening hard. Jaime knocked gently.

Silence.

'He has the kettle, the sink and the Nutrifeed in there with him,' I say out loud, my voice cutting into the fresh air.

'Yes, but we should call them now,' says Jaime, rising from the bench.

'Wait,' I say. 'I thought we were going to ring them from London. We wanted to be home, before it all . . .'

'We're the victims, we've done nothing wrong . . .'

But I know he is thinking of the blood seeping from Fate's arm, the baseball bat he wrestled from him.

'Maybe we should have looked harder for Gwent,' I say, even though we agreed it was futile: Fate would have buried him deep.

'I think he's probably somewhere in the garden . . .' he says, and the thought of his skeleton, nestled in the earth, makes me shiver. 'We must get in touch with his wife when we get home.'

Jaime goes to the public phone and presses the 9 three times. I hear his voice catching as he says 'ambulance'. The reflection of my face in the booth makes me start: its thin new shape. Jaime had to steal a belt to hold up his jeans. His coat looks as though he has inherited it from a larger relative. I've lost a tooth. Jaime's hair now curls over his ears, and he has a beard flowing down his chest. When we first stood in front of a mirror, we touched our reflections in a delirium.

'It's us,' Jaime said over and over in wonder, 'it's us.'

It seems to take a long time for them to answer Jaime's call. On the electronic board, the train goes from being due in fifteen minutes to five. Finally Jaime tells them there is an old man lying in a locked room in his cottage, and that he may be bleeding out. We couldn't call three days ago because he'd cut the telephone wires and we were still too weak to walk to the station.

'He abducted us,' he adds, 'he's a bastard abusing cunt.'

When he hobbles back to the bench, he looks shattered.

'What?' I ask.

'They say they can't come, he's not a priority.'

'*What?*'

'I know. It's mad,' he says.

In shock, we stutter theories: that a fresh round of government cuts has done away with public services altogether; that the NHS, long under immense strain, must have died. Should we go back? Should we call a private doctor? The noise of the incoming train steals our speech. We resolve to try calling again when we get to London.

There's a pause while we wait for the train doors to unlock, and in that interval, a terror starts to build inside me: a conviction that if I look back I will see Fate staggering into the station, beard blood-streaked, like a crazed Lear. The doors eventually slide open and I nearly trip in my eagerness to jump on. We sit down on baize seats. I tell myself that there's no way Fate could get out of that locked room, but I can't still my trembling. I am convinced that he is going to lurch into our carriage, knife in hand.

The train draws out of the station and we are safe for now. I exhale.

Jaime takes a can of Coke out of his rucksack.

'Do you mind if we have it now?'

'Let's do it, Mr Lancia,' I say.

We pass it back and forth, our kisses becoming fizzy. Jaime yawns and his head drifts on to my shoulder. In the honesty of sleep, he looks haggard. When we get to his mother's house, I'd like to see photos of him as a teenager, a little boy, a baby.

My mind surfs between waking and sleep. Images from Jaime's dream seep into my consciousness. A wolf running over a hill, a cloud frowning over him; the wolf wet under the assault of rain, the cloud chasing him. We've been twinned in the wombs of literary imaginations for a long time; it feels natural for us to still be joined by a psychic umbilical cord. As he wakes up, I see his disorientation as he glances round the carriage, realises, remembers. His eyes settle on my face, caressing my cheeks, my lips, my eyes. Then he pulls me in for a hug that crushes me; it almost hurts.

'It's OK,' I whisper in his ear, 'everything's going to be OK.'

He breaks the ring pull from the can and holds it by my left finger.

'I know this is really cheesy, but . . .'

I start to cry, and he does too. The pull won't fit on, it's too tight. I reach up, yank a lock of hair out of my scalp, and he knots it around my finger. As we lie back, I can't stop looking at it.

Trees blur past; sheep; suburbs; cities.

We get closer to London, but our carriage remains empty.

There are posters in the stations showing people separated by arrows. Jaime thinks it's an advertising campaign hangover from Valentine's Day. I suspect it's some art installation project. The thought of my canvases at home is a joyful hunger.

Paddington Station is virtually empty, with more pigeons than humans, strutting about as though they've taken ownership of the place. All the shops are closed, just as the buffet was closed on the train. People walk past with white birds covering their faces. No, the birds are masks. There are a lot of masks. A woman comes up to us.

'Can I help you?'

Her uniform looks reassuring, but the logo says Community Support Officer, which I fear is somewhere between policewoman and busybody. Jaime told me earlier that we needed to get our story straight; that we should just say we were drugged, nothing more. But now I see that Jaime is too numb for words, his eyes flicking over the street beyond, a look of horror on his face.

The woman's focus narrows on me. I try to speak, but my heart stutters. It's like the moment when I first woke up in Fate's cottage. I opened my mouth, but all I could manage were animal whimpers. Shock flooded my vocal cords and emerged in a scream. In the aftermath, my tongue felt strangely heavy as it attempted various shapes. I would look at a thing and wonder what sounds language had attached to it. Jaime called the telephone a surfer, the bedroom a prison, the table a chair, the chair a painting.

'We tried to call,' I manage, finally, 'but they said it wasn't a priority. What I mean is—'

'Where've you been?'

'Wales,' I say.

Her face darkens. I knew it would be like this; I knew nobody would listen; nobody would believe us.

'Have you been on holiday?'

'No . . .'

'I was sent to interview Augustus Fate,' Jaime cuts in. 'He didn't let us out for a long time.'

'I'm glad you were following the rules, but you need to go home now, otherwise I'll be forced to issue a fine. Remember: exercise once per day, infrequent trips for shopping.'

I open my mouth to protest but Jaime drags me away. We decide to head to my flat first, which is nearer than Jaime's or his mum's. On the tube platform, I stand too near to a middle-aged man and he gives me a fierce look. On the walk from Camden tube station to my flat, we see long queues outside Tesco. Empty buses trawl by.

My flat is a basement in a four-storey house on Hawley Crescent. I know there was enough in my account to cover the standing order for my rent, but I'm still worried that I might find I've been evicted. I kneel down and lift the japonica pot, relieved to find the key still there. When I unlock the door, the smell hits us: rot, rubbish, stale air. I open the windows and hear barking. In the back garden I call for Tommy and he wriggles through a hole in my neighbour's fence. I open my arms and he runs into them. I bury my face in his fur. He seems healthy and shiny and fed. Warmth fills my heart. I go to show Tommy my lock-of-hair ring, but it's fallen off somewhere.

Jaime calls his mother. She can't stop crying and he struggles with tears. His story – about going travelling, losing his mobile, finding himself in a remote part of Asia – is not very convincing. He keeps reassuring her, promising that he'll be over very soon. I am happy for him but I can't help but feel a cut of jealousy, wishing I could call my mother. He asks after her health, but all she can speak about is a virus and how the key workers are heroes and that she can't get any flour. We sit on the sofa, dazed.

A plague. Can it be true? In our modern era? Everything has shut down, Jaime's mother said. I picture all the buildings sitting empty. The cinemas in perpetual darkness. The libraries, where the sun slants slowly through the windows on to books gathering dust. Boarded-up churches where bats gather and the mice nibble hymn books.

'We're still in a book,' Jaime says slowly. 'Somehow, somewhere, we passed into another book. This can't be real.'

'But – you just spoke to your mum,' I cry.

'A projection, created from my memories.'

'So tomorrow we'll find a Booksurfer; we'll get out, we'll get back.'

'But how and where? Is this still Fate?' Jaime glances uneasily at the dusty windows.

'I don't know.' I bite my lip to still the trembling. 'I just want to be home.'

Jaime curls his arm around me and we sit in silence for a while as the sun fades. Tommy balls up on my lap and I part his fur with my fingers, down to every speckled fibre. I had forgotten how it felt to stroke him. This has to be real.

Jaime kisses my head and I look up into his sad eyes. Then something shifts in them.

'Wife,' he says lightly.

'Husband.'

He leans forwards, smiling, and gives me a kiss, and we jump, for in the distance is the noise of people bursting into wild applause, up and down the street, the cries and the clapping ringing out like bells across the city.

ACKNOWLEDGEMENTS

I first came up with the idea for *The Watermark* in the summer of 2010, and finally finished the book in late 2022, so I have many people to thank . . .

Thank you to my wonderful agent, Cathryn Summerhayes, for falling for my eccentric novel and working hard to get this deal, and to Anne Meadows at Granta for taking the leap of faith. Thank you, Dan Bird, for taking my book on with such energy and enthusiasm; for your stamina and patience through all the rounds of edits as we grappled with such a big book, and your publishing vision.

Thank you, Anna Wilson, for being such a good friend and introducing me to Cathryn when I had an agenting crisis.

Special thanks to Glen James Brown, who was my first reader. You gave me vital encouragement and feedback during the pandemic, when I lost all faith in the book.

To my dear Mum, who passed away on Christmas Day 2011, and was always so warm and encouraging about my writing from a young age. I was with my mother when I first came up with the idea for *The Watermark*, and I wrote 'The Prologue' not long before I lost her. One of the reasons the book took so long to complete was my broken heart . . .

Thank you to the team at Granta for taking such good care of my novel: Bella Lacey, Christine Lo, my managing editor,

Gesche Ipsen, my copy-editor, Kate Shearman, my proofreader, and my publicist, George Stamp.

Thank you to Christiana Spens for designing the artwork and the graphic novel section with beauty and flair.

My research for 'The First Story', set in Oxford in 1861, was aided by reading Matthew Sweet's superb *Inventing the Victorians* and Ruth Goodman's *How to be a Victorian,* which included so many useful details, from daily routines and food eaten to the letters embarrassed fathers would send their sons about onanism when first going off to school.

Thanks for love, support, and friendship: Zakia Uddin, John Ash, Susan Barker, Zoe Pilger, Sam Byers, Tom Conaghan, David and Leesha, Lyra, Catherine Taylor, Marina Benjamin, Jenny Bullen, David Hughes, Stephen Gill, Anna Maconochie, Alex Spears, Venetia Welby, Thom Cuell, Susanna Crossman, Ben Pester, Seraphina Madsen, Tristan R, Will Francis, Lola Jaye, Dylan Evans, Chris Power, Joe Thomas, Lucy Binnersley, Jude Cook, Simon Lewis, Tom Tomaszewski, Neil Griffiths, James Clammer, David Collard, Harold and the Shark and Matthew Turner.

A very special thank you to my dear Andrew Gallix.